The Best Dancer

The Best Dancer
Christoph Keller

Translated by Alison Gallup

Ooligan Press: Portland, Oregon

Sketch artist: Danielle Sorenson

ISBN-13: 978-1-932010-22-0

Ooligan Press
Center for Excellence in Writing
Department of English
Portland State University
P.O. Box 751
Portland, or 97207–0751
ooligan@pdx.edu
www.ooliganpress.pdx.edu

The Best Dancer body text was set in Sabon LT Std 10/14, Optima LT Std
10/14, and Century Expanded LT Std 12/14. Titles were set in Optima
LT Std 36/36. Headers were set in Century Expanded LT Std 8/10.

For Jan
And my family

for Bill & Alice
with love,
Chester.

This gave me that precarious Gait
Some call Experience.

  —Emily Dickinson 1/7/14

Epilogue & Prologue

Spring Morning, 1995

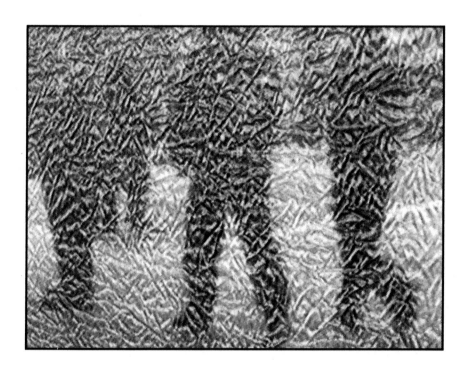

The gallery occupies just a single room on the ground floor of the house. Sometimes the old gallery owner allows the art to spill into the hall leading back to his office, where he does what he likes least: waits for clients.

It is four o'clock in the morning.

The front door isn't bolted; ring the bell and come right in. He used to greet each visitor at the door personally. The wait for the master of the house, duly prolonged by the same, turns those waiting into buyers: who wants to waste time on bad art? The longer one lingers at the door, the better the art awaiting him on the other side. Those who have already disappeared by the time the gallery owner arrives have earned his double appreciation: they've helped him get a little exercise and haven't taken up his time. His doctor strongly advises him to exercise, only when? His lap feels damp. But perhaps it is only sweat. It's muggy, muggy and airless.

He thinks he hears voices outside. "Take it easy!" he shouts. Nothing. Silence. Nobody's coming.

Since his stroke—or rather since the negligible series of "tiny ministrokes," which he wouldn't have even registered if he hadn't woken up that morning on the floor of the atelier and gone to the doctor about a pain in his knee—since then, his clientele has had to do without the wait calculated to further their appreciation of art: the walk from his office to the door has become too long for him.

On an easel, close to the front entrance, Ben Vautier's blackboard and white-chalk text greets the visitor: ART IS SUPERFLUOUS. GO HOME.

What fun it is, the gallery owner thinks, to poke fun at the art lover. Pity, in a way, that you can no longer offend someone who thinks himself a true admirer of art; spit in his face and he'll buy your saliva off you as it's drying on his cheek.

Upstairs, where the gallery owner performs one of his many other functions, that of antiques dealer, the rooms are overflowing: Thonet chairs, iron clocks, mortar, rusted stethoscopes, Tiffany vases, *oignon* pocket watches, old Victrolas and album after album of His Master's Voice shellac records (Satchmo, his favorite), Rosenthal china, birdcages, antique Christmas tree decorations, wind-up Japanese dancing dolls, masks from Urnäsch and the Congo, garden gnomes from Thuringia, a medieval tooth extraction set in a quilted wooden case, porcelain music boxes, and everything imaginable made of pewter.

It is from up here that, in the winter, when the trees are leafless, he can see the roof of the house that was once his.

This house, however, where he now spends most of his time, was once his friend's studio, the painter Max Falk, which is why everybody still calls it the *atelier house*. The largest room, with its old walnut table that once stood in a tavern and now serves as his office desk, has since been divided up into a small labyrinth of cubicles, separated by partition walls. Not that he has a large staff. Apart from Ms. Meili, who greets visitors during the gallery's opening hours, it is he alone who fulfills the various necessary functions: gallery owner, antiques dealer, bookkeeper, publicist on his own behalf, keeper and administrator of the remnants of his ruined collection, but also curator of his new Collection K, letter-writer and plaintiff in court, soldier and holy warrior in the battle against the ineradicable Huns who ravaged his city a second time—only this time not pillaging and plundering the abbey and its library, but his life's work, his collection, him.

He looks up. "No more!" he shouts. What was that? Silence. They can all go to hell.

In the dusty semi-darkness he can see the narrow flight of stairs, steep as a ladder, leading to the mezzanine, and how the mezzanine projects into the space, set off from the rest of the room only by a rickety banister. When was he last up there? He has furnished this quasi-suspended room with a dresser, a peasant-style painted wardrobe from the Allgäu filled with old dolls, a chair, a bed: his bedroom, just in case. What makes the staircase special is the banister, a genuine mooring rope that everyone wanted to touch, whether it was a compliant young woman who climbed the stairs ahead of him, or an eager client who followed up after.

"Watch out, here I come!" he hears his youngest son, one of three, followed by his giggle and the battle cry—"Ahoy there, king! Prepare to be boarded!"—or something like that. Clinking down the stairs, and preceding his son's own thunderous descent, was the beloved metal spring; *clonk-ffft, clonk-ffft,* then *thud-thud-thud,* the son himself on his rear end, hesitating as the spring did, pausing anew at each step, catching his breath, summoning his courage before tackling the next one, as if stairs were something to be feared.

For a moment the gallery owner thinks he sees a flash—a boy's eye? a coil of metal?—but he wipes the image away with a movement of his arm. So much work on his desk and still more upstairs on his workbench. Clocks that tick but can't give the time. The invitation for the show is a matter of urgency. His invitations are simple: the name of the artist and that of the gallery printed in black on a glossy white background. Still, they cause him such headaches. Are they what's making him so weary, as if before the exhibition even opens the artist is already complaining that he's sold too little? Nonsense. And yet: are there any people more ungrateful than artists?

"Yes," the old man sighs into the desolate space, "there are," and bending lower over his invitation card, his glasses clink against the loupe he is holding close before his eyes. The clear, high-pitched sound reminds him of the doorbell, a slightly rusted bell from whose clapper a cord hangs. This too, of course, an antique; he himself had screwed it off of a farmer's door, with the farmer's after-the-fact consent.

He'd stationed Ms. Meili behind a small table in the corridor where she could see the entrance door and receive visitors. On the table are several copies of the gallery's schedule and anniversary brochure; the stapled-together letters to the editor regarding Roman Signer's fountain, which—it had been established—drove the pigeons, along with the old hags that fed them, out of their park; the catalogue, also available in English, of his bird cage collection, which was without parallel in Switzerland; as well as a few of his youngest son's books—his favorite being the one in which, just a quarter of a way into the story, he had been reduced, together with his house and library and collection, to ashes.

Where is Ms. Meili anyway? He looks at the clock. Almost five. He can't remember giving her today off. It's not the first time she hasn't turned up. The good soul may well perform her watch free of charge, but he still needs to know if he can count on her. Well, not quite free of charge. He'd just given her a lithograph, an unnumbered one by a local artist, which she, as expected, didn't notice. He mustn't forget to remind her, and, taking up his thick green felt-tip pen, he starts, slowly and carefully, to write the letters of her name.

What was that? He listens for the creaking of the door and stares into the murky space thick with billows of smoke from his cigar. Not a sound. He sighs; then loudly curses the local philistines, who today, once again, have stayed away in droves. He pulls his bookkeeper's cap, a sun visor and rubber band contraption, further down on his forehead, holds the loupe in front of his glasses, and bends over the invitation card. How do you spell *preview* again, and *invitation*?

The doorbell!

This time he takes immediate action. Hoisting himself up, he grabs his cane and shuffles down the hall to the front door. It's closed: nobody there. The dust floats upward in the column of light formed by the door's window. Again, he looks at the clock. Again, the hand jumps forward. The gallery is open from two until five, and it's now five. Time to go home.

Outside, it is as bright—or as gloomy—as it is on other milky-misty days. He shuts the door behind him, turns the key twice, and jiggles to ensure it is locked. Holding onto the doorpost, he takes the first of the stairs backwards. Backwards, because this is the position he's in anyway. Then, seized by a playful confidence, he makes an elegant pirouette, and takes the next two steps neatly. What if he'd forgotten his cane? He chuckles to himself. He couldn't have forgotten, because without a cane he wouldn't have gotten this far. His mood darkens again.

Now the cobblestones, with their projecting edges and covered with moss. Did it rain? That would make the uneven path even more slippery.

Marching forward, swinging his cane out in front of him, he's able to safely negotiate the path, which leads through an impeccably overgrown garden with a few sculptures. The crankshaft of a VW Bug is his work.

He'd found it in a scrap heap, given it a base, and placed it among the other sculptures. Some of the pieces are no longer distinguishable from the undergrowth that surrounds them. Should he sell some of it as art? He'd have the blessing—in the form of a foreword—of Jolanda Gut, the leading art critic of the region, who, though she can't tell a urinal from a Duchamp, nonetheless decides who can feed at the money troughs.

It's an idea in any case: uproot the undergrowth and exhibit it in the gallery. As his last show, with which he'd bid his farewell, and as his final comment as to what he really thought of St. Gallen's connoisseurs, Jolanda included. He could see the article already: "...driven by a love of truth and the love of good art...after his fateful year, 1978, when his collection, business, and family were taken from him, he'd made a living dealing in antiques, as art didn't have to be a money-maker" (what a load of garbage!). Then, an old favorite, his remark (had he really once said this?) that he has to get close to artists, as people, otherwise collaboration is out of the question. And when he took his leave from the gallery, this would appear in the newspaper again, whether he says it or not: namely, that he is interested in young people, who still have their lives before them and whom he supports as if they were his own sons. Only he won't be leaving. He'll be a hundred and twenty years old, as he'd always proclaimed, and afterwards, immortal.

At the end of the path, the parking lot opens out before him. He begins to hum something that sounds like "Do Not Forsake Me, O My Darling." Squinting across the broad space, as if the sun were actually shining, he is now Will Kane, the sheriff of Hadleyville from *High Noon*, and the parking lot is Hadleyville, Switzerland: Land of Freedom, Land of Heroes.

Main Street is deserted and Will Kane knows why. Betrayal has swept the town clean. The first to walk out on him was his deputy sheriff who'd wanted his job. Following suit were his bookkeeper, who'd cheated him for years; his so-called friends; his three useless sons; his dog; and, finally, his wife, who'd hopped on the last train out of Hadleyville just in time. Hounds, Huns, everyone!

Yes, there were a few attempts to beg his forgiveness. The most recent one was made a year ago, by his youngest son. After not having been heard from for a dozen years, he called because he'd learned—from whom actually?—that his father was nearing his end. The gallery owner had no intention of doing him, or anyone else, this favor, but he did agree to meet his son: once, on neutral ground (at a café, as his wimp of a son had demanded), then, on his own turf (at the Hirschen, his saloon), and another time, at the gallery. He even took him to see his own works of art, which he stored in an air-raid shelter. That he ultimately let himself be talked into allowing his youngest into his apartment was a mistake he corrected—and not too late—when he saw him being carried up the stairs in his building, fireman-style, on the back of a friend. Which, to put it mildly, was a curious sight.

Will Kane looks around. The Hadleyville-ians' betrayal of him is so absolute they don't even watch him from behind drawn curtains. He checks the time on the clock over the watchmaker's shop; the hand jumps to the next digit. Even the saloon is closed—at this hour! The saloonkeeper, that coward, that traitor, is cowering under the counter, trembling for his life. He shivers. It's colder than he thought. The song fades out as he readies to cross the square. And out of the silence steps the gunslinger Frank Miller.

He has a plan: he'll lure Miller down to the river. He swirls, shoots curses over his shoulders like bullets, and runs, hearing Miller's heavy footsteps behind him. Reaching the river, he plunges in, and with his rifle gains purchase on the uncertain bottom; a boat chugs forward, its paddle wheels whip water into his face. He becomes dizzy, curses, and nearly falls, clutching desperately on to his rifle. Hell, he's no Will Kane anymore— what kind of hero has to be saved by his wife in the end! No, now, he's Sheriff John T. Chance from *Rio Bravo*. John T. doesn't ask. John T. acts. John T. lifts his rifle and—*bang-bang!*—bullets whistle through the air.

John T. is satisfied: at least two dozen Mexican bastards and Frank Miller, too—gotcha!— bleeding to death on the riverbanks. Served them right—WANTED: DEAD OR ALIVE—whoever tangles with him is a dead man from the start—*bang-bang!*, *clonk-clonk*—he pulls himself up on the far side of the river.

Scarcely having secured himself, he raises his walking stick, brandishes it in the air, and curses after a honking car.

Damn, his leg throbs. He must have taken another bullet in the knee.

Past Café Zimmermann—also closed!—and up the eight steps leading to his building's entrance, and he's home. He's trembling. Tears?

No, just the wind blowing the desert dust in his eyes. He'll make it. Step by step, he maneuvers himself up, gripping the railing; inside, another four steps to his door. Exhausted, but also proud of the hurdles overcome, he rummages up his apartment key, turns it in the lock, throws open the door, and bellows: "John T. is home."

Only now does he realize how tired he is. He manages to throw his jacket on the chair in the corridor and falls onto his bed—never mind how damp it may feel between his legs, never mind how much his knee might hurt, never mind.

Today, once again, wild with joy.

Lost the rubber tip of my cane this morning: Now I clack when I walk. (Only on hard surfaces.)

The first thing I test on the first day of the New Year is not whether my computer still functions, but whether my body does. This has nothing to do with the New Year, it is something I do every morning. I don't care if my PC has the Y2K virus: a neuromuscular sabotage program lives inside of me and is slowing me down step by step. My body has SMA, Spinal Muscular Atrophy (Type III, Kugelberg-Welander).

Whoever lives with a progressive disease makes a routine of testing daily what still functions. Am I still able today, the first day of the new millennium, to get up out of my office chair? Go into the kitchen? I know that one day I'll no longer be able to, and I have to reckon with this day, well, daily. Can I still make this step, get over this threshold? Can I still waddle to the bathroom (with the clacking of the cane announcing me)? And back?

My Muscle Book: So that I can write about my life with this disease, so that I can clarify for myself what

Marcel Duchamp,
Bicycle Wheel, 1951

it means to never really know what's still possible—what I am certain of is only that one day every movement, even breathing, could be impossible—I have resolved for the year 2000 to keep this journal.

Jan lifts the wheelchair out of the trunk. As usual, somebody is standing by, watching—are they interested? bored?

When we met at a writers' colony in upstate New York, Jan, who is now my wife, and who was there working on her poems, took me at first for two people: the one who'd come rolling up in a wheelchair, and the one who, sometimes in the evenings—as if after a quick change of clothes—made his way from his room to dinner on foot.

I'd almost had to turn around and leave because the "special room for wheelchair users" was accessible only by mounting a step and had a door through which a wheelchair couldn't fit. The director, who before my departure from Switzerland had assured me of the "wheelchair accessibility" of her building with a vehemence that implied I was ridiculous for even inquiring, arranged to have a bed moved into the library of the main building, a space which was supposed to be available to all. Otherwise I would have had to leave. Otherwise I wouldn't have met Jan. Otherwise I would have lived a different life.

Like every New Year's, a version of Jules Verne's Journey to the Center of the Earth *is on TV. Once again, Professor Lidenbrock and Axel won't reach their goal. Once again, they'll be flushed out of the volcano onto the surface of the earth. Once again, it will be just in the nick of time.*

Summer Morning, 1968

Surely there is no being so miserable as to be without a retreat to which he can withdraw and hide himself from the world. Such a hiding-place will contain all the preparations our journey requires.

—XAVIER DE MAISTRE, *Voyage Around My Room*

T*ick.*

Kasperli landed so hard on the crook that he was
unconshuss. Then he dragged him off to jail. From
there he was allowed to travel to America and three
days later a letter came...

There's something ticklish on my cheek, as if a warm finger
were gliding over my face. It feels like a wasp, nature's model for the
"helicopeter," which I was recently able to add to my toy soldier army.
But THE RULE says it's still too early for scratching. It's even still too
early for eyes to be opened.

Dear Kasperli, so you kept your word. That makes
me very happy. Do visit us for too days. We'll have
a party for you. The money is on the back. We'll be
expecting you. You will come with the whole family,
won't you? Okay, come at the appointed time or not!
Föschä Gingenschlag, prison warden of Sing-Sing
in—*tock*—New-York, sends best wishes to you all.

Morning wafts into my room carrying with it the aroma of freshly
cut grass and damp earth. This is because I am digging a hole in the
shadow of the fir tree, in the back near our garage. I found an ancient

Icelandic parchment in the ground, an invitation—so dirty it was barely legible—to travel to the center of the earth. I'm headed in the right direction and my hole is already three-quarters of a meter deep! And in the afternoon—

Stop! I have to be honest. That's what THE RULE says, and my mother too, who is unyielding when it comes to honesty. I didn't really find the ancient Icelandic parchment in our yard, no, I found it in the best book I've ever read. But while I was reading it, and *this* you can believe, I *did* travel to the center of the earth, and on the way I made up a story that takes me to this "New-York," where the tallest buildings are found and where I've also never been. *Tick.* Then again, if I wasn't almost at the center of the earth, my pants wouldn't be so dirty. Okay, caught again. My pants got dirty from digging, not from reading. It's true though, that sometimes I can no longer tell the difference between reading and digging.

> On the back: 20 doller for the trip.
> "Let's all go: Papa, you, Gritli and me."
> "Yes."
> "What!" the father shouted, along with Gritli.
> "We can go to America for free!"

And again: Stop! Question: Why do I have to tell the truth at all costs when this Jules Verne is allowed to lie whenever he wants? Even in the title of his book he promises we'll get to the center of the earth, but anyone who's read it knows that Professor Lidenbrock and his nephew and assistant, Axel, never arrive there. Us, yes: the professor, Axel, and me—we were spewed out of the earth by a volcano.

"You were shit out of the earth," my father said—*tock*—when I turned to him with my traveling problem.

"Shh, Föns!" my mother hissed, but my father was already on his way to the attic again where he organized his collection. This took up a lot of time—about as much time as is needed to dig to the center of the earth with a plastic shovel.

> "Yes."
> "Hooray!"

"Yippee!"
"Ollay!"
We packed up. Then we loaded everything into the
car and set off.

I'm not going to take Axel. Because he was secretly engaged to Gudrun, the ward of his uncle Professor Lidenbrock, he'd already hesitated to undertake this excursion the first time around. My concerns are too great that he will once again use every opportunity to chicken out of other trips with me as well: around the world, under water, to the moon. I think Axel would even shy away from driving to the market with my mother.

I have decided to take Kasperli; Kasperli is my favorite hero anyway. He's been around for ages, this wooden rascal. That's what my mother calls him. She thinks he was already around when she was a child. That means he's always been around. *Tick.* Kasperli is a cheeky little guy with eyebrows like pieces of coal, a red pointed cap, a blue T-shirt, yellow tennis shoes, and a long nose, which isn't as long as Pinocchio's though, for Kasperli always tells the truth, or most of the time, anyway, just like me. Kasperli doesn't hold back. He always has the last word, and if he doesn't, then his mallet does, and with his mallet he fearlessly strikes anything that gets in his way, be it the devil himself, which often happens, and there's no way he'd let any volcano spew him out like *shiiii…*!

First they drove through Lugano, Chiasso, Milan,
and then they drove onto an ocean liner which took
them to America (from Genoa).

Isn't it still too early to get out of bed? My bed is at least three years old, or did my father say three hundred? I can smell the dried oil of the painting over my head. It smells like orange cat with green spots. *Tock.* The cat's about to jump but doesn't, no matter how long I stare at her; if she jumps when I look away, I can't say, because then I'm not looking. What is she running from? Sometimes I spin around to see if someone isn't disappearing into the mountains in the back of the painting. I'm not fast enough. And if I were, could I still save the cat? Her body is cut up into pieces, as if she were a roulade, and the roulade pieces hang down on threads from a surprisingly cruel house-pet heaven.

But the cat is not dead. Don't you have to be dead to go to heaven? I know you don't have to be dead to go to hell, for Father Mutt says, I'll be cooked alive there if I don't watch out. *Tick.* Today is Sunday; today I have to watch out. Church is at eleven. Father Mutt is already heating up the soup pot. But I don't have time. I have to sail with the ship anchored in the attic to America, and in the afternoon—you know already. My father would call what I have a "conflict of interests," but my mother and I have an agreement: If I am still sleeping, that is, if I manage to be in bed again by ten pretending to be asleep, then I don't have to go to church.

It's still not even six. I examine the picture that hangs over my desk; it shows a black elephant. Unlike the cat, he has no smell because he is behind glass. I know that elephants aren't black, but at least this one isn't cut up into pieces of roulade. Is that the sky? No, the sky is in the jam jar on the sandstone wall near the rose bed—*tock*—in our garden. Nora and I filled the jar with water and rose petals and it already smells like our next summer when she'll be back from Sicily. Of course Nora knows nothing of my hole in the yard and my trip to the center of the earth. Otherwise, she would secretly get engaged to me, then she would worry about me, and I, like Axel, who wavered because of his fiancée, might not set off at all. In the end, I'd be married to Nora and I'd no longer even dare go to the vegetable market. My cheek itches again. Now THE RULE commands: *Scratch!* and I do so with pleasure.

"Is Sing-Sing far from New-York?"
"No," says the father, "and Menhetten is the port
city of New-York!"
"Ah, how do you spell Menhetten and how do you
spell New-York?"
"M-e-n-h-e-t-t-e-n N-e-w hyfen Y-o-r-k!"

I can see the curtain of dust that divides my room. *Tick.* That happens every time a new episode of *Star Trek* is on TV. The rays of the morning sun beam the dust up to the ceiling, just like the way Cap'n Kirk is beamed to the Klingon planet, which only proves that the dust in my bedroom is Cap'n Kirk on his way to the Klingon planet. Not too long ago my oldest brother Puck scientifically supported my theory with his recently acquired knowledge of modern physics.

"Beaming," he said, examining his hair as if it ought to be longer, "is nothing but the breaking down of the human body into its smallest parts and then sending them on their way at the speed of light. And believe me," Puck grinned, "there's nothing faster than light. As soon as the particles have arrived safely on Klingon, they are reintegrated into their original form. The tiniest particles of the body are atoms, you see, and atoms—*tock*—are, as everybody knows, nothing more than little specks of dust. This is how life works. *Capito?*"

"Why does it need a hyfen?"
"It just does, Kasperli," says the father with authorty
"there is a city called York and there is a city New—
newly added so it was written with a hyfen. New-
York. *Capito?*"

Although Mix is the sandwich brother, I have the sandwich room. To my left is Puck's room, which still floats in last night's haze of cigarette smoke, house-shaking music, and the dandruff of a horde of teenage boys. *Tick.* Mix's room is a theater of war; the carpet the battlefield where Rommel's desert army, Robin Hood's merry men, Caesar's Praetorian Guard, and Hornblower's unsinkable fleet all clash—the sea begins where the carpet ends—the Crusaders under papal supremacy conquer the Holy Land, and the Swiss mercenaries under the supremacy of whomever pays them conquer whatever they are paid to conquer.

Mix often asks me to join his bedroom battles. My task is to lead the losers to their historic defeats. He prepares our battles carefully. I'm the Germans on Omaha Beach, the Austrians at Morgarten, the Turks at Gallipoli, and the Evil at Armageddon. Once, I grabbed one of the books he was reading in order to conquer me and threw it at his army. With a single blow, his troops were obliterated, and I jumped up and ran away. I always win this kind of battle: by the time Mix is on his feet, I'm long gone. But even if he could catch up with me, he'd never hoist the white flag and admit his defeat; he would merely solemnly proclaim that I couldn't change the course of history—in any case, not in his bedroom.

"M-e-n-h-e-t-t-e-n everyone disembark," a voice shouted all of a sudden across the deck. It was the cap'n of the ocean liner.

Silence: *tock*—except for the muffled heartbeat of the clock over the landing. With a daring leap, I make it over the white rug next to my bed that overnight almost always turns into snow. I land safely on the wall-to-wall carpeting, test with my toes to see if the rug really is snow—the answer is yes, although the snow feels surprisingly warm—and slip out of my bedroom. In front of the stairs, I take a deep breath. So as not to lose any time, I take two steps at once.

At the landing, my father materializes under the clock in order to show me its mechanical parts. All I understand is *tick-tock*. And that everything in our house, occupants included, is ancient. My father vibrates in the morning sun and proudly explains that this clock is four hundred years old. I'm not impressed. I want to tell you what's old. I am old. I am four, six, in a second—the time it takes a sound to travel through your head—nine years old. My father puts his strong hands around my shoulders and lifts me up to show me what he calls the bowels of the clock. I see how the tiny gears interlock, how they cry out *tick*, and once again I understand in an instant why time flies and why grandmother's face is so wrinkled.

"The small wheels are all made of wood," he rhapsodizes, though his voice sounds so far away. All I need to do is nod. My father puts me back down on the floor. If this doesn't happen in time, he's doomed, according to THE RULE. My spectral father dissolves into dust particles, which are even smaller than atoms, and is beamed down the steps, through the closed door, and into my parents' bedroom to sleep again in his snoring body next to my mother. The best quality of a vision is that it doesn't get loud and wake up the whole house when it realizes it's time to turn to dust and disappear.

They drove right into the center of New-York. Soon they found Sing-Sing, the prison. They asked for Mr. Gingenschlag.

(CONTINUED IN NOTEBOOK 3)

20   Christoph Keller

Nana, dancing through the air, sings "Beware of entering Atticland!" *Tock.* Her gigantic bosoms are yellow, speckled with green and red dots. The lazy sunlight sifting through the pale curtains in the stairwell makes them glow. But where is the breeze coming from? Did my father forget to close the window after we left the half-finished parrot in the workroom last night? Otherwise, Nana wouldn't dance. Nana's what my father calls the plump, buxom inflatable doll that hangs over the attic entrance, hovering over all who have the courage, or are foolish enough, to come see my family and lose themselves in the labyrinth of my two-story attic.

"Hello, Nana," I whisper. I stand on my tiptoes to tap her yellow foot. She starts to spin faster; I am stronger than the breeze. That's all there is to it. I'm in.

(CONTINUATION OF NOTEBOOK 2)
"Here," the father cried. They rang for the attendant to come down. "I speek German not wery vell, my maaster caan better, wery guud!" The half-German-speaking attendant knew the last word only in English and that's why he said it like this. *Tick.* Then he said, "Mr. Gingenschlag is expecting you."

Head-Foot, who's lurking in the stamp room, is more dangerous than Nana. How he hates his pet name! It's a sore point. It reminds him of his limitations, of everything that he doesn't have: chest, hips, legs. "Nana wouldn't even so much as glance at you, pipsqueak! *Woof, woof!*" I try to sound as mean as Rott when he barks at the Chihuahua with the pink bow that belongs to our neighbor and I push open the door to the stamp room. The floor is yellow, the walls are green—because of Head-Foot's foul breath. As soon as I've turned on the light, I can see him grinning nastily—stiffening. He's currently nailed to the wall, imprisoned in his frame, and illuminated by the naked 60-watt neon bulb.

The Lithograph-Monster, his face now frozen in an imploring expression—THE RULE: never feel sorry for a monster—*tock*—lives behind glass over a wide metal cabinet which holds one copy of every single lithograph in the world. A few of them are even nastier than Head-Foot, and that is also why my father locks them away. Lying on top of the cabinet are the albums in which all the stamps of this world are to be found—only none, unfortunately, from another world.

> They went into a front room with pretty pictures
> and a big carpet, then there was another door, that
> the attendant opened, and they went into a hall.
> There clocks and pictures that tick and tock hung
> everywhere.

In the stamp room, I can trick my father, who hates traveling. He thinks I'm there, but I'm not. Not really, anyway. Without saying a word, my father hands me a Queen Elizabeth II 5p with a pair of tweezers so small they can no longer be seen between his fingers, and I place the stamp between the Queen Elizabeth II 3p—*tick*—and the Queen Elizabeth II 10p. Beneath the mistrustful eye of the trapped Head-Foot, I look at the stamps on the piece of blotting paper in front of me, zoom in closer with my camera eye, and already I'm traveling through the fantastic places depicted on the stamps: England, Taiwan, even the Principality of Liechtenstein. Yes, that's what I want to do, so it's also what I want to be, a "travler." My father never asks me this question: What do you want to be when you grow up? Doesn't that make him an unusual father?

Yesterday I proposed we didn't limit our journeys to stamps, but we could, like Phileas Fogg, travel around the world in a balloon. My father isn't interested.

Might he have something against the balloon?

No answer.

"We could go by airplane." I know my compromise rules out the possibility of being eaten by cannibals in Africa.

Still no answer. *Tock.*

"By car?" That would bring the cannibals back into play. "By foot?"

"Nonsense," was all he said, and that was also his last word on traveling. My father is the Phileas Fogg of the attic. Maybe it has something to do with his job. When somebody asks what my father does, I don't simply say he runs a big business, ruling over a genuine empire—which is what *he* always says, as if otherwise people would forget.

I say with pride, my father is a collector.

"Of what?"

What a question. "Of everything!"

I shut out the light, and with it, the stamp room. I stand in the corridor and try not to breathe. It's quiet. Not even Nana, who is surely still dancing through the air, is to be heard. I wander through dusty Bookland...

"Be welcome to my home. I am very pleased that
you have come. You will stay with us, won't you?"
"How do you do, Mr. Gingenschlag? We are very
pleased that we could come, but we'd prefer to stay
in a hotel." *Tick.*

...heading toward our cinema at the end of the corridor. Three seats, ninety-centimeter-wide screen, Super 8. Slapstick in black and white, cartoons in color. There's no other sound except the rattling of the projector, and it's up to me to make up and add words to the pictures, just like the way you have to think up and add pictures to the words when reading a book. At least half of the imagining is my job. Don't forget to bring a Coke and peanuts, because nothing is served during the show. I sit down and next thing I know I'm riding in the great wide prairie. I'm a hysterical Mickey jerking to and fro on a steamboat, or the skillfully unskillful Charlie who gets caught in the gears of a giant people-devouring—*tock*—machine, but then smoothly glides through the dangerous wheels. I'm the starving Yogi Bear laying siege to a beehive, Laurel poking Hardy in the eye or Hardy being poked in the eye by Laurel, or, I'm the younger version of myself in a homemade film in which I fearlessly shoot down the two-meter-high hill in our yard on a pair of skis.

On my way back through Bookland I slip into the workroom, which is now warm from the sun. Everything is as we left it yesterday. Even the smell of glue still hangs in the air. I pick up the tube of glue and unscrew the cap. Easy, too easy, I think. What good is a glue that can't even keep its own cap glued firmly on? The parrot is lying naked in a bed of its own feathers: burgundy, green, blue. Its body is made of oak—my father cut the shape with his saw in the workspace on the other side of the attic.

I filed—*tick*—sanded, and polished him until he turned smoothly in my hand. The parrot consists of whatever my father brings home from work. Yesterday, it was colored sheets of copper, so my parrot had a copper-sheet-feather-dress. My father promised that today we would glue the feathers that I cut out—with a pair of now-broken paper-cutting scissors—onto the body of the parrot, but with my father, yes, well, you never really know.

He loves to work at his table on the little elevated area next to the window in the workroom. Up there in his cigar-smoke cloud, he collects his collection. He photographs everything he acquires because this way he can also collect the photos of his various collections, as well as the albums in which he artfully arranges the photos. He develops the pictures in the darkroom next to the workshop, then pastes them into their respective albums—*tock*—and labels them with names like, "Helen Dahm, *Black Elephant*," "Erich Staub, *Slit Cat in a Fantastic Appenzell Landscape*," "Horst Antes, *Head-Footer*," or "Nikki de Saint Phalle, *Nana*." He also names the albums and places them on the shelves behind him. There are also albums of us, with names like, "Son 1: *Puck—Handicrafts*, 1961," "Son 2: *Mix—Christening and First Steps*, 1958–1960," "Son 3: *Stöffi—Skiing*, Winter 1969," or "Ruth: *Honeymoon*, 1953."

And now Foot, who knows the secret of motion: It *is* true that I have to nudge him on and then run downstairs so that I can see how he… walks?…crawls?…flows is surely the right word, but as soon as he starts moving only the end of the stairs can stop him. Unlike Head-Foot, Foot is all foot from head to foot. He has no head at all. When he's in the starting position—*tick*—he is maybe five centimeters tall. If he stretches himself out to flow down the steps, he can get up to thirty centimeters long. When my father and I hold him at his ends (he has only ends, no beginnings), and my father stands near the stamp room, I can walk down the corridor as far as the cinema because his body is so stretchy. We don't do that very often—we don't want Foot to overstretch his muscle because that's all he has, his muscle, and that's all he is, a metal muscle. *Clonk-ffft, clonk-ffft*, Foot flows down the steps to me step by step, always one at a time, until the landing stops him. *Clonk. Thud. Tock.*

What keeps Foot moving? What's his secret? The steps, of course. All that Foot needs is an endless flight of stairs. But Foot only moves downwards. I pick him up, carry him upstairs, and send him off on his journey once more. This time I let him sit on the landing. Here he'll wait until I come back. He stares at the stairs reproachfully, as if they were an insurmountable obstacle.

> Evening fell in a flash. "Can't I have 20 more minutes, please!" begged Kasperli. "Very well, get undressed and come back again." And when he came back he finally went to bed. Then the next morning at twelve Kasperli came into the kitchen sleepy-eyed and shouted "Mamma it's seven thirty. I… Oh God, I have to go to church! But no, there isn't one single church in Menhetten!"

Tick.

I t occurs to me—*suddenly? like a slap in the face?*—*why I rarely need new shoes. I hardly use them because most of the time I'm sitting. I look at the almost unblemished soles of my old oxfords and for the first time I get it.*

The hiding place I headed for so early on those Sunday mornings while everyone was still asleep—and not just to avoid church—was reached through two small doors. They were left and right of the only window on the second attic story and on a platform—a later addition—one step up. The walls were also later additions and they created my corridor, a narrow catwalk between the slope of the roof and the larger space hung floor to ceiling with church tower clocks. The doors were so small because they weren't intended as entrances or exits; rather, they had once been the double doors of an armoire. My father had succeeded in salvaging the doors, but not the rest of the *Appenzell* bridal armoire; and resourceful as he was, he had been able to make use of them in the reconfiguration of our attic.

Typically a portrait of the bride would be found on one of the doors of these "newlyweds' wardrobes," and the groom would be depicted next to her on the other. But we had separated the married couple again. The groom hung to the left of the Alps, which I could see through the window beyond the tops of the fir trees. But I always turned to the right and made my way into the corridor through the bride. It felt as if I were climbing into an armoire without a back: the first step landed me inside and then, from the second step on, this armoire was the armoire that every kid dreams about, or should dream about. By plugging in the miner's light that hung on a nail inside the door, I managed to penetrate the back of the armoire—pure darkness—and thus strode forth courageously, all the dangers of the world ahead of me and the bride, for now, behind me.

Not that one can get lost in a sixty-meter-long corridor that follows the slope of a roof, but the cord of the miner's lamp helped me imagine that this precisely could happen, and that I was no longer in an armoire but in a labyrinth with an extensive system of branched paths, dead-end alleys, and trapdoors. If necessary, the cord would show me the route back. It was always important for me to lose my way and at the same time to know, with every step, exactly where I was.

Did Axel feel this way too when he descended into the mouth of the extinct volcano with Professor Lidenbrock? He held his torch high—he couldn't rely on the cord of my miner's lamp—hesitated one last time, and then set out after all. Perhaps he was only being cautious and the Professor irresponsible. I followed Axel, I followed the Professor, I followed Hans—I thought of Axel's fiancée, whom he had had to leave at home—but I couldn't really catch up to them, for they were always just disappearing around the next corner.

A crib materialized at the edge of the light cast by my lamp and then dissolved again into the darkness. A marten-gnawed trunk made a sound, the only remaining wheel of a bicycle began to spin as I went past, and something—I didn't want to know what—crawled away from me and under a bed sheet. Everything that was old—and everything became old from having been in our attic—was waiting to be resurrected by father. It didn't matter that the center of my earth was only a dirty square meter of wood floor between two roof supports. I had carved my name with a

Axel, Professor Lidenbrock with the miner's lamp, and Hans, their guide, on their way to the center of the earth.

rusty nail in the supports and thrown a sheet over the top of them to make my roof. A couple of blankets that nobody wanted anymore hung down from the supports, and these were my walls.

My furnishings consisted of a moth-eaten pillow; a few ancient piles of dried bat droppings; prune, plum, and peach pits; and an apple that had shriveled up long ago. I didn't even tell Nora, my summer love, about this place. I didn't even bring a pencil or a notebook for my stories. When I was six, I could still stand upright; at nine, my head was hitting my ceiling, the beams, the roof. I huddled in my secret, little space—it wasn't much bigger than the bureau in my bedroom—on a dusty pillow, the protection of the bed-sheet-roof above me, and dreamed up the stories that allowed me to travel wherever my heart desired. Was there really any difference between real journeys and imagined ones? If the rain pattered down on the shingles, my hero in America, Kasperli, got wet too.

Later, back downstairs, when my mother, perhaps with Mix, had gone to church, I wrote the stories down. One day my father took my exercise books to a bindery. After two weeks, a book had been made from Kasperli's eight *Adventures and Heroic Deeds*—so read the subheading—which was also called "a children's story" by the author to alert the target audience. Richly illustrated, just like Jules Verne's books, in color and black and white. With a "Note on the Contents," which the author, nine years old at publication, provided with five examples of his signature, one with a proudly displayed spelling error. The book was hardcover and had a jacket for which the son, along with his father, took artistic responsibility. "Number of copies of the 1974 special edition: One." The book was immediately out of print.

There's no doubt that it was less dangerous to access my center, the attic of my attic, than the center that Axel didn't actually get to in the end. If I were to be discovered I wouldn't have to deal with a sea monster or any other kind of monster, but only with Father Mutt at the Rotmonten church. Where was the volcano to save me from him? I had to hurry. The door of the armoire was open, the bride smiled coolly. Along the cord, down the stairs, *clonk-ffft, clonk-ffft, thud-thud-thud, tick-tock*...almost nine o'clock already, Nana was dancing wildly in the wind, and I was as far away from my bed and my pretending to be asleep as...as...from..."New-York-with-hyfen"...

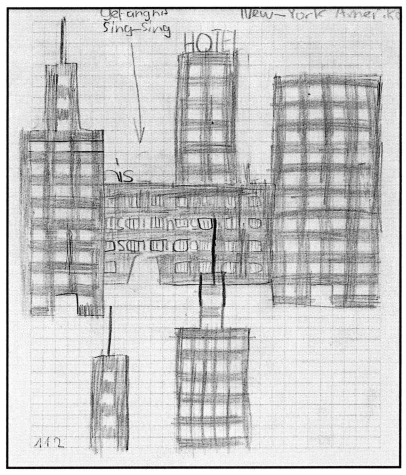

Drawing from "Kasperli as Mailman" by Christoph Keller, *Kasperli: Adventures and Heroic Deeds. By Children for Children. A Children's Story,* story number 4, notebook 6 (continued from volume 2), pp. 112–113, printed and published by CK; binding: G. Fischer, St. Gallen; jacket: CK and AK, 1974.

The extendable cane with the ski advertisement on it is not what I want. We are standing (actually, I'm sitting in my wheelchair; Jan is standing) in the—what's the name of it?—the Hospital-and-Nursing-Supplies-or-Something-Store in St. Gallen. Just like the wheelchair is my lifeboat in the car, so that I can get from the parking lot to the restaurant, the folding cane in the string bag on the back of the wheelchair is to be my lifeboat from the wheelchair parking spot to the urinal.

If I have to relieve myself when we're out and about, Jan helps me out of the wheelchair in front of the public bathroom—that is, assuming we even find one that is accessible to me—by putting her arms around me in a bear hug and pulling me up. She opens the bathroom door, which is often too heavy for my arms, and I set off. Up to five meters, ten, even twenty, no problem. I hold onto the wall, the sinks, the hand dryers, while Jan waits outside. Sometimes, she tells me, she waits for me in the wheelchair even if the—questioning? reproachful? appraising?—looks of the men passing by her are unpleasant.

"A cane can't prevent me from falling," I contend in the Hospital-and-Nursing-Supplies-or-Something-Store. Buying a cane would mean admitting I'm getting a little worse again.

"Not true," Jan says. "Your cane will send a signal that you're not as sure on your feet as you appear. It will make people aware that they need to be more careful."

The cane department of the Hospital-and-Nursing-Supplies-or-Something-Store is also the incontinence department. Mostly plastic, some glass. Who wants to go in glass? And where do you put the glass afterwards? In your briefcase, in your coat pocket? Is it really leakproof? Not now, I'm not incontinent; I'm here for a cane, which I don't really want either. But I could use such a container. In case of emergency, Jan could push me to a discreet spot; I could stay seated in my wheelchair and do my business under the shelter of a tree. Would the police be sympathetic toward a public offense of this sort? It's true, I'd be thumbing my nose at the law, but I could tell myself, isn't the law likewise thumbing its nose at me, in that it makes most public bathrooms inaccessible to me? What sort of equality is it that doesn't even include the right to equal peeing?

My bladder is trained—for impracticable cities, long evenings with friends whose bathrooms are either up or down stairs, the flight from Zurich to New York: seven hours and fifty-five minutes plus two hours to get on and off the plane. I make it to Manhattan without a visit to the bathroom, even though with customs and the taxi ride it's another two hours. As of late (and when Jan isn't there), it's true, I have kept a plastic cocktail shaker next to the bed at night, but I've learned to be

The third sex. The sign hangs near the public bathroom of the St. Gallen Stiftsbibliothek, the collegiate library in the cathedral precincts, above which I attended school (third floor, no elevator, railing on the right) from 1977 to 1979.

silent about such things. My Russian friend Yu, who has helped me up from the toilet—always flush immediately!—says I should write about this; no one else is writing about such things. Okay, I'm writing about it, but I'm ashamed; I'm ashamed when peeing and when writing about it. We have a saying in German: learned is learned. Once you've learned to be ashamed, you're ashamed...

Even the manufacturers are ashamed to manufacture such products. Otherwise, why would they give the Uribag such a childish name? What does it feel like to be in the Nursing-Supplies-or-Something-Store? Just like in a sex shop in a strange city. Hat on. Don't forget the sunglasses. Tock.

...where you gonna run to now...
The voice seeps from Puck's room. I hear my mother's steps. The harder I press my eyes shut the more convincingly I convey the impression I am sleeping. Rott barks, a seldom occurrence. Now (I hold my breath) my mother is standing at my bedroom door.
...hey, hey...
A thirteen-legged spider crawls over my tongue. It's the velvety touch of the toasted, buttered, and "that's-not-good-for-you!" salted Sunday morning braided bread that I was going to miss. Church or breakfast. The door handle lowers (I blink), and the guy calling for Joe

in Puck's room raises his voice. *Tick.* It's eight minutes to church for me and seventeen for Mix. The path is steep but we still walk sometimes: asphalt, gravel, a few stairs, low and wide. I take the stairs with big steps; Mix clings to the railing that separates the meadow from the path. He swings his leg back for each step to get the momentum he needs. For the particularly steep spots at the end of the path, Mix, already a bit exhausted, slips his arm through my mother's. Puck doesn't go with us anymore because he is allergic to incense, as well as to Father Mutt's babble.

Father is too thirsty to hold out for an entire mass. It's not his fault that church doesn't allow one to attend to a natural need, and thus he considers the Church to be an unnatural institution that he'd prefer to stay away from. Drinking less is out of the question. It's also not easy to decide what he is supposed to drink. Orange juice makes him itchy and if he drinks black tea, he can't fall asleep. Mineral water gives him hiccups. The only thing left, heaven knows, is wine. Of that he can drink as much as he wants: no itchiness, no hiccups, no headaches, and sleep?—he can sleep like the Lord himself, sometimes even during the day on the floor of the stamp room in the attic. Some wonder about my father, but no one understands that better than I do. If his RULE says: *Drink!*, he has to drink, and his RULE says that a lot. One can't do anything about it.

"Turn the music down!" *Tock.*

How is Puck supposed to hear that? Anyway, it'd be better for him if he turned the music off completely. What if father gets angry again? One night a little while ago Puck was late for dinner, and although it turned out that his motorcycle broke down, father didn't want to go pick him up. "That should be a lesson to him!" father roared, whereupon our mother asked, "What should be a lesson to him? That he can't get home on his own two feet?" Father screamed that Puck should have thought about that beforehand, and our mother wanted to know what Puck should have thought about beforehand, that his motorcycle could possibly break down? "End of discussion!" he yelled, and climbed upstairs and sat in the bathtub, whereupon mother snuck out of the house to pick up Puck.

I would have almost actually fallen asleep, but sensed my mother bending over me. She knows I'm only pretending to be asleep and I know she's only acting as if she didn't know. How I'd like to open my eyes and look at her. How we'd laugh.

Bam!

I start: They nabbed Joe. The guitar roars one last time and then it's quiet. I hear the scratch of the phonograph needle searching for the next song and at the same time the click of the latch as my mother lets the door shut. The last time I went to mass, Mix fell on the ice out on the square in front of the church and couldn't get up. We rang the doorbell at the rectory, but the housekeeper informed us that Father Mutt couldn't help, for if he did his midday meal would get cold. We asked to use the telephone in the vestibule to call a friend, but the housekeeper could not oblige. She worried that this might disturb the Father as well. My mother promised to keep her voice down, but the housekeeper shook her head, added that the Father, too, was only human, and slammed the door. Two passersby helped Mix to his feet. His legs were so cold he had to lie beneath a blanket half the afternoon.

Puck's song starts again from the beginning, and this time it's loud enough so he can hear it in the shower.

...hey, hey...

I count the strokes of the church tower clock. It's eleven. Father Mutt, followed by two altar boys, glides to the altar, adjusts the microphone, and preaches the Word. He says: Love thy neighbor as thyself. He says: Refrain from sin. He says: Mercy, mercy. He says: For heaven's sake, let not thy lunch get cold. He says: Joe, run to save your soul.

...where you gonna run to now...

As always, Kasperli was lucky. He doesn't have to go to church in Menhetten because there aren't any there and he gets the toasted braided bread with butter and as much salt as he wants.

Tock.

Dear Lord, let there really be no churches in Menhetten!

The saleswoman in the cane and incontinence department of the Nursing-Supplies-or-Something-Store brings me a folding metal cane made of a shiny coppery material with a firm grip. I'm unsuccessful in opening it and folding it up again. Jan tries, also in vain. I make my disabled-people-also-have-to-be-athletes remark. The saleswoman, embarrassed, smiles the Uribag-smile. Also not managing to make a cane out of the four parts joined by elastic, she gets another model. It takes both the saleswoman and Jan together to get this one to work. I'm at phase three of four. To cope with phase four, you have to take the cane in both hands and jack it straight with one swift motion. My arms are tired, but it is a good exercise. I buy the cane and let it disappear forever in the wheelchair string bag behind me. I'll buy the Uribag as soon as they've given it another name.

I once asked a policeman in Paris if the public bathroom he was pointing to with his nightstick was "accessible." He looked at me in astonishment (looked down at me in my wheelchair in astonishment) and said, before turning away, "Theoretically, it should be accessible to everyone." It wasn't.

Part One

On the edge of the bed, socks for the next day; on the breakfast bar, the book for my morning break, Rühmkorf's next-to-last poems. In my head, the thought with which work might begin.

Today it's this thought: Putsch! Down with the totalitarian regime that predetermines my day to the last detail, that robs me of my spontaneity and rigidifies my daily life. Each step is calculated in advance, every movement already foreseen. If I bring my cup from the bar to the kitchen—a mere quarter turn on my own axis—I can save myself a trip by taking what's left of my grapefruit at the same time. As I have to increasingly be stingy with my movements—soon each one will be determined for me beforehand, inscribed in my thinking—my walking will become a close-meshed network of sparse muscle activity that maneuvers me through the day and allows me to think of nothing more than my next motion.

When a thought takes shape in my head I simultaneously think of the route I have to follow to get to my desk to write it down: doorframe, the middle bookshelf (Bulgakov's selected works at shoulder level, my favorite place to grab hold), the back of a chair, my office chair. What's most important with each step is to be careful that I don't stumble: the edge of a carpet or a pencil is all it takes. Increasing my speed—I can quicken my step a little—increases the risk of a fall. My thought pushes me forward, but I have to concentrate on walking. I have to see the step *before executing it. My thought better make it to my desk, otherwise it doesn't deserve to be written down. If it gets there, it's a good one.*

It used to be that my father, when he was home—when he was still at home—could more often than not be found in our two-story attic where I had dreamed up my first stories. On the third and fourth floors of our house on Alpsteinstrasse, which floated in the *foehn*, halfway between the mountains and the city in its high-lying valley, he reigned over his kingdom. Up there was where he oversaw his collection of everything: photographing it, organizing it, and, equipped with loupe, cigar, and bookkeeper's visor, numbering it, determining its value, and with his Collection K stamp, designating it irrevocably his own.

As the collection grew, various off-site storage facilities were required: the attic of our garden house, our tool shed-turned-shooting range, the double garage (where the clocks soon hung in two rows and, in the early days, frightened my mother when she parked her car), and the atelier house, which would soon be crammed equally as full. He expanded into empty apartments and soon emptied apartments in the buildings that his business bought as tax deductions. No unused corner in his factory was safe, and soon the same was true for the used ones. Paintings hung close, one above the other, transforming the corridors into galleries. Sculptors came to have their sculptures welded together by the factory workmen. In a barn outside the city he hoarded old furniture that he breathed new life into (or had others breathe new life into) as soon as he had the time or money to do so and as long as the furniture hadn't already mildewed, moldered, rotted, decayed, or whatever its particular way of departing this world was, rendering the remains useless, even to my father.

His father, who was also named Alfons, had done his share of combing through the flea markets too, though he limited himself to old weapons and pewter, and, most of all, to the spatial constraints of his apartment, which he was prepared to adhere to. Alfons, Sr. didn't need much and by sticking to his limits he may have been what those in St. Gallen call *brötig*—literally "bready," meaning bourgeois. And even though this might be the worst insult that the good citizens of St. Gallen may have devised for themselves, my modest grandfather always seemed to be a satisfied man.

The only boundary he overstepped with certainty—and gusto—was the German-Swiss one at Lake Constance. The German-born Alfons had, as he liked to tell it, marched into Switzerland as a traveling journeyman plumber. Burst pipe after burst pipe, clogged toilet by clogged toilet, he advanced on Switzerland from the Allgäu, ultimately taking the country by storm, and drain. He also liked to recount—taking care that Alfons, Jr. was within earshot—how his father had taught him a lesson in modesty. After asking for an increase in pocket money via a color postcard, he received a refusal from this father that was penny-pinching, even with words: "If you can afford a color postcard, you certainly don't need more money."

In 1926, Alfons, Sr. settled in St. Gallen. He joined Dornbirer's tinsmith shop, founded two decades earlier, and the two of them ran the business—an "& Keller" added to the name of the shop—at the Platztor on Sankt Jakobsstrasse outside the old town. The tinsmiths became fitters and the tinsmith shop, "Gas, Water, and Drain Fittings." Following Dornbirer's retirement in 1940, and the subsequent retirement of the "Dornbirer &" from the company sign, "Gas, Water, and Drain Fittings" became the more modern "Sanitary Installations."

The bells of the St. Mangen church woke my grandfather each morning, meaning he never had to get himself an alarm clock. He met his wife, Maria Wetter, in her parents' bakery where he bought his morning roll. So she wouldn't have to spend her whole life working her fingers to the bone behind the counter of a bakery, he married her, he proudly explained, "across the street," for that's where they settled, and she spent her whole life making bread for him instead. This was how he started a family and brought his days on the road to a close. He was also modest when it came to children, having one son and one daughter. Nothing enticed him away anymore. No travels in the motley world: St. Gallen, in its misty high-lying valley, was enough for one life. The honeymoon took them to the Allgäu, perhaps in order to bid a final farewell to his journeyman years. He moved into an apartment only once in his life, and with good money, he furnished it such that it would outlive him. He moved out only once too: a few years after my grandmother passed away, he went to a nursing home, where he died.

Grandfather's apartment was located on the roof of the building in which Dornbirer & Keller had its premises. Once he ran out of space here he declared his pewter and weapons collection complete and stopped collecting. He put one or two boxes of pewterware, which he had been able to replace inexpensively with better pieces, in storage, and even that nagged at him. His little blue notebook, in which he listed each item of his collection, lay on the buffet by the entrance to his apartment; once the collection was concluded, space was made for the notebook in the top drawer.

The pewter items decorated the apartment. He kept the weapons, however, in a little house that stood on the roof terrace. It was reached through the kitchen over two steep steps and through a small sitting area equipped with a pergola for the summer sun. In his later years, when I was five, six, perhaps even seven years old, I often spent an afternoon at his apartment. I'd sit at the living room table and assemble the same model house over and over again. It was a difficult task—the walls had to be erected from beams and each shingle placed individually on the roof. If I had assembled everything properly, I was rewarded by a light turning on inside the house. When grandfather, who didn't want me to play in the little roof house by myself, opened the door to the terrace, I would drop what I was doing and follow after him. Already a bit stooped with age—hardly noticeable for all his corpulence—he was forced to hold onto the doorframe. He took a gulp of air for each step and gave himself the heave his body needed to cope with the height difference— breathe in, breathe out, *heave!* breathe in, breathe out, *heave!*—until, using his portly self as an air pump, he had hoisted himself outside. As I write this, these "symptoms" sound eerily familiar to me.

Just as everything had to be a little bit bigger at his son's, everything was a little bit smaller in the little roof house—out of protest, chance, or just because. A small gabled roof, a tiny chimney, which supplied a scaled-down fireplace with the means for smoke to escape, small shingles, two small rooms. To enter the little house grandfather had to bend down. Like the doors that led to my attic corridor, the doors here were also on the small side and even if they weren't quite as tiny as mine—after all, they had to grant my grandfather entry—they, too, were the doors of a long-moldered armoire that had been finally put out to pasture.

In my memory—the little house and the building on which it stood are no longer—the furniture seems suspiciously small, as if it had been specially made for me. I sat comfortably on my chair at the little table while my grandfather, a giant who swallowed the chair beneath him, had to squeeze into the corner across from me. Here, everything was as tidy as my father's attic was untidy. Everything had its place, while for my father space seemed to exist solely to be conquered by accumulated objects. Even the dust seemed to conform to these two opposing principles of organization: there, the kingdom suffocating beneath its weight; here, the dust-free zone designed to last an eternity.

The weapons, weapons from all epochs and wars (as Mix confirmed for me), were the only things in grandfather's little roof house presented in their original size. Yet the halberds, morning stars, crossbows, sabers, knights' armor, and the rifle grandfather had used in World War I, seemed more harmless, not more threatening, in the scaled-down surroundings. The armor I could slip into, the sabers I was allowed to whish from their sheathes (as well as I could: the sabers came up to my chin). I cleaned pistols—though they were already spotless—with a long wire brush, lubricated them with invisible oil, and stuffed them with imaginary powder. Then, using my left arm to position, I aimed at the armor in the corner, the hunting horn, the twin pistols on the wall, the family coat of arms, the St. Gallen bear, and pulled the trigger. *Click, click* the enemy I didn't have would always die straightaway.

When grandfather died in the early 1970s the valuable pewter collection, as well as everything else, went in equal parts to my father and his sister, who had a particular knack for inheriting. His share of pewter teetered on the sofa while hers, the larger of the two, towered on the living room table. What she didn't know was that her brother had tricked her, passing off the inferior pieces as the whole of the collection. "The stupid cow," father boasted when he arrived home with this carload of pewter and proudly presented his loot to us—his share of the inferior stuff and all of the valuable items—would "never find out anyway."

Alfons, Jr., "Föns" to his friends, completed elementary school in St. Gallen as well as an apprenticeship at his father's plumbing company. Even as a young man he was an overpowering presence: beefy, robust, heavy-boned, with a hairline already in retreat. He combed the strands back, making his already prominent brow even more powerful. He had charm, humor, was surprisingly romantic, vulnerable, and ponderous.

He moved with unmistakable authority, as if one of those mysterious Easter Island sculptures that made such an impression on him had broken free of its petrified state.

The cathedral, centrally located and open on Sundays, seemed to Föns to be the right place to scout around for a bride. While he envisioned the altar as a workbench and the altar rail as a fence for the garden he didn't yet have (but without a doubt would have) his gaze remained fixed on the white neck of an unknown beauty. Her light brown hair set off the crescent of her neck, which was bisected by a modest, yet valuable (he could tell) and properly polished silver chain. Was she not an optimal fit for the Hollywood swing in his future backyard? Style was what this neck-crescent promised, tenderness and grace, why, simply everything that was missing

Carl Liner,
portrait of my mother, 1955.

in his life. When she turned around, briefly exposing first the magnificent curve of her right cheek and then her long, elegant nose, he knew it made no sense to wait until mass was over, for the Hollywood swing, which would have a blue cover and white buttons, had already started to rock gently in his head.

Max Falk, who sat beside him on the pew, would be given the job of finding out the name of the unknown beauty. Not that patience was Föns's strength, but having his friend also ascertain, while he was at it, whether the altar might be purchased and, if yes, for how much (and whether there was any wiggle room on the price), and would the bishop (or whoever was in charge of such matters) accept a few free plumbing hours as payment, was something he saved for another occasion. He elbowed Max in the side and, with an upward movement of his chin, drew his friend's attention to the object of his desire seated seven rows in front of them. That one? No, not the old bag, nitwit, the one next to her. The task was clearly a delicate one for the devout Catholic, and so Föns whispered to the painter that he'd buy a drawing off him or, better still, as a token of his affection, he'd give him a refrigerator. Though for a refrigerator, he said getting up, he really also ought to get an oil painting: ideally a portrait of his future wife. Föns let the cathedral door bang shut, and Max, the prospect of a refrigerator in his head, said his amen to the amen of the mass.

Föns took the antiques route home, envisioned "sold" tags on several pieces of furniture he saw in shop windows, and thought about where he would put these items in his future house.

Max followed his friend's intended as she crossed the square in front of the cathedral accompanied by an escort, an older gentleman (her father?). He decided he'd portray her seated.

Meanwhile, running into Fräulein Biedermann at the market place, Föns decided to involve her in his marital plans as well.

Max's fiancée, who would certainly be impressed by the new refrigerator, had stood when he'd painted her. She was cold because he could not afford to heat his studio (the atelier house), and she was cold because he painted her nude.

Yes, Fräulein Biedermann would do Föns the favor of inviting his bride-to-be to one of her soirées, as the conceited cow called her social functions, and soon he would make his future wife's acquaintance. Thanking her, Föns headed to the next antique store.

The stranger and her father went into Café Pfund on the Marktplatz where she bought (as she did every Sunday after mass) a selection of the chocolatier's trademark *zwanzgerstückli* (pastries costing twenty centimes apiece). She emerged holding the shop's small, pink, eight-piece selection gift box tied with a ribbon in her long, graceful hands.

In order not to sin in the eyes of the Catholic Church by doing a nude painting of the woman with whom he would enter into the bonds of marriage, Max—the already quite respected portrait painter of Catholic saints in St. Gallen—had taken precautions: he'd lent his fiancée the face of an arbitrary woman. But because he sincerely loved his bride-to-be, the sight of her naked caused him to render her face with such a level of arbitrariness that her body ultimately appeared as if it had been created by God while her head seemed the work of an amateur.

What was keeping Max? Föns had already sat down with his parents and sister to Sunday dinner (roast beef, peas, mashed potatoes, red wine; Föns was the only one who always had second helpings of everything). He had seen so many pieces on his antiques route that he had not only furnished his future villa (twenty-four rooms) but had also, in his head, rented a barn where he could store the other items.

But maybe this was okay, Max reasoned. This way he could, if need be (for instance, to heat the atelier house), sell the nude of his betrothed, with its arbitrary face that didn't recall a single woman in this world (or any other). In doing so, however, might he not only be sinning against the church, but also allowing this shoddily done visage to tarnish his professional honor?

Max would have nearly lost sight of Föns's future wife and mother of (ideally) two children (first a boy, then a girl), when the banging of a garden gate reminded him of the obligation he had to his friend. The mystery woman followed her father (for he was her father) over stone steps and into a modest, whitewashed house with a gabled roof. No sooner had they disappeared than Max approached the mailbox and noted down the name: The Franz Josef Hämmerle family.

Max breathed a sigh of relief. First, he could restore his professional honor by painting the face of Fräulein Hämmerle particularly well. Second, he could save his soul at his next confession. Third (and as additional penance), he could sell—as a precautionary measure— the nude of his fiancée with the unsuccessful head, presumably to Föns, who had already approached him once about buying "something of the sort." And, on top of all this, he, Max Falk, would get a refrigerator. Everything, everything would fall into place, just like everything always did, when one entrusted oneself to God.

Although she was not acquainted with Fräulein Biedermann, Ruth (for this was Fräulein Hämmerle's first name) gladly accepted the surprise invitation. It provided her with an opportunity to spend an evening outside her father's four walls and sphere of influence. She told him that Fräulein Biedermann was an old friend with whom she'd lost touch. Franz Josef set her curfew for eleven and said he would be waiting for her watch in hand.

Föns danced with Ruth once that evening, with the unwieldiness of an Easter Island statue that had lost its way on a Swiss dance floor. Before driving her home shortly before eleven, he shook her hand as if it were a client's whose burst pipe he had just successfully repaired and informed her that their paths would undoubtedly cross again soon.

He started the siege the next day. Having estimated how long she needed to walk to the transport company where she worked, he waited in front of her house at the calculated time. When she came out, he pushed the car door open. On the passenger seat was a package of one dozen *zwanzgerstückli*, mostly cream slices. She told herself she would accept the sweets this once and said thank you. He drove her to work, as he would everyday henceforth: mornings, afternoons, evenings, for two years (on and off)—tirelessly, always punctual, always distrustful.

From the very beginning my father called my mother his collection item no. 1. Though he may not have reconditioned her the way he did his other pieces—it really wasn't necessary—he did photograph her, arrange her in numerous albums, and assign her captions and numbers:

My mother, five years old, in a white lace-trimmed dress that was no doubt a product of her father's textile company; he was a textile merchant. She is standing in front of her family's magnificent house in Austria—built the year before, in 1934, in Lustenau in Vorarlberg. A house the local authorities had had their eye on even before Austria's *anschluss* to Germany. Since Franz Josef's wife, Hermine Hämmerle-Kessler, had consistently refused to return the new salute when crossing the border, an obscenity the German authorities entrusted the Austrian authorities to handle, the takeover of the house moved one gratifying step closer. In Munich, my mother's parents were expelled from a hotel after Hermine, upon noticing the lack of butter at breakfast, summoned the manager and informed him that it was better for a country to make butter than guns. But before the local authorities, encouraged by the German authorities, descended upon the house, they'd often taken occasion to requisition grandfather's sedan, a black Fiat, for the arm-pitching parades that were held with ever greater urgency in Vorarlberg. The Fiat was covered with flags from top to bottom and my grandfather recognized it on the street only by its license plate, a letter-number combination that stood for paradise only once he'd lost it. When Austria officially decided in favor of Germany in 1938, my grandparents fled. The family reached Switzerland with their three daughters in two cars via different border crossings. Franz Josef had not taken his son along: the tuition for the current semester had been paid in advance and Franz Josef was a businessman after all. At the Stella Matutina Jesuit School in Feldkirch, his only son remained behind to see the new rulers dismember the crucifixes and piss in the holy water fonts. A "good Nazi," who didn't want to believe his new God was capable of such atrocities, drove

my young uncle personally to his parents in Switzerland. Meanwhile, the Fascists filled my grandfather's house with babies bred according to their standards, rearing them to replace those who failed to fit the new trend. When the war was over the Allies needed quarters. They, too, preferred grand houses, and so my grandparents, with the help of the mayor, arranged for the babies (now no longer the future of the Aryan race), who had grown up in Franz Josef's former home, to remain where they were for the time being. It was better for the house to accommodate toddlers and their caretakers than the marauding soldiers of a victorious army. When the house became my grandparents' property again they chose to remain in St. Gallen. They discovered that they—because of the house? Or because my grandmother hadn't returned their silly salute?—had been on the list for Buchenwald. They had escaped deportation because the local authorities—thanks to their continued lack of experience—had arrested my grandfather's brother instead. "Traitors," their neighbors had called them when the nightmare was over. "You ran off and had a grand old time when we'd have needed you most." "Really?" Hermine retorted, having lost none of her quick-wittedness or penchant for confrontation while in Switzerland. "I had the impression we were raining on your parade."

More pleasant photos: My mother, already in Switzerland, as a ten-year-old pupil in front of the Catholic girls' boarding school in Menzingen. She escaped the daily morning mass and the endless kneeling on the hard wooden benches with the aid of a gentle tap on the side of her nose. This caused a weak vein to burst and blood to flow. Allowing a drop to fall on her thick wool dress she'd throw her head back to get the attention of the mother superior, who, in turn, would immediately send my mother out of the church—thus preventing a major bloodbath. The miracle of the nose-that-always-bled-during-morning mass was something the mother superior never got wise to.

My mother as daughter, between her parents, the beloved brother, who died young, and her two sisters; my mother on a bench in the municipal park with her father; my mother as a would-be fashion model, flirting with the idea of a career on the catwalk—supine, her long hair thrown melodramatically over the floor. This picture is followed in the album by my mother on a stage in Bregenz, the one time she was able to fill in for a model who had fallen ill. My mother as a bride. My mother in one of the countless north Italian churches my father dragged her to on their honeymoon. My mother with my brothers and Dora, our housekeeper, who refused to put the feather duster aside even for the photographer. My mother as a newly minted homeowner proudly standing in front of a bed of roses in what was now her garden. My mother pregnant with me, although the idea had been to stop after two sons. And from these pages on—I'm leafing through faster—my mother as mother: in weatherproof loden coat, with the dog leash in her hand and windblown hairdo, her cheerful face slightly weather-beaten and marked by fatigue, the good sort—out and about with the boys and Rott, the dog. My mother happy in a glade, my favorite picture.

If I want to sneeze, I have to stop. The wind I produce recoiling could knock me over despite my cane.

My father, who married my mother in May 1953, was a big eater and drinker. He enjoyed company. After midnight my mother opened the living room windows, letting the cold air in, to remind the guests to bid their farewells. "We have two small children who have to sleep," she would say, although she also liked guests. "I have a bottle of wine that still needs drinking," my father would reply. The guests would slip into their coats, wrap scarves around their necks, put gloves on, and set about drinking the new bottle of wine Föns had already opened. My parents spent their leisure time at the Lions Club, on the golf course, in artists' studios, at flea markets, in Fröhlich's five-story antique store near the cathedral, and—though often my mother went alone with her sons—with friends on the lake.

At first, Föns had more money than he needed to pay the outstanding invoices. As he earned more and spent even more, he started calling his acquisitions "investments." Whatever he dragged home was never anything less than a *trouvaille* and the seller a "complete moron, who understands nothing of his business. I guarantee you, Ruth, this piece is just going to increase in value," as if he ever considered parting with an object voluntarily. The collection "diversified itself," as if it had become an independent being, the collector helplessly at its mercy. His reinsurance was his business and business was better and better, for the business was now him (which was also the reason why he never allowed it to incorporate). After his father retired, the enterprise was his entirely. To "Keller Sanitary Installations" was added "Keller Mirrored Cabinets," and then, quickly growing larger, "Keller Metalworking."

Every day he brought home something new: a turret clock, a crossbow William Tell might have shot with, a Fabergé egg that had belonged to Catherine the Great, a rusty saw from an abandoned sawmill, a little oil lamp from a plundered Etruscan tomb, an evil "Negro sculpture," as they were still called then. Once, when he was quarreling with a supplier about an unpaid invoice, he placed this last item in the stairwell of his business where the steps were steepest. The very next week the supplier stumbled on it, breaking his ankle. If that hadn't been a worthwhile investment!

"I don't have to pay for it right away," he said, when he saw his wife's worried look.

"You have to pay for it at some point. Let's save for the business. How do we know times will always be like this? And for the children...," Franz Josef's good daughter said.

It didn't occur to my mother to ask for jewelry or a designer dress or that weekend in a many-star hotel on Lake Maggiore, or even simply for more money for the household. Had she asked she would have gotten it: he was always generous. But she frequently said that she didn't need these things. That was her way of telling him he should save his money. What she didn't get would earn interest at the bank, she imagined. But it didn't work that way. What his wife didn't want—and hadn't he offered over and over?—didn't turn into savings but into the chest of drawers at Fröhlich's, the one with the "reserved" label already dangling from it.

Because even he sometimes felt uneasy about this course of action, the presentation of the acquisition at home would be endorsed with a "Ruth, this is for you."

"What am I supposed to do with another painting by Carl Liner?" she promptly replied. "The walls are full. Plus, we already have one of his Brühlbach oils. And if you're really getting all this for me, next time I'd like to be there when the selection is made."

"And this here is for Puck!"

"How come I never see any of these things again—after you've brought them home for *me*?"

"You yourself just said the walls are full, didn't you? You never come to the workshop where I keep the paintings. I'm happy to show you my collection."

"*Your* collection."

"It's all for you, the woman at my side."

Franz Josef had taught her (and the war him) what had value. Cash had value, solid walls had value, a house with a roof that didn't leak had value. Her husband's dust collectors, however, did not.

My mother, already the master of and-another-thing, said, "You're paying for it all in the end."

"Of course." But there was no stopping him. He was already onto the next idea. "We need more space."

"For things?" Having more space was something she feared as much as she longed for.

"For you. You're pregnant again. And there's a house on Alpsteinstrasse made for us. I was just there. It has a first floor apartment with seven rooms. Plus we'd get a spacious basement and two attic rooms, where I could set up my workshops. The house is bigger—and nicer—than your father's! What do you say? Agreed? I've already signed the lease. You'll love it, you'll see!"

The house on Alpsteinstrasse, ca. 1960

And he was right. What a magnificent house it was, with a yard like a park. The family of four moved in on December 1, 1957. Initially, they lived in the spacious apartment on the first floor. High ceilings, huge windows. The large hall window framed the Alpstein panorama—after which the street was named. Max Falk mixed a dark violet for the living room ceiling; the artist friends stayed even longer. Tall larch trees and flowering rhododendrons generously bordered the yard. The garden, a small park laid out in the English style, contained trimmed hedges, rose bushes, and gravel paths. The convent on the opposite hill gleamed white at night and floating over everything, in the *foehn*, the mighty Alps.

After three years, Franz Josef bought the house on Alpsteinstrasse, all four stories of it, for his daughter and her family. His son-in-law, whose money was now being oh-so-profitably invested, tried to persuade him to put it in his name, as it was proper, he said, for a house to be registered in the husband's name, after all. Franz Josef let him know in no uncertain terms that if it was the fate of one of his daughters to live in a flea market at least the flea market should belong to her. Each of his children had received a house from him, not even a war had been able to take his own house away for long, and now it was his youngest daughter's turn to get her fortress for life. Four children, four houses: the *Lustenau ur-house* had quadrupled.

Where to begin? When did it start? Was there an incident? There is no date in my diary I can tick off as the exact day the muscle weakness, the slowing down, set in. Was it the first time I had to support myself on the armrest to be able to get up out of our low lounge chair? The first time, groping, I grabbed on to the banister? Was it much earlier, when I suddenly demonstrated an inexplicable clumsiness while jumping rope—and if that was the beginning, when was that exactly?

Two are enough, my mother thought in 1963. The boys, her husband, the house, the garden, the feisty dog. Dora, who had a room in the attic and helped out. Föns now visited the flea markets, antique shops, and artists' studios alone. He only rarely showed his finds; if they made it into the house at all they sat in paper bags on the stairway and disappeared into the attic after dinner.

When Max Falk, his wife, and three children moved out of the atelier house to live outside the city where it was cheaper, Föns took over the lease to surprise my mother. As she wasn't able to summon the necessary enthusiasm, he said he was only doing it, after all, to relieve the strain on the Alpsteinstrasse house. But relief didn't come. On the contrary. And surprise was something my mother felt only once it emerged that her husband had already been renting the atelier house for a year.

Did he show her his treasures less and less frequently because she would only just say it wasn't necessary and couldn't they use the money for other things? He would tell her there was plenty of money. Did she not have enough housekeeping money? Of course she did. The sons? They also had everything. The bills? All paid. She shouldn't worry about these things. She was his "goddess," hadn't he discovered her in the cathedral? She didn't like hearing that; it sounded like heresy. Plus, she wasn't comfortable on the pedestal on which he placed her.

Sometimes the dark living room ceiling weighed heavily on her. Upstairs lay her ailing mother. In between caring for her she fed a five- and a seven-year-old. Ruth had to give her mother an injection every four hours to relieve her pain. A year after Josef's death, Hermine had fallen on the kitchen floor in her apartment and hadn't been able to get up; Ruth and Föns had decided to take her in. This meant they'd had to renege on a promise. For a quarter of a century, a widow had lived on the third floor. She donned white gloves when she dusted and whenever she wanted to watch the boys playing in the yard from her living room window she asked their parents' consent. My mother felt like a traitor. They had promised the woman, who was approaching ninety, that she could die in her apartment.

Now it was her own mother who was dying there. She could hear the coughing through the ceiling. Each cough had her running upstairs to comfort her, but no sooner would she reach the third floor when one of the boys would start bawling or the dog would bark. Twice a night Föns got up to give his mother-in-law her injections. The weight of the bed sheets hurt her bones, which were crumbling to dust. If she moved her arm, it might break; a violent cough had already caused her to crack a rib.

No, this was not the time for a third child. What could she do? Talk to Föns about it? Could she still talk to him about such a thing? What could she talk to him about? What did they still talk about? She'd bring up the boys; he'd speak of collector's joys. She remained in the kitchen long after their rushed dinners, while he disappeared into the attic or drove to the atelier house. If she was still awake when he returned, she could smell the alcohol announcing him. She went to an internist. He recommended an abortion, because of her low blood pressure. Even God himself could have no objections, for surely, ensuring her survival was not a sin.

But her gynecologist knew his audience. "You were raised a Catholic, Ruth," he said. "That means this child, if aborted—not that

I would do it—will haunt you the rest of your life. You're not the type. And for what? Your husband earns enough money and you have enough room." Then he reeled in his catch. "Whatever might go wrong in your life, and something will always go wrong, you'll attribute it to this sin. An abortion is a curse. I don't know a single woman who has really gotten over an abortion. And it would hit you harder than it would other women."

So while her mind submitted to God's will, her body sought a solution for which she couldn't be held liable. And she might have succeeded. What she did was the following: She worked more and harder, lugged heavy things around, bent down quickly only to straighten back up just as quickly, jumped whenever the opportunity presented itself, bounded up and down the steps even louder and more frequently than the men in her life, tirelessly mowed the steepest patch of grass in the yard—

"And what now?"

Could one get eternal damnation for lawn mowing?

"What do you think?"

My mother pregnant with me, 1963.

Even the gynecologist couldn't say what exactly had brought on the bleeding.

"I'll tell you. You need to decide now. There are only two possibilities. Either I give you an injection and you stay in bed for eight days, not one day less, and you'll have your baby. Or I don't give you the injection."

It had never been a real choice.

At any rate, I do know the exact date I reached for a cane for the first time: November 17, 1998. The only way into Jan's small apartment in New York's West Village was via seven steps, so we lived in a sublet on the Upper West Side. C., a professor of Medieval Studies (I found a facsimile of the St. Gallen cathedral in his apartment), was paralyzed from the waist down after a car accident and dependent on a wheelchair. Maybe that was why he always let us have his three-room apartment for such a low rent.

I'd been following the advice of an American doctor and trying out a new drug, a steroid that athletes use to build up their muscles. For three weeks it made me stronger, restored me "muscle-wise" to where I was two years before. My pace picked up; I walked on air. Then, also overnight, it was all over. Whether it had to do with the drug, with which I experimented a bit, I don't know. Nobody really knows, even if the research is getting wiser to SMA's tricks.

All the same, since that November day I haven't taken a single step without a cane or without holding onto Jan's arm, or onto walls, the backs of chairs, picture frames, or even the stalks of plants. A roughly 130-centimeter-long slender piece of picture frame that I discovered behind a wardrobe in the living room served as my first cane. It was rickety, junk; why hadn't C. thrown it out? It would have buckled had I really tried to support myself with it. But what I needed was stability, or, to be more precise, the illusion of stability. It was enough for me to hold that slender length of wood in my hand and, with it, to establish contact between my hand and the floor so that I could balance my way through the room with some degree of safety. I only bought my regular cane (whose rubber tip was now missing) once we were back in St. Gallen. It is a slim, black, aluminum rod, for which I am constantly complimented.

My parents on my father's fortieth birthday, April 20, 1964.
He was a passionate hunter.

While the "worsening" is happening, it seems to cover up feelings and command compensation to make up for weaknesses—my body almost always comes up with a way out. If my body stops having ideas, I have to have them: Instead of a breakfast table, a breakfast bar; instead of climbing stairs, a stair lift; for walking distances beyond the apartment, the wheelchair; and sometimes, now, the cane for equilibrium. This must go on. It always does somehow. Already a wooden frame has turned up behind a wardrobe; a moment earlier, it had been garbage, now it is my stopgap salvation. At first I am pleased with the chance discovery, with my ability to solve a problem. Later, what I must really feel becomes apparent: helplessness, rage, fear, powerlessness. Resignation. What is draining is that I will constantly have to rely on newer and newer stopgap measures. Feelings, too, are compensated for. Onward, onward...

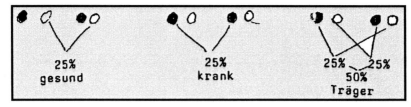

Hereditary factors

What I lost on that November day in 1998 was not equilibrium, but the idea of it. Afterward, as I moved like a tightrope walker, the black aluminum cane became my balancing pole. My next loss was open space. Although I didn't have to hold onto the walls, I needed their reassuring closeness. Now, when I walk, the reassurance of the walls is no longer enough for me. In one hand, the cane, while the other seeks, with each inch I move forward, something to grab onto: the bureau, the back of a chair, the walls, which, I notice, I always touch in the same places. My fingers leave gray traces on the white surface, abstract drawings that change daily. Sometimes I think I should have wooden frames made (as an homage to my picture-frame cane?), hang them over the drawings, and sign the resulting pictures.

I remain sitting and wait for what will happen. In my head, sentences happen. Sentences, strong as muscles, that gain, not lessen, in strength, and I realize that it is the same strength, only it has shifted.

As the feudal period, when we still had all twenty-four rooms on Alpsteinstrasse to ourselves, was drawing to a close in the 1970s, I would often, weary from reading, lie awake at night for a long time in my bed—itself a collection piece, of course, and likewise numbered. It sat directly under the nerve center of my father's collection in the attic. With closed eyes, I—collection item no. 4, after my mother and my two older brothers—would try to extract a direction, a purpose for the ceaseless creaking of wood caused by the steps above me.

The third floor of the house was where we slept: four bedrooms, my mother's dressing room, two bathrooms, and, the site of the secret high point of the day (secret, because the appliance found here was intended solely for my father), our parents' WC, behind the brown paneled door, with its Clos-o-Mat. Those were the days when I first read Rabelais, whom I had discovered in father's library. I found the three volumes untapped in their soapy, waxed protective paper and deduced they were meant for me, the finder. Nearly every page contained a drawing, which would expedite the reading of the fifteen hundred pages, as if the speed with which one completed a book mattered. Rabelais' crude wit, not unlike my father's, was something I took notice of. Natural things were spoken of naturally, in the way one wasn't allowed to speak of them unless one was a dead classic author or my father, who defied everything. It was obvious to me that Gargantua would not have chosen his "neck of a goose, that is well downed, if you hold her head betwixt your legs" as the best of all ass-wipers, but rather our Clos-o-Mat had he sat upon it just once.

Nowadays, when terms like *ass-wiper* are no longer supposed to be used, everyone knows that a Clos-o-Mat is a toilet installed with a hands-free, paperless mechanism for washing one's bottom, that is, a fanny washer. At the push of a button, the unmentionable area of the sitter, male or female, is cleansed with a jet of pleasantly warm water, and the little hairs are even given a bit of a blow-dry. However, back then, in St. Gallen (in fact, in all of Switzerland), not a single soul knew anything about a wonder of plumbing of this sort, because such a thing was, of course, only built for kings. And, as everybody also knows, Switzerland has never had a king, and never will, as our best and most incorruptible of all democracies would never tolerate such a thing on the throne. Only not everything everybody knows is always true, as everybody basically knows; and only I, and I alone, had the proof, and with it the power to transform our entire country with one single word into a monarchy.

Did I say the word? Of course not, because I was not a subversive boy; because it was enough for me to know that our country was secretly a monarchy, even more unshakable than the English one; and because back then I didn't want to share my king with anyone. The fact that there was a Clos-o-Mat toilet in our house meant nothing less than that the king lived with us. And that king was my father. And I, though the youngest of three sons, was heir to the throne. As a result, it was my natural right of succession to profit from the royal insignia whenever I felt the urge (or the call of nature).

For years (it was the mid-1970s), I saw my father—this went through my head as I lay in bed and tried to fix the position of his steps above me—as the Supreme Ruler of All Helvetians and The Whole of Helvetia, particularly of my small two-and-a-half-thousand-square-meter Little Switzerland on Alpsteinstrasse, which was neatly fenced in and fitted with two locked entryways. Yet now, sleep eluding me and my gaze directed at the ceiling, I was old enough to realize that the creaking kingdom above me had already long since perished. Though, nothing was said. Certainly nothing that mattered. So I kept quiet, kept quiet more than ever, for the progressive, incurable, always fatal illness called becoming-an-adult, which had been diagnosed in me around this time and would henceforth take its irreversible course, silenced me.

Perhaps this is why I am only now wondering, seeing that I am suffering from all the symptoms of being-an-adult, why this story, which for me began in many respects like a royal fairy tale, turned out the way it did. Is it because childhoods are fairy tales told in reverse, because the kissed prince turns into a frog, because the imagination is hopelessly clouded by the grind of everyday life, as if it is forever November on Lake Constance? Or because, in the end, an ass-wiper can only be a Clos-o-Mat and that gargantuan "wonderful pleasure, both in regard of the softness of the said down and  of the temporate heat of the goose, which is easily communicated to the bum-gut and the rest of the inwards, in so far as to come even to the regions of the heart and brains" can no longer be felt at that unnamed area, having been replaced by the speechlessness of assholes clinically cleaned?

Just as father filled the Alpsteinstrasse house—which was his in every respect except on paper—in order to appropriate it, he also bought books mostly only to possess them. While he at least leafed through the art volumes and consulted them as references for his collection, he no longer even took the literature titles out of their protective paper. Through the possession of an object, that for him, the non-reader, seemed to pose a threat, he was able to subjugate it. Did he suspect he had only to unpack one of these threatening beings and read it for all his big talk to fizzle into air?

My father thought of himself as a conqueror, and he conquered literature, so he may have thought, by buying up as much of it as he could.

He had instructed a local bookseller to send him, in weekly deliveries, every book on art and antiques as well as (a boon for me) the entire ongoing publication list of the Zurich publisher Diogenes: drawings and cartoons from Flora to Searle, contemporary Irish literature from O'Connor to O'Flaherty, the Americans from Bradbury to Highsmith, and my favorites: the illustrated Jules Verne editions and the anthologies, from *Murder* to *More Horror Stories*. To my knowledge, however, my father never dignified any of his purchases with a second look.

For several years he had the money for this, as well as the space in our large house. I secretly relocated the literature section of his library, book by book, to my room. At first, I was modest about what I took, out of respect for the reading materials but also for fear of my father. I think what drove me to take the books without asking was his phrase, "what's mine is yours," which sounded a little bit more like a threat each time it was repeated. The books also seemed to gain in value when I treated them as smuggled goods, thereby restoring the worthiness my father's lack of discrimination had taken from them. Although I may have told myself at the beginning that I would return them to the attic, the books ended up remaining with me as the quiet protest all good books are anyway, but also as proof of the reading services rendered—not to mention as another partial victory in an undeclared competition with Zack, my school friend, for the biggest and best book collection.

The collecting virus had attacked us both. I know where mine came from, but don't know where Zack had picked up his, maybe from me. Our rooms were similar: we had put up posters, predominantly of scantily clad female singers, on our walls; we kept records, predominantly by male singers, on our shelves. We cut out everything that had anything to do with music and glued these cut-outs onto prepunched sheets that we filed away alphabetically in a rapidly growing number of binders, thus making us chief investors of glue sticks at our local supermarket. Zack and I were St. Gallen's Stone Age version of the Internet: click on a name and within seconds we'd have isolated a minimum of five pages of material on the desired topic, plus a dozen links to related subjects. When working on the entries for the male singers, one of us would call the other. New findings had to be discussed and certain ones withheld so as not to jeopardize the information edge gained. When subjecting female singers to the scissors, no phone calls were made, just the shared solitary visit to the bathroom of our respective homes.

Bookcases, record shelves, cassette stands. The rack Zack had mounted over his desk, a towering five levels of tapes, collapsed on his head during one of our analytic discussions. I laughed as I heard the clattering, crashing, and cursing through the telephone. This mishap set him back weeks, if not months. Complete years of Swiss pop hit parade had fallen on him. Ultimately, he won the competition anyway by constantly using my means—my pocket money—for his own ends. If he couldn't convince me to lend him money, he wheedled me so effectively that I ended up buying the record he would have bought himself with the cash he'd wanted to mooch from me. He had enough time on the way home to talk me into lending him my new purchase overnight so he could tape it.

While my father wanted to possess books physically so he wouldn't have to read them, I read books (and so did Zack, I believe) so I could possess them. I had to render a service that justified the way they became my property—theft? transfer of possession? permanent loan? I started to read at an early age, wherever I was and whenever I could. And I always wanted to have what I had read close to me, as proof of the service rendered, as assurance that the experience I had had while reading would not be erased from my memory with the giving away of the book.

I fought on the books' side to foil my father's campaign against literature. The world of Montag, the fireman in *Fahrenheit 451*, a world in which the fire department's job is to set fires not put them out, scared me. Montag destroyed books until he read one of them and was infected. This infection was life-threatening: Montag was hounded by the book haters and would have been hunted down and killed had he not escaped to the book lovers. Did my father know of this danger? And if he did, why did he then take the risk of keeping the contaminated objects in the house? Or was he no longer aware of what was being delivered, of what he himself was lugging home daily in bags, boxes, and baskets?

Montag found shelter from his pursuers in a world of books where not a single physical book existed: literary masterpieces were memorized and recited constantly so they were not forgotten and could be passed on before death. I was also one of the infected. As long as nobody hounded me—father didn't set any fires, at least no concrete ones—and as long as

I could possess the books without having to memorize them, my destiny as one of those incurably afflicted by the book plague was all right with me. (And yet, in the film I found the walking books disconcerting—they were so sad, so sullen, so without a future).

A disease progresses step by step, they say, which in connection with my disease isn't without a certain irony.

If quiet reigned above me I knew my father was in his comparably modest corner of the workroom, the nerve center of his collection, amidst the dense smoke produced by his cigar. At the smoke's bottom, the desk surface, he would fish around for a photograph, push it into photo corners, and glue it onto a preprinted, prepunched sheet headed *Collection K.* If I heard him cough, I had fixed his position correctly. I pictured how he adjusted the eyeshade fastened to an elastic band on his forehead, or how he knocked against the loupe with his horn-rimmed glasses. Creaking above me indicated he was pulling a binder off the shelf. Energetic, more vigorous creaking meant he had stood up and gone down the two steps that separated his corner from the rest of the room. Once this had happened, the acoustic trace faded away and usually I fell asleep.

Father was up and about in the vast attic where nothing, not even the dust, was what it seemed. Was he en route to the workshop, where three broken clocks disassembled into their still functional components waited to be reassembled into a single mechanism, which, even if no longer stylistically true, would stubbornly tick on? Was he standing in the darkroom where the next set of photographs was drying, before bringing the new pictures into the workroom to resume the cataloguing of his collection? Or had he stood up in order to replace the bottle of wine, already empty again, with a full one?

The first bottle trickled away in his 130-kilogram body—his, as he would say, "personal best weight"—during dinner and without any obvious effects. Perhaps he perspired a bit more, perhaps he perspired faster. The second bottle made him cheerful, boisterous, a charming and witty entertainer. This wit, however, segued into sharptonguedness, braggadocio, and aggression as the contents of the third bottle were emptied. I whispered to my brothers, or to my mother, "Watch out, Number Three." Or, if he was within earshot, held up the corresponding number of fingers, for it was best to get out of his way. The warning system functioned, even though Number Three (after the detour of his walk with the dog) normally drove him to the attic and his collecting anyway. We'd be sure of a safe distance of two floors and one bottle—until Number Four brought him back down again.

For some reason or another he had made it a rule not to stock wine in the attic, although he could have best concealed the bottles there. Instead, he chose to become a master stair climber: fifty-six steps, with the empty bottles, down to the wine cellar and just as many, with full ones, back up again. Didn't he know that his youngest son counted him out, night after night, bottle for bottle, as if he were a ring referee and his father were boxing against the only truly unbeatable world champion heavyweight? Number Four made him tired, whiny; my father surrendered to a drunkard's sentimentality. This followed the aggression of earlier in the evening. He no longer yelled, "You'll see, now I'm getting mad, it's all over now!" He now had the need for warmth: human, or, at the least, canine.

He would plop himself down in the middle of the living room sofa and beg, in a thin whine, for anyone within hearing distance to come sit and watch a film with him. He preferred Westerns, in which Gary Cooper, or even better, John Wayne, would assume the task of doing the yelling on his behalf. Father considered the shoot-out to be the highpoint of the tradition of dialogue in the Western world. A threshold behavior made its appearance in the transition from Number Three to Number Four. If aggression hadn't yet completely dissolved into sentimentality, he'd switch to his film without saying a word, unconcerned whether one of us was watching something else. Whoever left the living room in protest could go to hell for all he cared, though just a glass, or even a sip, later we'd hear him call: "Come on, come sit with me, you can watch what you want…"

I was the youngest, I was the heir to the throne, I endured the abdicating king the longest, I hoped the most desperately. Even once the bottle-counting era dawned, I still sat with him. Thigh to thigh, his in corduroy, mine in jeans. His as big as my waist, mine the size of his upper arm. Wine glass, Sprite bottle; the cigar between his lips. He coughed, spit tobacco, lifted one of his gargantuan butt cheeks and joyously let it rip. James Stewart drew his Colt—finally…with him the film was always almost over, his town half wiped out, his family long since buried, before Jimmy also let it rip. "Ah, finally!" father and son breathed a sigh of relief, sometimes at the same time.

"Come on, come sit with me!" he'd shout again and again. Soon the man enthroned on the living room couch, stinking of alcohol, tobacco and sweat, was someone I more and more wanted less and less to do with. Soon I had saved enough pocket money to buy myself a flea market TV, which found a spot on the bureau opposite my bed. In the living room, if I heard him coming, I hoisted myself out of the ever lower—or so it seemed to me—lounge chair, and waited until I knew he was at the

The boys' playroom in the basement, which, after a failed attempt to replicate St. Gallen in plaster, was called the "padded cell." Subsequently the padded cell served as a storeroom, my father's last bedroom in the Alpsteinstrasse house, my student digs, and as a bedroom for two subletters. Today this room is my office.

front living room door so I could disappear out the back one. If I heard him shout my name, I tried to climb the stairs faster. Once he no longer called after me—had the king seen through this castling maneuver?—he called for the dog and rattled the box of biscuits.

All that was left was bottle Number Five. If he managed to make his way back up to the attic he'd pass out on the floor of the stamp room. If he couldn't make it, he lay on the steps, so that sometimes, when it was time for Zack to go home, Zack and I had to step over him—an Alpine massif of a body, especially as by this time I had already started to lose physical strength. On such nights, Zack and I didn't linger at the front door as we usually did, talking about movies and books; instead, we exchanged embarrassed goodnights, and Zack left quickly. We never spoke of these incidents, because, for my part, I was ashamed. For Zack—he had his own father he didn't want to, or couldn't, talk about.

If the creaking above me had ceased and I still lay awake, I sometimes sneaked down to the cellar. Although I had developed the skill to infer from his conduct the exact amount of wine he had already imbibed down to two or three glasses, I nevertheless had to see what I didn't want to believe. For the contents of these bottles my father was giving up everything that had, for such a long time, been most dear to him: his entire kingdom, the queen, the heir to the throne, and his vassals. I had to touch the bottles, warm the cool, green glass in my hand, as if with the warmth the secret the bottles had to hold for my father emerged—and I had to do this before he emptied them and then destroyed them the next day.

Bottles stacked to the ceiling. Bottles in cardboard boxes. Bottles in wooden crates. In the good, very good times, father drank his way through the expensive B-list—Beaujolais, Burgundy and Bordeaux, Brunello, Barbaresco, and Barolo. In the very bad times, he contented himself with Chianti in two-liter straw-covered bottles and the cooking kirsch. A collection of corkscrews lay on a small table in the wine cellar. Beneath this, there was a basket intended for corks, which was always empty, and standing next to the table was the bottle crusher, which he had experimented with. The machine, however, did only an incomplete job of destroying the evidence, cracking and crashing and such that the broken bits of glass flew across the room and could be found by my mother in father's pants pockets. Standing in one corner were three three-liter bottles of Marc, one bottle for the birth of each son. These, at least, remained untouched.

So this dreary room—lit only by a dusty bulb, with a cold, damp earth floor that I stood barefoot on—was the laboratory where my father's metamorphosis occurred. Of course I knew that the metamorphosis was not tied to one location and that it also transpired sip by sip, making two people out of one, only to halve him once more into a single person. But even if this person still looked like my father, he didn't have much in common with him anymore. And what he still had in common with him—his outward appearance—made the transformation into this loathsome character even worse. Why did he do this? Did he no longer have any choice, like that good Dr. Jekyll, who'd been so imaginative, as my father once was, that he had come up with a way to transform, via a strange concoction, into, of all people, someone like Mr. Hyde—until he no longer needed the concoction because in the end he was only Hyde?

Surely this was true for father as well, who wouldn't have had to drink another drop ever again to no longer be my father, but did so—just to be on the safe side?—nonetheless. Did he not see what sort of person he was becoming, or had already become? Or, was he already so much this other person that he could no longer see who he had once been, the person he could have remained being? All of us, not just me, could have used *him* so much.

"Haven't you noticed he's ruining everything with his boozing? That it's better only one of us goes to the dogs rather than all of us, especially as he's past saving anyway? That mother is only waiting for you so she can get a divorce because she doesn't want to take father from you?" Of course, Puck wasn't supposed to tell me any of this. My mother wanted me to realize it all on my own, when I was ready. "You don't have a father anymore. Get it?" It was all very well for my brother—he was in Bern, at the university, where he had started studying law, and came home only for the occasional weekend. As Mix was completing his commercial diploma at boarding school, I was the only one left in St. Gallen, alone with my mother and what had become of our father.

If I look at the ground I am afraid of heights. This little bit of height frightens me? That balancing is a muscular act is something I have only known since I have no longer been able to do it.

Sometimes I wish I had pulled bottle after bottle from the shelves and smashed them. Had done inestimable damage no one could ignore anymore. Instead, I simply walked out of the wine cellar, closed the door as softly as possible behind me, and climbed up the thirty-six steps to my room on the second floor without turning on the stairway light.

The proprietor of a pub downtown that I visit once in a while sometimes doesn't recognize me in my wheelchair. Only when I enter his restaurant

King and heir to the throne on the Hollywood swing, ca. 1969

on foot again—because I found a parking space close by—does he remember who I am and is glad I am doing so much better.

B. paced out the terrain for our meeting; we can't go to one bar because the bathroom is on the second floor, another has steps, and a third is too far from a parking space. We should color code this terrain, I tell B.: a project Peter Greenaway could get excited about (see the picture of Stairs on p. 154). St. Gallen. Red carpets to indicate areas walkable and wheelable for all; blue carpets to indicate areas accessible for most (one or two steps easily taken with assistance, narrow corridors, slight incline); yellow carpets to indicate inaccessible areas (see also the Muscle Book entry on p. 142). After a month the carpets are rolled up. But maybe by then people will realize what's missing.

I ask Mix whether he feels fit enough to come to my place. Sure, I'm doing pretty well, he says. But he can't get on my barstools anymore, he continues, that's something he can no longer do.

In Flims, in the Grison Alps, my oldest brother Puck won a ski race in February 1968. He was twelve. He came to a stop after the finish line with a daring swerve, then elegantly, protractedly, as if in slow motion, slumped to the ground. He was so taken aback by having "just collapsed," as he said afterward, that he still wore the victor's grin on his face even as he lay in the snow. From there, he watched as the losers—second place, third place, and the no-longer-worth-mentioning places—sped by him, slowed down, and came to a standing stop.

"It's nothing," he said to his mother, who was quickly at his side. His skiing teacher looked down at him. His skiing buddies. The girls, too. Shame and anger prevented him from feeling the cold, but he felt the looks. Neither the rush of victory nor an obstacle hidden in the snow had brought him down. Nothing broken. No cramping. No pain. Why didn't he just get up? It was as if someone had turned a switch inside him to "off."

"You're not hurt," the ski teacher said pulling Puck back on to his feet. And there he stood again, propped on his ski poles. Though he felt his strength flowing back he continued to shake. The muscles in his thighs seemed to flutter, whirr, as if something were crawling inside. That "ant feeling" he would soon know all too well: ants using his muscles as an autobahn. His fingers twitched, and his hip felt numb for a few minutes. He insisted on trudging home. Of course he didn't let anyone carry his skis for him, especially his mother. Had she not been there he would only have told her he'd won the race.

The next day the village doctor diagnosed a knee strain. He prescribed an ointment, for use twice daily, and a few days of rest, which, just by looking at the ruffian, he could tell wasn't going to happen. "Nothing we need to worry about, Mrs. Keller. The cold grabs hold of us sometimes without our noticing it, and then, just like that, we're lying in the snow getting even colder. That can, as in Puck's case, lead to muscle contractions. The worst he has to fear is a catarrh. Still, I suggest you consult a doctor once home so treatment can continue."

Puck knew of nothing that needed treating. He'd administer his prescribed rest on the slopes, twenty times a day, as long as they were still there. He'd make himself fall-down tired so there'd be a reason to fall down.

"It doesn't hurt," Puck said without being asked, when our family doctor in St. Gallen examined him.

"Of course it doesn't," the doctor said. "It might be better if it did. The diagnosis is correct. The muscle is strained. Rub the ointment on twice a day, take it easy, and come back again in fourteen days."

When they went back the doctor had the X-rays. "It's seems quite possible the fall has caused a hip problem. I'm referring him to a neurologist at the hospital."

"Should I be worried?" my mother wanted to know.

The neurologist took a look at the X-rays, and then, skeptically, at the seemingly strong boy. Puck's bones glowed on the illuminated glass mount. "Cap'n Kirk took a picture of my skeleton." He tried to make me believe this after he came home. The pictures'll be beamed to Vienna (via trusty Swiss Post), he continued, where they'll materialize on the desk of the chief physician at the Orthopedic Hospital.

"That the boy just collapsed like that—it doesn't make sense. The hip is fine," this doctor said over the phone. He recommended seeing a muscle specialist. And so Puck's now international medical history (once Austria had been included) set out for Bern, where another doctor—not satisfied with the work of his eastern Swiss colleagues—had another set of Cap'n Kirk images made. Once he saw these, he suggested a muscle biopsy; ideally for all three boys, as it was perhaps a question of a hereditary disease, he added. Hadn't the mother mentioned the second boy sometimes moved a bit ponderously? Did she herself perhaps suffer from muscle fatigue? No? Her husband, then? The grandparents? Well, we'll see.

We have American guests and I want to show them the Stiftsbibliothek. I call to find out whether the famous abbey library is wheelchair accessible. If it isn't, I have to wait outside. I am informed over the phone that there is an elevator, but I'll have to send someone up to get an authorized person to operate it for me. For two years, I attended school in this building. For two years, every day, I climbed the stairs and passed the entrance to the library and the felt slippers lying outside. How can I resist asking whether I, now in a wheelchair, also have to wear the parquet-protecting slippers? What was intended as a remark to lighten the mood silences the woman on the telephone. She'll have to ask, she says.

In the St. Gallen Stiftsbibliothek, Anno Domini 2000

No one, not even I, five years old and schooled for life by my attic, would have suspected that in the museum quarter, lurking behind the walls of a harmless-looking townhouse (painted in the chocolate blue of the packaging of my mother's favorite chocolates), was a Frankenstein laboratory. Gloved men in green lay me on an examination table, asked my name—"Kasperli," I divulged—and told me to count to three. They placed a plastic nose over my own nose, but rather than be able to breathe twice as well, I could barely breathe at all. Strange experiment! What I inhaled smelled as if someone had distilled Nora's and my perfume from rubber. I counted to one. When I woke up the aliens had cut a wound the length of an index finger in my right lower leg and thigh and sewn in a micro receiver. Mine registered "negative," which was positive, while Mix's and Puck's transmitted a "positive," which was not good. In fact, it was bad, yucky, phooey, a shame and disgrace. For anyone in its clutches, not in the slightest way positive, but rather, well, without beating around the bush—it was shitty.

I roll out of the Stiftsbibliothek's narrow elevator but don't get very far. The elevator's light barely illuminates the anteroom in which I find myself. It is hardly larger than a cabinet. The woman accompanying me—is it the woman I spoke to on the phone?—locates the light, which in turn locates a step. She busies about taking the step with me in my wheelchair. As she clearly doesn't know what she's doing, I have to stop her in order to prevent an accident. I explain she has to press down on the bar mounted to the back of the wheelchair with her foot so that—with the wheelchair tipped backwards—we can overcome the step. Once this is done, she noisily unlocks a door and I roll out of what actually is a cabinet—a sacristy cabinet—though without a back, and from there, surprised, and exposed to the surprised looks of the visitors, I roll into the Stiftsbibliothek.

After the tests had been completed, Mix, age ten, and Puck, age twelve (I was five and stayed home) heard Dr. Louis Feller—who, as an orthopedist, wasn't really the right sort of doctor, but he was a friend of the family—tell our mother that soon this something with three letters would force her boys to give up all sports, in fact, running around of any sort, and ultimately walking itself. They would have to spend the rest of their lives sitting in a chair. And furthermore, before the wheelchairs could no longer be avoided, they would be dependent on crutches for some time. As SMA took its course, it was possible a respirator would be required, which would necessitate something known as a tracheotomy. There was, Dr. Feller played with his letter opener, no chance of a cure, no chance of improvement, no chance of even checking the progress of this illness, which was still little researched in 1968— unless, of course, one wanted to get involved in that futuristic adventure called genetics (which, frankly, he didn't have much regard for). No, he didn't think it could do any harm to light candles in the cathedral, he added absentmindedly, as he made a few concluding notes about this really quite unusual case of two sons in a single family simultaneously stricken by a hereditary disease—a disease the chances of getting were statistically negligible.

While Louis spoke, Puck was busy tying the bands of the brawn-o-meter (or, whatever the muscle-strength-measuring gizmo was called) around the arms of the skeleton standing next to the desk in the hopes of scientifically determining how much weight a dead man could lift. Mix, whose bedroom battles had him embroiled in the third decade of the Hundred Years' War, sat impassively—the absentminded smile, which had earned him his reputation of being an introverted boy, on his lips—as he devised a particularly cruel form of torture for his prisoners of war. As different as the two were, and still are, my brothers share a well-developed sense of self-protection; so ignoring this enemy inhabitant from another galaxy, who had fallen from the sky to concoct this nonsense from an oversized executive chair, wouldn't have posed a problem for them.

My mother couldn't get around what Louis had told her. Sometimes I found her on our living room floor, dead for a few minutes, and then, just moments later, she'd be in the kitchen busily preparing dinner for five. Her fainting may be a textbook example of chronic low blood pressure. But the textbooks should also explain why she first lost consciousness in Dr. Feller's office when he told her in no uncertain terms what the future had to offer her sons. "What's that supposed to mean, Louis—no muscles?" she said, once she came to again. She realized she was holding a glass of water in her hand. She also realized she was ashamed to have passed out in the doctor's office. Surely she knew how busy the man was; busy as all men essentially were, at least as soon as she was dependent on their support. "It just can't be, can it? Puck *has* muscles."

"You're right, of course," Louis said impatiently. He was the eight-minute, two-question doctor—much as he might like to, he could no longer afford to give any patient more than this number of minutes and questions. "I haven't been clear. The biopsy of your boys' muscle specimens exhibits discernibly pathologically altered skeletal muscle with an indication of primary neurogenic atrophy and distinct secondary myopathy. The histopathological image is typical for Atrophia musculorum spinalis pseudomyopathica Kugelberg-Welander."

My mother looked at the doctor helplessly.

"I'll try to explain. Spinal Muscular Atrophy, or SMA, is the collective name for a group of hereditary neuromuscular diseases. All forms of this disease affect the nerve cells we call motor neurons, which govern the muscle movements we control intentionally. SMA causes the lower motor neurons at the base of the brain and spinal cord to disintegrate, thus preventing the transmission of the electrical and chemical signals on which normal muscle function depends. Muscles we do not intentionally control, such as those that govern the bladder and intestinal functions, are not affected by SMA, nor are sight and hearing. Studies have shown that children with SMA can be of exceptionally high intelligence. There are three types of SMA, of which the first two are fatal. Most of those afflicted with Type I die at or before the age of three; those with Type II can be expected to reach an average age of eighteen years. SMA Type III, or Kugelberg-Welander, is a milder form of the condition and doesn't manifest itself before eighteen months of age, normally appearing between ages five and fifteen. A weakness in the muscles governing chewing and swallowing is rare, and the respiratory tract is generally not so strongly affected as in the first two forms of SMA. As a rule, children with Type III have a normal life expectancy. If problems with the respiratory tract arise, this constitutes the greatest threat to life."

"But Mix has muscles, too," my mother mumbled.

The clock, the clock. The clock crouched before him, ready to pounce. Not that he had actually set it for eight minutes, yet the alarm signaling that the end of this visit (and the beginning of the next) was long overdue rang unceasingly in his head. Louis sighed. "Admittedly the term atrophy is somewhat misleading, as it does describe a gradual disappearance of muscles caused by a lack of minerals. Your boys, however, have muscles. Of course they have muscles. They look muscular. They will always look like strong young boys. Only that's exactly what they are not."

She tried to feel her own muscles. How did you feel muscles when you had them? How did you feel them when you didn't have them although you really had them? How was all this to be comprehended? While Louis spoke of wheelchairs, Mix fidgeted about in his seat and Puck jumped up, anxious to get on his bike again.

"At a certain point, you'll have to consider whether prostheses might be a good idea. To counteract scoliosis."

"Scoliosis?"

"When muscles lose strength the skeleton is forced to bear more of a burden. The spine begins to curve; this curving can be counteracted with metal supports. Surgery, too, might be a consideration. Bones will become more brittle with physical inactivity. Have the boys pop calcium pills. Keep an eye on their weight, Ruth. Excess weight will also make it harder for them to walk. I'll prescribe vitamins for them. Don't bother trying physical therapy. There's no point. You can't train atrophying muscles. So, no exercises, got it? From this point on no more gym class; I'll give you a doctor's note. Unnecessary movement only causes strain. Occupy them with reading or watching TV."

Louis pushed the button on the intercom to call in the next patient. "Just imagine having a sack of potatoes on your back that's getting heavier and heavier as you're getting weaker and weaker. Best for them to stay in bed and not fall out." Then—to soften the blow?—he added: "But don't worry about them finding wives. Women like taking care of men. I'd be seriously concerned if you had girls instead of boys."

The mention of the female sex must have directed Louis's attention to my mother. "And what about you, Ruth? Have you thought about going to a specialist for these fainting fits?" As he led her to the door, he said, "I wonder about the youngest, if we shouldn't... On the other hand, three out of three boys in one family, that would be like you winning the lottery three times in a row...but can one be sure? Best if you bring the third boy in for regular check-ups, too. My secretary will schedule an appointment."

Dr. Louis Feller, the physician for the national soccer team—and as such, responsible for the best muscles in the country—was a good doctor, renowned for his dexterity with a scalpel. His careless words may not have been the direct cause of my mother's fainting—she was already in treatment for her inability to cope well with nervous stress—but what she called her wheelchair dreams started after Feller's diagnosis. Night after night, for years, she dreamt of trying in vain to climb a hill. She would then see what the hill was, a pile of wheelchairs, and each time she made this discovery, wheelchair upon wheelchair would break away from the pile and fall towards her—and she would wake with a start.

And once awake she'd go to the cathedral to light the candles that, according to the latest medical research, it couldn't do any harm to light. "Lord," my mother prayed on the cathedral pews, whose hardness she had grown accustomed to during her convent school years, "you have already given me two handicapped sons. I accept my fate. But that's enough, don't you agree? Let the youngest be spared."

As the youngest I received the clothing my brothers had grown out of. But that wasn't all: I was also prescribed the same medical measures, as if their hereditary disease, which I had not been diagnosed with, was already mine as well. What harm did it do to take vitamin pills, or perform the isometric exercises, which Dr. Feller believed would do no good in our case, yet still ordered for us because he wanted to fulfill my mother's need "to do something." Perhaps because he was an orthopedist, we all got shoe inserts that were supposed to achieve something orthopedic, but mostly were uncomfortable. Sons one and three removed them from

My first bicycle. Christmas 1968.

their shoes during unsupervised moments, while number two forgot about them entirely, whether they had been inserted or not.

Swimming was good, he said, for those weak in muscle move through the water as if on the moon. But *ne quid nimis*, as the Latinists say, applied here as well, proclaimed Feller—another Latin quotation bubbling on his lips, one he fortunately swallowed just in time—and, with a raised old-man eyebrow, having grown bushy at too young an age, he translated: nothing in excess. He couldn't caution my mother enough. The first procession of the SMA Brothers took place on the stairs of a neighbor's pool, which we were allowed to use on a regular basis: Puck and Mix—each with his right hand on the railing, right leg first, followed by the swinging of the left leg, helped along (like grandfather when he had to contend with a steep stair) by an occasional huffing and puffing—vied for second place with each step they took, while I, the Spared One, raced ahead of them, already in the water upon their arrival.

Did my mother suspect before my diagnosis that the authoritative word medical science had delivered with regard to my health was not incontrovertible? She later told me she often stood at the large window in the hall watching me as I played badminton in the yard. Like my brothers when they were four or five, I knelt in the sandbox instead of squatting down. Like them I ran, "breaded like a *Wiener schnitzel*," into the house, laying a sand trail through the hall into the parlor and up the stairs to my room. That posed a housekeeping problem, not a medical problem, and was easily solved by vacuuming. Both of her oldest sons were already suffering losses; how could she have imagined a potential third case?

The lengths our mother went to find a cure, or at least relief, for the incurable disease! Without Dr. Feller's knowledge, so behind the back of orthodox medicine, she wrote to an Albert Josters, M.D., in Westphalia. With his very own "unique Josters dietary regimen," Josters claimed he could cure everything and so, Mrs. Keller, he wrote back, why not a muscle disease, too? Muscles need nourishment. Your sons' muscles, he said, are lacking something—a protein, a mineral—and even if science does not yet know what sort, his diet should nevertheless be thought fully capable of a cure. And although Dr. Josters self-confidently added that he had even already cured cases of SMA, the missing mineral was not, in the end, to be found in his diet.

My mother was not to be discouraged and wrote to others. On the recommendation of a Mr. Wendelin, she contacted a Dr. Helms-Meyer from Nuremberg, by whom she was to inquire about the possible success of a cell therapy. This was how she also heard from a Dr. Martino Grossi, who, "in haste" from Riehen, told her of a Prof. Ruckmann whom he soon would have the pleasure of consulting in Biel and who would perhaps know more. That led to a Dr. Wrorbrough from Oxford, MA, in the United States, who recommended a Dr. Kalinkaya at the Children's Hospital Boston, from where the matter was referred back to Switzerland, as this was where a certain Dr. Preston Gschwind from Brookline, likewise MA, USA, was currently to be found; Gschwind in turn commended his fellow countryman Dr. Joseph M. Frielinghaus, place of residence at present unknown. Somehow or other she found out about the Parisian acupuncturist Amadou Xuan Wu, who had to, however, send her a negative answer, here "negative" really meaning negative, "*je regrette vraiment, chère Madame*," and from there— anyway: What was with each response a disappointment for my mother proved for me—a budding writer, after all—to be an invaluable source of names I could bestow upon my invincible heroes, or villains.

What was accepted by orthodox medicine, so what was useless, as SMA was a disease medically proven to be incurable, was covered by health insurance; and what was covered by health insurance Dr. Feller prescribed for us, though never without adding that, in principle, we could also forget these things. If a therapy promised the least hope it was banned by orthodox medicine as unorthodox and thus not covered, as if hope were something bad. Incurable was incurable and consequently whoever promised a cure in our case was a quack—on this the men with the scalpels were agreed.

My mother started reading the wheelchair stories in the waiting room magazines more attentively. Sometimes she even bought one of these publications at the newsstand. Sparingly, at most once a month— here, too, the Latinist's *ne quid nimis* seemed to apply—one of these stories, always with its "there's-no-hope" beginning and yet somehow predictably happy ending, turned up embedded amongst the reportages on victorious tennis players or fabulously rich beauties. In the past she had read a few pages of these accounts and lamented the tragedy of fate having snatched a person, preferably young, from a life of activity, only to thrust him or her down into one in a wheelchair. Apparently, there were no old disabled people in Switzerland; in any case, they weren't to be found in the magazines my mother read. The elderly were all bursting from the pages with vigor and good health, quite the opposite of those my mother knew. In the past she had been glad that the newly wheelchair-bound started to come to terms with their life-altering fate in an exemplary manner—and always reliably in the sixth paragraph, which somehow always coincided with the arrival of the magazine crew. There she would stop reading, and turn to the rest of the magazine, happy that none of the truly fortunate and forever incredibly beautiful rich people with their winning tennis games were in wheelchairs or just had breasts that were too large.

Now my mother read the wheelchair stories through to the end. She hid them in the secretaire—at which she also conducted her household correspondence—in a little folder that she kept beneath the little folder with the bills. There were children in wheelchairs because of mysterious viruses—wasn't the defective SMA gene a mysterious virus of sorts? Just a few weeks earlier, these children had played ball and climbed trees, and now here they were smiling bravely into the camera (even if with contorted faces) from the metal contraption that henceforth would take the place of their legs. They made things for their grandmothers, and composed poems—little telegrams to the dear Lord—that their father photocopied for the neighbors and one of which was reprinted alongside the article. There was the ski racer who had broken his back during a fall and a few weeks after his operation was already beaming from his shiny new wheelchair, as if instead of paralysis, an Olympic victory had landed in his lap. Never a word of dissatisfaction. Of bitterness, only that it had been overcome once and for all. A lot about God. Of other values stumbled upon, and the empty pleasures one had been content with before—this "before!" If there was talk of fate, then it was of how well it had been mastered, an example for all. If in the end one hadn't mastered his fate, which was permitted to happen in the magazines on average once a year, he was called a hero, his suicide a release, as if the deceased were Jesus Christ and killing oneself were suddenly no longer taboo.

The more hopeless the case, the longer the article. Hope for recovery, already severely shaken, could nevertheless still sometimes be found at the ends of the stories in the form of an address. If the scalpel no longer helped, there was a radiation treatment that—and how to get your head around this?—could be fatal for the healthy but curative for the terminally ill. Beyond chemotherapies miracles lurked. This was the gray area of hope, the land of ludicrousness. The laying-on of hands in the Alps, distance healing, conjuration, black magic, voodoo from the South Seas. If there were good forces there were also evil ones that, properly deployed—conjured—could in turn promise the absolute good. Should she travel to the South Seas, believe in straw dolls in whose heads needles were stuck? Go to Russia where the head of state's ailment— what sort was a state secret—could be healed hundreds of kilometers away and over the Urals.

Even death was curable. My mother started to read books by Murphy as well as Kübler-Ross's on encounters with death. Was death perhaps the greatest hope? Was there really something like recompense in the hereafter for misfortune sustained on earth? One time, out on the street, a neighbor had congratulated her on her disabled sons. "What an opportunity! What luck!" he had exclaimed enthusiastically. The hard lot that had befallen her sons at such a young age in this life, he said, would give them an enviable boost in the next, and her too, the mother, who suffered with them, of course. The man, who bought his villa with stock market money, had three healthy children, a beautiful wife, and an even more beautiful mistress, seemed to be unconcerned that, with so much happiness, a demotion in the next life was a distinct possibility for him.

For a start, perhaps as a concession to the church to which my mother still belonged at the time, she asked a healing sanctuary in England to include her in their prayers as offered in their brochure. It was a free service—overall, she found English healers unpretentious and altruistic—so it was probably not a scam. After this, it was one short step to the warm-hearted Appenzell layers-on of hands, who looked away with embarrassment when she placed a modest donation on the dresser. Appenzell was only a half an hour's drive and nobody had to be told. At least the faith healers didn't laugh at her and they took the time to listen when she explained her sons' fate. Those desiring to be rid of their warts were required—because the warts had to go—to appear during the waning moon; it was thus during the waxing moon when those seeking to strengthen their muscles were to come. The warts the dog had disappeared after a single session, while the sons said that at least the hands on their skin was a nice sensation, and that they also felt better afterward, something they'd never been able to say following a visit to Dr. Feller.

Suddenly people were coming around the Alpsteinstrasse house with divining rods, locating harmful water flows; this resulted in aluminum foil having to be buried to protect the house and its inhabitants from dangerous currents. Others went through the rooms with a pendulum looking for good and bad forces, which meant moving the beds from one corner to another and, when a new diviner appeared on the scene, having to push them back again. Someone recommended placing consecrated particleboard, pointed in a southerly direction, under the mattresses as a way to put an end to all the bed disarranging. With a few cables that were clipped to sleeves and waistbands as if to a battery, the influx of cosmic energy could be secured from the living room couch. By means of a thought experiment over a distance of hundreds of kilometers somebody ascertained that all three sons, including the One Still Spared, had transmitters in their bodies that had to be surgically removed to release them from alien control.

In the early 1970s, my mother took Puck and Mix to Manila, where a healer, without any anesthesia, reached into their flesh with his bare fingers. Even though the stains on their underwear turned out to be pig's blood when tested at home, Mix and Puck felt better for six months and, what's more, their school performances skyrocketed. So hope did help after all, even if administered by a charlatan. For the same reason, we all went (this time me included—as a preventive measure and because my mother didn't want to leave me home alone) a total of seventeen times to a high frequency radiation treatment therapy at Dr. Runikoff's institute in Upper Austria. For three weeks, twice a year, we were forced to spend our vacations amongst old sick people. In a darkened hall, an electric wand was passed over the half-naked bodies of the institute's patients, regardless of whether the disease being treated was gout, SMA, or rheumatism; the idea being to reactivate muscle cells. The only things ultimately activated, however, were the blue sparks that flew through the mysteriously dimly lit space.

I, the Not Yet Diagnosed, resisted spending every vacation at an old people's clinic. I proclaimed that travel, preferably around the world, if not farther, would be therapy enough for the disease I did not yet have. Now the time had come, hadn't it? The swimming pool as moon had not been able to replace the attic, for which I had now grown too big. My mother recognized this, let me go, and after that no one went to Dr. Runikoff's institute anymore. For the first time, I translated one of my attic journeys into reality, went to Venice, from there made my way by boat, island by island, to Athens, where I climbed the steep hill to the Acropolis with what was already noticeable effort.

For the third time, my mother looks on as one of her sons resorts to a cane, no longer able to carry a cup of tea to his desk, and despite the cane, slinks along the walls, employing them as additional support. She sees how the third now seeks to conceal this; she sees that I know that, of course, I cannot conceal the cane. I joke how elegant it really is, black and made from shock-resistant aluminum. But she has been a housewife for too long, too long already and forever a mother, not to recognize the black marks on the white walls as the traces of my hands in search of a hold. But she doesn't see, as I see, how she grows a third leg for the third time, because she now has to walk for the third son as well. I don't know if she knows that I know how she has resolved in her head to remain fit for another ten years so that she will be able to help all three.

The first time Dr. Louis Feller made an attempt to diagnose me with the muscle disease he had already discovered in my brothers, I was five; the eleventh time I went to him, I was fourteen. He still didn't succeed in reducing me to this something with three letters. Why didn't he finally lay down his arms and surrender from behind his pompous desk? Would I have to keep reporting for checkups, year after year, usually in spring, until the doctor got a result that pleased him?

May 1978, springtime: SMA season. What a shame to have to fritter away yet another entire afternoon with Dr. Louis Feller! Again, I'd have to listen to his chatter, watch him busy about with his doctors' toys. His twingers and tweakers, his scratchers and stingers. This year, too, like a crazed tailor, he'd fasten the loop of his most ridiculous gadget, the brawn-o-meter, or whatever it was called, around my arms in order to measure how many pounds I was still able to lift.

For years this had been too childish for me—basically since a friend from elementary school and I had sat in my driveway and tape-recorded my second work, likewise published in one copy, the play *The Grisly Crimes of Dr. Morton* (1976, still not premiered, and available for such). In it: a young beauty who strays into a castle during a fierce storm; a mad scientist inside the castle who brandishes about all sorts of silly medical gadgets; and, of course, the hero, imbued with Kasperli's courage and Axel's sensitivity, who had to put a stop to the villain's shenanigans before sixty minutes had elapsed, for that was when the cassette was over. Now I was old enough to know that I had to keep quiet about such influences and instead profess to be reading *Ulysses* in the original and secretly working on a twelve-volume opus worthy of a venerable prince among poets.

Louis followed THE RULE that dictated his ritual. He made me wait in his anteroom beneath the panels on which a hand-drawn woman demonstrated how to lift weight without sustaining a back injury. Once my mother, who didn't want to let me go to Dr. Feller's alone, had sat down across from him, he said his usual "so"—his way of expressing that he wanted to know how I was doing. After half a sentence he interrupted my report with an "I see" followed by his "well then, shall we?" Meaning I was to take off my shirt. I hopped onto the examination table. Had he noticed how effortlessly I did this, quite unlike my brothers, who had to hold on to the table with both hands before they could seat themselves on top? Dr. Feller felt my pulse, lay the cool cylinder of his stethoscope on my chest, and pressed a few buttons, which only a doctor could find, on my back.

"His respiratory system is all right," he mumbled as he did every visit. Then he pricked me with a tie pin-like thing that was the color of tarnished silver.

"Good," he said.

"Good," he said again as he rummaged for his little rubber hammer, then tapped my knees and elbows for reflexes. None this year either. Which would prove, in what had in the meantime become a decade-long field experiment, that I didn't need any. But he didn't let up and hammered away once more. Again no reaction. And I jumped with ease from the table I knew my brothers could barely get down from.

The doctor then wanted to see me walk. So I walked for him. The faster I walked the sooner I'd be able to get out. Any moment now I'd be rewarded with the sound of his thunderous voice telling me what I already knew, namely, that everything was all right. If he let me go right away I could still have an hour before dinner to read on the lawn, the cool grass under my bare stomach. With my chin raised I strutted over to the skeleton that hung swaying by the window. It grinned back at me, and when a breeze blew in it clattered like a wind chime. As I stood in front of the poor guy, who would never leave this office, Louis barked, "On tiptoe, boy!" as if wanting to test my hearing as well. Not wasting the opportunity, I swung my arm skillfully above my head to demonstrate how I had scored the deciding point during my last team handball match. The doctor was still not impressed.

As the examination's finale, Louis ordered me to climb up on a chair that he moved to the middle of the room. I hesitated, looked first at him, then at my mother. She nodded without saying a word. I lifted my left foot onto the chair, reached for the backrest, and swung my right leg up. Standing up straight I let go of the chair back. All my movements were executed correctly, though I had to admit they were a bit slow, all of a sudden a bit slower, just like sometimes—when we had trained for a long time—I got up a bit, just a bit, more slowly off the judo mat. It had taken me a little more effort to lift my second foot onto the seat of the chair, as if I could only do it if I concentrated. I sensed this effort was noticed, but I also knew that I had to be observed very carefully on a good day like this one. With a little luck Louis hadn't even looked up from making his notes. For him, too, it was the same every year.

"You can get dressed," he said. "We'll do a new biopsy. But I'm positive, Christoph—"

He was silent.

What?

My mother looked at me, and I avoided her gaze; still standing on the chair, I looked at Louis's white head beneath me. He noted something else in my file. Then, as if wanting to award us—me? her?— one of the diplomas that so liberally populated the wall behind him, he squinted meaningfully over the rims of his glasses. In a businesslike voice, which intimated he could have said what he was about to say a year earlier, he proclaimed: "Christoph has it too."

SMA progresses in phases, yet I don't know what rhythm my phases obey. A phase doesn't cause any pain. A phase doesn't announce itself. I don't even know what a phase does exactly. First my strength goes, then the memory of this strength. Once both are gone the phase is past.

"My sons have what? They're saying my boys are what? Ruth, don't be silly!" Föns said in 1968.

"The fall, Föns—"

"Puck won the race, did he not?"

"His teacher says he's always the slowest at school."

That, too, only made him laugh. "Guess what place I always came in? Someone's always the slowest runner."

Puck's teacher also thought he should practice jumping rope.

"Are you kidding? Jump rope? The moronic jackass can't be serious. That's girls' stuff. I'm proud my son can't jump rope!"

And what about the biopsy, the histological results of which had been authored by the renowned Insel Hospital in Bern?

"Spinal? Genetic? Histo—? Both of them? That's just a way of saying I-have-no-idea! And you're buying it, too!"

"Louis knows very well what he's talking about. He's—"

"—a scoundrel!

...a...a...a..."

Hounds...

Father stuttered.

...Huns!

Cliffs soaring heavenward, sand as far as the eye can see, the saddle leather cracks. They'd indulged in the cool darkness of the Hadleyville saloon; the whisky still warms their throats. Who knows when they'll next sink their teeth into a hunk of bread again. The sun blazes mercilessly; their buckskin shirts are drenched with dusty sweat, emitting a stale odor. But the brute energy of their horses is already coursing through their own bodies once more. They've left Hadleyville to go after the bad guys like real men. They'll hunt 'em down, cost what it may—

...and someone would have him believe his sons would soon no longer be capable of mounting a horse?

"Capito! My sons are okay. Do you hear, Ruth? They're just fine."

His body contradicted his words—or was he trying to keep his thoughts on a tight rein? His face had turned red and sweat pressed from his pores as if the desert sun over Hadleyville were actually beating down on him. Will Kane, no, even better, John T., from *Rio Bravo*, trembled with rage, shouted with frustration. Shouted at his wife. Shouted louder and louder.

You don't die from SMA III; SMA III is a lifetime of slowing down. At five years of age you can romp around just like all the other kids, you can ski at ten, still play a little handball at twelve, still climb the steep hill to the Acropolis at fifteen, still wander through halves of cities at eighteen, still get up from just about any chair at twenty-two, still go up or down almost any stair at twenty-seven, still take quite a few steps in your apartment at thirty-seven, still slip a sweater over your head without assistance at forty-two, and still bring a fork to your mouth at forty-four.

Here, father, is where I grind to a halt. What comes with forty-two and forty-four is something my brothers model for me; I see it every time I see them. That is as far as I dare think, that is as far as I have to think and want to think even if, despite experience to the contrary, I always talk myself a little into believing that maybe it won't all hold true for me. But beyond that?

But he also said: "You realize, of course, where my boys got this disease. It can't possibly be my genes. Look at how I'm built. Strong as an ox. Nothing can knock me over. And you? The slightest breeze! These constant fainting fits. Just take a guess where your sons got this dis—this stuff from."

Dressed for Fasnacht, ca. 1969

The guy keeps asking questions. Is it getting worse? What's it like being pushed through St. Gallen, all those places you used to be able to walk? Is it hard? He just keeps asking. It's good. I keep talking. I want to be asked. Who's still interested? Everyone has long gotten used to my disability, except for me. Gotten used to the fact that the worsening will continue unchecked. Then this brazen guy, whom I don't even know very well, comes along at the perfect time. Finally, someone who's asking the Grail question.

"Hey!" someone shouts in the movie theater, a guy I know even less well; he heads over to me. "That's my seat," he says, meaning my wheelchair. We talk about everything but, until the film starts. Finally, someone who acts normally.

But he also said: "Why do you think I started drinking? Why I have to drink? How's a father supposed to cope—two handicapped sons. That'll knock the strongest ox off his feet."

Or he said he started to drink because he had been so very lucky; mostly, however, he said he didn't drink.

He said his license hadn't been taken away for drunk driving because he had been drunk but because some gutless rat squealed on him.

Once there was no longer denying—and more alcohol no longer helped—that his sons really were cripples after all, he said he didn't have sons anymore and confined himself to drinking.

Sometimes I dream of a cure that I owe to a fire, a conflagration. I awaken, see the flames, which have already encircled me, and leap out of bed—although I can't possibly leap—run out of the apartment, up the flight of stairs... (In the more gallant version of my cure-dream, I carry Jan up the steps in my dreamily strong arms and take her outside where the fire department, surrounded by pajama-clad neighbors, is putting out the flames.) Would it also work when awake? Should I set fire to my bed or hope—as, of course, I have to be surprised by the blaze—that a fire will break out in my house one day? But wait! I never dream of myself in a wheelchair, so, when I dream, I'm always already cured...

In 1978, ten years later, when I received my diagnosis, my father didn't say anything at all. For this year was, as he would claim over and over again from this point on, his fateful year: the year in which everything— business, collection, family—was taken from him.

Have finally replaced the rubber tip of my cane. Now I no longer clack when I walk and can once more sneak around like a cat.

W ith each slower and slower step I emigrate further and further into SMA land, into my exile; am essentially writing emigrant, exile literature in my muscle diaspora...

In common parlance SMA is called muscle wasting, and this constant losing of muscle even feels like a wasting away. Although that is precisely untrue: it's not the muscles that waste away—the muscles are there—it's the energy they should be communicating. Where does the energy disappear to? The energy, as they say, fizzles out. I feel the fizzling out as a whirring. This "ant feeling" is the only thing I feel: I don't have any pain. The muscle whirring is pleasant, a cozy feeling that comes with the ever-present weakness.

Energy is information. My muscles get this information only in fragmentary form, communicating to me with their whirring that they are ready for deployment and waiting for the command. I give the command, but it—the information—gets lost en route. Where does it get lost? On the route from my brain to my muscles by way of my nerve fibers.

My body is a room in which the light only flickers. The switch works, the bulb is intact, the fuse turned on, and yet the electric impulse arrives at its destination incompletely, because the cable in the wall is rusted through. The information says: light!, it says: energy! And the whirring

*in my body starts again, especially in my legs, which want to be up and
running. It creeps and crawls. So much unexploited energy!*

Light!

Father swore and ate and drank and was soon so worked up that his
cusses and curses took shape, flying from his mouth as peas and half
chewed chunks of meat. Had he really shot and killed all the people he
mercilessly and vociferously had declared he'd bump off at the dinner
table, St. Gallen would have been a ghost town long ago. The fact that
he never actually translated any of his threats—or, as it would turn out,
only one—into action, disappointed me at first. My father was not only
no longer a king—something I had been forced to realize in the now
almost empty wine cellar—he also wasn't one of those Western heroes
we had admired together for so long.

"I earn three times more than they do!" he ranted and raved
night after night from his place in the dining room beneath an early
riverscape; it had been painted by an Appenzell artist who, due to
persistent demand, had done a series on the subject. "...and with just
a few years of elementary school! Now, when I really need their damn
money for once, they're cutting off the supply on me. Me! And they've
built their big-shot villas with *my* money. Without me, there'd be no
Goldene Rank!"

The Goldene Rank—the Golden Loop—was St. Gallen's gold coast,
though it was a coast without water as Lake Constance was fifteen
kilometers away and could only be seen through the occasional attic
window. This was where the lawyers, architects, and doctors, as well
as a handful of politicians, settled in a density that was surprising, as
if they wanted to seek shelter in their reserve of white single-family
homes with Eternit-brown roofs. If my father chose to go as far as verbal
genocide at the dinner table, it was the professional caste he'd always
eradicate first.

The "they" he cursed with such powerful eloquence were the
bankers. When the 1970s didn't actually prove to be more lucrative than
the 1960s—a situation that even baffled those who earned their money
with money—"they" refused to help him prevent his business from going
bankrupt. The volume of orders had fallen off to a level in keeping with

the old factory, but the new building had been completed, the company logo nailed up, the corridors hung to the ceiling with paintings, and each and every corner provided with a surprise in sculptural form. All that was left was for the machinery to be fed.

What had happened? Was it because oil had become a bit more expensive? Had the coffers run dry? Had the bank been broken? Just recently, during the 1960s, anything had still been possible and now all of a sudden that was over? "Who applied the emergency brake? The bankers! The big cheeses, of course, those spineless bastards lazing about on their crisis-proof salaries doing nothing!" Up to this point money had been available to him for the taking—"Your good name is enough, Mr. Keller"—now his accountant spent days on end in bureaucratic red tape and couldn't get a single centime. The owner had to appear in person, "wait in their stuffy halls filled with bland bank lobby art letting them savor their little bit of power," to find out that his good name was now one they avoided like the plague. Eventually, his name no longer even registered, as "they" no longer even bothered to decline his requests. The faucet had been turned off and no financial plumber could turn it on again, let alone a plumber's son, which my father, of course, was.

He'd been warned in good time, hadn't he? Yes. By his accountant, whom he then promptly replaced, only to stand trial for fraudulent bankruptcy half a dozen years later with the successor accountant; by his wife; by his anxious employees. But heed the voices of warning? Only a sissy does that. The enemy must be confronted; the duel fought. Third bottle, fourth bottle, fifth bottle. The streets of Hadleyville, swept clean. There was no one, not even someone with whom Will Kane could duel, or whom John T. could ambush. *Betrayal has swept the town clean. Do not forsake me, O my darling.* The train pulled out; the bankruptcy proceedings commenced.

"Can we do anything else for you, Your Majesty?" father screamed, wrongly supposing he still sat firmly in the saddle at the Alpsteinstrasse house, a saddle he continued to believe would belong to him. Even the riverscape behind him would soon be taken from the wall and hauled out of the house by "those who called themselves bankruptcy clerks to conceal their theft from the law."

"That's how they came crawling, the Mr. Bankers, you should've seen them. May we shove some more money up your behind? But no, of course not, we don't think your factory's new building could ever be too big—it can't be big enough. Is there any reason why you shouldn't have an office in which a member of the *Bundesrat* wouldn't get lost? We believe in your visions, and do you know why? Because we believe in you! Can we get you another million, Your Majesty? All of us, the bank administration, the board, and the whole fucking management of our fucking bank think that what your factory-palace *really* needs is a tower of solid gold, one that's higher than both cathedral towers combined and at least as tall as the Eiffel Tower— though naturally not as rusty—from which you, Your Majesty, can piss on all of St. Gallen, the whole of Switzerland, and ideally on the entire world as well, just like Gargantua pissed on Paris from the roof of Notre Dame! That, nothing more, nothing less, is exactly what these goddamn—"

But wait, the Kasperli word of honor: I promised to be honest. Did father really say this? The honest answer: yes. But did he say it in this way? Well, he did swear, you can take my word on that, and there are still plenty of people who can testify to this even if they may cross to the other side of the street before I can ask them. But had he worked Gargantua of all creatures, that giant's son, that pissing Gargantua, into his speech? Could he have read, of all books, Rabelais's book—one I did

claim, after all, he hadn't even taken it out of its protective wax paper?

"This done, he considered the great bells, which were in the said towers, and made them sound very harmoniously. Which whilst he was doing, it came into his mind that they would serve very well for tingling tantans and ringing campanels to hang about his mare's neck when she should be sent back to his father, as he intended to do, loaded with Brie cheese and fresh herring. And indeed he forthwith carried them to his lodging."

It doesn't matter. What is remembering, other than the thankless process of reinventing your own past; thankless because you have to reinvent something that already once was?

As if catching me in the act of thinking these things he scrutinized me closely and then exclaimed triumphantly, "That was *exactly* how they spoke to me! And now what?"

I shrugged my shoulders. When father—*my* father, *the* father, *this* father, the *ex-king, John T.*, (would he soon really be shooting? And can I keep him at bay if I call him John T.?)—when *he who sat there* didn't know what happened next how was I supposed to?

A flick of the wrist and I'd be out of commission. If I press the height control of my desk chair I plunge to the depths. One to two centimeters, depending on how fit I feel, is what separates me from no longer being able to get up from this chair. For a while now there has been a pillow on the seat. I tell myself it is more comfortable this way. And it is, but the pillow serves first and foremost to raise the surface. This way I can more easily stand up. Or even stand up at all. On less muscular days I can't do it without the pillow. I touch the height control. If I press it I plummet twelve, fifteen centimeters. Do I want that? From down there I don't even have to try standing up anymore, for I know I can't do it, and I see this certainty as a relief. My bungee jump into the depths. What an adrenaline rush that would be! My little adventure, stranded down below. My survival episode in the safety of my own office chair. How big is the risk for those who, surrounded by TV cameras, test their ability to survive in a fairly tamed wilderness? Half the world subsists on beetles anyway, so what? My risk is small too. I have my telephone. Yet for a minute, I imagine as if I am cured. I let go of the height control. The thought is enough. Refreshed, I continue writing.

"And now what? What happens now?"

John T., who always got the biggest steak, hacked off a piece, put it halfway in his mouth, left an end peeking out, and whistled for the dog—all while continuing to rant. "Now they don't talk to me at all. Their gold has suddenly corroded..." Rott trotted over, sat on his hind paws, and barked impatiently. My mother, who was returning with the coffee, had long given up on her "please-not-at-the-table." Father leaned forward and snapped his fingers. Rott snatched the piece of meat from his mouth.

"Did you see how gently he does that?" He wiped the dog saliva from his lips with his sleeve. "My dog! We'll go for a walk in a minute, Rott, let me finish eating. Good dog, what a good dog. Everyone's betraying me, Rott. I can't trust anyone but you. Maybe my youngest will come with us. He's still a little on my side. What do you think, Rott?"

The next piece of meat, which Rott didn't let out of his sight, father cut for himself. The drop of saliva hanging from Rott's chops lengthened until it broke off and fell to the floor. Father washed his food down with wine. Though my plate was now empty, I didn't dare stand up. Of course, I wanted to go along; of course, I didn't want to. I loved these evening walks after eating, before the film, even if they were getting shorter for me as time went on. I loved my dog. I had loved my father once. I imagined he once loved me too. Of course, I'd go along. I couldn't have guessed it would be our last walk together.

"And what do the Mr. Lawyers do, the ones who got me into this situation in the first place? Send me reminders. And when I call I'm told the Mr. Lawyer, Esq., is away from the office, or in a meeting, when he's actually standing right there pinching his secretary on the ass. Let's go, Rott!" He belched. Stood up. His napkin got stuck between his stomach and the table edge and then fell to the floor. "Not while I'm around! You'll see! Now I'm getting angry! You'll see, when I'm back in the saddle again, I'll buy those guys, I'll own them, one by one. Better still, I'll shoot them all dead, those, those—."

"*Rio Bravo*'s on TV tonight," Mix announced, looking up from the newspaper he'd been reading.

"Big surprise," I said.

"Maybe you shouldn't go out with the dog today," my mother suggested, adding in a somewhat quieter tone, "in your condition."

"Who's going where?" Mix, deeply absorbed in the TV listings, wanted to know. My middle brother deeply absorbed in something has to be envisioned literally—as if his upper body sought to absorb the newspaper or the book he held, he sank deeper and deeper into his reading. Sometimes father shouted at his second-born to get his attention, and Mix would look at him with genuine astonishment. This meant Mix was on the high seas, an expression he owed to an essay he had written a few years back, when he was still in elementary school. Whenever he became immersed in his thoughts at school, or actually really was reading Forester under his desk, his teacher would say: "There's our dreamer, on the high seas again, Captain Hornblower." This wasn't merely a rebuke directed at Mix for not paying attention, but praise—sunk, in typically Swiss manner, in the subtext—for a brilliant essay about Hornblower on the high seas. This was where— and maybe this was the reason for his mental absence—he was relatively safe from father.

"It's okay. I can go," my mother offered. "After I wash the dishes."

"I'm going. Now!" my father said. "That means now. Coming, kiddo? Rott?"

My mother gave me a look that was at once pleading and resigned.

"Why doesn't anyone ever tell me anything," Mix muttered and continued reading.

When I go to the bathroom I take the phone off the hook. I don't want to miss a call. But that's not the real reason. I am afraid a call could come at the wrong moment—the ring of the phone could strike at a bad time. Strike is the right word. The hollow of my knees is where the ring would "strike." The muscle-nerve connection. It hasn't happened yet, but on a weak muscle day the ringtone, a lightning bolt of sound, could strike the muscles in the hollows of my knees—they freeze, they stiffen up, I buckle, sink to the floor, lie there.

Cliffs soaring heavenward, sand as far as the eye can see, the saddle leather cracks. John T. Chance rides again. Bang-bang! Time for our walk.

Along Alpsteinstrasse, across the intersection to the meadow with the No Dogs Allowed sign, and back again. At the halfway point, we passed a Labrador who barked at everyone and raced back and forth in his yard behind a wooden fence until those passing by had hoofed it out of his territory. It was, if I remember correctly, the house and the dog of a doctor or a lawyer, in any event the dog of a species endangered in eastern Switzerland. Father stopped to allow the evening's supply of anger to run dry. Quietly, but loud enough to drown out the yapping, he carefully explained to the hotshot mutt everything his fearless fighting machine would do to him and his master's diplomas at his command—the command, after all, of a brave *hauptmann* of the victorious Swiss army.

"Seize!" the commander shouted, and although Rott—a dog having already approached middle age, anxious for his retirement years, a dog of the same magnificent embonpoint as his master and as much of a stubborn old mule—yes, although Rott did bark at the neighbor's dog, he didn't give a moment's thought to seizing. And how would he anyway? The wooden fence separated the two dogs. That's why it was there. And what dog would be crazy enough to shove his nose through a fence into the jaws of a Labrador?

My brave dog defeated the Swiss army all on his own once, when the army was rehearsing for the big moment in our yard. It was the Russians who had to be fended off, back then, when they were still a menace on the rise. And in the end, it was *"der Russ,"* the mighty Russian, who sounded even more threatening in the singular, who was fended off—by a half dozen men in their late thirties, mid-forties, mid-level managers with mid-level beer bellies, who had, for the purpose of national defense, dressed themselves up, painted their faces, and crawled under our rhododendron bushes. Although Switzerland hadn't been attacked in some time, the threat during World War II had led to the so-called *réduit* strategy: a Swiss form of conflict resolution that my father would also resort to. It consisted of abandoning the lowlands—women, children, the aged, and the crippled included—to the enemy without a struggle so the army could defend itself by safely retreating to bunkers hollowed out of an Alpine massif. When Rott tore off after the soldiers, the attacked army beat its disorderly retreat—according to regulation—out of our yard. Those who didn't make it to the street climbed up into the trees. For one part of the troop, however, retreat was cut off, so that the sergeant found himself obliged to negotiate with the enemy. He rang our doorbell. Just the evening before, my mother had warmed up consommé for the soldiers, but she knew nothing of military exercises in her *réduit*. Of course she had heard the dog barking, but Rott, she told the sergeant, mostly only chased after the Chihuahua with the little pink bow from across the way, who, incidentally, had never once taken flight. She whistled Rott back from the rhododendron front and apologized to the soldiers who insisted on climbing down from the trees only once the attacker had been taken into custody inside the house. There the commanding officer of the troop rewarded Rott for his dedication with dog biscuits and an especially fat mortadella. There were no casualties.

"Forget it," I said to father who was still rattling the garden gate. We were only about two hundred steps from home. I wanted to watch the evening film: *Taxi Driver* for the first time, not *Rio Bravo* for the fifth. But more importantly, I didn't want to be seen with my father on the street a moment longer. Baring his teeth, the Labrador jumped up along the fence.

"Father, just leave him!" I shouted, which to his ears may have sounded like "father, seize him!" for he now squeezed his hand through the fence. Rott snarled. I tugged at father's sleeve, but his hand was now between the slats. Could the gate be opened this way? He never found out. When he wrested his hand from the fangs of the neighbor's dog it was a pulsating piece of red flesh.

Utterly perplexed, yet proudly holding his hand out in front of him as if it were a trophy of war, he tottered home. On the sidewalk behind him, a trail of blood and curses.

My mother drove him to the hospital. As she had hoped, the doctor on duty was Dr. Farmer, who had treated Puck after his ski accident and stitched up my knee after my bike accident. The fact that Föns was so stinking drunk did have its positive side—he wasn't experiencing much pain, Dr. Farmer said. The patient had lain down on the bed and fallen asleep.

"It's not so bad," he said, after he had taken a look at father's hand.

The emergency nurse washed out the wound. Dr. Farmer gestured toward the visitor's chair and my mother sat down. I positioned myself behind her, the dog leash still in my hand.

"How bad is it really? I mean, at home. One hears things."

My mother sighed. She had covered up father's traces where they could be covered up, had kept silent too long when she should have said something.

"He drives a car in this state," my mother complained for the first time to an outsider. "He says, if you can't walk anymore, you should drive, and thinks that's funny. The police brought him home once and I protected him. That was ten years before the bankruptcy and before the president of the *Chaine des Rôtisseurs* suggested the time had come for him to leave the club. But because he was still a person to be respected, the police turned a blind eye. I told them it really was an exception. I lied to the police, lied to perpetuate what's been destroying me for years. Yet what I wanted most was to throw myself at one of the officers and beg him: 'Take him with you, please! Take the drunk off my hands! Take his driver's license away so nothing happens, so he finally comes to his senses and sobers up. At least take his gun away, the one in the glove compartment. If you won't do that either, then take me with you, please...'"

"I'd best give you something," the doctor said.

He kept father for a few days in the clinic "for observation" although the wound only required outpatient treatment and a more fitting description would have been "for sobering up." He prescribed treatment at a health resort, and his diagnosis, "shattered nerves," ensured that insurance bore the costs. Otherwise father wouldn't have gone, for, after all, he didn't drink.

I can only get out of bed because I am an athlete. I tense my muscles, six seconds long, again and again. It seems to work better with closed eyes. I feel the muscle energy flowing through my waking body. To distract my thoughts, however, from the chair I will climb—as if a rope, hand over hand—I am currently reading Dante. It is my time for poetry. If Dante gets through a circle of hell, then I will manage to get out of bed. I throw the comforter back. If the cover lies too heavily on my leg I push it aside with my hand. I pull my right leg over the edge of the bed, then the left. With enough momentum the left leg hoists my upper body up with it, if not, I use my arm. I sit there, watching and waiting, the chair opposite me, dust clinging to its cross supports. My palms become sweaty. I throw the clothing off the chair because I gain time by doing so. The rug, too, must be smoothed out. The books aren't standing back to back. Now. The telephone. In case it rings while I'm standing up. Now.

Not yet. I put on my glasses—that is important. Is the cane where it needs to be? I extend both arms, feel their heaviness. I hold them out for ten, twenty seconds because the heaviness is good. It reminds me that I have muscles, even if they may not be very strong. I take advantage of this moment. My fingers take hold of the edge of the bed,

my muscles tense, bottom goes up, knees click into place, hands touch the floor. I am the human jackknife; left hand grabs left armrest, head on armrest, right hand lifts my upper body up from the seat of the chair—I am standing. How about that, it works, worked again today! The cane is where it needs to be: in my hand. I rely on it while I move my feet closer together, then we're off, my cane and I—nothing can happen to us now—toward the kitchen where I can already smell the coffee I haven't even made yet.

In the bathroom mirror I see the three red pressure marks on my chin; they come from the back of the chair where I propped myself up using my chin.

And on the way to coffee I see myself, vain as I am, on a stage, see how an actress gets up, stands up, the way I do, following the Stanislavsky method. Yes, it should be a woman, with the requisite grace, an actress. Curtain! And I see the actress, how she plays me. I see what sort of fragile, delicate, dignified sequence of moves it is, how graceful she is, see the magnificent chair, a throne really, that had been discovered in the props room. She allows her body to rise and it is as if her essence floats away.

She understood, the actress, who, to be able to play me must also be a dancer, the best there is. She understands me, she is standing now, standing for me, spinning for me, and I bow slightly in the hallway mirror, and the ballerina—is dancing.

By the time I changed from the Catholic to the cantonal school in 1979 my steps had become heavier. As if someone had started hanging weights on my body, as if somebody were whiling away the time by filling my cells with liquid until I wouldn't be able to walk anymore. Only after I no longer had sufficient strength to play tennis was I capable of imagining no longer being able to play tennis one day. Yet now, I was no longer capable of recalling what it may have been like once, only a few months ago, to have played tennis.

How on earth had I ever done that? I started to ask, as if I'd lost faith in myself. I thought back to the tennis court, saw the reddish granular surface, saw my tennis partner on the other side of the court, saw how she served the ball. I saw how the ball gained speed in the air, how it flew over the net towards me, saw myself as I ran to meet it, bringing my racket back. But as I readied to take a swing, the memory broke off. For although I had made these movements so often in the past years that my body—my muscle and nervous system—must have internalized them, I didn't see what came next. Perhaps I wasn't capable of remembering that I had quite recently still been able to perform this movement? Of course, I knew what came next. No doubt I had walloped the ball with my racket and masterfully countered the shot—or, what had been more frequently the case of late, had misplayed the ball. But that wasn't the memory of how I had played tennis but rather my knowledge of how tennis was played, which (if need be) I could have refreshed by watching any old tennis match on television.

What did my memory have to do with my muscular strength? Was it powers of imagination that ultimately made muscles move? Did SMA blot out this memory? Did I merely have to have a powerful enough imagination and remember each of my movements as accurately as possible to be able to play tennis again? Were there memory cords that corresponded to muscle cords? Were muscles remembered movements? Were the origins of muscles memories? Was there something like a muscle memory?

Before burying my tennis racket in the closet under the bag with my Boy Scouts stuff, my elementary school notebooks, and the exercise books in which I had written and illustrated my first stories, I tried to mimic the movements I had mastered so well only a short while before. I swung back to hit an imaginary ball but something stopped me just prior to the imaginary impact of the ball on my very real racket. It was the same hesitation—a lack of muscular courage?—I had also sensed when I imagined the movement. My powers of imagination were no match for my loss of strength and as a result—since then—the memory of these movements has also remained on the sidelines.

As little as I was no longer able to imagine what had once been, was I able to imagine what was to come. I saw that Mix now needed ten minutes for the twenty steps that led upstairs; during the breaks he was forced to make on both of the landings, he read a book he carried with him specifically for this purpose. I hadn't failed to notice that Puck, who around this time was living with his girlfriend (it hadn't been easy to find a building with an elevator), now only managed the front steps with effort and avoided the upstairs. I myself reached more and more frequently for the banister to be able to take the steps at a still undiminished speed. Louis Feller had also pronounced his judgment on me, clearly and unmistakably. And yet, I wasn't capable of imagining that one day I would go up stairs as slowly and awkwardly as my brothers, let alone that I would one day simply no longer be able reach my room on the second floor on my own two legs.

For several months already I had had trouble getting out of the low-slung lounge chair in the living room. Even before my diagnosis I had started avoiding this particular piece of furniture. As I now had my own television and wanted to avoid father even more than the chair, I retreated to my bedroom. And yet what I noticed in my brothers—how they got up out of the chairs they still could manage—was something I didn't want to accept for myself, not for my future in five, seven years from now.

Puck turned his chair away from the table and moved a second chair in front of him. Using his right arm he raised himself up from the chair on which he sat so that his upper body tilted forwards. To extend his legs—something his muscles no longer did—his backside disengaged from the seat of the chair and literally soared into the air. His stomach lay flat on his thigh; his chin touched the floor. With his left arm he propped his upper body on his knee so that he could free up his right arm, which supported his weight, in order to raise himself up from the second chair. Once his upper body was straightened up he could take his left arm from his knee in order to safeguard himself on the backrest of the second chair until he stood firmly on his own two feet.

For Mix a second chair proved unhelpful when standing up. The arm strength required to lift himself using this method was something he lacked. He had to use the table our mother cleared for this purpose. Sitting on his chair he bent forward until his weight started to shift from the chair to the table. To prevent his sliding from his chair he clutched the table edge opposite him and began to pull himself slowly onto the tabletop. Lying thus, with his upper body on the table, Mix rested briefly before starting the centimeter by centimeter "army crawl onto his legs" as he called it. His method of standing up took longer than what I called Puck's "jackknife method," and it was the latter that I would appropriate for myself.

Certainly, I sensed that what I saw would apply to me too, in a still-to-be-seen but predetermined way, and just as certainly, I did not want to admit this. How to live with this prospect? How to go on when one day going on foot would be a thing of the past? How to maintain distance when the distance separating us was to become smaller and smaller anyway, and not in years, but in muscular strength? And was I now really like *them*, my brothers, and no longer like *me*? What had I been like? How *different* from *them* had I been and how *similar* was I now? It was no longer only *their* disease, it was now *our* disease, and *they* and I were suddenly a *we*, the SMA Brothers.

As if my muscle weakness countdown started only at that moment when Dr. Feller put my own SMA certificate into my already slightly trembling hand—granted, it was a somewhat exciting moment as well, as if I were being given the dirty Icelandic parchment that promised a journey full of wondrous adventure, like the one to the center of the earth—our disease joined us together in a way that no one could want, least of all brothers.

The SMA Brothers in front of the basement steps, ca. 1968

Despite the five and seven-year-age difference—I was fourteen, Mix and Puck were nineteen and twenty-one and had little use for me, the latecomer—my brothers crowded me. They embodied my future more explicitly than was good for me and than is even normal among brothers, and I unconsciously had to keep my distance from them during this time, a time of major physical difference between us, just as they may have unconsciously kept their distance from me. In their eyes, I probably embodied a lost muscle paradise. Maybe it was a good thing that my brothers were only rarely home at this time. Mix was completing his commercial diploma in central Switzerland (at an elevator-less institution) and Puck was studying law in Bern (at the university there, which was only partially accessible). Maybe this is why I could bear it: because after my diagnosis I grew up as an only child. And maybe the reason I wasn't able to imagine this step-by-step worsening was because it was so clearly before my eyes.

So where did my journey go now? For the first time I heard the term "muscle fibers." Carpet fibers, yes—but muscle fibers? Did I have to picture my muscles as a carpet? One that was fraying? Whose strength frayed away? Why didn't anything hurt? Surely, loss hurts—it has to, doesn't it? The muscles—or their fibers?—whirred. It felt a little bit like a muscle ache, but there wasn't anything concrete, nothing that could be comprehended in words, nothing that I could really understand. The only thing that was (and is) comprehensible—*measurable*—and even then, only inaccurately so, is the slowing down. And sometimes, and this is still even hard to understand, there was only the impression of slowing down, which heralded and prepared the way for the actual slowing down. So was there a feeling after all, the feeling of slowness?

Something that had been inside of me since birth had begun to alter my body; only now, after my diagnosis, did the disease seem to really break out. Of course, something had begun: My body was in the process of growing from a boy's into a man's. My body, however, transformed itself in two ways, and it did so in opposite directions. As if it were the most natural process in the world, I was steadily losing strength at the same time my classmates were steadily gaining it.

I grew as well—got taller, put on weight. I did not, however, develop the strength to keep my ever heavier body moving at a corresponding pace. I, too, stood in front of the mirror each evening; Scotch-taping a strand of hair back so overnight it would finally get used to the spot I had assigned it. Against Dr. Feller's advice, I worked out with dumbbells, attempting to keep up at least a little with the steeled upper arms and thighs of my classmates. Although I was not overweight, my body started to deposit fat around my waist while my shoulders became bony and pointed; my muscles slackened bit by bit.

As a good citizen, you had to stand on your own two feet, didn't you? Wasn't that precisely what I'd be less and less able to do as time went on? I found a part-time job as a sorter at the post office where, sitting, I tossed thousands of letters into their pigeonholes. I avoided discotheques—too loud, too humiliating. Who wouldn't make fun of a grotesque dancer like me? No hikes with friends, no more exploring the world beyond well-worn paths. My muscles had already disqualified me from the playing field. During my last year at the Catholic school, I had still participated in sports week from the substitutes' bench. It was a good thing I went along, because I was able to spend the journey and the evenings with my friends; it may have done me good that I walked the stretch from our ski camp to the ski lift's valley station with everyone, but having to wait in the valley station instead of being allowed to return to the heated camp was something I felt as punishment for my difference. Freezing, I read one novel after another to forget that only a year before I had still been one of the skiers now roaring and shouting past me.

At school, I was excused from gym class. The PE teacher, however, believed as much in the trainability of a muscle as he did in the unparalleled laziness of the high school student. I rebelled with the strength-building exercise machines that ultimately took away the strength they were supposed to give me. I simultaneously battled the soldier mentality of my gym teacher and the pessimism of my doctor. SMA made a first decision for me: those able enough on foot could choose between drawing and music; otherwise, it was drawing—for the drawing classroom was on the ground floor while music lessons took place on the top story of the school building.

I wasn't actively shut out, but passively, yes, as nobody thought it necessary to remove a single obstacle that stood in my way. I started walking other routes, which became longer and yet more arduous. I still didn't see the signs—the wheelchair symbols that are now found everywhere but at the time were still a rare sight—and yet I started to follow them obediently, already driven by necessity, for lack of a world more accessible. The steps became higher for me, and that, too, limited the possibilities. Once I was also excused from the weight room with a letter from Dr. Feller I did, it's true, gain three hours per week that I was able to spend reading in a café or at the park. Only, I was alone in this. If the others played soccer, I read; if the others showered, I read. If they went off on sports week, I read at home.

Girls. Finally!—after the all-male Catholic school on the cathedral precincts, where I could only imagine replacing the poster girls on the walls of my room with real ones, now there they were, to the left of me, in front of me, behind me, everywhere. I sat in their midst, next to Zack, who had changed schools with me. Yet I didn't translate the bold plans I had once envisioned in detail into action, but instead, thought up new, sound reasons why a girl couldn't get excited about someone like me. I was ashamed. My body was in the early stages of no longer being suitable for normal life. I didn't speak to anyone about what was happening to me, and no one asked. I sat there, already somewhat slumped, my stomach bulging, my shoulders tapering, and waited to be spoken to, while at the same time sending a signal to leave me alone.

What is my life expectancy? I get asked this sometimes. Normal, I say. What you might expect from any life.

I had the needs of a young man and the abilities of an old one. Was I becoming an unbelievable character, one that should exist only in literature? There was the old man in the boy's body, the dwarf who doesn't grow, the person who negated nature. "Nothing can be done when one person's burden is heavier than another's," I read in Günter Eich, and I didn't have to be told that twice. Could Peter Weiss's bitter *Leavetaking* have fallen on more fertile ground? His dictum why he wrote—because he wasn't cut out for anything else, as he put it—applied to no one better than it did to me. The place he was destined for, Auschwitz, where his name had been on the death list, disturbed me. I could empathize, which for someone who grew up in Switzerland was neither presumptuous nor even ridiculous, but rather confirmed my weakness: for me, the teenager, the weakness I shared with others—my being an other, an outcast, chosen in a negative way.

I discovered Wolfgang Hildesheimer's *Tynset*, his withdrawal-from-the-world book, but also enjoyed his early satires as an antidote to the *weltschmerz* taking root in me at such an early age. I wrote Hildesheimer a long letter so overladen with my problems it would have frightened even an optimist. He refused my desire to meet him by postcard, saying he already knew too many people. Dürrenmatt's labyrinths followed, in which I found my way with alarming effortlessness. In the insane asylum of *The Physicists*, where a sentence once thought can no longer be taken

back; in a world in which, as I read later in *Lunar Eclipse*, a priest thinks nothing of preaching to empty pews; and a cerebral one in the *Gedankenfuge* of *Stoffe*, where one makes journeys without getting up from one's desk and which showed me an alternative beyond all physical journeys.

What was I, who would I become? Maybe not a "travler" after all, but rather a yet-to-be-classified—and to be embodied by me?—variation of Dürrenmatt's prosthesis lady from *The Visit*: the *Teenagergreis*, the teenage-old man?

SMA, my SMA, behaves like an unwelcome lodger you hear rumbling around in the attic not knowing what she's up to. You only know she's up to something and, what's more, that her steps can't possibly augur well. Will she start a fire, maybe even tonight? Yet all you can do is roll over in bed and try to get used to the noise, and perhaps even the prospect that one day, at any time, the house could burn down. What you can also do, of course, is talk yourself into believing that what you hear and what's giving you such a scare is just the warping of the wood, for you do live in an old house after all.

Yes, she. *SMA: Though she's already so dangerous, though she's already so incomprehensible, the TEENAGERGREIS lets his body be linked to the opposite sex at least in this abstract way. Now however—after the diagnosis—everything is different; now everything that had already been suspected but couldn't be admitted has come true. And it's come true in that it's been given a name. The LODGER has a name and her name is now SMA. In his house, his body, she plays the part of the squatter, because she is residing in him illegally without his consent and without paying rent, for it is he who pays the rent, the TEENAGERGREIS.*

Now it's no longer the wood that's warping. Now it's his body that creaks and squeaks and rumbles. Now SMA, the squatter, who can be imagined in the film version of his life in the most splendid clichés, is pretty, blond, tender, and loving—not the deceitful and cruel being she really is, as it emerges when it is too late because he has already fallen madly in love with her—and she should be sexy and maternal, in a nutshell: a teenager's dream.

The steps at the entrance to the cantonal school in St. Gallen that I went up from 1979 to 1983. An elevator was installed only in the 1990s.

At my high school there were no elevators, no ramps, no ground level entrances, and no one who was bothered by this. Back then, people still wanted none of this buildings-adapted-to-humans nonsense, not even at a humanistic high school, and the result was that anyone who, like me, still could just barely adapt, *had to* adapt to the building, while those who couldn't—well, there were simply correspondingly few people in wheelchairs at my school and countless others in Switzerland. There were no signs hanging at the doors barring entry to wheelchair-dependent students and teachers, and there was also no such law in the school regulations. But this wasn't necessary. The steps were enough.

"Oh, steps, oh, stones, nothing can be done when one person's burden is heavier than another's" was the lesson THE BUILDING repeated to me every day, as if I wasn't only unsteady on my feet but also slow on the uptake. If I asked why a ramp couldn't be installed even by the back entrance, where the trash cans were found, I was told such a thing mustn't be done, for renovations of this sort would disfigure THE BUILDING: "Just imagine, the beautiful sandstone ruined by a ramp! Why, that would be downright criminal, not to mention illegal, for it's a landmarked building, you know. There's a law that protects beautiful buildings like these, you see. Incidentally, nothing personal. The building cannot be modified in any way whatsoever, and that's not just on account of someone like you; you need to understand this in an objective way."

I nodded and from that point on tried to understand it in an objective way. After all, I did go to school in this building every day to understand in an objective way how my city, my country, the society and world in which we all lived, functioned and, for example, treated someone like me. So, there was an indispensable law protecting old buildings, but not one to protect people who didn't conform completely to the norm. This wasn't obvious, you had to be taught it, and this was no doubt one of the reasons why I went to school. Now I, too, no longer wanted such a magnificent building like the St. Gallen cantonal school to be disfigured on my behalf. But how would I have been able to know that; after all, I didn't even know, for example, that garbage cans lying around all over the place weren't regarded a criminal disfigurement of a historic building, whereas ramps, which would have provided me with easier access and made access possible in the first place for countless other students, were. In order to really grasp this I would have to learn to feel even more ashamed. How had such an idea even occurred to me! "Ramps! Elevators! Stair lifts! What next? A student cafeteria accessible to all?" No, no, I was the problem, not THE BUILDING, and step after step this became more and more clear to me. Had THE BUILDING been the problem, someone would have long since come and fixed it. And as there were laws that protected buildings, I had to be happy that no one removed me, for I, of course, basically disfigured the building the way a ramp or a stair lift did.

Really, no one wanted to see the way I struggled through this building each day, up and down the stairs! Didn't it mean—for I was offending against the preservation order—I was acting illegally, so was a criminal? "Have you ever thought," THE BUILDING asked me "that maybe this is why there are no wheelchairs at this school? Have you ever considered that maybe this was the reason no one comes and sands the steps out of existence?"

"No, I..." went THE PROBLEM.

"And," THE BUILDING continued, "isn't it true that according to your Dr. Feller it won't be long anyway before you'll also be wheelchair dependent? Don't you know that your muscles have only given you a reprieve, so you'd better watch out and make sure you wangle your way on your wobbly legs through to your senior year final exams. And if your muscles," and here THE BUILDING clicked its tongue with immense pleasure, "conk out before this, then you'll—"

"Quiet! Shut your trap!" THE PROBLEM shouted loudly, and loudly it reverberated off the walls of THE BUILDING, causing a girl, and not an unattractive one—you can take my word for it—to turn around, look, stop, and give me a questioning stare. Despite the strain of getting from the German room in the basement to math class on the second floor without being late—I had seven minutes, just like everyone else—I attempted a smile. THE BEAUTY said nothing, however, but merely raised her forehead, nose, chin, and then her already rather short skirt, and, as quickly as possible, taking two steps at a time, left me standing in her wake.

"Quiet," I whispered, and now knowing better, I kept the following to myself: Be quiet, you just want to get finals over with, don't you? And then hightail it out of this building, ideally to another city. You want to go to college, right? Ideally, study architecture, for this is how you can best change the world. But with these muscles you're really only good enough for literature—doesn't matter, because everything will be different there, wherever "there" may be. So be grateful, ask for nothing that won't be given to you voluntarily, but most of all keep your mouth shut and save your strength for the steps, for until finals there are, after all, still 263,356 to go—

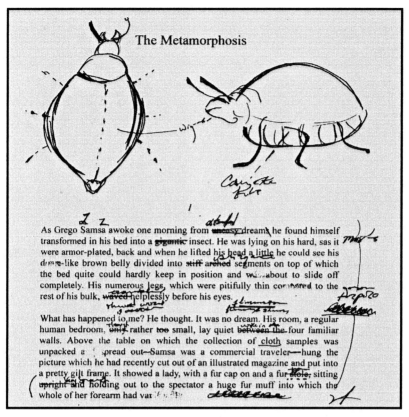

Gregor Samsa as a beetle. The Samsa apartment.

Pity that Gregor Samsa simply grows weak and dies. The Samsas were too easily rid of him. Kafka shirked his responsibility. I'd have liked to have known what would have happened to the beetle outside the protected world of his room, what the outside world would have done with him, but that was something Kafka couldn't, or didn't want to, envision.

I would have liked to have read how the beetle scuttles down the steps, encounters the "butcher's boy with his tray on his head." How the charwoman with the "little ostrich feather in her hat, which stuck up almost straight" might perhaps hold the door open despite her disgust—it's possible, isn't it? How Gregor hastens across the street, to end up where? With an insect enthusiast? In a research laboratory? At the zoo? With a traveling circus, in a cage next to the hunger artist?

What if he falls in love and fathers little Samsas? The very idea of it, perverse! Or so we'd think. What idea? That a creature that has ceased to fit the norm could find happiness? Kafka was no optimist. He lets the charwoman push Gregor away with a broom: as if you could simply sweep off a beetle as big as that! And while the charwoman sees to "that thing next door"—once it is disposed of, she's to be sacked—the Samsas treat themselves to a spring walk. The last thing Kafka can still think of in The Metamorphosis *is Gregor's sister stretching her young body.*

Rereading The Metamorphosis *I am struck by the many ways Gregor's situation could have paralleled mine, and I can already see the headline: SAMSA HAS SMA! Kafka describes it exactly: Gregor's muscles weaken, they atrophy, each movement is an enormous expenditure of energy that leaves Gregor lying on his bed for hours, tired of living. Soon he can no longer make his way through the apartment, and then he can't even get out of bed. Even his family won't help him anymore. Wouldn't it be best for everyone if he died on his own; and next thing you know the Gregorbeetle does them all this favor: dies of muscle loss, starves, because no one feeds him any longer, ultimately suffocating, because of his enfeebled muscles, under the weight of his body.*

The more stairs I put behind me the more difficult they became. In the first year, when I was fifteen, I could still manage them well. The banister was on the right side, so I'd swing my left leg first—was this why it would become my stronger leg?—and then drag the right one up behind. I held my schoolbag in my left hand. What we were studying, whether I went to school for two or for five classes, or which classes they were—none of this was decisive yet. But as time went by math ended up being the easiest—the lightest—subject because we wrote on loose sheets. I found French increasingly difficult—heavier. It was also harder to predict. Bringing the grammar book along for each class, whether we needed it or not, meant a base weight of 450 grams. Always having *la lecture* with me as well, in case *le professeur* should be so inclined, could mean a daily difference of 85 grams (*Le Grand Meaulnes*) to up to a kilogram (*Les Misérables*, three volumes). In addition, there were the chemistry and physics books, poetics, the world atlas. All the same, in the first year I still mastered the material for up to eight classes, (a) to (h), plus 250 grams for my sandwich, over on average fifty meters of corridor and allowing for a time factor of seven minutes from class (a) to class (b) up to class (h) multiplied by the number of steps (40; 32 cm high). Question: Assuming student K. has six classes on a given day, how much strength does K. need? Answer: With increasing frequency K. arrives late to class.

Later, former classmates, who I hadn't noticed, said they remembered me. Of course, they didn't really remember me either, but that peculiar stair creature, that crawly beetle who, or so it must have seemed to them, tirelessly burrowed his way though the system of holes and hollows that was Swiss education—that steps-freak the cantonal school offered them free of charge.

This was why no one spoke to me back then. Four and a half years, they all climbed past me; for four and a half long years, each one of my fellow students left me in their wake, outdistanced me. Not a single teacher (all our teachers were male; we had a female only once, when the French teacher was sick and his daughter was allowed to substitute) spoke to me. Not the biologist, who surely knew a lot about mutations; not the physicist, who could calculate how much energy I had to expend per step (SMA as a function of my age minus step height); not the English teacher with whom we spent an entire year reading *Hamlet* in insanely painstaking detail and only got as far as "Words, words, words!" in the second act; not the history teacher, who taught us what, for example, the Nazis had done with the Jews but not what they had done with the cripples; not the Latin teacher, who had helped me render *mens sana in corpore sano* into perfect German; and not even the Germanist—who had confided to us that he liked blond women most, had married one, and that his absolute favorite thing to do was to zip around Tuscany with her in their car, listening to Brecht/Weill; with him, we read Kafka, first *The Metamorphosis*, then *Before the Law*, and finally, *In the Penal Colony.*

Bitter today? Yes, I'm taking it off and allowing myself a comfortable bitter day in front of the fire with a glass of red wine and Beethoven's last sonata.

A good many friendships also became more difficult for me; in Zack's case this was directly linked to steps. I had met Zack when still on foot, on a snowy day on the way to school. We shared an interest in music and literature, for endless conversation, as well as the impossibility of approaching the opposite sex—Zack because of his pimples, I because of my waddle walk, and both of us because of our fathers about whom we had been so very silent since the beginning of our friendship four years earlier. We were our own two-member private club and met daily wherever we might happen to be—in the schoolyard, in the record stores, in the second-hand bookshops, at the flea markets—spending hours plotting our future as publisher and author, though it wasn't yet clear who would be what. For starters, Zack wrote a portrait of Billy Joel for a pop magazine; I wrote on death for the *St. Galler Tagblatt* newspaper.

We were also rivals when it came to girls. Each of us seemed to have resolved to pick one out independently of the other, one with whom we could fall in love from afar. I was at least able to tempt one girl to a short and—I thought—clearly romantic evening of roasting chestnuts in the cellar fireplace, while another got me to rest my feet on the windowsill and howl at the moon to the recently released *Songs in the Attic* as the summer evening breeze blew in my face. Here, too, the rivals did anything within their power to achieve victory in the undeclared war—from alarming misappropriations of allowance money, all the way to *schadenfreude* when one of us lost something the other didn't yet have.

Can it be a surprise to anyone that for an entire winter we pursued the same girl—one of seven hundred at the cantonal school and not from our class? Never, not once, did we speak a word to the other about this one girl, so pretty, so blond, so tender, so sexy, so maternal, and yet in the end, so deceitful. After a weeks-long siege, she went down as *l'inconnue de Saint-Gall* in our just begun *journaux intimes*, as neither one of the rivals succeeded in learning even the name of the willful beauty.

I picked Zack up every morning. He started thanking me for this by keeping me waiting, at first only because he was by nature a bit chaotic, then, to show me that the possession of a seven-year-old Toyota (which I was able to drive when still sixteen because of my SMA—the legal driving age in Switzerland is eighteen), made me not so much a demigod, but more like his personal driver. I lived in the bigger house, had more pocket money, and now a car to boot. If I waited for him after school he'd sometimes tell me the day was too beautiful not to walk home; if it rained he let me drive him, without comment, to his front door.

I was there each morning without fail, but I always had to ask Zack if he would carry my school bag up the steps. If I didn't ask, he'd have already leapt out of the car; if I didn't ask quickly enough, he'd have vanished inside the school. If I did ask quickly enough—before bringing the car to a stop— he snatched up my bag with an "of course, what sort of friend do you think I am?" look, and then would hurry off with the same hasty "goes without saying" attitude. All that was left for me to do was lock the passenger door, hoist myself out of the car, and climb the steps. Unlike me, Zack, who had kept me waiting, was not late for class. With speed he could beat me, humiliate me, with speed he could emerge the winner of our competition.

I found my bag at the top of the steps and leaned on the wall—its gray paint felt somewhat slimy but it gave me the hold I needed to bend far enough forward—to pick it up off the floor. Now that a real weight hung from me I walked even more slowly along the corridor.

A teacher and a classmate help me over the rocks near Viareggio so I too can see where Shelley drowned.

SMA takes my bicycle away from me and gives me—in exchange?—a motorcycle. Then it takes my motorcycle, but in exchange, I receive a car. It replaces someone who can only envy me with a new friend.

Life, however, seems to have something like poetic justice for stair-climbing. The bag that Zack left lying at the top of the steps was soon picked up by another classmate. Ralph put it on the desk that Zack and I shared. Soon Ralph offered to carry me up the steps, fireman-like. I positioned myself behind him, he squatted down; I placed my arms around his neck, he took hold of them; he raised himself up, and I hung from his upper body. Sometimes he ran with me on his back up the stairs faster than all the other students. We arrived at the top laughing and out of breath.

From then on, Ralph carried me up half the world: as far up the Sagrada Familia in Barcelona as was possible, as far as one can get on two legs in the Uffizi in Florence, the Catherine Palace outside St. Petersburg, and the Kremlin in Moscow. What is etched most distinctly in my memory is the descent, and, even more, the ascent, of the steep spiral staircase in the Paris catacombs, I on Ralph's back and Ralph forced to keep apace with the other tourists. He carried me up countless private stairways, at the end of which the door would sometimes open and we'd be received with an indignant "What, drunk already?" Once, when we visited the cathedral in Lausanne, Ralph, engrossed in the Latin inscriptions, climbed a small staircase without waiting for me. I hesitated whether to call out to him, but he came right back, apologized, and said that he didn't think about steps when he was out with me.

Walking is going better—or am I only happy about a "muscular day" because I have already gotten used to much less? SMA progresses in phases and wears away at me in layers, in steps and thresholds. Some days I feel "more muscular" even if in the long run nothing is gained. But what counts is today. And today is good. And good is good. Only my Muscle Book is gradually turning into an obsession. Already looking forward to the next entry...already today can't wait to see what will be on my mind tomorrow...

I nstead of using the main entrance to the Kunsthaus Zurich, I have to content myself with the museum's delivery door, although it's just two sets of two steps that would have to be surmounted, were there a ramp. So Jan has to roll me away from the entrance for normal Swiss people and push me—with wheelchair, coat and shopping bag on my lap, it's more than a hundred kilograms—over rough cobblestone, around the Kunsthaus, past the Swiss Arts Council (public building, two steps, no ramp), to the entrance for non-normal Swiss people.

We stop short on the sidewalk, for the museum's delivery area can only be reached via an unusually steep entryway. What if the wheelchair slips away from Jan? What if no one opens the door? What if Jan can only push me up part way? We chance it nonetheless. After all, art needs to be an adventure.

The sign next to the bell above the garbage cans by the delivery entrance informs us that during work breaks it can take longer for an ill-tempered (that's not on the sign) assistant to come and welcome the museum's more special guests. I, in turn, inform the assistant, who after a few minutes makes his appearance, sandwich in hand, how easily the main entrance could be made accessible. He dismisses this impatiently, however, saying he's tired of hearing it as literally everyone he lets in this entrance tells him that, and, especially, as it's not his, but management's responsibility.

The elevator that brings me up is marked "freight elevator" and is filled with bulk refuse and artworks sealed in plastic. Through a door *set into the wall I burst smack into the middle of the* An Unrestricted View of the Mediterranean *exhibition and—now having myself become an item on display, a* Wheelchair is Beautiful! *rolling installation—all eyes turn to me.*

After seeing the unrestricted view of the Mediterranean, at least in part—I was blocked from some of the walkable installations due to steps or doors that were too narrow—we realize that not even all of the regular exhibition spaces are accessible, meaning stepless and rollable. Steps are everywhere, and almost everywhere sufficient space for the ramps I can envision perfectly. Visitors offer their help, though it isn't so easy (plus, it's dangerous) to carry a wheelchair and its contents up a set of stairs. Jan, who had never visited the Kunsthaus Zurich before, tells me she doesn't care if she sees all of it or not.

But now with the wheels of a mission that could no longer be stopped in motion (and fearing a second encounter with the sandwich-eating assistant) we decide to give the "normal" elevator a shot. If I remove my feet (that is, the wheelchair's leg supports) I am able to fit, just barely. The door presses against my knee; the wheelchair feet dig into my thighs. During my one floor journey in the narrow elevator I give myself over to visions of being buried alive, while Jan runs down the steps to receive my delivery at the bottom. A visitor who witnessed all this says she can't

believe wheelchair users are treated with such contempt in a country as rich as Switzerland. Another visitor holds the heavy main entrance door open, and a German tourist helps Jan maneuver me, tilted backwards, out of the museum.

This action should really be captured on video (Pipilotti, help!) or better still, staged several times a day. Man in wheelchair comes rolling along! Rolls over the Kunsthaus Zurich! Rolls over the buildings denying us access! Obstructs the streets of a rich Switzerland that spares no expense to level our country for cars, but pinches pennies when it comes to adapting and adjusting our country for people! Overthrows a government that

The building—the Guggenheim Museum in New York—as ramp: the elevator brings visitors to the floor of their choice and anyone and everyone, whether by foot or in a wheelchair, can view the exhibits.

permits three quarters of all public buildings to remain inaccessible for a large part of the population and doesn't even deem it necessary to make our parliament a place that all can effortlessly enter!

Ah, America, you have it better, your buildings are accessible, for you can sue if they aren't...

J an flew back to New York, where we spend a good part of the year. She has to prepare for the university where, as a poet, she teaches creative writing. In six weeks I will follow her, my manuscript in my luggage. In the meantime, I once more have to take each step on my own.

A woman around fifty lies on the floor. She has fallen and cannot get up. Helplessly, she extends an arm. The ground plan of her apartment appears on the screen, including three telephones that begin to flash. Focus shifts back to the woman, who is now flailing her arms about, and the viewer understands: if only the woman had what the company is about to offer! Without this product, however, she'll die. Should she fail to heed this warning, her body'll have already decayed by the time it's found by the neighbors—they'd have followed the strange smell— for, of course, the disabled always live alone in the wonderful world of advertising. When I saw this commercial in the United States for the first time I was initially preoccupied by whether the woman was really disabled or whether an actress was playing the role, and I couldn't decide what I would have found more cynical. It was after this that I felt the jolt so desired by the marketing strategists, the one that's supposed to force me to reach for my wallet, for now it was I who lay helpless on the floor.

Onward!

The anti-collectors started their work in the cellar where, in the same room as the fireplace, there were halberds, heraldic drinking glasses, mortar, and "stabellen" chairs to clear away, as well as Max Falk's trilogy of St. Andrew (painted when Puck was born), St. Michael (painted when Mix was born), and, (the not yet uncanonized) St. Christopher, with the Christ child on his muscular shoulders, painted when I was born. The numbered red stickers signaled which objects were to be taken away.

From the cellar, they burrowed through our house, gnawing their way from room to room, from one floor to the next. They rooted through the kitchen and found silver and crystal. They opened closets where they were met by falling vacuum cleaners, collections of old toys, talking Bohemian dolls, and Neapolitan *crèches*. They took down paintings that had hung in the stairwell; here a Liner, there a Spahni, here an Eggler, a Brignoni, a Roth, a Tinguely, and a Poliakoff. By way of sculptures, works by Luginbühl, Spoerri, Adler, and Thalmann, they reached the attic—my attic—where neither Nana nor Head-Foot could scare them off.

They deflated the protectress of the attic kingdom and rendered my stamp-room monster harmless by switching on the light without knowing THE RULE. They made sure not a single lithograph was left in the drawers. They plundered the labyrinth library, marauded the cinema, and leafed through the Leitz binders that collected father's collection. They even took Foot, my stair-climbing spring that I had left on the second floor of the attic. They lifted the bride and bridegroom doors off their hinges, slipped into my secret corridor, lit the miner's lamp, and worked their way forward—at first stooped over, then on all fours—to my secret little room, the attic's attic, where I had thought up every story imaginable, except this one.

Of course, I take my steps on my own when I am alone. Yet, once more, I am surprised how much a disability can be delegated. Is it that banal? When Jan is here, I feel more secure although I am really not. Were I to fall she wouldn't be able to catch me even if she were at my side quickly enough. Even so, she could go get someone who would help me up. For this reason I put the cordless phone in my pocket when I'm up and about the apartment on my own. It is my feeling of insecurity that I delegate to Jan—she absorbs it for me and that makes her somewhat insecure. Now, however, for the weeks until I follow her to New York, alone, I am once more my own insecurity; I walk again for myself, think again for myself. A good lesson.

For a few days—it would be five—a half dozen workers, under the direction of trustees and bankruptcy clerks, set about emptying our house in the absence of the party responsible for the whole tragedy. As word had gotten around that Mr. Keller would bump off anyone who stood in his way (not, however, that he had never done such a thing), the clerks seized their opportunity once they heard the newly minted bankruptee and potential madman had withdrawn to the Grison Alps to recuperate. Before they invaded our home, however, a secretary called to make sure the man of the house had really beat his retreat and to ask whether my mother had briefed her sons, who were in touch with their father no doubt (which was not the case), to treat the pending transaction as confidential.

It wasn't difficult to keep father from the chaos he had wreaked. He savored his Alpine exile; there, he needn't worry about a thing, neither the bankruptcy procedures nor how his family, which was suddenly without an income, would get by. Now he, the bankruptee, was sick, perhaps even sicker than his sons, who didn't have to spend months at a clinic. Maybe he even saw his bankruptcy as a disease, as something that struck through no fault of his own. And the fact that he had been sentenced to fourteen months probation for negligence would have done nothing to change such a perspective. On the contrary, it reinforced his conviction that there was a conspiracy against him, for he had never done anything wrong, of course.

It was now up to our mother to provide for the family. After a quarter century as a housewife, this was no easy task. To pay the bills that were already piling up, she took out a mortgage on her house. It was her steadfastness that made this possible—just a few months prior to the inevitable bankruptcy, when father sought to persuade her to entrust our Alpsteinstrasse home to the bank as surety, she had refused. Otherwise, we would have lost the house as well.

However, as all of her sons were still completing their educations—Puck was at university, Mix was finishing up his commercial diploma, and I would be in high school a few more years—and as she couldn't just mortgage her house indefinitely, she had to look around for another source of income. Of all things this presented itself in the form of the sanitary installations with which father had begun his professional life, and which at this juncture was only a small share of the business, a business that had temporarily grown to eighty employees. My mother was able to release this part of the company from the bankruptcy assets, and when Puck learned that, in addition, it would be possible to take over the even smaller division that manufactured mirrored cabinets for bathrooms, he decided to break off his studies and further safeguard the financial survival of our family. And this is how the budding attorney became a small businessman and the housewife and mother, a small businesswoman.

Before the bankruptcy clerks had even started to comb through our house, a few days had been fixed during which my father's art collection would be exhibited

Nana on my bike simulator. It is not the original attic Nana but one I found in a Niki de Saint Phalle souvenir shop on the Ile de la Cité in Paris (one step).

in the Kunstmuseum St. Gallen. Interested parties could then follow it to Zurich and purchase the desired objects at an auction. This all came full circle for me, when years later, at an exhibition of eastern Swiss art at the Kunstmuseum, I found myself once again face to face with paintings across from which I had once eaten breakfast.

I already had the key to my apartment in my hand, and had nearly reached the door on the stair lift, when I noticed I was floating in water on the lift's platform. I succeeded in stepping from the lift into the water and opening the apartment door, but that was as far as I could get.

The clinic in the mountains of the Grisons proved to be an idyllic place, where although father may not have achieved everlasting sobriety he did, at any rate, become an artist: what had been pent up inside of him during his decades of collecting found release. Over the course of his seven months at the clinic he did hundreds of watercolors, collages, found-object installations, and sculptures, and at the end of each workweek he took his pieces to the village carpenter and had them framed or pedestaled. His room was filled with hundreds of things he had created during this seven-month period, and what he did with these things was what he always did with things, animate and inanimate alike: he collected them. His bookkeeper's visor tightened around his head, his loupe pressed to his horn-rimmed glasses, he sat once more, hunched in the thick smoke of his cigar—though it was forbidden to smoke cigars at the clinic this prohibition did not, of course, apply to him—shoving photographs into their corners, gluing them to sheets, and labeling the sheets: *Untitled*, 1978, 40 x 40 x 7 cm, found material, partially painted, or *Vegetation*, 1978, 29.5 x 21 cm., collage, painted. What may have spurred him on was Werner Bergengruen's saying, which he had tacked to the wall in front of him: AND THE END WILL FOREVERMORE REVEAL ITSELF TO BE A GLORIOUS BEGINNING. The first Collection K had yet to be liquidated and the seeds of the second were already germinating. Unaware of the undoing of his collection, he collected onward in the Grison Alps. Nevertheless, he must have suspected something, for this time he proceeded more judiciously. Now he was his own art business, A to Z, for he was artist, archivist, curator, critic, board of trustees, patron, and sole buyer all in one. This collection would not be taken from him—because no one would find out it existed. He would keep it secret; create it only for itself. It was to have no value, or rather solely the value of art. Wherever the collection would be stored, this storeroom would be its museum, a museum that admitted no one.

Father's return to St. Gallen was heralded by countless boxes and crates that arrived by rail and post. These were followed by the artist himself—thinner, sober, with rested nerves. And he was, in turn, followed by the village carpenter's second reminder that the artist's bill needed to be paid once and for all.

Telephones flash on the ground plan of our apartment that I see in my head: one in the living room, another in my office, and the third in the bedroom. The water is a few centimeters high. I am careless. What if I get stuck on the stair lift? I am negligent. What now? Back to the car; but then I hear the front door and there she is, my mother, who had been out with her dog. As always she's there when one of her sons needs her. On her arm I circumnavigate the soaked carpets, wade through the apartment, the water seeping into my shoes. I am surprised I can walk in water. I sit on the barstool, an island from where I alert the fire department and, once they have arrived, I watch them at work. My contribution to the clean-up operation will be to describe it in my Muscle Book.

And so here he is again, the king, finding his kingdom plundered. Scepter gone, crown gone, they fell upon him like Huns. He's forced—he finds out only now—to dwell in the basement dungeon, like a prisoner. Because his wife can't take him any longer. Wasn't a problem when the money was rolling in. Nothing from the sons anymore either, now that the cash no longer flowed. No one visited him in the clinic when he wasn't feeling so hot, not a single call, not one postcard. He'd been shunted off. Tricked. They'd watched as his collection was torn to shreds. Standing here again, he curses, curses and throws a fit and makes threats. Slams the dungeon door shut. Why don't they just lock him in at night, too? In the morning, he finds his clean laundry in front of his room, but that was the least the queen could do for him.

The firefighters suck the water out. I explain to each one of them that I unfortunately cannot lend a hand, my muscles. Jan—I call her later in New York—has a guilty conscience because she isn't here. Because she can't do what my mother is doing, what, I think, I should really be doing.

He's bankrupt and as such is not permitted to own anything. It's his turn now, isn't it, to be spoiled. Hadn't he slaved away for his family long enough? His wife can see what it's like to feed a bunch of ungrateful brats. Had no idea what it means to support a family. Bills every day, it never stops. Amazing what accumulates, isn't it? And then there are the exhausting hassles at work as well. So she'd really learn her lesson, he leaves her with the carpentry bill for his art. To be debited under "special" in the business expenses. The art itself goes in a newly rented air-raid shelter where it is really safe and the rent—well, how he pays the rent is his affair.

He sleeps more and more often in the atelier house—only coming home to get his clean laundry and this or that collection piece the Huns generously let him keep. And it's in the atelier house where he's busy building his new life: a gallery, where he'll support young artists, an antique business, and a workshop that specializes in repairing old clocks. In his absence, the Huns have also plundered his atelier house. Not quite, grins the gallery owner, for he already sees himself as such; they overlooked the basement, not to mention the room he, not one to be outsmarted, had walled up just in time.

And so, raising his sledgehammer: *wham!* for the bankers... *wham!* for the architects, without whom he would have never built so big... *wham!* for the doctors... *wham!* for the Huns ...for his offspring—they'll see all right! *Wham! Wham!* The wall caves, he tosses the hammer aside, tears at the bricks, *ahh!*, lying before him is a treasure worthy of Ramses—or whatever that guy's name is from *The Valley of the Pharaohs*, which he recently saw on TV again. And here—he already sees himself surrounded by young artists, female ones in particular, who admire him, the patron—here's where he'll hold his exhibitions, *Wham!* Glorious will be his beginning, revealed in the end; they'll see all right! And whose end it would be still remained to be seen! *Wham! Wham!*

The apartment is dry again but the furniture is still "wrong." It's in my way, literally. Wary as a cat I register each change in the apartment. Like my own cat I internalize the changes, but while my cat then ceases to be interested in them, I have to incorporate the changes into my daily trajectory. What can I hold on to? What might I trip over? Where will I get stuck? Before long, my new "cat path" is set.

Sometimes he needs to look in on the business, or what's left of it, to show his offspring, who were doing everything wrong anyway, how a businessman conducts business. It goes like this: anyone who comes to the door is informed that he's the boss, and, damn it all, never mind whether the boss's fly is open or not. It's also of no relevance that it was an errand boy with whom the boss had wanted to strike a deal. Doesn't matter. What's really bad is arrogance; arrogance is the end of every company. If the phone rings, the boss'll sometimes take the call, though usually he has to slam the receiver down on the desk once the caller turns out to be an asshole. Respect: that's the end-all, be-all of a successful businessman, and no one knows better than he does how to get it—this shitty respect. He explains to his wife, who's busy fussing with some nonsense or another, that it's the secretary's job to hang up the boss's phone call, after which she hangs up the phone and asks whether he didn't have matters to attend to in the atelier. Did he? He sure did, for a boss fights on all fronts, but first he has to order another ten-year supply of letter paper. This was the way to get a better price.

I tell L. that the painting he loaned me has sustained slight damage. I was holding onto it while in search of a new "cat path" when it fell. Walking isn't going so well anymore, so I needed the walls. Don't worry, says L.

He now goes walking with Rott alone, for his youngest son has even turned on him, having been systematically set against his own father. The accusations—that he never bothered about school matters and (now this one, out of the blue!) that he never cared about this disease (what was it called again?)—these were nothing but a pack of goddamn lies. And it's all because he'd been systematically excluded from these things, just as he'd been excluded from everything else!

He *does* care about his sons' illness. He watches his youngest get up out of the lounge chair—just barely managing and only after several attempts. "You've seen better days too, huh?" he says encouragingly, but all he gets is an impertinent look after which his youngest sets about crawling up the stairs to get away from him. Well, let him then! Only he won't be fast enough—if anyone's going to up and leave then it's going to be him!

Once again an item from his collection (no. 4) had proved itself irreparable. Everyone knows that when *he* throws out one of his pieces it really was past saving. Hadn't exactly been a *trouvaille*. Well, even he was allowed to make a mistake now and then, wasn't he?

After three months of orange juice, which causes him to itch, and black tea, which won't let him sleep, he starts drinking again. This is his eldest boy's fault. He thinks his father has earned a little glass of wine on Christmas Eve, just for a toast. Ah well, Merry Christmas. Three hours later three bottles are empty and he's passed out on the living room floor, legs stretched under the Christmas tree, candle wax dripping on his feet.

I wait. I can't do anything. I wait for the water to evaporate out of the floor and the walls. The cordless phone sits in front of me on the kitchen bar.

Had he heard correctly? Did collection item no. 1 really just walk up to the collector and say: "I no longer belong to you"? It can't be. Unbelievable. A collection piece can't just go and say such a thing. It's Easter. Happy Easter.

The petition for divorce he receives over the summer also can't be. Nonetheless, he shouts: "I'll destroy you, commercially, morally, financially, in every way possible, you and your crippled sons as well!"

I move into the study where it's dry, eat breakfast here now too, read the paper, avoid, it turns out, the living room and the kitchen for weeks.

The police inform the mother and three sons that they can only take measures toward their physical protection when something physical has happened. When asked what, all the police know is that Mr. Keller is still Mrs. Keller's lawful spouse and thus the head of the family. That he still lives in the house is evidence of this. The guns, loaded and lying about everywhere cannot be described as an immediate threat; a shot has to—It *has* been fired, his wife blurts out (as he learns from his sources), in the attic, two years ago, when he wanted to rid her of her fear of guns. The bullet whistled past her ear and lodged in the spine of a book. Since then her hearing has been worse. Her husband didn't apologize; instead he cursed the gun manufacturer. She could be dead, my mother says, but the police need to know if there were witnesses. Since there weren't the police can only advise her to be careful and next time to report the incident in a timely manner.

Twice he throws a steak knife at the oldest, but misses both times. He tells the middle one that if he weren't already a cripple he'd beat him until he was. The youngest, he'd already noticed, avoids him, but does the youngest know that this suits the father just fine? They can all go to hell. Happy Assumption Day.

The sentences I want to write—for example the one that says the "wrong" arrangement of the furniture disturbs me—lead me through the apartment as if along a handrail. If I have a sentence in my head, walking goes better because my mind is distracted. Were I to stumble— literally—on a sentence I'd be able to retain it.

From now on, the mother locks herself in the bedroom with her youngest son. The oldest sought shelter in an apartment of his own and the father won't carry off the middle one, who's getting heavier and heavier. Still, the mother tells Mix he should bolt his bedroom door, which is something Mix sometimes forgets to do. But the father has no intention of stealing one of his sons.

Up until the very last day, the mother does her husband's laundry and places it outside the door to the padded cell.

Walk the south route from bathroom to bed along the right wall. The abyss of an open door.

Once, after bottle Number Four, the inhabitant of the padded cell decides his wife is to fulfill her conjugal duties. She manages to escape and lock herself in her bedroom. Nothing happened because there were no witnesses.

The court order arrives. The creature dwelling in the padded cell has to leave the house by the last day of the month, but all he does is tear up the letter and trudge off. Late at night a deep bellowing can be heard from the basement vaults of the Alpsteinstrasse house.

I stand before the dismantled armoire and can't lend a hand. Everywhere, objects within my reach. It was only rain after all. Rain that overtaxed the sewer system for a few hours and was thus able to enter our basement apartment through the pipes. I want to chop wood, mow the lawn, rake, weed. I want to rage.

I want to reach the end of my strength, not just use my strength to reach the end of the corridor.

I want fatigue, healthy fatigue, not to be fatigued after a few steps. What is real exhaustion, healthy exhaustion after physical labor, exhaustion that makes the expenditure of energy worth it? What is healthy desperation, rage, what is fury? I could smash my coffee cup. I could erase today's work from the computer. I could shout with anger. I open my mouth and am silent. This constant not-being-able-to. This eternal being-dependent-on-assistance. Always having to wait, always having to watch. This little bit of water.

When father arrived home the morning of his court-arranged moving day he discovered his key no longer fit. Standing in front of the locked door (so I imagine, I was at school), he swore to himself that this time, for once, he'd carry out his threats. A security officer waited a few meters away. Father drove to the atelier house and called my mother at the office. He screamed that he'd make sure she and her brats would never have another peaceful day again, for the rest of their lives, and hung up.

As both of my older brothers were already of age at the time of the divorce, it was up to them whether and how often they wanted to see their father. In my case, there was a court-ordered visitation right, and there was even a "regulation for Rott." The latter—drawn up by my father, stamped, and in his opinion, legally signed—decreed that the dog was to be picked up by Mr. Keller daily at a time to be determined by him, for which reason Mr. Keller was to be provided with a key to the Alpsteinstrasse house. Should he be unable to come, a note to that effect would be left on the steps. The dog's food was stipulated: meat, bones, and six eggs. It was to be left by him in the refrigerator each Friday. Another of the dog-delivery-man's obligations was to see to the dog's dessert: dog biscuits rolled in slices of mortadella.

He justified the fact that he didn't support his sons by claiming, bankrupt as he was, that he was a poor man forced to live at subsistence level. This didn't prevent him from keeping his two apartments, the atelier house, and an unknown number of storerooms complete with contents. He accused us of living luxuriously. As evidence, he cited unnecessary expenditures we'd allowed ourselves, like the 734.30 Swiss francs for the changing of the door locks. Instead of paying child support for me, he sent me a hundred franc note on two or three different occasions. Although this would have allowed me to make quite a splash at the flea market, I sent the money back to the addressee. The first time I did this my mother replaced it; the second time, having matured morally, I did without the compensation for the loss incurred. My father answered by return mail that this was bad-mannered. He didn't blame me, however, for, of course he knew he said, who was behind it all. In the transcript of the divorce hearing he stated that, as a voluntary concession and as a sign of his good will (and as pocket money), he would transfer a weekly sum to his youngest son in the amount of 30 Swiss francs, annually 1,440 Swiss francs, a sum that he'd deduct from the child support. It was telling, wasn't it, he said, that this pocket money hadn't been returned. And by the way, he added, being taken to court for the child support (which he didn't pay) didn't faze him in the slightest.

Nor had he fought for his dog beyond the "regulation"; he fought only for objects. My father just couldn't be sure about living things. Anything with legs, even weakened ones, would run out on him. Did he delude himself into thinking that my mother had also set the dog against him? Anyone who wasn't for him was against him. Rott was against him. It was my mother and I who now walked the dog after dinner and usually we spoke about father. We only heard from him regarding Rott when the dog died. Within a single day metastases had caused Rott's body to swell. I held my dog as the vet administered the injection. Via my father's lawyer, I learned that he knew "through his channels" full well that we had killed Rott because the dog had been in our way.

Already during the divorce he threatened to sue us. We received a first, still unofficial list of all the objects he wanted—or their monetary equivalents—typed in the large-point, space-occupying, possession-claiming font of his mechanical typewriter. To my amazement, I find references in the court files to bills from a gardening company dating to August 1958—a year after my family moved into the house—in the amount of 53 Swiss francs, and invoices from a tree nursery dated November 13, 1959, for 45.40 Swiss francs. I find an entry, "crystal chandelier," and payment for a "circulation pump": he'd prefer to take these things with him? He wanted money for the "rework on the heating," "painting," and "roof repairs," as if after twenty years all this work hadn't become long overdue again, and as if he himself hadn't also lived in this house for two decades and taken up more than half of it all on his own. Our old curtains were on the list, and as he didn't have an invoice for this entry as "proof," he cited the curtain salesclerk as "witness." I find the building of the entry area, the tool shed, and the double garage, and as "proof" the name of the architect—as a witness for what? That he built these things? I find everything in our yard that was suspected of being art; here the artists serve as witnesses, with names and addresses provided. He demanded reimbursement for the work his own company did on the house two decades earlier and which he himself had presumably never paid for. I find a bill for 79 Swiss francs, a donation to the home for the blind in St. Gallen. He wanted this money back too, as well as the 16-franc stamp fee for the entry of the house in the land registry.

As I write this, I see my father in the corner of the atelier house where he set up his office. Against the backdrop of the windowed façade, which is covered with white bed sheets, and surrounded by his binders, his bookkeeper's cap on his head, just like in his attic days, he seems to float in the smoke of his cigar. Lying on the desk next to him, neatly organized and ready to be numbered and filed—he never threw anything out, of course—I picture the many letters his sons had written imploring him that if he didn't want to support his family to at least not harm them further with lawsuits, especially as he knew better than anybody how unjustified they were. But all he does is cough, wave away our pleas (and our mother's as well) as if they were merely smoke from his cigar. And I can hear him muttering his mantra: *It all belongs to me!*

Feverishly, he pounds number after number into his adding machine—this, too, an antique purloined from the bankruptcy assets. Only once it spews out the total, including a rough estimate of the interest and the interest on the interest, rounded up in his favor, does he pause. Second thoughts? Is he thinking of Puck, his oldest son, who has said he wants to come by to "discuss something?" Is he hesitating to consider what it is he's actually doing? Maybe, maybe not. I don't know. Then, glancing once more at the sum he divides it by three: two parts for him, one for his future ex-wife and her sons. Thinking his offer generous, he double-underlines it, provides it with three exclamation points, and writes beneath it: *I could do this differently!*

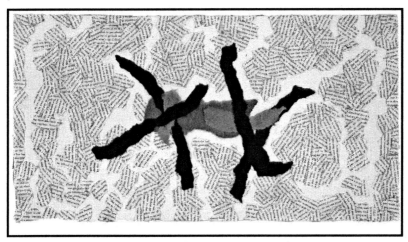

Kurt Adler, *Chromosomes III (Hereditary Factors Series)*, collage employing a first edition copy of *Patrimony* by Philip Roth, 1994, private collection.

I go out into the yard for the first time this year. Because Jan isn't here I wait until my mother is around. The steps up I can still manage well, without assistance. But the steps down—these scare me. I risk it and it goes okay, but not well. Each step requires new courage; each one deals a severe blow to my right knee. My mother stands next to me. She is quiet, saying only that we need a solution, as I should, after all, be able to go into the yard on my own.

It is the first nice spring day this year and it makes me sad. I want to go into the yard and now that the snow has melted, I can't tell myself that it's the snow preventing me from doing so. Now it is my legs, my muscles, me. I'm stuck in my apartment. Is nature now only there for me to look at? I draw the curtains and dream of snow.

I meet U. for dinner. While he pushes me from the parking lot to the restaurant I tell him that it is hard for me on days like this to not just be able to leave my apartment, especially as my work has also come to a standstill. U. is quiet, nods, is concerned, but not concerned enough to suggest, "Call me next time and we'll go out together." I don't like to ask him; I'd only ask those who'd offered.

Later I mention a film I would like to see that's playing in one of the few movie theaters in St. Gallen accessible to me. We're both interested in the film. I tell him I have written a letter to the owner of the theater asking why eight of his twelve theaters are not wheelchair accessible. U. thinks that's cool.

The next morning I call him up to arrange our movie night, but U. no longer has time. He doesn't say he has too much to do at the moment and hadn't realized it yesterday; he says he's had his fill of films for the time being. I wonder if he says this because he knows I haven't. Have I given him a reason to hurt me where it really hurts, and what sort of reason could that be? Presumably, it is not intentional, but I don't like to ask him that either.

I receive a letter from the movie theater owner in which he informs me, somewhat offended, that he had, in fact, equipped one of the theaters I listed with a ramp. The other seven theaters, which remain inaccessible, are not mentioned. Next time, I plan to do my homework more carefully.

Fall Afternoon, 1980

S teps. That's all he can think of. Before he can even see the eight steps that lead to the building's entrance, they appear in his head, along with the four that lie behind the closed front door. As a test: Will he still pass it? Surmounting a flight of stairs means only that he'd managed it once, perhaps he'll still manage it for a few more months, maybe years; it does not mean, however, that he'll be able to surmount it henceforth and forever.

Anything requiring muscle strength resonates with a *still*: he can still get up from his couch, though not from a low wall, for example. He can still climb out of his Triumph Spitfire—which he had restored himself, with the help of a friend—but he can no longer crawl beneath the car; a mechanic friend, whose prices are good, does this for him. He can still push down on the accelerator, pedal to the metal, and screech past the sidewalk cafes in town. He can still shower without help. He can still dress himself. He can still get up from the toilet. He can still raise his arm above his head to comb his hair. He can still bring a full glass to his mouth. He can still breathe.

Still, still, still.

He reaches for the railing. It is cool, unyielding, fixed firmly to the wall. It makes him feel strong.

He is twenty-four. Most of his friends sail and horseback ride; one is about to take his helicopter exam, while he—he swings his left leg onto the first stair—already walks like an old man. It feels like his muscles are shrink-wrapped in rubber. No matter how great the effort, his speed remains the same.

Is his left foot firmly placed? This is important when climbing steps. For a brief moment this foot is responsible for everything. If it slides, he falls. The rubber soles of his shoes have been scratched with sandpaper to provide better traction. With luck, the steps are rough granite (as they are here); if the stone is polished, however, a few drops of water are all it takes for him to slip. One time he'd had to ask that the stairs be dried off before he stepped on them; the girl he was visiting was one he'd have liked as a girlfriend. She knelt down and wiped the stone with a dishtowel; their repeated exchange, however—his increasingly embarrassed *Just a little more*'s to her frequent *Is that enough?*'s—led to the step-by-step obliteration of their mutual desire to further the friendship.

Today, however, the sun has been shining since morning and the steps are dry. He reaches his right arm out in front of him. His left leg, which now anchors his body on the step, and his fully extended right arm form an axis—the tilted position of his body resulting from his maneuvering—and from this axis, he gains the leverage needed to heave his right leg up one step. As if skeptical of his achievement, he removes his hand from the railing, rubs it, then grabs on again. He'll manage the remaining eleven. What comes afterward is something he'll presumably not succeed at; nevertheless, he owes it to himself and, as the oldest son, to his family, to try.

He doesn't really walk like an old man. Waddling like a duck—an old duck—is a better description. He has a duck rump, he says so himself. It wiggles with each step. It bulges as far out in the back as the paunch he is developing does in the front. The duck rump is the result of the slightly forward lean of his walk. A muscle that is still strong has to do what a weakened one no longer can. As he cannot fully bend his knees anymore, he compensates with his still flexible hips; thus he, St. Gallen's dandy (whose hair, admittedly, is getting shorter and shorter), sometimes swaggers along Multergasse, St. Gallen's Champs-Élysées. His compensatory strategy sometimes tempers his duck walk a bit, so that he swaggers more like a stork, which looks somewhat better. A stork with a duck rump. His legs thrust forward, his hips wag to and fro. A woman once shouted after him asking whether he thought the way he walked was cool, and if so, she'd wanted to let him know that his stupid come-on wouldn't work on her. Another woman spent an entire evening promising she'd be his legs, now and forever, but when she saw the effort it took for him just to stand up, she no longer wanted to give him her telephone number.

He's reached the top. He stands on a threadbare carpet in the no-man's-land of the stairwell, whose light the timer had once more shut off. He looks up; if he lived here, he'd have to switch the light on again at every floor and would still be forced to climb half of each set of stairs in the dark. Today he managed the stairs and the front door in two minutes. One hundred and twenty seconds divided by twelve steps comes to ten seconds per step. The concentration distracts him; even when he factors in the time he needs, he is sometimes grateful for the delay. The way becomes longer, the thoughts clearer. Though he may be losing muscles, he is, nevertheless, gaining time. So here he is. Now he'll ask—beg? force? compel?—the occupant of the apartment whose bell he is ringing to please (please!), for heaven's sake, stop what he is doing.

"Welcome, son."

The son brings himself to shake the father's hand. It feels rough, a roughness that's familiar. The father turns and disappears around a corner. The son follows as fast as he can.

It is dark in the apartment. Actually, shadowy is the more apt word; light appears to be the only thing the apartment doesn't have a lot of. The many objects cast shadows everywhere, shadows that flow in and out of one another. In the hallway there is a lamp whose shade is so discolored—from tobacco smoke?—that the light it gives off suffices only to call attention to itself. Anything more distant—including the father, who has already walked beyond the lamp—is bathed in semi-darkness. There's another reason why the apartment is so dark: the windows are all covered up. He passes a single-door armoire—didn't it once stand in the living room of the Alpsteinstrasse house?

Everything seems somehow familiar, although this is the son's first time here. The rooms are hideaways, the corridor a ravine in which all, not only the weak in muscle, have to take care not to stumble. Three rooms, one for each of the repudiated sons. An existence amongst stone bears and plastic garden gnomes, Christmas tree angels and wooden flea market dolls. Empty birdcages. Carpets from Persia, Burma, and Peru in piles, oil paintings in rows, lithographs in stacks. Oceanic masks, framed fragments of old wooden armoires. Clocks ticking in the drone of a radio. Rust, dust, bones, shards of glass, moldy bread.

The apartment reminds the son of an abandoned archive, a warehouse. Overwhelmed by the sheer quantity of things, he's almost forgotten the father, the person who'd dragged all this stuff here. He is surprised when he sees him poking out of a room others would use as a parlor—the archivist, the stocky warehouse worker, the bearded chief who'd lost his tribe, the native withdrawn to his reservation.

"You see how I'm forced to live," the father says.

The son holds onto the handle of the parlor door.

"Why didn't you listen to anything we said?" he pleads.

Before he sits down he has to make sure there is a second, unoccupied, chair opposite him, so he'll be able to get up again. At the same time he's struggling to find a suitable way-in to a difficult conversation. But he's already smack in the middle of it, isn't he, and isn't it already going wrong? Is it supposed to go wrong? Maybe that's why he's here? Because he knows, deep down, that it will go wrong, because the father can't help it and because he, the son, needs to be able to confirm this, one last time.

"*I* wasn't the one lacking in goodwill."

He isn't sure whether the father has really said this or whether it's just his imagination.

The son is mortified to have to ask the father to bring him a second chair. What stings even more is having to accept help from someone who has decided to bring him down by judicial means. They'd only shaken hands and already the conversation had become a legal proceeding. He wishes he hadn't met the father here, but in a restaurant, on neutral ground.

The father brings the son a second chair, mumbling something like "of course" and "what's mine is yours." The father offers him a glass of mineral water and says, "See, no alcohol. Such a load of nonsense."

"Father," the son says hesitantly, taking a sip of water, "if you withdraw your case against us you'll still have three sons. Otherwise, you'll have lost three sons."

The father just grins.

"You can't expect us to visit you when you're suing us at the same time."

The father says nothing. Instead he rummages up a Polaroid snapshot from a stack of papers on the table and holds it out toward the son. It is a young woman sitting on a chair. Her head is not in view; her legs are cut off at the knees by the edge of the picture. She is naked and her legs are spread. With her fingers she's pulling open the lips of her vagina.

"I don't need your mother," he says. And then, "I'd like to know what sort of woman spreads her legs for you. Do you always have to pay for it?"

Once the father had held a condom out to the son's girlfriend and when she turned away in anger, he grumbled she shouldn't make such a fuss, it had only fallen out of his pocket. A few days later he boasted that the son's girlfriend had tried to slip him a condom.

"Can you even get it up? It's a muscle too, isn't it?" the father says.

The son reaches for the chair and jiggles it to check its stability. He hopes he can get up in one go. The father, as if wanting to show him how easy it is, jumps up. He stands in front of him, legs apart, hands on his hips.

"If you and your brothers don't want to visit me, don't. It's okay with me. Saves me time. The suit's going through, don't fool yourself. I'll sue you all until I have what I want."

The son pushes on the seat of the opposite chair. Torso down, duck rump up.

"I'm in the right, and I'll get what's mine, you can be sure of that. Everything belongs to me. Every single thing you have is mine. Everything!"

The father is standing dangerously close to him.

If the chair, or one of the chairs, doesn't matter which, slides now, he'll end up on the floor, lying at the father's feet. What if he is forced to rely on this man's help to get up?

"Now I'm getting back what belongs to me. You'll see. You'll all pay, just like I did!"

What if the father knocks him down? A gentle tap would be enough. He pushes with his right arm, raising his upper body so that his head is now level with the father's hip.

The father moves closer to hold the Polaroid of the naked girl in front of his face.

"You've got it backwards, my dear boy! It's not you who sets the conditions here. If you want something from me, come crawling. I'm still your father, don't forget that."

They're almost touching.

At last, the father takes a step back.

Laughs.

Points to the door.

Waves the Polaroid.

Says, "Unless, there's something in it for me, of course. Then we can talk whenever you want. But what are three cripples worth?"

I, too, understand that stairs have an aesthetic function, even though it's one that limits me and puts me in my place. But a world without steps is as absurd as a world without the color yellow.

Summer 1999: We were subletting from C. on the Upper West Side again. After eight hours, interrupted by four excursions to the bathroom, I want to move from my desk chair to the couch. It's already after six; Jan won't be home for two hours. I can't get up from the couch without assistance. What if the building burns down? IN CASE OF FIRE USE STAIRS it says next to the elevator.

I toss a selection of books onto the couch: Raymond Queneau's The Blue Flowers *in Italo Calvino's Italian, Eugen Helmlé's German, and Barbara Wright's English translation; Paul Virilio's* The Conquest of the Body; *an American Jules Verne biography; James Baldwin's* The Fire Next Time; *the newspaper. In case something happens to me on the way from my desk to the couch, I stick the telephone in my pocket. I push myself out of the chair, reach for my cane, and sally forth. In front of the couch I turn around, press my hands on my knees, bend forward, and allow myself to fall. How soft the pillows feel!*

The first thing I think of now that I'm settled is that what I really want to read are the Raymond Carver stories sitting on my desk. Beyond my reach. I'm tired, work isn't going well, the apartment is overheated. The Americans are capable of flying to the moon and bombing countries whose names they cannot even spell, but heat a building properly? The telephone in my pocket rings. It's Jan. She forgot her key.

It's too hot or too cold and the pipes are hissing and hammering. Whom to call, whom do I make race through half the city to help me from the couch to the chair? How will this person get in the apartment? I don't even know the number for the doorman. Is the key on the living room table in front of me? No, all that's there is a dried out peach pit. I throw the pit toward the door and immediately regret it, as Jan will have to pick it up.

I am shaking; it isn't my muscles shaking, it's my anger, toward their weakness. A siren sounds. Police? Ambulance? What if Jan gets hit by a car? What if I get a call from the hospital? What if she needs an operation, and I'm stuck on the couch. It's a fire truck. Is the building on fire? Stay calm, remain seated, in this city there's always a siren going off somewhere. But what if the building really is on fire? Our emergency plan goes like this: Jan steers me in my wheelchair to the stairwell, helps me onto a wool blanket, and pulls me down the steps, one at a time, as well and as quickly as she can. Hoping the fire takes its time. Hoping someone helps. Hoping the fire department is fast. IN CASE OF FIRE USE STAIRS. It is nine stories: two flights of stairs per story, twelve steps per flight of stairs, making two hundred and sixteen steps. How many bones does a person have? Doesn't a person have two hundred and sixteen bones? Will I break one bone per step? The siren fades away. Nothing has happened, nothing is burning. I'm just sitting by myself on the couch. I understand, of course, that our absurd plan only works if Jan is with me. I want to stand up. I want to try. I don't even know where I want to go if I should succeed in standing up. I just want to be away. Away from the couch, away from the staircases, away from the signs that tell me that in case of fire I am not provided for, away from the signs that show me the way, I want away from my fear.

I push the table aside and pull one of the chairs within my reach toward me. It is stable. Am I? I might be able to manage it. The couch is about half as high as the bed. I haven't tried this in years. Just don't think about it. Don't calculate how high, how long, don't weigh, balance, consider anything. I grab the edge of the couch, raise myself up, and the couch slides away. It bangs against the wall behind me and I fall back. It's pointless. The heating pipes hiss.

At least the couch is now jammed in tight. The chair is on the carpet, so it won't slip. The second attempt likewise fails; the couch is too low, but I'm able to get a little higher. Third attempt, fourth, my arms are getting tired, fifth attempt, my rear end hangs in the air, right elbow's on the seat of the chair, I sweat, see flames of heat. Give up? No way! If I don't succeed in standing up I'll wait. I'll read, I'll try to calm myself so Jan doesn't notice anything when she arrives with the super; so my powerlessness won't infect her—the man must be the strong one, after all. With complete aplomb I will sit here and compare the three translations of The Blue Flowers...

I make another attempt. This time I succeed in grabbing the back of the chair with my left hand. Only, no hesitating, otherwise I'm back *sitting on the couch; a lurch, and I am standing. I hold onto the chair, reach for the cane, slowly, carefully, I toddle from couch to table, from table to chair, from chair to wall, from wall to hall door, and as I push the door handle, I hear the key in the lock. It's Jan, who'd found her key in her coat pocket. "Wow, it's hot in here!" she exclaims cheerfully.*

Once, at the Bronx Zoo, when I wanted to visit the gorilla enclosure, I was forced to affix a tag displaying the international wheelchair symbol to my wheelchair. I wanted to know why this was necessary; whether one couldn't recognize my wheelchair as a wheelchair without the wheelchair tag. Securing it to my chair, the attendant explained that wheelchair occupants might, unannounced, leave their wheelchairs.

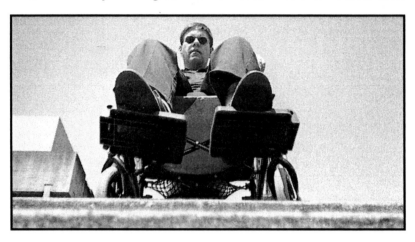

Empty wheelchairs left behind on paths could be dangerous for other visitors. For this reason, the wheelchair has to be identified with a numbered wheelchair tag, which, she continued, must be turned in at the ticket office upon leaving the gorilla enclosure.

In my head, I have a map of the places I have already been. It reminds me of Mondrian's Broadway Boogie Woogie, *which shows the street network of Manhattan reduced to the colors yellow, red, and blue. Since seeing the painting for the first time it has become my personal street map, applicable to everyplace I go: accessible buildings are indicated in blue, red is for accessible routes, yellow for inaccessible ones. For me, Mondrian's painting is alive, because it changes. It is getting yellower and yellower.*

Part Two

W hat's left to visit? Everest? Around the world in a motorized balloon powered by the millions of a bored billionaire? I have better reason to undertake the journey to my bathroom.

That between 1980 and 1994 my father and I so rarely bumped into each other in our little city was due to the fact that we both had clearly staked out our territories. His tiny area, the size of a public square and a few streets, was in the east, between the Eternit high-rises of the hospital grounds, the noisy autobahn approach road—concealed, in a makeshift sort of way, by indestructible vegetation—and the silvery gray shopping center whose lipstick-shaped tower could be seen from our yard.

The atelier house, where I had spent so much time because it seemed like an extension of the attic, marked the western border of his small republic—or was it really more of a ghost town where the sheriff had finally ensured peace and quiet? This two-story wooden structure, with its gabled roof and wide, windowed façade (where Max Falk had his studio), was concealed behind a multi-family house; the two buildings shared access to the street. As the atelier house couldn't be seen from the road, a modest sign on the garden gate informed visitors of the existence of the hidden gallery. Father only used this entrance when he needed the car, which he parked on the street, already beyond the limits of his territory and in the shadow of the willows of the cemetery on the other side. He had suffered a series of small strokes in the spring of 1994, and since then he sometimes drove the short stretch to his apartment. Normally, however, he exited the atelier house through the gate in the back. From here, he could get to the Hirschen quickly and without being seen—it was just a few steps through a parking lot. After he'd eaten and had his wine all he needed to do was cross the street, pass Café Zimmermann, turn the corner, and climb the twelve steps to his apartment—the one in which Puck had once asked him to refrain from suing his own family.

Every so often he'd add a new storage space. But even these expansions of his territory shifted the borders of what seemed to me—and perhaps to him after the many Westerns we had watched together—like Hadleyville by only one, maybe two, streets. Only the air-raid shelter, where he kept his own art (the works he did at the clinic and in the period that followed), was some distance away, about half a kilometer from the atelier house. The former king's kingdom had become small, though commensurately manageable and defensible.

My territory was correspondingly large. It consisted of the Alpsteinstrasse house, which, admittedly, had become smaller not long after father's departure, when we converted the second floor and the attic into apartments as a source of additional income. Mix and Puck had both moved out. My mother set up her bedroom in the former parlor on the ground floor and during the summer months when I came home from Geneva, where I was at university, I occupied the basement room that was once our playroom and, for a few months, our father's last bedroom in the house. From Alpsteinstrasse, my turf extended down the steeply sloping hill to my high school, and out across the entire city—with the exception of Hadleyville, which I avoided—and beyond, to wherever it might take me. Hadleyville was enough for my father; he left the rest of the world to me.

I moved to Geneva right after high school. The fact that I didn't have to do military service and therefore could go straight to university was a gain. All in all, I saved roughly two years of my life. No muscles—but no mud either. If that wasn't a deal.

The price to be paid for this privilege was a high one, even if for the time being it was seemingly only a matter of one single word. Given all the stamping Switzerland had already undertaken, most horrifically the "J" in the passports of Jews seeking refuge during World War II, my being branded "unfit" four times at once, twice in my military record book and twice in my civil defense one, was enough to send a shiver down my spine.

II. Sanitarische Entscheide über die Tauglichkeit, Untauglichkeit oder Zurückstellung

1. Entscheide über Einsprachen

Entscheid der 1. Instanz
(Vertrauensarzt der Gemeinde)

__untauglich__

_____

_____

_____

_____

Datum   8 . 3. 1983

Stempel und Unterschrift

```
F. Brändle
prakt. Arzt
9015 St. Gallen
```

Entscheid der 2. Instanz
(Vertrauensarzt oder vertrauensärztliche Kommission des Kantons)

_____

_____

_____

_____

_____

Datum

Stempel und Unterschrift

4

An *invalidus* was someone who wasn't suitable for Roman military service. While it's true, of course, that the Roman army no longer exists, many languages have still managed to preserve the word's meanings in a millennia-long maneuver. In German "invalid" means: *schwach* (weak), *krank* (sick), *ungeeignet* (unsuited), *unfähig* (unable), *zu nichts nütz* (of no use); in English, if stress is placed on the second syllable instead of the first, the result is "in-*val*-id" (as in an invalid bus ticket); in French, *invalide*: "infirm," "unfit for work," "unfit for duty," "in-*val*-id"; in Russian, too, the in-val-*id*, here emphasis on the third syllable, has also held its ground; in Spanish, *válido* is prefixed with a *minus* to form the word for physically disabled.

My military record book was stamped by a captain (with whom I was not acquainted), acting on behalf of the Swiss authorities. My civil defense record book was stamped by an independent medical examiner, who, as I had never met him in person either, never actually medically examined me. What was it exactly that went through the minds of these rubber stampers as they went about stamping people?

THE RUBBER STAMPERS
A Mini-Drama

Hanging on a wall beneath mounted deer antlers is a diploma in Swiss Rubber Stamping. Two wooden tables stand on a shiny green linoleum floor. Rubber stamps and inkpads fall in line, ready for deployment. At the right, the CAPTAIN *sits in front of his gray pile of to-be-stamped record books; at the left, the* INDEPENDENT MEDICAL EXAMINER (*hereinafter,* DOCTOR) *sits in front of his yellow pile. The books are open, their spines broken. Moving to the same rhythm,* CAPTAIN *and* DOCTOR *pull book after book from their respective piles, read out the names of those to be stamped, and bring their rubber stamps down on the corresponding pages with resounding thuds.*

DOCTOR
humming

Ta…

CAPTAIN
humming

…taaaa…

DOCTOR
humming

Ta!

CAPTAIN

Ha!

DOCTOR

Yours?

CAPTAIN
Keller, Christoph, unfit!

DOCTOR
Ha! Mine too: Keller, Christoph, student, unfit!

CAPTAIN

Student? Definitely unfit!

DOCTOR

Studying languages…

CAPTAIN

Girls' stuff! Not another fag?

DOCTOR

And, unfit! Maybe your daughter's type. Imagine that.

CAPTAIN

Marlis? Disgusting! If I got a hold of him out on the drill grounds…I'd cure him of his unfitness for good, all right. Ta…

Raises the rubber stamp for a strike, but the DOCTOR *stops him.*

DOCTOR

Looks like he's really got something.

CAPTAIN

Into the mud with him! Push-ups! I'll make a man out of the sissy in about two seconds flat. A queer who might defile my little Marlis? I'll make short work of him! Ta…

Raises the rubber stamp for a strike, but the DOCTOR *stops him.*

DOCTOR

Spinal Muscular Atrophy Kugelberg-Welander. Says one Dr. L. Feller.

CAPTAIN

Kugelander what? Kugelander my ass! Freeloaders, all of them. These parastites—

DOCTOR

Parasites.

CAPTAIN

What?

DOCTOR

Parasites.

CAPTAIN

That's what I said. Plebiscites! They should all be…Ta.

Stops himself.

Back when you still could. Ha! What they cost the state! Just think what could be done with all that money! More F-18s! Mountains bunkered to the hilt! Doubled severance pay! More concrete! Anti-cripple campaigns!

Looks up, a mischievous expression on his face.

You know, doctor, what would really be the cheapest solution?

DOCTOR
mischievously
I know, captain, I know.

CAPTAIN
Too bad.

DOCTOR
Too bad is right.

CAPTAIN
Back when.

DOCTOR
Ah, yes.

CAPTAIN
Well?

DOCTOR
Oh well. And...

readies his stamp for a strike

C,

and stamps.

CAPTAIN
readies stamp
...for cripple!

and stamps.

DOCTOR
Wait!

CAPTAIN
What do you mean wait?

DOCTOR
You stamped three times.

CAPTAIN
Yeah, so?

DOCTOR
stamps
First twice ta-taah!, then the third time. Like this! *Ta-taah!*

Unfit! Unfit!

Stamps two times quickly.

And then *Ta!* Unfit!

Stamps.

CAPTAIN

Ta-taah! Unfit! Unfit!

Stamps two times quickly.

Ta! Unfit!

Stamps a third time.

DOCTOR

Unfit!

Stamps. Both pause; they look at one another. Smile.

CAPTAIN

Shall we?

DOCTOR

You want to?

CAPTAIN

Ready when you are.

DOCTOR

Who's the chorus?

CAPTAIN

I am!

DOCTOR

You, again? Well, all right. You do have the better voice…

CAPTAIN

Drill grounds voice.

DOCTOR

But next time…And…

taking a breath.

For walking?

CAPTAIN

Unfit!

DOCTOR

For standing?

CAPTAIN

Unfit!

DOCTOR

For screwing?

CAPTAIN

Unfit!

DOCTOR

For being Swiss?

CAPTAIN

Unfit!

DOCTOR

For having a well-paid job?

CAPTAIN

Unfit!

DOCTOR

For serving on a board of directors?

CAPTAIN

Unfit!

DOCTOR

For living in a villa in the fancy part of town?

CAPTAIN

Unfit!

DOCTOR

For being a normal person?

DOCTOR/CAPTAIN
stamping

Unfit!

Stamping.

Unfit!

Stamping.

Unfit!

Stamping.

Unfit!

And so on.

The CAPTAIN *and* DOCTOR *continue to stamp and shout until the audience members realize that nothing further will happen during the performance and leave the theater.*

I was still—but for how much longer?—not completely unfit for staircases, though it's true I was *more unfit*. "No such thing!" I heard the CAPTAIN bellow in my head to the rapid firing of the DOCTOR's stamp. "You're either fit or you're not. Into the mud, 263,356 push-ups, unsoldier Keller!" And thus as my SMA gradually—in steps? phases? levels? thresholds?—waxed, my ability to manage steps waned.

From this point on, steps had to be lower for me to climb them. While the average step is roughly thirty centimeters high, I was still good for twenty. Ideally, I tackled step climbing early in the day, when I was well rested. If the banister was on the left it wasn't long before it was hopeless for me to even try. I started to dream about steps and thought of steps and nothing else, not of the seminar material to be discussed or the friend who awaited me at the end of the stairwell. I now inquired about steps before setting out: How many? How high? On what side was the railing? (If there was one.) Is there an elevator? My questions often came across as reproaches, and occasionally the answers provided were mistaken and impatient. "Oh, you mean the two steps? I don't notice them, even when dashing into the building." But somehow it would work out in the end because a branch of a bush next to the entrance would qualify as a railing ("See, not a problem after all"); or sometimes when it didn't work, because the branch proved to be too pliable and I fell in the bushes ("Can you get up yourself or do you need help?") I beat a weakened retreat; or if ascent were hopeless ("Because of the two steps?") we'd relocate the meeting to a stepless restaurant.

The dormitory had four steps—low and wide, so suited for me. A twelve-meter-long corridor led to the elevator. Fifth button, fifth story, no problem. Room with a kitchen, view befitting of a student dorm (the back courtyard), and matching *ambience*: every weekend, disco noise pulsed from the basement through the water pipes up to me. On the ground floor there was a restaurant with unsavory customers, unsavory food, and even more unsavory management. The bathroom in my room was tiny, but that was good, for this way there was always something within arm's reach that I could hold onto when showering or standing up from the john. The desk chair I could raise myself out of (and still could on April 17, 2003, when I went through these pages prior to the German printing of this book, but now no longer can, as I check the text today, August 31, 2007, for the American edition), I brought from home.

The only adaptation to the room was the second mattress, which I had the building super put on top of the bed. Though I hadn't renounced the two-chair method, I had acquired an alternative technique for standing up: turning myself over on the edge of the bed, I would get onto my knees, and, provided the bed was high enough, I would then hoist myself onto my legs.

The university buildings were located at the foot of the hill in Geneva's old town, scattered across a slightly ascending terrain. I studied Spanish because there was an elevator to take me to the Spaniards in the main building, while the Italians were not physically accessible to me. Russian could be reached from the parking space I had in the chained-off professor's parking lot via an elevator at ground level. To get to my classical studies seminar, I had to go up a half dozen steps, which I would manage through to the *demi-licence*.

In my second year I replaced Spanish with English; not because of steps, but to be able to counter the Russians somewhat—it was 1984. It was a serious decision, muscle-wise, as there was no elevator up to the English department and, what's more, the building itself was on a rather steep slope. I only attended morning seminars and showed up to class with the relevant texts photocopied from the *Norton Anthology of English Literature* as the book had become too heavy for me to carry. This way, my bag hung lightly on my shoulder, freeing up my arms for balance and the upward propulsion I required. Because I didn't want to admit to myself that I needed a break for the five-hundred-meter stretch to class, I stopped to buy a newspaper at a kiosk halfway along the route. I was happy when people were ahead of me in line, because this way I could rest longer. I'd patiently dig around for the necessary change, carefully fold the newspaper, stick it in my bag, and, with an additional

In Geneva in 1994 Peter Greenaway set up one hundred staircase-like structures. These could be climbed and the postcard-sized peepholes peered through in order to view city subjects chosen by the artist. The difference, according to the stair-building artist, was that you saw reality and not an image of it reproduced on a postcard.

two hundred and fifty grams, I'd embark upon the remaining two hundred and fifty meters.

Oh, Geneva. Geneva wasn't a city for me; instead, it became a yardstick, a linear measure of how much I could still manage each day. For me, Geneva shrank to the size of Hadleyville; on foot, it was only a few streets, corners, and buildings. Across three streets with six rampless curbs, it was about eight hundred meters from my room to the main building of the university; these eight hundred meters became a test route for my muscle strength. When I began my studies I could still manage the distance well; three-and-a-half years later, in the spring of 1987, I had to drive the route. Eventually, I decided to leave Geneva to complete my degree at the university in Constance. At least, I was taking the finished manuscript of my first novel with me.

Our territories, my father's and mine, overlapped only when one of my father's artists exhibited in a different gallery. He viewed this as a success, not a betrayal. The (not always applied) principle of his gallery was only show an artist one time, the first time.

During the divorce, I often saw him patrolling Alpsteinstrasse in his Golf. He noted down who went in and out of the house and when. If it was the electrician at the end of the workday, he concluded my mother was having an affair with him. If my mother left the house in the evening that meant, in his thinking, nothing other than that she was on her way to a lover and, moreover, that Mix and I were going hungry, because the inconsiderate act of leaving the house ruled out our getting dinner. Because his lawyer was able to convince him that his snooping wouldn't persuade the court as to what a loving husband and caring father he was, a private detective ultimately assumed the surveillance duty. The detective's task was to substantiate the affairs my mother was not having, while the detective's client generously overlooked the easily ascertainable fact that it had been he, not she, who had committed adultery—and serially, for my father did everything in series. The first time (as we learned once he'd finally moved out) was back in the first year of their marriage, with the neighbor's au pair; later, it was whenever he knew his wife would be safely out of the house, for whatever reason, whether she was bearing him a son at the hospital, or away with her sons at a health resort for treatment. The detective trailed my mother over "incredibly long distances" as stated in his investigation and observation report. One time she took the autobahn "in torrential rain," the hapless detective stressed melodramatically, to nearby Lake Constance. Because of my mother's daredevil-like driving, he gave up and exited the highway as soon as he could. Severely shaken by her "downright irresponsible behavior behind the wheel," he dispensed with any further chases and set to work on his conclusions.

Once, probably around lawsuit no. 4, I saw my father coming towards me between the shelves of wrenches, light bulbs, pots of glue, and cans of paint in the do-it-yourself section of a supermarket located midway between Hadleyville and Alpsteinstrasse. I knew he'd seen me, but he didn't come over. Why should I have gone up to him? He passed by without speeding up, without slowing down; he passed by me with firm resolve. I tell myself it took effort for him not to look at me. I stood in my rather inept yet adequate hiding place awkwardly holding a bike lock, of all things, which I had grabbed without thinking. Had he slimmed down? His hair, at any rate, had thinned. The beard he'd grown again had a coppery tinge. There was dandruff on his black shirt and his face glowed a seething red. Was he still drinking? Was he drinking again? I put the bike lock back and watched my father pay for a set of nails and then run away, just as he always had.

He burglarized us twice. The first time, he climbed over the backyard fence and tried to force his way into the house, but the solid doors and the grates he had installed (and which turned up on the list of items demanded back in his next lawsuit) held up against him. So he went after everything in the yard that wasn't nailed or screwed down. He spent a half hour ripping up the grass trying to drag off a two-meter-high, roughly two-hundred kilogram iron sculpture before the police stopped him. He was more careful when he broke in the second time. One day we discovered that a small sculpture that had been mounted to the outside of the house was missing. We filed a complaint against persons unknown and the insurance company compensated us for the loss. As chance—and the carelessness of my father—would have it, a representative for the same insurance company, whether as a client or out of detective-like curiosity, turned up at the atelier gallery one day and found the sculpture hanging on the wall. The insurance company's decision was Solomonic: we had to repay half the insurance money and father could keep the sculpture.

156   Christoph Keller

Now and then I saw him coming out of the post office. Although there was one in Hadleyville, he refrained from relocating his P.O. box there. Aside from the court, the mail was the only point at which our lives still crossed: in the form of endless attorney correspondence and bills that he actually should have paid (but didn't) as the losing plaintiff. Dodging him at the post office was easy. He popped in mornings, around a quarter to ten, before he opened his gallery. This was when he'd also mail the postcards that, for years, he sent us as accompaniments to the lawsuits. I imagine he slid them proudly to the clerk behind the counter, writing side up: "Just two today, Fräulein Fischbacher." It was always cards, never letters, for this way he could also let the postal workers in on just what sort of people they were delivering the mail to each day.

The cards were always blank, white A5-80-gram paper; back then, they could be purchased fifty to a packet, at first for 80 centimes and then for 1.20 francs at the Migros supermarket; I used them myself for my music archive. A photograph from a film was always glued to the card. As we had the same TV magazine I was soon able to guess which picture would reach us over the course of the week. Squire Pengallan from *Jamaica Inn* enthusiastically welcoming his horse to the dinner table; Travis Bickle from *Taxi Driver* brandishing his gun in front of the mirror; Harry Lime from *The Third Man* pointing from the Ferris wheel toward the ant-sized people in Vienna's Prater, people who were worth no more to him than ants; Dr. Strangelove hoisting himself out of his wheelchair;

Will Kane, of course; and, over and over again, John T. Chance, his revolver aimed at the viewer. At the top, double-underlined with his fat green felt-tip pen, and followed by three exclamation points, his—well, his tough talk should be familiar by now. I wouldn't be surprised if my father copied the cards, numbered the copies, and filed them away in a binder; after all, they were collages, and he was now an artist.

If the cards came with the afternoon mail delivery—which we still had back then—I was able to intercept them; if they were in the morning mail, my mother would see them and I could tell from her face that once more "something" had arrived—a court order, a letter from the lawyer's office, but I always asked about the cards first, for these left the deepest marks, maybe because they were so irrational. "Dogs, Do You Want to Live Forever?" Soldiers dying in black and white in the German movie of the same name about the Battle of Stalingrad. "Again?" Was the only reason this one kept coming because this film was constantly on television at the time? In the end, the cards were boyish pranks that always screamed the same thing, "I am right!" and "It all belongs to me!," and maybe we should have simply ignored them. But it was the childish tenacity, the defiant dogmatism, the stubborn obstinacy that threatened us more than his ridiculous American gunslingers aiming their pistols at us. Our mother took these threats seriously, too seriously, for she took them to heart. Because he was so adamant and always made his claims using the same words, she asked herself again and again whether she wasn't perhaps to blame for everything after all—for the failure of her marriage, for his infidelities, his drinking, cursing, and even maybe for his bankruptcy. Maybe everything really did belong to him? Maybe it really was her genes and hers alone that were responsible for all three of her sons falling ill with a rare hereditary disease? Each one of the cards triggered a small crisis for my mother that forced her to relive it all—the cursing, the drinking, the whoring, the bankruptcy, the divorce, the clearance of the house, the lawsuits.

Accompanying the lawsuits were the anonymous calls—mostly a mere rustling in the receiver, sometimes broken by an uncontrollable smoker's cough with which I was all too familiar. I don't remember anymore if once I actually took the phone into the bathroom and flushed the toilet, or if I just saw someone do that in a movie. Now and then, however, I would scream into the rustling, "Say something, you coward!" One time, I uttered a desperate curse, but I never received an answer from my father other than a sudden click.

Dinner with H. tonight. I call the restaurant to ask whether I—"in a wheelchair," I say, simplifying matters, even though I can still take a few steps—will be able to get to the second floor. The waitress says she doesn't know. Does the building have an elevator, I ask. That she does know: "No, it doesn't." Then, impatiently answering my own question, I say I probably won't be able to get to the second floor. "Yes," she says, "you probably won't."

Another restaurant, second try: I ask whether the restaurant is "wheelchair accessible"—my attempt at ridding my way of, ideally, all physical obstacles with two simple words. The hostess on the phone apologizes, saying, unfortunately it isn't, but it won't be a problem: "We'll just carry you up."

In airplanes, the international wheelchair symbol is sometimes found on the otherwise unaltered bathrooms, as if this solved the problem.

"Thank you! Thank you! Thank you! Thank you! For holding the door open for me, thank you! For helping me out of my chair." Usually I am happy to say, whisper, mutter, aspirate, chew, swallow, digest my thank you, but not today. Today I want to be unthankful.

I have to let the waiter touch me. He's helping me stand up—nice guy—but for two seconds, I hang in the arms of a stranger. It's too close for me, and no doubt for him too, and sometimes I don't want to let a stranger touch me, sometimes not even when one wants to help me, sometimes not even when I have to stay seated as a consequence.

Dinner with H. cancelled in the end because of snow: too slippery.

"*Sports for the disabled" on the Swiss Television Network: What am I supposed to make of this? I don't have the urge, the drive, "to be like the others" (and what are they like?), or even "normal" (and what is that, anyway?). At any price. And least of all at the price of my dignity, physical as well as mental.*

Isn't being "not normal" already the biggest compliment that so-called "normal" people have come up with for the "un-normal" or even the "abnormal"? Wouldn't my "wanting to be normal" be merely a radical denying of my physical state? Wouldn't that constantly make me want to be that which I cannot be? With my radical denying, don't I make those who don't want to, or can't, do these sports—or those who do these sports seemingly voluntarily even though, in the end, it is social pressure compelling them to participate—into even less "normal people?" Wouldn't I even be doing harm to these people, as I'd be contributing to making the difference between "normal" and "not normal" even larger by feigning a "normality" that isn't given?

Of course (the show isn't on yet), even here, amongst the slowest, the fastest will have to be determined. How on earth can a person with a disability, who's been given the gift of slowness, the benefit of time, subject himself to the test of speed?

I imagine carefully conceived differences in the classifications. The one-legged amputee can't be pitted against the two-legged paralytic. Sports need to be fair. There has to be one-crutch and two-crutch long-distance races; wheelchair steeplechases, sponsored by wheelchair

A woman in the museum looks at *Le Chariot*, sees me in my wheelchair, looks at *Le Chariot* again, and turning once more to me says excitedly: "That's you!"—"Yes," I cry, taken aback, "that's me, *l'homme qui roule!*"

makers and disability insurers, that have to be split into separate motorized *and* manual *classes. Carcinomas are a world of their own. And, what class does bad breath compete in? Blind boxing, on the other hand, I imagine, is easy and, above all, of high entertainment value. But where to put the epileptic—her unpredictable attacks could speed up her ski run, which potentially constitutes doping? Are life-sustaining medications classified as doping? Is the hunchback allowed to bobsled?*

The Swiss system of determining degree of disability, which is used to calculate disability benefit amounts, should also be applied to sports for the disabled. The 25-percenters compete amongst themselves, as do the 52-percenters and the 99-percenters. As my disability is progressive, I can participate in a different class every year—and I already envision myself being disqualified on the victory podium because I was selected for the 72-percent class but my archrival's doctor is able to place me unambiguously in the 71-percent class. The highlights, however, are the biathlon, triathlon, pentathlon—the ultimate events for the "not normals" too—because the so-called multi-disabled can do these. This is where the cancered, hunchbacked, hand-amputee competes, or the mentally deficient, atrophying, drug-addicted, corruptible politician... ah, but now we're getting into something else... cut to black.

Excursus: Human herd behavior, tested in an experiment on the stairway entrance to the Theater am Kirchplatz in Schaan and got a real scare in the process. *"Theater Steps," inspired by Turrini, Bernhard, Handke, & Jelinek.*

Inside the theater Peymann and Beil rehearse, refusing to let anyone in through the theater's only ground floor entrance, including those in wheelchairs, so I freeze outside. Nevertheless, friend F.-P., spurred on by Peymann's merciless screw-you-stay-out stance, plunges into the pit of the theater's stairwell and tries to persuade someone to open the door. But it isn't that easy.

I sit with my back to the theatergoers, who have to pass me to get into the theater. As guardian of the stairway, I am enthroned before the very steps I am unable to conquer. Ladies, alone or with partners, make their appearances, smile at and/or greet me. Gentlemen sometimes offer their assistance; do they want to help me or impress their female companions? I thank them but continue to wait for F.-P. as I freeze outside in front of the door, because inside Peymann and Beil, as I found out later, are reading from their own correspondence, something they have to rehearse apparently.

Once the stream of theatergoers is set in motion, a line forms, which no one steps out of, no one breaks, and gone is the solidarity, never mind how cold it is. All that counts then is the stream, the streaming, which mustn't be interrupted under any circumstances. There are no smiles left for me, no feminine hellos, no masculine overtures to help me surmount the steps; the little twosomes and threesomes merge and form a crowd; crowd is power, power is muscle, and muscle marches, tramples over everything. Avoid eye contact, onward, march! March!

Epilogue in hell. *That a theater, and a relatively new one at that, can have built such a wealth of steps with such insensitivity! Ask the politicians, who by virtue of their official positions are, naturally, already extremely sensitive to the issue, and admittedly they will all give the same reply: We'd like to, of course, but it is too expensive to completely rebuild, unfortunately, unfortunately, the money, the money, bye.*

A visitor says there is an entrance somewhere in the back. The ticket boy, who reappeared after ten minutes shrugging his shoulders, has no idea and vanishes again. Not even the high threshold of the "ground level" entrance—three people are needed to get me in my wheelchair over it—has been removed. I'm inside and gradually warm up. Nothing is gained without a struggle, not even in the liberal paradise of a theater.

I have to skip the reception in the basement where Peymann and Beil are signing programs after their performance. Doesn't matter; I see only asses at receptions anyway.

So I watched the "sports for the disabled" program and finally understood that any and all satire will arrive too late.

First, a report ("thematic programming") on disabled children who require prostheses is shown. A boot is being pulled on the prosthesis of a young girl.

GIRL *(ca. 9): Ouch, you're ripping my leg off.*
BOOT JACK: *Doesn't matter, we can reattach it.*

During the commercial break there is an advertisement for an upcoming health program that deals with excessive weight and excessive sweating.

On this evening's NZZ Format TV magazine there'll be a segment about Thomas Mann's death in Zurich. Then the new SF Swiss Television Network's station identification comes on. It shows an untalented wannabe suicide victim who hurls himself off of a dam and into the depths on a bungee cord. Although catapulted back up by the momentum of the cord, the acrobat does not—as the laws of gravity would have it—smash his skull on the dam wall. Instead, a gigantic logo comes into view, informing us viewers that we're watching the Swiss Television Network. The sports show follows: normalo-sport, the main program and abnormalo-sport as the pre-primetime amusement.

Fireworks.

The disabled band Sympa plays African music. A voiceless blind man sings the Paralympic anthem. To cheers and jubilation, the wheelchair delegation (the announcer informs us) "marches" in.

Cut.

Someone becomes world champion in the ultimate discipline, downhill skiing, in the "lower leg amputee class"; another gets the bronze in the "upper arm amputee class."

The victory runs are staged by the camera—the usual rapturous celebration of the body, only here and there an arm or a leg or a torso is missing. At the finish line everyone is the same again, athletes, who, panting and puffing and coughing, spout nonsense: took this curve like this, that one, unfortunately, like that.

"...'tunes up' his artificial leg to racing strength..."

"...racing material..."

"...special joints..."

"...foot molded in a stiff ski boot and then screwed tight..."

"...the paraplegic bobsled prototype ETH simulates movement sequences 'normal person'..."

"...a normal person, indeed a standing person..."

The "forearm amputee class" competes. Then Nordic skiing, where there are only three classes: "the visually impaired class," "the sitting class," and the "standing class." For this, the "degree of disability is

164   Christoph Keller

reflected in percents." So I was right! Those who can show they have higher degrees of disability, stipulated by disability insurance, get a head start!

Three winners of the "sitting class" sit behind three small white podiums; from their wheelchairs they can barely see over the structures. Apparently a ramped victory podium couldn't be constructed, even for this occasion.

Some of the stump athletes have to be "psychologically prepared" so they stay the course. A torso with head, strapped to a cross-country ski equipped with a plastic box, drags himself panting across the finish line, coughs a few words of victory, nearly dies on camera, and is wrapped in a warm blanket so that he doesn't completely die, at least not on camera. He's given encouragement. His head is patted. Whole thing looks alarmingly real. It is real, unfortunately. It looks like a heart attack, but the stump is pleased with what he has achieved of his own accord and is already looking forward to the next time.

A female athlete ("Nordic standing class") injured her knee and, she suspects, broke an arm. But it doesn't matter, she says, the arm is already paralyzed.

Cut.

Switzerland's President Ogi appears on screen. Couldn't be at the competition, unfortunately, unfortunately, but now he's here. From the Swiss point of view the Paralympics were a success: twenty-two medals, "one less than last time, but who's going to complain, given the festive mood." Ogi—who'd recently publicly lamented the fact that he too, not even fifty-three years young, now had to wear glasses, and, as head of the Federal Department of Defense, Civil Protection and Sport, thus considers himself to be an expert on disabled issues—thinks the athletes will "make the most of their fates" and in them he sees an "example" that touches "us all in our hearts" and "goodbye, everyone!"

Helicopter, fireworks...

How will walking stop? Will it be a fall, a fracture, a crying out, a stiffening of muscles; will it be utter astonishment at what's happening to me?

My mother was nervous as she handed me the telephone receiver.

"For you. A Jolanda Gut. Isn't that..."

I nodded. Father's little art fart friend. Who regularly wrote about openings at his gallery, articles in which she never failed to mention that the gallery owner cared for his artists as if they were his own sons; articles, which if I saw them in time, I tore out of the newspaper to at least prevent him from intruding in our life in this way as well. What did she want? To cancel the next studio visit? That was all right with me. Why on earth had I gotten involved with her group visits to local artists' studios in the first place? These were artists whose names were largely familiar to me because I'd been forced to watch as their works were taken from our house. My mother seemed to suspect something else and opened her mouth to speak, but then walked out of her bedroom, where she'd answered the phone, without saying a word.

After Ms. Gut congratulated me on a prize I had won (a one-kilogram E.T.A. Hoffmann doorstopper of a book, for some of my clumsy poems), she said: "He misses you, Christoph."

"Who?" I asked, as if I didn't know.

"Your father."

"Oh, does he?"

"He'd like to see you."

"Why?"

"Well, Christoph, he's your—"

"Did he say that?" I interrupted.

She faltered. "No, not exactly…"

I remained silent. I had no reason to make things easy for this woman.

"Your father doesn't know I'm calling you."

"Is he not allowed to know?"

"Yes, he is, of course, I only thought—"

"No."

"No, what?"

I cleared my throat, sat down on my mother's bed and burrowed my feet in the dog blanket that lay on the floor. The bed was low, but I'd be able to stand up. I'd still managed it the last time. And I didn't care if I couldn't this time.

"No, I won't see him. You know he's suing us. For the second time already?"

"Not you and your brothers, only your—"

"What's the difference?" I interrupted. "If he wins, what will we live on? His goal is to take the house from us because he can't live here anymore. Where would I live then? With him?"

"I… I don't think that's right either."

"My mother can't take it much longer. Sometimes she nods off on the couch. Later she says she fell asleep. But she didn't fall asleep. She fainted."

"Maybe… maybe it's just the way he is. Maybe he just can't approach you and your brothers, so he—"

"Has to sue us? Maybe that's just his way of talking to us!"

"Christoph—"

I interrupted her again. "You know he didn't even call me when I was diagnosed. Not once!"

"I understand you are very hurt. You have to try to get past it. He was sick himself, Christoph."

"From drinking!"

"His nerves."

"Do you know what he said about us, when my brother visited him for the last time, three years ago?

She didn't. I told her.

"That's terrible, I...I am sorry," she mumbled.

"Why should I want to see him, Ms. Gut?"

"Because...because he's your father." She was silent, then continued, although she knew I wouldn't give in. "Won't you at least give it some thought? He's had to start all over again. He's suffering; it is very hard for him, that he's lost everything. He speaks of nothing else. 1978, he says over and over again, was his fateful year. Everything gone, his business, his collection, his family. He...he doesn't have it easy."

"Neither do we, because of him," I said and hung up.

That was in the spring of 1983. Jolanda Gut made her second attempt to reconcile me with my irreconcilable father in February of 1994 without our having had any contact over the intervening years. This time she wrote. Blue ink, yellow stationery. I was thirty-one, but she still addressed me with the familiar *du*, which she'd used when I was a nineteen-year-old high school student. She wrote that my father had suffered "a series of mini-strokes," and since then walked with a cane. He dragged himself with great difficulty from his apartment to the gallery, she said—where he'd sometimes keep watch at four in the morning because he thought it was daytime.

For Puck, it was a fall in an auto repair shop in the spring of 1993. He had to go to the bathroom, which was in the basement. The friend who was with him carried him on his back, but he stumbled, or slipped on something. My brother—who, at that time, was as old as I would be in 2000—doesn't remember exactly what happened anymore. They were lucky, though, as the friend could have broken his back. "You really had to go to the garage?" our mother asked despairingly. At the hospital it turned out that Puck had broken his kneecap. Dr. Feller, almost seventy and all but retired, operated. The very next day a bottle of wine appeared at the hospital so doctor and patient could drink to a good recovery. SMA may well have laid him up in bed for weeks, it may well have put my oldest brother in a wheelchair permanently, but it did not take away his courage, his cheerful nature, or his optimism.

"And how do you see that happening?" Puck said. "We'll drop in on him from time to time? Go to his openings? Buy a painting? He'll give us a buzz now and then? Come by for a glass of wine to chitchat about the good old days? He'll push us through the zoo in our wheelchairs? He hasn't even ever seen all three sons in wheelchairs at the same time! It's all the same to him. He's been spared all of it. For ten years he sued us, and then his hypocritical bosom buddy Max Falk sued us on his behalf. It's only since he lost that lawsuit, too, that things have finally calmed down. No more burglaries, no more threatening postcards. Do you even know if he wants to see us? And what about our mother? Haven't you thought at all about what she's gone through? Now that it's finally over?"

Mix set out for home after closing time (this was spring 2000), slipped off the scooter he uses to get from the office to his car, and banged his knee on the concrete floor. At the hospital it turned out he'd torn his kneecap. Our mother feared Puck's fate would now be repeated, seven years later, with her second son. There was hope the kneecap would heal without surgery. "With good behavior," the doctor in attendance said, there was a distinct possibility the bone would mend itself within four weeks. Mix did well and was soon back on his feet again.

In response to my proposal that I scope out the situation with father, Mix, who now worked in the office at Puck's bathroom mirror company (which my oldest brother had made into a successful business) said he wasn't interested.

Didn't he miss father?

"Well, sure," Mix said, "but not this one."

Once Mix is on his feet again, he needs two canes to get from one of the two chairs in his apartment he can still get out of to his bed, the bathroom, or his scooter. He takes the scooter to the balcony or to the underground garage where his car is parked. If he's not feeling strong enough for the two canes, a four-legged walker is at the ready. He drinks less water so that he only has to go to the bathroom (with Clos-o-Mat) when he's up and about anyway. "It won't be long before I won't be able to walk." He's been saying this for years. Anyone who

asked him how he was doing would always hear he was doing well,
sometimes very well, and now and then, really well. But not *well? No,*
never. Mix was never not *doing well.*

When our mother read Jolanda Gut's letter, all she said was: "If he is
calling you from his deathbed and you want to go, then you have to go.
You'll have my blessing."

"Just watch it doesn't happen to you," Mix warns me. I don't know
what he means exactly. His falls? He falls a lot, almost once a month. A
crack between two tiles where the toe of a shoe can get caught is enough
to bring him (or me) down. But more and more he falls because his
muscles are overtaxed and can't hold his body up. It is as if they stop
working for a split second, and because he no longer has the strength—
or the reflexes—to activate against this brief power failure, he collapses.
Once it was in his kitchen, with a slice of pizza in his hand; another
time he fell backwards down a staircase, though he managed not to
injure himself.

"I heard you're not doing well. Call me if you want," I wrote on a
postcard-sized piece of paper, added my first and—to be on the safe
side—last name and telephone number, stuck the note in an anthology
of Russian prose I had edited, and sent it to the atelier house.

   I placed the card on page fifty-six of the book, the start of Ivan
Bunin's story "Kasimir Stanislavovitch." In this story, Kasimir
Stanislavovitch, who leads a wretched and lonely life in Kiev, receives
an unsigned telegram consisting solely of the message "on the tenth."
He travels forthwith to Moscow, a city where he'd seen better times—
what sort we are not told— and treats himself to a rare feast. After
visiting one or two sites from his life (a life we know is bungled), he
sits down in a church where a young couple is getting married. He
does not reveal himself to the bride and groom, nor does he reveal his
relationship to them to the reader. The young woman proceeds past
him "like a princess," and even grazes him with her bridal veil—it
may be their first contact, for Bunin tells us the young woman doesn't
know of Kasimir Stanislavovitch's existence. Kasimir Stanislavovitch
cannot take his eyes off the young girl and by the way he observes

her, it appears that she may, in fact, be his daughter. We learn nothing further about their relationship, nor why they don't have one (at least anymore). After the marriage ceremony, he retreats to his hotel room. He tears the cord from the window curtain, but realizes he doesn't have the strength to take his own life, and drives back to Kiev. In the hotel, the farewell note he left behind is found: "No one is to blame for my death..."

The phone rang the next day. I heard a familiar rustling, a hoarse wheezing, a reproachful—or so it seemed to me—cough, and I already started to regret having made contact. Would putting down the phone dissolve the vision I had conjured?—the same way the father I had loved used to dissolve on the first landing of the attic steps after he'd materialized there to explain the nature of time to me?

"Hello." I heard the timeworn voice of an old man. "This is your father."

I don't ask Mix what he means exactly by his warning that I should just watch out, but I've also resolved to behave well. Don't stumble. No wrinkles in the carpets. Nothing on the floor. Eat less. The heavier I am, the more weight I have to schlep around. More calcium. The less calcium in my body, the more brittle my bones will become. Go to physical therapy more often; do the exercises more conscientiously. Pop the vitamin pills, regardless of what color they are this year. All in all, I intend to remain in motion, to not shy away from any journey, be it around the world or simply to my bedroom and back again.

A half hour before our meeting at Café Zimmermann, I called my father to remind him— Jolanda Gut had advised in her letter that father needed reminding. He picked up the receiver quickly, but then, caught off guard by his own speed, he didn't seem to know what he was supposed to do with the damp plastic object he held in his hand. I heard his labored breathing. Something—the book I'd sent him?—fell to the floor. I pictured my father in bed, protected by objects, the blocked windows, the dust of miserable years.

"Are you there?"

Now he responded quickly, caught out, reproachful: "Of course I'm here!"

Shouldn't I have made sure he'd keep to our planned reunion? Or, should I have chanced it—that his desire to see his youngest son again would win out over his new conception of time? Should I have spent a half hour at the Zimmermann hoping he wouldn't come so I could have told myself I *had* tried again, hadn't I?

"So, ten o'clock?"

"Is that you, son?"

"Yes."

"We said the Zimmerman, right?"

"Yes."

"See, your father forgets nothing. I'm on my way."

As I wanted to be there first I set out immediately. Three minutes later I was in the car and in another five on his street. There, within walking distance of the Zimmermann, I parked in a no parking zone, my international wheelchair symbol (which displayed the license number of my car and the year, 1994) indicating that I was permitted this maneuver, which was illegal for others. I threw open the door— did the door to his building, which was just a few steps away, open at the same time?—and, holding on to it, pulled myself up and out. Yes, the door to his building had burst open, but all that came out—like a shot—was a ball, followed by a young boy, who chased it into the quiet street. Using my car as a railing, I walked around and surmounted the curb. No father in sight. From here, ten meters to the street corner, from there, twenty to the Zimmermann. One step up, five meters through the bakery, five to the corner table.

I wanted to meet in Hadleyville—under no circumstances did I want to lure him away from there—but I didn't want to meet him in his headquarters, the Hirschen, on the square opposite. He would know the Zimmermann, but not well, just as I still had only a vague memory of the café and bakery where we'd picked up our Sunday bread in days gone by. As if now I was the one doing the spying, I'd driven through Hadleyville to find a suitable place for our meeting. The Zimmermann had only one step at the door, and I called ahead to ascertain something of the make-up of the café's interior. I didn't want to meet him, as Puck had, in his apartment, and I wanted to come alone—my brothers had entrusted me with this—but I also wanted to be sure that I'd be able to stand up without anyone's help and certainly without the help of my father.

I wanted to be early, and I was. I wanted to be there before my father, to see him coming; most of all, I didn't want my father to see me coming.

The waitress—was she the one who'd described the accessibility of the café to me, at first somewhat sullenly and then as if granting me a favor?—asked what I wanted. Coffee, black. I'd sat down heavily, observed by her with displeasure, maybe even with distrust—she hadn't realized she'd, in turn, been observed by me.

Would he be punctual, or would he keep me waiting, put me in my place? Once again, I regretted having come. Even more so, however, I regretted having ordered coffee; it would make me more nervous than I already was and expose me to the risk of having to go to the bathroom.

And then there he was. Approaching slowly, slowly. Unsteady, but without a cane. He didn't limp. But the rhythm of his walk had become another rhythm, a slower one, a scuffling one. His hair was white, and he wore it longer. His bald spot was larger. His beard had also grown and white had replaced the rusty red. He was dressed in black—shoes, pants, shirt, all black. He'd lost weight. Was less imposing; was no longer one of those overpowering Easter Island figures he'd reminded me of in the past. He disappeared from my field of vision, and it took some time before he negotiated the doorstep, covered the ten meters through the bakery and café, and stood before me. Did this make me happy? I didn't know yet.

"Who thought we'd meet again." Which one of us said that? His hand reached for the back of the chair, a gesture resulting from the awkwardness of the situation, but which he combined with the search for a hold. His shirt was buttoned up, his zipper half down. When we shook hands dandruff fell, some of it on my arm, on my bare skin. The opening sentence was not followed by a question mark, so it could be both an observation and a reproach—this sounds more like my father and I now remember he was the one who'd uttered it.

So, there he stood before me, my father, my worst adversary, my most difficult love, and I was amazed, simply amazed, that I'd needed so long to comprehend why I'd committed to this meeting, why I'd suggested it, had sought it for years, decades. It was so I could spit at him. I couldn't ram my fist into the bastard's face, but at least I could spit in it. Spit in his face for all his cruel and constant taking, or maybe even more so for his earlier giving, which he'd then taken from me, too. I would spit for his having shown me, in the attic and in the atelier house, what could have been. Spit in his face and then, as quickly as I still could, walk out on him once and for all and finally live my life and my life alone…

But I didn't do it. I just sat there watching him seat himself, an awkward and involved procedure. After his opening remark, he said nothing at first. Finding a topic of conversation was my affair. Had he wanted to see me, or I him?

"Yes, who thought we'd meet again," I said.

Pause.

"So, how are you?"

Good question, I thought, and said: "Fine."

Ah, be proud, always keep up appearances, always walk tall, never speak the truth! Why didn't I say that physically at least, I wasn't fine; that I was suffering from an illness that was steadily worsening. Why didn't I say how difficult that was? Why didn't I tell him all this, so that he—the one who'd shirked all responsibility—would also not feel so fine?

"And you?"

"What do you think! Lousy."

We ordered coffee, my second, his, as always, as before, without milk and sugar. Any second now he'd say: "Have to watch my weight." And then he said it.

"You?"

"What do you mean?"

"Don't you have to watch your weight, too?"

"Yes," I said, and he grinned smugly, our begetter, as Puck called him, his meager attempt to keep him at arm's length.

"This time with cream!" I called after the waitress.

"See," he said, leaning back, without so much as suspecting that I—that anyone—might have a problem with him, without suspecting that his youngest son was sitting so quietly only because he wasn't in a position to ram his fist into his face and didn't dare spit at him. Was it so difficult, was it so impossible for my father to say what I had hoped to hear from him: Yes, you are right, and I (for once!) was wrong, yes, I did something (something!) wrong, forgive me, son, and believe me when I say I am truly sorry, forgive me for everything, for all that I did to you and our family, I hope we can make a fresh start...

"You do take cream, then," he said and, after a pause, "pretty fattening to pour cream in your coffee everyday."

Pause.

"And the gallery?"

"What gallery?"

"Yours, of course."

"What about it?"

"How's it going?"

"How do you think—you know you can't live off art. Or have you managed to?

"No, not really..."

"Not really! That means no, right? So how are you getting by then?"

"Not with any help from you, in any case."

"No, not with any help from me. You don't get anything from me. And why should you? I don't give you money so you can blame me. Is that why you came? To blame me? To get what there still is to get? You should've thought about that before."

"What, being your son?"

"My son! Do I have sons? Where are my sons? Tell me, where were my sons all that time I could've used sons? Tell me!"

The waitress saved us with our coffees. I felt the pressure on my bladder. I hadn't ascertained whether I'd be able to get to the bathroom or not. How long had I been here already? How long had it taken for us to be completely out of sorts? The waitress set the tray down on the table between us, placed my father's coffee in front of him, then mine in front of me, quickly, too quickly. Did she know my father? Did she also sell bread in the bakery, had she waited on him in the past, did she serve him on a daily basis, was she simply waiting until I left?

"You were telling me how your gallery was doing."

"How do you think?" He took a sip, splattered coffee, cursed. "Roman Signer, he's a famous artist now..."

"So?"

"I made him after all, and now?"

"What?"

"He's showing everywhere!"

"He should, shouldn't he?"

"And what about me?"

"You'll show the next Signer."

"Exactly."

"But that's good."

"Yes, it is."

"You can be proud of that."

"I am."

I tore the top off my container of cream—it had a picture of a Swiss Post horse-drawn St. Gotthard Pass mail coach from 1858 on it—and poured the contents on to the linoleum tabletop.

"Are you proud of your father?"

The sugar cube crumbled well over the cream puddle. The result was a crystalline trail I'd originally thought could be a border demarcating the cream territory, instead, though, it now led spiral-like from the center to the outer boundary.

"I was proud of you when your first book came out. With me in it as the crazy father, a crazy daredevil of a guy, that's me all right! Then you let me burn with the house. Good work!"

Salt didn't make much difference, just messed up the sugar's crystalline spiral. So it had to be pepper, and I peppered pepper onto the sugar cream landscape.

"That was our attic, wasn't it, that you let burn, right? The book labyrinth..."

I hesitated about whether I should use the Zweifel paprika chips and then decided against it. What self-respecting artist used Zweifel paprika chips? I dipped my finger into the lower right edge, but my signature would prove only temporary—the cream lake instantaneously closed in over it.

"I stopped reading after you burned me to death. Why should I have continued? You know I sell all your books in my gallery?"

Ketchup lent the landscape the requisite agitation, Maggi sauce, well shaken, well jiggled, the essential Pollock-ness, served and preserved by Spoerri. I placed the horse-drawn St. Gotthard Pass mail coach in the middle.

Then, boastfully, triumphantly, a little short of a victory for him: "Then everyone up and abandons me again!"

The waitress reappeared. I smiled, seeking to make her my ally. She nodded in my father's direction, however, refusing me the satisfaction of any sort of verbal reaction to my daubings. Instead, she placed a few paper napkins in front of me.

"Two more coffees," he said.

I picked up one of the green napkins, unfolded it, and lay it over my work. The cream, the Maggi, and the ketchup pushed through the light paper turning it dark green.

"So, you're a Russian major?"

"I'm finished with school."

"Nice," he said pointing to my smearings. "Do you want to show with me?" Then, his finger now pointed at me, he added: "So, you're a communist."

"Then I would have studied Marxism-Leninism."

"You didn't?"

"Just a little."

"I had to find all that out in the newspaper! Everything! What you do. Your books. That you got married. That you're a communist."

In reality, my father has been dead a long time. In reality, he is dead at long last. In reality, everything is finally over, for death freed me from my father. In reality, his fifth tiny mini-stroke felled him, once and for all— and with a single stroke, not even a stroke of lightning, just a mini-stroke, his immortality came to an end. He died in the atelier house. He'd been able to cling to the ART IS SUPERFLUOUS. GO HOME sign for a half minute. Then he collapsed, elegantly, protractedly, as if in slow motion. This is how Jolanda Gut found him; she'd been in the process, yet again, of writing a portrait of his gallery, his fateful year, 1978, and his artists, whom he cared for as if they were his own sons. She found his last words, which he'd also wanted inscribed on his tombstone, on a note in his pocket: "Blame the doctors for my mini-stroke, those—." The note also said he wanted to be buried in the Cripple Creek cemetery on the other side of the Rio Bravo near Hadleyville. Jolanda Gut informs me of this in her dense, scrawly handwriting via a sentimental postcard and asks me in closing to come to the funeral. On the postcard is a reproduction of the horse-drawn St. Gotthard Pass mail coach from 1858; leaning out of the coach is John T. Chance, shooting at anything and everything he doesn't understand. I don't go to the funeral, of course, but I do go to the grave, while it is still quite fresh. Meaning, I roll there: first in my car, past the no-cars-past-this-point sign and into the Cripple Creek cemetery, until the rows of graves become too narrow, and from there I roll in my wheelchair. And then it happened. The wheels of my wheelchair plow into the soft earth and I am stuck in my father's still quite fresh grave.

"See," he says grinning.

Will it be a fall, in my case, too? Could it also be a stiffening, a "warm freezing," the way I sometimes picture it when I get stuck in that ravine of space between the kitchen door and the bar—frozen in a movement. Like what's been happening to Jan's father more and more frequently of late—all of a sudden, on his way down the hallway of his apartment, he stops; he doesn't fall, he doesn't walk, he just stands, unable to even eke out a single sound—a mini-stroke, blood vessels opening, closing. What do I know what they do, what they cause? But Jan's father is eighty-nine and played tennis until he was eighty-two, while I am thirty-eight and stopped playing tennis at fourteen. When Jan's father freezes, his body loosens up after a few minutes and then continues on. I have to shout a command at mine, "Go!" is enough for my muscles to pluck up courage. My stiffening is only a seconds-long fear, for a moment later, I am off, nearing the far bank of the Rio Bravo—there it is, the barstool that receives me, here it is, the bar counter that supports me. SMA, my lovely SMA, when it comes to preparing me for the moment when I'll no longer be able to walk, you are so tender, so loving, that one day, when I relinquish my cane and can let myself fall into my wheelchair once and for all, it will be a relief...cut to black.

"I forgot my cane. Can you imagine forgetting your cane? And I can't even walk without it. Not a single meter. Says my doctor!"

Pause.

"Doctors!"

Pause.

"And? Could they do anything for you?"

Pause.

"See! Why don't you listen to your old father?"

Pause.

"But then who's listening to your old father anyway!"

Pause.

"I'll tell you who is. A whole lot of people! Mainly women. Girls, one or two of whom you'd like, too. But we're not quite there yet, my dear boy. You can put that out of your head. Girls! You've no idea how many work for me, for free. One looks after the gallery, for nothing at all, and you know what? I can barely get her to leave at the end of the day. But she's too old for me. Fifteen years younger than I am, but too old for me! (*Laughs.*) Another comes every Saturday morning, gets down on her knees in front of me and scrubs the floor. She's not quite right upstairs. So you see, the women all listen to your old man, just not your mother, that, that..."

"Please, we agreed—"

Pause.

"The one who scrubs the floors paints, too."

Pause.

"She's hoping I'll give her a show."

Pause.

"She can keep on scrubbing!"

Pause.

Pause.

"I'm *sorry*, what was that you said?"

"I didn't say anything."

"You said not about your mother. That's what you said."

"I said please."

"Please what?"

"Please not about my mother. We can talk about anything else, just not about her."

"And why is it not permitted to talk about the holy saint of Alpsteinstrasse?"

"Talk, fine. Only you don't really talk, you just curse her. You immediately start to shout."

"I never shout!"

"You're shouting now!"

"I shout when I want to!"

"Then I'm going."

"Go then!"

Pause.

"If you could just talk."

"Let's talk! What do you want to talk about? You can talk to me about everything. Ask my artists."

Pause.

"She screwed me over."

"You screwed us over."

Pause.

"You're married now, aren't you? Or aren't I allowed to ask that either?"

"Of course you can ask me that. Viktoria and I met six years ago and—"

"Then you'd better be good and careful, my dear boy," he interrupted me. "You can never be too suspicious when it comes to women."

"We're doing very well," I said.

Viktoria, or Tori as I called her, had gone to Italy for a few months as part of her Romance studies degree. Even if we hadn't talked about it, we both knew that this was not the only reason for her semester abroad.

"Couldn't be better."

"She'll screw you. They all do, sooner or later."

During our Sunday morning phone call—Tori said she could only ask one call per week of the distant relative with whom she was living—she'd encouraged me to meet my father again, in spite of everything that had happened.

"You see how I've fared. Your mother—"

What if he really is dying?

"Please—"

After he died I'd reproach myself, wouldn't I? For having not even tried one more time?

"...is..."

What if he'd changed?

"...a..."

What if it was just the way he was?

"...a..."

Wouldn't I then at least know where I stood?

"...damn..."

Huns...

My father stuttered.

Maybe, Tori had said, the only reason he kept suing us was because this was the only way he could communicate. A communication problem, I'd mumbled, and Viktoria had nodded—or at least I had imagined her nodding in her room in Ferrara, the way she had always nodded when we'd had a thought at the same time. A communication problem, like my disability, she said. Nerves that wouldn't communicate. Nerves that wouldn't tell my muscles what they were supposed to do with the strength, you know, that my body would store somewhere.

...Hounds!

Before Viktoria hung up because she had to free up the line for the distant relative, she'd said I really should write about "it" someday. What did she mean, exactly, I asked. My SMA *and* my father, she answered. Basically, I had two disabilities, two progressive illnesses, she said. If I'd ever be able to separate them from one another, then that was the only way to do it.

Cliffs soaring heavenward, sand as far as the eye can see, the saddle leather cracks.

When my father saw me slide to the end of the bench and pull the chair closer that I needed to help me stand up, he asked: "What are you doing?"

"I'm going."

"How come?"

"Because you aren't sticking to our agreement. Because you never stick to an agreement."

"I always stick to my agreements. What did we agree to?"

"Not to talk about my mother. Not to speak about the past at all. Father"—a first, tentative *Father* that made my mouth dry—"we have no common past because you deny it, every day and every minute. Because you can't accept anyone's point of view but your own. Because you won't even listen when someone *really* wants to talk about something. You're afraid that that could have an effect on your view of things. You are dogmatic and deaf. And I didn't even come to criticize you. I came in the hope that we could see each other once in a while. But, to be honest, I don't know how that's to work if we can't speak about anything that really concerns us, because you immediately start to blame everyone else."

He hesitated.

"What am I allowed to talk about?"

"I don't know. About yourself. How you are doing. How the gallery is doing. What you do."

"You want to hear something about me. How I'm doing. How am I supposed to be doing? I had to start from the beginning, for the second time in my life. I had nothing, again, nothing. From zero to a hundred, then back to zero again. I..."

He was silent. Reflected for a moment. What was he thinking? That every sentence he spoke, no matter how it started, turned into an expletive?

"I have my gallery, as you know, and the workshop. Clocks, mostly, but I repair everything. You know I was always pretty handy with things."

I nodded. He smiled.

"We made a lot of stuff together, you and I, do you remember? Somehow the whole business also had its upside. I can really live for art now. Am an artist myself. Maybe I'll show you some of my stuff sometime. I don't show my things to anyone. The gallery isn't doing well, of course. Am constantly broke. You must know how that is. Do your books actually sell?"

"I can't live from it."

"So what do you live on?"

"When a book comes out, the readings are important. Sometimes there is a prize, a grant. There's also a small disability pension, which also helps a little."

"Do you have to pay rent?"

"Why shouldn't I have to pay rent?"

"The Alpsteinstrasse house does belong to your mother after all."

"I want to pay rent."

"You do? Figures. Everything she does is okay, and everything your father does is wrong. Was always that way." Then, abruptly: "You never even said thank you for the flowers."

"What flowers?"

"The ones I sent you for the premiere of your first book. The one in which I go up in flames."

That was six years ago, in the spring of 1988. The flowers were already on the reading table when I arrived and remained there during my reading. It was only afterwards that I discovered the note with "I am proud of you, father" written in thick, green felt-tip pen.

"You could have said thank you."

"I gave them to the bookseller."

"Ingrate!"

"You were suing us. For the fourth or fifth time."

"And I sent you flowers anyway."

"Anyway?"

"Yes, anyway! Is that not proof of my generosity? That I, unlike everyone else, can forgive?"

Pause.

"I wasn't invited to your wedding either."

"Please…"

"I'm also not allowed to talk about my youngest son's wedding?"

Pause.

"How do you think I felt!"

"Like Kasimir Stanislavovitch?"

"Who?"

"Never mind."

"Never mind! The way you speak to your father! I was non grata! Non grata! Me, your father, not welcome at the wedding of his own son. The oldest didn't invite me to his either. And the middle one? Is he married too?"

"No."

Pause.

Pause.

"Bring her with you the next time."

"Who?"

"Your wife. What's her name again?"

Tori, as K. saw her

-1-

The first time Tori disappeared she was three and a half. She didn't get far, of course. Still, she said, she'd made it to the train tracks. There she faced southwards and let the wind tousle her hair. She waited for the train in the frost and ice. One came; others came at various intervals. Even if none stopped to take her with them, this was nevertheless how she acquired her belief in redemption via the railroad. She'd have gotten on the train, Tori swears today, and would have gone as far south as she'd been allowed to go.

Half an afternoon later she was back in the kitchen where her mother, who hadn't missed her, was stirring pots for dinner. Upstairs the second-born was screaming; her mother's belly swelled with the third. When she turned to the turnips, the mother noticed the state her daughter was in.

"No doubt you've been playing in the yard too long, building snow caves, blue with cold as you are. That's for boys. You should know that!"

"I ran away, Mama. Almost all the way to the south!"

"At least you're properly dressed for the cold weather. But don't you think it excessive, wearing a hat with earflaps *over* your wool hat?"

On this afternoon, as an exception, Tori was allowed to run a bath, but she had to swear she'd be on time for dinner. They were not in the habit of speaking at the table, or only the father did. He was the mayor. This was why everyone in town had been to their house; their second floor served as the Town Hall where callers could call on Herr Mayor. This made Tori sad, for she, too, had many questions for Herr Mayor. Once she had gone from house to house, ringing everyone's doorbells, saying she was calling on them. For this she was rewarded with a smile, in some cases an apple, an occasional piece of chocolate, but never with a peek into anyone else's home. Wasn't that unfair? She told her troubles to her rabbit, who nibbled his unpeeled turnip, and she resolved to enter the home of every person on earth at least once in her life. For this reason—there wasn't a doubt in her mind now—she wanted to be a "caller" when she grew up.

Occasionally Tori sat in the waiting room upstairs. Her mother encouraged this, for this was where Tori learned how to wait. As daughter of Herr Mayor she was, moreover, a Fräulein Princess Mayor of sorts, who had to show herself to the public in her new, always self-tailored, clothing. If the bell sounded and it was her turn, she hopped from her chair and sashayed—fully aware of the eyes of the other "callers" following her—out of the waiting room. She was also certain of what the mayor would say: first, "You again?" then, "Isn't your dress just a bit too short for such a little girl?" and, finally, without having listened to a single one of her questions, "Tell me, where are your little brothers, Tori?"

The second time Tori disappeared she was eight and managed to get further. The postbus heading north stopped in front of their house. She stood at the stop for the southward-heading postbus, which was on the other side of the street, in front of the grocery where she was already allowed to do some small shopping for her mother. Because the Missus Sonderegger, as Herr Mayor called the widowed proprietress, left her apartment door (located in the back part of the shop) open, Tori had been able to at least sneak a peek into her vestibule. As she climbed onto the postbus, her school satchel rattled promisingly; inside was a cheese sandwich wrapped in a napkin, the *oignon* watch that was a gift from her maternal grandfather, and the arithmetic problems for school. She paid with her savings and bought a return ticket—because it was cheaper, not because she wanted to return. The bus driver made sure a fellow bus driver, whose route he crossed down in the valley, drove her back. He told Tori to give his kind regards to her parents. Tori called on her father and the driver received a commendation from the mayor.

The third time, she was twelve. She took the bus again, but this time she said she was visiting her grandfather and showed the bus driver the *oignon* watch as proof. She savored his impressed "All by yourself?" and was certain that this time his colleague wouldn't bring her back forthwith. She stayed away overnight, snuck into a barn and kept warm next to a sheep. The following morning she went out and stood on the road, but no one stopped because they were looking for her (though others stopped). Tori began to sob. On the kitchen table at home, she found a note in the town hall clerk's handwriting informing her that Herr Mayor and his family had gone to the maternal grandfather's. The latter will certainly be sorry, the note continued, not to have been able to receive his favorite granddaughter among his rare visitors, especially as she always carried his watch with her, signed *Father (dictated, and signed in his absence)*. Tori decided she'd let them come home to find her cleaning the house and planned to cry out "Oh, there you all are! Have a nice time?" as soon as they walked in, but she fell asleep on the sofa before midnight.

Alas, the stories from her youth were the usual ones and mainly revolved around the dining table. Woe betide whoever made a sound while Herr Mayor listened to the news on the radio during the midday meal! Everyone in the village raised his hat when he appeared, so one was surely allowed to expect an ounce of respect at home as well. It wasn't until Tori was seven that she understood that the father often meant himself when he said "one." But already from an early age she'd known that one had to eat without making a sound and that "one" in this context was everyone else. No slurping, no lip-smacking, no giggling, not a peep. Of course the cutlery clinked a bit, and that was permissible; he who dropped his fork onto his plate, however, was expelled from the table. He who returned found the table cleared, never mind how much he (which, for all intents and purposes, was never anyone other than she, Tori) had already eaten. The father, spurred on by the bad news from the radio—all of which, without exception, he had seen "inevitably" coming, so much so, that Tori sometimes wondered why the world didn't seek her father's advice more often—ate intently, eyes closed, and with unerring aim.

It was never Tori who broke the silence. As the firstborn, however, she had to learn what it meant to accept responsibility for the family.

If one of the sons and heirs—in whose succession she had irreparably
meddled—made a peep, she was punished. Tori was forced to squeeze
herself into the bottom of the hallway closet, which had been emptied
for this purpose. The mother closed the closet door and turned the key,
while Herr Mayor never looked up from his plate. The sons kept silent.
Tori watched the light fade, heard the key rattle, then the muffled radio
voices, which she imagined were thunderclouds over the dining table.
All she had to do was will it and everyone at the table got wet.

Soon Tori was too big for the bottom of the closet and the space
could once more be used as storage for the Christmas decorations. It
was about time, the mother said, and unscrewed the cellar light bulb
so Tori could ponder her behavior in the dark down there. From that
point on, anyone wanting to go into the basement had to take along
the miner's lamp attached to a long cord that hung on a hook in the
kitchen. Crunching sounds beneath one's feet could be assumed to be
bursting pill bugs, which caused the boys to giggle and show off their
slippery prey. One time the father nearly tumbled down the steps and,
it occurred to him afterward, that Tori's basement banishment could
be combined with the provisioning of white wine. Was she not already
down there? Could she not then bring a few bottles up and stash them
in his private cabinet? So they had their secret, father and daughter, and
were one. How smoothly everything functioned at the Town Hall after
all! No sooner was Tori locked up than the table noise stopped. Nor did
she ever complain of hunger.

Family lore also had it that the daughter frequently sat beneath the
mayor's desk while he decided the fates of his callers. If Herr Mayor
didn't notice her, she bit his calf in the spot where the gray wool sock
segued into the paternal flesh, gently, like a kitten bloodying its teeth
out of love. Consequently the mayor would let out a little cry, which the
caller seated opposite would find inappropriate. And consequently the
mayor was seen by his constituents as being increasingly odd. Sometimes
little Tori—with her rosied chubby cheeks and little *Trachten* dress that
she ironed herself—chose an inopportune moment to burst forth from
beneath the table. For example, when it was imperative to bring the
basket of eatables standing in solitary splendor on top of the table in
contact with a perfectly reasonable building project whose only obstacle
was a perfectly nonsensical zoning ordinance. Transactions could usually

be saved despite the bite wounds and Herr Mayor's verbal eruptions. The basement banishment, which sometimes lasted until morning, fortified Tori both mentally and physically. Nevertheless, the time had clearly come for her father's political promotion and the family's move to the cantonal capital.

The apartment they rented in St. Gallen was so big that from the kitchen window the two cathedral towers appeared as one, while from seventeen-year-old Tori's room they'd seemingly moved so far apart again that they once more stood side by side. This meant that sooner or later her mother brought every single one of her guests to Tori's room so the phenomenon could be observed firsthand. Her mother found a friend of steadfast faith in Dorothea, with whom she went to mass in the cathedral on Sundays. All the old hens decked out in their pastels and enough confessionals that one feared for the souls of the city's citizens. The ex-mayor recuperated at the district court from the strains of the country, extolled the small city's big city atmosphere (so many train stations!), and put his party membership on the table—albeit with a guilty conscience—when something higher became available in the halls of justice.

It turned out that the tracks alongside which Tori had stood for the first time at three-and-a-half had, in fact, pointed south. Postcards and posters restricted the south to Florence, to Urbino, Ferrara, and Siena. A distant relative who had married an Italian man was living in Ferrara and Tori now wanted that, too. Gone, at seventeen, straight to *Italia!* Tori notified her parents on the third day of her disappearance; her mother said she'd thought as much, and Dorothea blessed her. The father wasn't home.

In Ferrara, Tori thought of a new way of running away without really having to run away. She more or less stopped eating, in order not to add any unnecessary weight to the already overloaded world. Wasn't there enough for everyone and didn't some (1%) have so much and others (99%) have so little? She almost always sounded irritated. In Italy, of all places, she set about improving the world. She shot reproving looks at the *ragazzi* who flicked their still-burning cigarette butts onto the street, and raised her shoulders higher in indignation when they whistled after her. What an unholy racket the *motorini* made, and those louts, who couldn't give a damn about the damage the constant roaring of their exhaust was wreaking on people, animals, and the environment! The twerps revved their motors, *rmmm! rmmm!*, ensuring, along with their fathers—who thought nothing of drinking their espressos while their Fiats idled outside—that Italy remained covered by a cloud of smog and that Tori woke in the mornings with a headache. Yet, she'd decided on Italy as her paradise, and that was that. Further expulsion was not an option.

Soon she could eat what she wanted and yet she became scrawny and scrawnier. This led to a hospital stay, after which her mother wrote her in Ferrara, saying it was about time she came to her senses, meaning returned to Switzerland. Prior to this, Tori had had an affair with her psychiatrist, or so her mother claimed. Tori's first lover, however, was no psychiatrist. It was her cousin, who, that spring, had also felt drawn to the south and their distant aunt. His room was right next to Tori's and soon he was visiting her in hers, from which the tower of Santa Caterina could be seen. Tori's body came and went; the doctors couldn't do anything. The thing with her cousin fizzled out. In the church, she lit a candle for Santa Caterina for a thousand lira. And she'd only mentioned the whole business with the psychiatrist to get her mother's attention, as any psychiatrist, even a made-up one, would have known. The father's attention could no longer be gotten.

At home, Tori accused her distant relative of rummaging through her drawers, sniffing around her underwear, probing into her acquaintances, and reporting the "facts," spiced with fictions, back to Switzerland. Tori, now eighteen, moved back into her childhood room and sewed heavy, dark purple curtains for the windows. When, at nineteen—with a little more flesh on her bones and cutting a more cheerful figure in general, less irritable and more tolerant of her surroundings—she had passed her university entry exams, the mother organized a party for the neighbors' twins, who hadn't passed anything. The mother forgot Tori's birthday, but she asked Tori to lend a hand in the preparation of her brothers' birthdays, which occurred in quick succession.

The boys weren't everything Tori's parents could have wished for either, but they were boys at least. One of them seemed to be developing an impairment of the motor nerves—or was "special," as the devout Dorothea thought. Every now and then, when they'd been invited somewhere for a visit, the oldest would get up, pull a beetle out of his vest pocket, and pop it between his thumb and index finger, causing Tori to relive her hours in the basement and the muffled giggling of her brothers through the door. Tori wanted to go to college, whereupon the necessary amount of money was frozen at the bank for the sons, who didn't want to go to college. The daughter's tearful protest resulted in the father pointing out, in heavy alcoholic slur, what it cost to raise a child these days, until it was finally self-supporting. He now read the news in the newspaper at lunch alone. Tori drew the curtains in her room and unscrewed the light bulb using a handkerchief. The mother said she should come to her senses. She and her father, the mother told her, would need the money for a trip they wanted to take around the world that would, God willing, bring all of them together again. Surely, Tori didn't want to stand in the way of this with her selfishness, did she?

Tori started working as a secretary to pay for her studies and naturally, according to her mother, had an affair with her boss. Tori started an affair with her boss when she heard her mother had already insinuated she'd been having one. She moved into a tiny apartment with a stray cat, drafty windows, and feeble central heating. This way she could save for college. Sometimes it was all right with Tori that her mother saw her studying at the only table in her apartment, wearing a shawl and clutching a cup of hot tea in her numb fingers. She'd leave the windows open before her mother came, but her mother usually cancelled the invitation at the last minute or suggested they meet in a cozy café in the old town. Before Tori set off, she called her father and told him how well she was managing. Two days later, there was always a 50-franc note in her mailbox, accompanied by an, "I am proud of you." In the café, her mother said Tori had kept her waiting a bit, but it didn't matter.

Tori was a good secretary and earned more than either one of her brothers. Since she'd had an affair with her boss, her mother sometimes called her daughter a whore. Her father, who in the meantime had all of a sudden "stepped down" from his position at the court, after having been "honored" for his service, sometimes phoned her at three in the morning to tell her how lousy he was feeling and how his wife, whom he was going to divorce—just wait and see—got on his case every chance she could, all because of this hypocrite Dorothea, may she go straight to hell. Tori wasn't able to fall back asleep after these calls and wanted to just be the whore she was already taken for. Her father didn't follow the news any more, although he now had the time for it and there was no longer anyone who'd disturb his listening.

Tori cut stories out of glossy magazines for her father, stories about women who financed their lives, or their studies, through prostitution. In one of these stories, a student said she was always amazed at how easy it was to earn money in this hypocritical society we live in and that it would be a cinch for her to be kept exclusively by a sugar daddy, but she didn't want to give up her freedom for all the tea in China. Tori highlighted this sentence, stuffed the lavishly illustrated articles into envelopes, which she stamped but never mailed, and which I found after Tori had left me and—for the nth time—had disappeared again.

Looking at the photos of prostitutes I am reminded of the one time I myself went to a prostitute, years before I met Tori. Did it really, as I imagined for a while, solve all my problems in one fell swoop—or at least my unfitness problems, which had been state-certified? And was the prostitute I went to one of those who'd prostituted herself to pay for college? Was this what Tori could have become? And what about me? Should I not also decide to be the person society already turned me into?

-2-

Ultimately, I went to the whorehouse because of Buñuel.

Buñuel, Luis. 1900–1983. Spanish filmmaker, subtle provocateur, clever quick-change artist, spy, alcoholic, gun fetishist, frequenter of brothels. His father is said to have taken the young Luis along with him to a brothel, to initiate his son—a ritual that would turn into a lifelong habit. K. (who considered himself fatherless to the same extent Buñuel was considered godless—both were untrue) saw that the time had come for his own initiation.

Well-worn plush, dusty lighting, imported strippers with restricted residence permits gyrating beneath a disco ball and shedding their clothing every half-hour to the beat of the music. The ritual began at the bar, as this was where the to-be-initiated could find relative safety. This was where one sat and pretended not to notice that a scantily clad female had occupied the adjoining seat. Spoke to him because he'd caught her eye. Wanted something from him, no doubt about it. Who would be so rude as to deny her his attention?

Part of the ritual was the invention of another identity. In the semi-darkness of the *etablissement*, K. became a documentary filmmaker, calling himself Pierre, in honor of the doctor who is shot in Buñuel's *Belle de Jour* and ends up wheelchair-dependent as a result. And the woman who'd sat down next to Pierre was named, of all things, Séverine: What an accident of fate! This was the name of Pierre's wife, played by Catherine Deneuve in the film! She spoke English with a French accent, and the well-placed lulls she inserted into the conversation hinted at an exciting double life. Once introductions were over, Pierre's hand was permitted to alight on Séverine's leg, even if, for the time being, only in friendly proximity to the knee. And in doing so it turned out that his film was such a daring cinematic work that even—*ooh!*, Séverine interrupted him, *how much* she loved champagne! How arousing her accent was! Parisienne! For Séverine was nothing other, and the celebrated documentary filmmaker found himself ordering champagne. But all he could afford was a piccolo, at 38 francs, and with his beer, the total was already 53 francs. The hell with it! Live for today! What did Pierre have an expense account for, anyway? Itemize it under "research."

Wouldn't they be more comfortable in one of the plush booths in the corner? Once there, Séverine suggested an entire bottle of champagne, but that was really breaking the independent filmmaker's bank account. Nevertheless, she permitted his hand to forge ahead into the magical intermediate zone of her stockings and miniskirt. When he started to trespass beyond the boundary of the hem of her skirt, however, Séverine squeezed her muscular thighs together, effectively checking his movement. Her enchanting smile reminded him that that which Shakespeare is said to have called "nothing" or even "hell" (George Steiner seminar, Geneva, c. 1984), could only come full bloom if he accepted her invitation upstairs. Of course, K., gentleman that he was, did not inquire about the price, but Séverine named it nevertheless, as she didn't expect him to come in vain. Expensive? No more expensive than two subsidized seats at the Zurich opera. Or sightseeing by helicopter in the Swiss Alps, the Eiger, Mönch, and Jungfrau mountains as climactic points.

"Take a real good shower and come in through the backdoor. I'll see you after midnight," Séverine whispered, slipping away to take her turn again gyrating beneath the flickering colors of the disco ball.

Midnight. Feeling courageous, freshly showered, and with enough
Swiss francs for two opera seats in his pocket, K. crossed the (low)
threshold of the back entrance. The banister: on the right. He hadn't
even inquired about the stairs. Had he hoped they would prove
insurmountable at the last minute? Step after step the narrow staircase
wound steeply upwards. No blood-red Buñuel baroque here, just some
artificially lightened IKEA cherry wood. A bathroom with a shower,
three doors, one of which was open. Inside, Engelbert Humperdinck was
singing. The waiting room, however, was empty. He didn't sit down,
for the chairs seemed low and he was already a bit tired from having
climbed the steps. What to do? He could find relief in the bathroom now
that he'd overcome the real challenge—the two flights of stairs. At least,
there were no magazines on the little table; no multi-board-member
types (Swissair, chemicals, arms trade, culture, nuclear power plant,
National Council) zipping up their flies on their way out of a room. A
hand beckoned to K. from the opened door and he tottered inside.

"Be comfortable, sugar," Sugar said.

Hanging on the wall was a poster of Marilyn in *Some Like it Hot*,
and for this reason, Sugar's name was Sugar—Sugar Kane, the sister of
Will Kane, the town marshal of Hadleyville from *High Noon*. Sugar
was also from Paris, Séverine's closest friend, she confided to K. in a
Brazilian accent.

"Why don't you be cozy with me, sugar?"

Because K. was loyal; unfit, but nevertheless a valiant Swiss soldier
who knew what was right and proper. Sugar Kane closed the door behind
her. The bed was low, but he would manage it. He wiggled the chair that
stood by the window closer, left-right, left-right, until his little dance
had moved it to the desired position. He needn't worry about the chair
slipping away when he had to stand up: wall-to-wall carpeting. But K.
still wasn't "comfortable," for unforeseen questions had arisen: should
he wait for Séverine, should he make himself "comfortable," and if so,
how "comfortable"? Should he allow her to make him "comfortable"
and was that included in the price? What were the rules of the game here?
Did one shake hands? Should he have brought flowers? Should he light a
cigarette (he didn't smoke) and position himself, like in the movies, with
his back to the window? Why was it that K. spent his time at university
dissecting words like "nothing" or "hell" to their very cores while failing

to research such a life-altering step? Hadn't he studied initiation rights enough—even though there was always that fade-out right before the actual act of initiation and then a cut to the next morning when the to-be-initiated was now an initiate. And, most important: what about the instrument in question here, the muscle some claimed wasn't really a muscle—what was it then? Assuming he made himself "comfortable," what then? Wouldn't that be rude, an insult? Was it not rude of Séverine to keep him waiting? Was she taking a real good shower? What was she doing while K.'s body took over the thinking for K.? He unbuttoned his shirt and was horrified; for a moment, he saw himself lying naked on the bed, incapable of standing up, while Sugar ran off with his clothing. Police sirens wailed and then fell silent.

But he didn't care about anything now. He undid his pants and let them slip to the floor. Sat on the bed, which was lower than expected, unlaced his shoes, and was trapped.

He was here to have sex; and, to have sex, he had to separate the sex from his illness, which he believed was the only thing standing in the way of his having uninhibited sex. So to execute the separation once and for all he'd decided to experience heaven in Séverine's hell. He was here to screw himself into fitness. To screw himself to the level of a soldier-citizen recognized by Switzerland. Once he'd screwed according to regulation, everything would be okay, all problems would be screwed from the world, no one would sneak a suspicious look at his fly anymore, because self-confidence would finally pearl on his forehead. K. would be ready for a wife and children, 'til death do them part. Maybe even with affairs on the side.

What she wore? Not much. I remember something blue, something light. Something with spaghetti straps. A scarf reminiscent of a dishtowel. Gold-colored sandals. Red toenails. Séverine breathed a "Hi" into the room and made herself "comfortable." When she saw me pulling my leg onto the bed she said, "Take your time" and meant, "Don't take mine." She didn't even close the door.

And Buñuel? In a biography I read later I discovered that the young Buñuel hadn't gone to a brothel at all. He didn't have the money. Or the guts. He had to imagine his sex stories himself. But once he'd thought up enough of them, and also had the money, he is said to have visited whorehouses repeatedly. Until he entered the Kingdom of God.

- 3 -

They met at university. Neither one of them had been able to completely part with their shared hometown; Tori lived in a small, poorly heated apartment and K. in the basement of his childhood. Both commuted. Tori took the roundabout route to Constance, going by train. She had to change trains twice—three times on the weekend if she wanted to go to the library—and once she arrived at the station, she often had to wait forty-five minutes for the connecting bus. K. covered the same distance by car, including customs clearance, in under fifty minutes. Once he'd even managed it in just forty-three.

To speed up the border proceedings, which in his opinion were superfluous, K. tossed the badge with the international wheelchair symbol onto his dashboard. This showed, by means of a few broad strokes, a wheelchair with a male (never a female) occupant, reducing those affected to their physical restrictions. Applied discrimination. Still, K. didn't want to renounce his use of the wheelchair symbol at the German-Swiss border, for the customs officials waved him through as soon as they saw it.

That wasn't quite okay, Tori thought, once she'd started getting rides with him to the university. He was using his disability to gain an advantage and that was immoral, she said.

K. argued that he put the sign there so that every time he crossed the border he wouldn't have to explain to the officials that it was hard for him to get out of the car and open his trunk. The wheelchair symbol, however, produced a revealing misconception, he continued. From the fact that a disabled person sat behind the wheel, the officials inferred that this person, because disabled, was not to be thought capable of smuggling anything across the border. *That* was immoral, for it constituted discrimination, and that he gained this ridiculous advantage as a result was beside the point, given the context, and, what's more, was itself ridiculous.

What was immoral, Tori would not give in—Tori never gave in as he'd soon find out—was that with the sign he wasn't actually proving he was a disabled person who couldn't open his trunk himself, but merely *claiming* to be such. This claim, verified only with difficulty, rested on trust; not on the Darwinian the-stronger-eats-the-weaker but on the Rousseauian *contrat social*, upon which, in turn, Western Civilization was based, and it was precisely this, this basic trust, that he was abusing, should he still, in fact, be fully capable of getting out of his car and opening his trunk himself (something he was fundamentally required to offer to do for the trusting officers). Not only was he not doing this, but he was also leaving them to their belief that because he was disabled, he was a person incapable of smuggling, that he was, plainly and simply, morally better, and *that* was immoral. And, Tori said taking a breath, from that he was deducing his *right* to smuggle.

But he never smuggled more than the allowed pound of meat or a few liters of milk, K. mumbled.

That was irrelevant, Tori said triumphantly, for the fact that he smuggled at all only went to show that he was fully aware of the advantage he'd gained through his disability and the displaying of the wheelchair symbol. Where, she wanted to know, did he draw the line? Milk? Meat? Drugs? Money? Bombs?

And already Western Civilization was going up in flames. Tori savored his silence.

He would have the moral right of putting out his little sign, she said charitably, only when his illness had progressed to the point that it was impossible for him to get out of the car.

When he saw the twinkling in her steel-blue eyes, he was silenced and stepped on the gas.

"Slow down," she said, her feelings hurt.

Later it was Tori who tossed his wheelchair logo onto the dashboard; this way she didn't have to pay duty on the shopping they did in Constance every Thursday. But, for now, Tori and K. weren't married and didn't even drive to university in the same car. K. passed Tori's bus on the way to Constance, and she passed him on foot here and there in the sprawling corridors of the university. Waiting for him, the special student, was a special parking space behind a special fence, which only those special drivers—professors, delivery people, and special students— were permitted to go through who were able to place a special permit, provided with the University of Constance's stamp, on their dashboards.

His first attempt at finding the special entrance described to him over the telephone landed him in a storeroom where he found himself face to face with stuffed life forms, glass display cabinets with preserved innards, and deformed skeletons. So it was true, experiments were being done with living things, all biologists were Frankensteins, and he, the freak, would perish here, in this academic freak show, his limbs stuffed, his brain in formaldehyde, and his sperm in a freezer compartment. His second attempt got him to the right entrance. One floor down in the elevator, to –01, and a subterranean cement paradise at the University of Constance opened up for him, with a bookstore, a travel agency, and a branch of his bank. The ironic thing was, however, that literally every floor was reachable by elevator except for the one on which his Slavic studies seminars took place.

K. reached the mezzanine-level seminar room by taking the steps down half a floor from 03, and when the seminar was over he continued down to 02 where the elevator then brought him to 03 again. When descending stairs he had to step down on his right leg, as a result each stair delivered a hard blow to his right knee. For the sake of Pushkin, Lermontov, and the others he'd have—*thud, thud*—in a quarter-century, or even sooner, earned himself a case of gout or sclerosis, if not arthrosis. What's more he was gambling away any chance of an academic career with this time-consuming method of stair-mastering. The renowned Slavic studies professor, who drank coffee with Kristeva, followed by the doctoral candidates, who in turn drank coffee with the Slavic professor, hurried away after every seminar, taking the steps. Only those who could keep pace with the professor made it in time to the university café, where the various assistants' tasks that led to a bright academic future (copying, compiling, coffee-getting, calling Kristeva's secretary) were divvied up.

But it was thanks to these same steps that Tori spoke to him.

"Can I carry your bag for you?"

"It's all right."

He took the next step. *Thud.*

"I'll give it back to you at the bottom of the steps."

"Thanks," K. said, embarrassed.

Thud, thud.

-4-

K. was studying three languages (Russian, Czech, English), Tori, two (Italian, German). The only course they had together was "Visual Fetishism in the Work of L. Buñuel" taught by Professor A. Marinetti.

Professor Marinetti's smile was irresistible when she spouted incomprehensibilities about celluloid. Her silicon breasts heaved when she divulged delicious tidbits about Tristana (from Buñuel's *Tristana*) and Séverine, morsels marinated to indigestibility in Lacan, Derrida, and Foucault. She (A. Marinetti) also had full lips, which, as she told the class, without supplying any theoretical support, bespoke an unstoppable sensuality she put down to her Italian roots. It was in Rome, she explained, when overcome by a sultry southern night, her parents, both married to others, had yielded to desire and conceived her in an unlit corner of the Castel Sant'Angelo. Now, however, (she continued with a wink) back to Lacan, Derrida, and Foucault.

Tori and K. got to know one another better in the darkened seminar room where Marinetti was showing *Belle de Jour*. That led to a glass of wine in an old town pub where K. knew his difficulties getting up from a chair could be avoided by luring Tori to the bar. Bar stools were good, bar stools were high. In the semi-darkness, he held on to the bar and allowed himself to slide onto the stool. A beer for K. and a glass of Bardolino for Tori, because the waiter was Italian, or at least looked Italian. The drink was followed by a modest stroll through Constance's old town, during which K., thanks to his waddle walk, was able to slip his arm through Tori's. Wedged beneath the windshield wiper was a ticket. Had he deployed the wheelchair symbol, the privilege of parking where others were not permitted could have been his, but that would have pointed out an aspect of his personality that, at such an early stage of becoming acquainted, he didn't want to draw needless attention to. He pocketed the parking ticket casually; his momentary fitness had been worth it.

He brought Tori, who insisted on taking the train home, to the train station, where they had an exchange of glances that augured a kiss. Elated, he stepped on the gas and pictured her surprised face when she saw him outside the train station in St. Gallen. He would offer to take her home, or at least to the bus, and perhaps the kiss in the offing might materialize that very night. In front of the train station he discarded the idea as too childish and drove off, hoping she hadn't seen him. At home, he regretted not having waited. He couldn't sleep and poured himself a grappa. He was in love.

As chance would have it Buñuel's *Tristana* was playing that same week as part of a mini Spanish film festival in the only theater in the city not obsessed with Hollywood. The theater had obscenely low seats, which K. now simply decided to risk; somehow or other he'd manage to stand up. The man sitting next to him looked strong. Tori would also no doubt help, and this way he'd hang in her arms for the first time. Wasn't his muscle weakness actually a decisive seductive force, one he'd so criminally neglected all these years? Might he have had a girlfriend earlier on if he'd listened to his doctor, who'd assured him he needn't worry about finding a girl, as girls liked taking care of boys? He decided it was time to stop standing in the way of the happiness of all those young women out there... Only it turned out that the logistics of his getting out of the chair no longer played a role, for Tori and K. kissed while sitting. And they sunk deeper and deeper into the seats K. had been so afraid of just moments before.

-5-

What's striking about the two Buñuel films is that at the end of both, one of the protagonists is in a wheelchair: Pierre in *Belle de Jour* (1967) and Tristana in the film of the same name from 1970. K. was especially fascinated by *Belle*, and Tori by *Tristana*. They watched both films on video in bed, over and over, their preferences becoming interchangeable, the way preferences always became interchangeable between those destined for one another: soon Tori wanted to watch *Belle* again, then K. *Tristana*—this way they'd each come a little closer to unlocking one another's secret.

Tristana is unfaithful to Don Lope, but once she falls ill with a tumor in her leg she returns to her benefactor. She loathes him because he takes her in again and hates her lover for letting her go. Nevertheless, she marries Don Lope, because this way she can punish them both. Her leg must be amputated below the knee (see the picture on p. 215). Legs from the knee down, particularly feet (compare L. Buñuel's *Viridiana*, 1961), symbolize sexuality and its (dys)function for Buñuel. From then on, Tristana gets around by means of crutches or a wheelchair. Don Lope still wants her, for now the beautiful Tristana belongs to him alone: no one else will desire a disabled woman and a disabled woman cannot run off—literally. Professor Marinetti avoided looking at K. when she'd made this remark, while K. tried to remember later if this wasn't when Tori had first eyed him with interest. Don Lope is triply mistaken: first, Tristana locks him out of her room, even on their wedding night; second, her beauty fades within a few months; and third, she kills him. It could be argued (and Tori did this, equipped with Professor Marinetti's tools in K.'s bed) that he also would have died if Tristana hadn't faked calling the doctor, but what counts is the intention, and that was sexual crippling, followed by murder. As if she herself might be dying, Tristana sees her life running in reversed sequence, until "The End" reminds the viewer that it's just a movie.

Belle de Jour tells the story of Séverine (again, Catherine Deneuve) a woman who acts out her sexual fantasies. She works in an *etablissement* as "Belle de Jour," between two and five in the afternoon, allowing her to arrive home in time for her other life with her somewhat boring but kind husband Pierre. Fantasies intersect, as do realities. One of Belle de Jour's clients refuses to accept the limitations (time, place) imposed on him. One evening he appears at Séverine and Pierre's apartment, but is sent away by Séverine. The client shoots Pierre as he is coming home, paralyzing him. A "friend" enlightens Pierre about his wife's double life, but it remains unclear whether Pierre has understood the friend at all. Séverine's dream world, however, seems intact, if not perfect. At the end of the film, Pierre suddenly stands up to pour his wife a whiskey, as if he's forgotten his paralysis, or as if Séverine had imagined (wished?) this as well. Or, is it her powers of imagination that have brought him to his feet?

-6-

At first Tori's mother refused to acknowledge K.'s existence. Every three weeks Tori visited her mother, drank unsweetened coffee with her in the kitchen, contemplated the two church towers as if they were one, and tried to steer the conversation around to K.

She could go to hell, K. said. Anyhow, he wouldn't come crawling on his knees.

Tori was doing this just to annoy her, the mother told her friends. In the past, she said, all she had to do was mention to Tori that a certain cup was her favorite for it to be in pieces a moment later.

The friends, however, only remembered the little girl Tori, who—smartly dressed, a lily in her hair, and a perfect, well-rehearsed curtsy—served a cake she had baked herself, as a surprise, to the *kaffeklatsch*; to which her mother said, "But we already have a cake, silly!"

Of course even back then it was best to simply ignore her until she came to her senses, the mother said. She'd run away but would soon be back, tied to her mother's apron strings, sometimes both at the same time. It was always the same with her daughter. But she *did* always come to her senses, her daughter.

K. sometimes thought about whether the reason someone like Tori even slept with someone like him was because she wanted to know what it was like with someone like him. Didn't feel like that, though. What if Tori just plain loved him, without any *if*'s, *and*'s, or *but*'s?

The world belonged to them, and everywhere in their world, there was always a bed. It didn't even have to be a bed.

How sweet the daughter's revenge on her mother would be when it turned out that the Catholic daughter would put a little crippled kid on God's earth! A soulless, little cripple, whose damnation was written on his body and who had to atone for his sins, for all to see. How nicely it would punctuate her martyr's existence. Wasn't that always how it worked? Crucifixion, then canonization?

Nevertheless, as time went on, Tori's mother was able to warm to K.'s existence in the life of her daughter, even if she wasn't yet thrilled with the situation. K. and Tori, already secretly betrothed, owed their hesitant reception into the family to a particularly important Catholic holiday from which no one was allowed to be absent. K. chose not to be offended. Everything would take its course. Plus, he was hungry and the dinner table promised a lavish meal. It turned out to be a delightful evening. K. had a lively discussion with Tori's brother, a soldier in the Swiss army, about whether neutral Switzerland should buy the new F-18 fighters or not. The brother was for the F-18s; K., in theory, against. No one said anything about screwing cripples. The head of the family giggled for no reason, as if his daughter still sat beneath the table pinching him in the calf. In the end, Switzerland bought the F-18s.

The F-18 brother then wanted to get to talking about something else, "to be quite frank" with K. Now, K. really shouldn't take it personally, but "when it came right down to it," he considered a life like K.'s, "inferior." K., at long last able to look one of these "Unfit!" stampers in the eye, thanked him for his sincerity but couldn't promise him with any real conviction that he wouldn't, in fact, take what he had said personally.

K. had underestimated his longing to be a fit person among fit people. He should have thrown his beer in the stamper's face. He conformed as well as possible, something that was possible less and less frequently, or wasn't possible at all when chairs and steps were involved, which, when he thought about it, was actually always the case. So he resolved to stop thinking about it.

Tori used the important holiday—which, as every year, despite the Crucifixion, was drawing to its conciliatory, upbeat close—to announce her engagement to K.

It was around this time that Tori's father had gotten down to business with his drinking and brought an end to his existence in the apartment with its view of the cathedral. The divorce was on its way.

Tori's mother accepted being a fallen soul right in front of the church's very eyes, losing her devout friend Dorothea in the process. She acquired herself a Protestant admirer, who started spending the night more and more often. In the cathedral, she sat only in the last pew.

Nothing more stood in the way of Tori and K.'s marriage.

They stood in three rows, side by side, in rank and file on the top floor of the Nursing-or-Something-Supplies-Store—these chairs with wheels. These misassembled bicycles. These off-road office chairs. These muscle prostheses.

K., with pretty Tori on his arm, inspected the troops in statesmanlike manner. The gleam of chromium steel, the smell of leather. That one there? Wow! Even had a horn. Or what about this one? Was the container mounted on the back for ski poles? Oh K., Tori groaned, you and your clever commentary. She was more serious about the whole business than he was. The ski pole rack was, of course, for canes. For part-time walkers, like him. At the time, he didn't yet have a cane, but he did want a wheelchair. Tori was getting impatient. They took a few steps back to get a look at the whole lot. The wheelchairs snarled, hissed, bared their teeth, pawed the ground as if their wheels had hooves, charged him, rolled over him, tore him to pieces, ripped him to shreds. Dizzy, K. held on to his wife.

They were buying his first wheelchair for a long trip to Italy. This particular piece of equipment, which he didn't really need yet, would give them both more mobility. He could still walk distances of up to five hundred meters. On muscular days, he could even cover six hundred, and on Tori's arm, up to a thousand meters. After that, however, he had to rest. He sat in a restaurant or in the car and let his muscles relax so they'd be good for another few hundred meters or at least, depending on how "muscular" the day had been, a few dozen. What if he were to sit in a wheelchair instead and simply continue onward? Roll on while sitting? He'd have to get used to the wheels that would become his legs. But this also had the advantage, however, that he could accustom himself a little to that time when he'd only be able to move around this way, so that he could outfox his less-muscular future with the still-quite-muscular present. For the time being, however, and this may account for the euphoric humor he brought to the task of buying a wheelchair, he was delighted that he'd once again be able, with strong Tori behind him, to take more extended strolls through cities, to walk along (flat) seaside promenades, and even, when the trails were well-trampled, to explore woodland paths...

"Who is the wheelchair for?" the salesman who had joined them asked. Tori smiled. He could just as easily have asked whether K. had written the screenplay for *Dr. Strangelove*, K. felt so flattered. "For me!" K. cried, standing upright and relishing the salesman's skeptical look.

The salesman cozied up to Tori to find out what was behind her companion's statement. Smiling, Tori confirmed what had been said, while K. inspected the wheelchairs again, at an even brisker pace for the salesman's benefit. All that was missing was a pointer. No, not a battery-powered chair. It had to be light and foldable, so it would fit in the trunk. Most were foldable, but the lightest model was the titanium one, which was too expensive.

"Even here, there's the Fiat-Ferrari distinction," K. mumbled. "A disability is a luxury good you have to be able to afford," Tori added. The salesman nodded sympathetically.

K. dropped down into the expensive titanium contraption, the evolution of which, the salesman rhapsodized, had something to do with the American conquest of the moon and the consequent development of the Teflon frying pan and titanium metal, which was all nonsense, but K. let it go, gliding back and forth in the luxury chair. It *was* comfortable, had the easiest roll, but the price, the price.

He leapt out of the chair. The salesman gave Tori a questioning look. Was the guy making a stupid joke? She shook her head: no joke. Nor did K. really jump out of the chair. Inspecting the wheelchair troops had made him tired, and what he'd really done was grab hold of the armrests and lever himself onto his feet. He saw that the salesman wanted to ask his customer what was wrong (so young, so agile, such a pretty companion, and yet, a wheelchair?), but the Grail question seemed too intimate, even in a store like this one. Instead, the salesman went to fetch catalogues.

K. plopped himself into another titanium model, forcefully rolled himself a few meters, then applied the brakes so hard he nearly toppled out of the chair. It was like the toy racetrack he had as a child, where the main attraction was to speed up the cars coming out of the curves, only now he himself sat in the racing car. Parking the Ferrari back in the row he avoided Tori's look. Honked. Grinned like the child he would like to have been at this moment.

In the end, K. decided for an 11.5-kilogram model without a horn; aluminum, 2,800 francs, and with metallic paint finish for an additional charge. The seat cushion was extra too and could be purchased on the first floor. Oh yes, definitely necessary. Could they take the wheelchair with them now? No, it could be picked up the following day. The salesman still had to measure Tori. Since most of the time she would be the one pushing K., the handles had to be adjusted for her.

The bill (with ten percent deductible) went to the Swiss Invalid Insurance Administration, as it was actually called. K.'s independent medical examiner had already assured the invalid-processing administrators in writing that K. had become largely unfit to walk and thus was entitled to the reimbursement of the so-called "additional expenses to meet the needs of the disabled," which were a consequence of the invalid life he led. He left the Nursing-or-Something-Supplies-Store on his own two legs and the following day picked up his substitute legs for distances of five hundred meters or more.

- 8 -

Nevertheless the trip to Italy turned out to be a fiasco. Language course for Tori in Emilia Romagna; time for K. in the hotel room to write his story about the adventures of a women's lingerie sales rep. The wheelchair stayed in the car when they were in town. In the afternoon, he met Tori (Hanro bra, LaPerla panties) at a sidewalk café. Day trips to Bologna and Urbino in the wheelchair. In Ferrara, K. (on foot, his wheels stayed in the trunk) finally met the distant relative. She leaned over to shake his hand and he smiled up at her. In Ferrara, Tori and K. strolled the paths of the Finzi-Contini. Tori wanted to write her thesis on them: *The Jewish Element in G. Bassani*. She bought herself an inexpensive menorah at a flea market. The wall, behind which they imagined Micól Finzi-Contini in her short white miniskirt and holding a tennis racket, was too high to be able to see anything—for the seated as well as the standing.

All the same they had their best sex during the trip. It happened after an animated visit to a porn theater in the neighboring little town—a whim, nothing more. None of Tori's fellow students had seen them. Never before had they burrowed so deep in their down quilts. Even though she admitted it was "really nice" ("not that it wasn't usually nice"), she didn't want to go to the porn theater a second time. It started to disturb him that more and more frequently Tori was claiming certain things had been his idea. And it wasn't even important whether they were good or bad, whether the things in question were successful or unsuccessful.

The purchasing of the wheelchair started to become his idea. He was grateful to Tori that she'd stood at his side during this difficult step. Do what you have to do before you *really* have to do it, she'd advised. And he listened. Buying the wheelchair was an important and good decision. Painful, drastic, and yet helpful, because so much became possible again; a relief, because there was a lot he no longer had to take on himself. And yet it all of a sudden became his idea and his idea alone. It started when she said this was how one got to know the constitution of the world: steps everywhere, ramps nowhere, neither at the main post office nor at the zebra crossings. The world was filled with obstacles. For every stupid bird in the Brazilian jungle, Tori complained, there's a species protection law, but no such thing for people with disabilities. Then she'd suddenly surprised him by saying that she'd really prefer living in an apartment in the old town, only, because of the wheelchair, of course, that wouldn't work, as these buildings, she'd continued, often had no elevators. Soon he noticed the anger with which Tori would fling his wheelchair into the trunk.

Even their wedding became his idea. No sooner had they gone ahead with it than she gave him the feeling he'd talked her into it. Marriage, how bourgeois. In the registrar's office it turned out that keeping her maiden name at this point in the process would cost an extra fifty francs. Had she thought about this earlier, she'd have gotten her name (which already belonged to her!) for free. K. also found it unfair. He offered to pay the fifty francs and not charge it to their shared account, but he wasn't to get off so lightly. The registrar became impatient. Tori decided in favor of the fifty francs. As they posed in front of the town hall for photographs, the sun broke through the clouds for the first time that day, which was generally viewed to be a good omen for their marriage. Tori asked her mother to get the photos developed, but under no circumstances at such-and-such photo shop, as they had ruined her film once before. The mother didn't have to be told twice and the photo shop lived up to its poor reputation. The marriage lasted three-and-a-half years.

An incident during that Italian trip that K. has been unable to explain to this day because it was so singular in his life occurred in Urbino. He was waiting on the sloping old town square in front of a boutique in whose display window Tori had spotted a blouse in her favorite color (steel blue). Did he sense their relationship was nearing its end or did he no longer want to wait under the "NO DOGS ALLOWED" sign with its international dog symbol? Releasing the brakes of his wheelchair he let himself roll into a Volkswagen bus from Schleswig-Holstein. His knee hurt for days.

When Tori came out she said she did like the blouse but she already had enough blouses. He offered to buy it for her as a present but she declined. He noticed that she had gotten thinner again.

"My leisure-time chair," he called his first wheelchair.

"My convertible," because he thought he would only need it in good weather.

"My lifeboat," because he knew that with the help of the chair (and the person who pushed it) he'd be able to get everywhere again.

-9-

He blamed Italy. How couldn't it be Italy's fault? Tori's whole life leaned toward the south and he began to stand for the north. This was why she wanted to go without him to Italy. This had been her idea, the only one she didn't attribute to him.

They had planned a year, maybe two, maybe a life, in Rome together. He could finish writing his new book (after abandoning the story of the lingerie sales rep he started working on a novel about an unbeatable chess player for whom only one opponent remained: the ghost of a long deceased grandmaster) while she would teach German at the Swiss Institute. His hope was that the institute would install a stair elevator because of him. Soon he noticed that Tori spoke of the Rome trip only in the singular. When *I'm* in Rome. As soon as *I'm* in Rome. Once *I've* settled in Rome. When he asked her about this, she divulged some of her plan. She thought he could join her two or three months later, since he still had obligations in Switzerland, after all—his many projects—and, anyway, it wasn't so easy in Rome in a wheelchair, the seven hills and such.

The three months Tori wanted to spend in Rome by herself turned into a half year. Then they didn't speak about Italy at all anymore. The ultimate result was three months in Ferrara; Tori wanted at least to spend her semester abroad in Italy—"*I* wouldn't let her go," her mother said every chance she got—and stayed with the distant relative in Ferrara again. They spoke by telephone every Sunday morning, K. reporting on the progress of his projects and Tori on the progress of her thesis. The distant relative had perfected her spying. With Bassani's book in her bag, Tori prowled the alleyways of Ferrara, which, in view of what was done to the Finzi-Continis, seemed gloomy to her. She had no appetite and lost weight, as she had done during her first Ferrara stay. An imaginary knife bore into her bare back with ever more frequency. After six weeks, K. visited her for a few days. Tori had become alarmingly thin again but refused to go back to Switzerland with him. When she finally did return she was "skinny as a skeleton," as her mother said, adding, smiling at K.: "Really, what man would want such a thing?"

Tori wanted to have her own room. For Bassani, but also to sleep in. They put the double bed in the guest room, which was just big enough for it, and the pullout couch that had been in the guest room was moved into the bedroom. K. watched television, went out with friends, and fell asleep reading. Tori put up heavier curtains. Once he snuck around the house and placed a good-luck chocolate ladybug in her window, which she thanked him for but didn't eat (he found it in her ashtray). A kitchen knife lay on her desk; every time he saw it he brought it back to the kitchen, only to have it reappear on her desk a short time later. She said she drew the curtains because this way she didn't have to look at the grille in front of the window and felt less trapped. She said sometimes she could barely breathe. She felt threatened. The man with the knife was creeping about outside. *The* man with *the* knife, not *a* man with *a* knife. She knew he was imaginary, but that didn't make him any less real, she said.

She only spent the night with him sometimes. If he called out to her, she said she was coming in a couple minutes, but then usually slept in her room all the same. The last time they slept together was after K. had spent an evening with friends watching the Bulgaria/Germany game (Bulgaria won). A woman he met there kept returning her hand to his thigh. And K. found himself wondering with whom he had actually slept, or had wanted to sleep with, after Tori withdrew from him and, remarking that she still had work to do, disappeared into her room.

-10-
Almost All the Way to the South
Excerpt from a screenplay

Medium close-up: TORI *is sitting at her desk and has turned her back to the camera. She is wearing a steel-blue blouse. She winces, as if someone has hit her, but she doesn't turn around. Roses can be seen through the iron-grilled window. Beyond these, trees and the Alps in the* foehn. *On the bed is a suitcase, open, and overflowing with clothing.* K. *is standing by the bookcase, holding on to it.*

K.

What are you doing?

TORI

wincing again

The knives...

Outside someone passes by the window: a shadow dismembered by the window grille. Close-up of TORI *from behind.*

TORI

I want to move out. I've found an apartment. I... It isn't expensive. Just one room with a kitchen and a bathroom... I thought... until we can get along again, I... I can't go on any longer.

Turning towards him.

Do you want to see it with me?

Through the window a shadow can be seen darting by. The camera pulls back. A knife is stuck in TORI's *back.*

K.

offscreen

You're staying?

TORI *putting the clothing from the suitcase back in the wardrobe.*

TORI

My exams, I can't go now... will you help me study? I... the knives...

K.

Don't I have a right to know what you're accusing me of?

TORI
hesitating
You know… it's so hard for me… You… you… just can't
do everything.

She sits at her desk again.

K.
laughing affectedly
Of course I can't do everything. I'm not Superman.

TORI
That makes it so difficult. You and your clever commentary.
That's all you have, clever sayings for everything.

A knife bores into her back again.

TORI
hesitating, looking up, now firmly
I mean, in bed. If you really must know. It's in bed. You
can't do everything in bed! Are you satisfied now?

K.
unsure
What do you mean?

TORI
You know what I mean. You're no acrobat. You can't do
all the positions.

K.
Is there someone else?

TORI
angrily
No, there's no one else! Can there be no other reason
for you? If there is someone else then everything's my
fault. But I won't do you that favor. There's no one else!

K.
So there is someone else! You're carrying on with
someone else and blaming me for—

TORI
There is no one else!

An empty wheelchair can be seen through the window.

TORI
sighing
A year ago there was someone, I… nothing happened.
We kissed and… I sensed, because it was even possible…

K.

What?

TORI

That I could kiss someone else. That I wanted to. But that can't be. We have problems.

K.

To figure that out, you had to kiss someone else?

Through the window the shadow can be seen sitting down in the wheelchair.

K.

Are you still seeing him?

TORI

No.

A knife sinks into her back again.

TORI

My needs have simply changed.

K.

loudly

How do you want me to do it to you? From behind? Until you can't anymore? From the front? Standing? In mud? Should I throw mud at you? Should I screw you in the mud, you slut?

TORI

softly

Please don't be vulgar, like... like that time you talked me into... that film, please, I... It's not just in bed. I also want to be able to go skiing with my partner... up into the mountains, I... I want a normal life...

She looks through the window grille.

She is skiing. A MAN in a ski suit races after her.

K.

bitter

That... no, that I can't do.

TORI *and the* MAN *dash over the slopes. They stop in a little wood.*

K.

angrily

Is that what you're blaming me for? That I... have a disability?

TORI
at her desk
No, of course not... Only there's just so much you can't do and I... for example, going for walks... I... I want a man to be able to help me out of my coat... carry my suitcases... protect me... that he...

TORI *dashes through the little wood on skis; the* MAN *hurtles after her. She stops by a tree. The* MAN *races up to her, slows down, bumps into* TORI, *who cries out, then laughs. He presses her against the tree, tears off her scarf, kisses her neck.*

K. *is sitting on the barstool in the kitchen playing with a knife.*

TORI
entering
What are you thinking about?

Tristana's artificial leg.

- 11 -

When Tori finally called on Sunday afternoon—since Friday she'd been traveling by train back and forth across Switzerland (but not beyond, as her rail pass wasn't valid for other countries) to gain some clarity about their relationship—K. heard noise in the background, noise that sounded southern. He should have known. So much for back and forth across Switzerland. And the clarity?

Tori said she could barely understand what he was saying it was so loud. Anyway, she had only wanted to tell him that she was coming home Monday, late afternoon, and then they could talk.

Was she alone? he asked.

It's really loud here, she said.

He shouted, she shouted something back, then they were cut off. How good that felt! The neutral misfiring of an electronic signal, and suddenly, quiet. Everything gone. The south, Tori, whomever she may have kissed, gone. He hadn't reckoned on this: he'd expected dull, paralyzing despondency with the silence, but instead new prospects opened up. When the phone rang again, he ignored it, but when the ringing stopped he started writing a desperate love letter to Tori, one which he didn't send and didn't even end: "Dearest, beloved, darling, let's...! ... Is it really?... After all these years!?" The damn south. He was simply no match for it.

He slept well and spent Monday morning revising his new novel (about a mediocre civil servant who murders a member of the government in order to release himself from his mediocrity) and it seemed to him that his ideas were flowing a bit more freely again. Then, becoming sad, he stopped working, and called a friend to see if she wanted to get a cup of coffee. She did, for she liked analyzing other people's relationships— though, she wouldn't be heard from again for months if someone went to the trouble of subjecting one of her relationships to scrutiny. Over coffee they spoke about him and Tori and deliberated the pros and cons, the not-only-but-also, the staying-together and the splitting-up-forever. The coffee tasted bitter, but the post-coffee purchase of a "virginal" appointment book for 1995 proved illuminating and symbolic. Afterwards, they went to the movies where a German comedy with the fitting title, *The Unloved* or *Unmanned Man* or whatever it was, was playing. "Let me know what happens," the friend encouraged him after the film and kissed him on the lips. "It'll be okay," K. said, clutching his appointment book bravely.

Tori didn't arrive until eight. She sat with him at the kitchen bar and was silent.

And? What do you mean *and*? You have nothing to say? No, forget it. After all that thinking, nothing? Nothing! He played with the knife lying on the bar. She'd gotten even skinnier, in just three days. Hungry? No. So what about the clarity that the tracks of Swiss Rail—*Please*, she interrupted him. For heaven's sake, eat something.

He'd recently seen her naked in bed. How bony she'd become. She admitted to weighing fifty-one kilograms, meaning she weighed around forty-seven. When he thought about what her mother had said, he realized he no longer felt attracted to her. How long had that been the case? It consoled him a little that he wasn't the only one with a body that one could be scandalized by. His shoulders were as bony as her butt cheeks. Bone hills, ridge walks. His waist had gotten fleshy; hers barely still had any fleshiness at all. Her skin hung loosely on her back, just as his stomach muscles had gotten flabby in front. Was this what the south did to her? Was it him? Was he the reason she looked this way? Was this what her skeletal body wanted to communicate to him? Once it had been the father, then the mother, now him? He put the knife back on the bar.

"What now?" he asked impatiently and with a determination that surprised even him. "Tori?"

"What do you mean?"

Even her face was bony. Every bone was an accusation. He was to blame for every visible bone. Was this why she was eating less and less: to make her accusation more barbed?

"You know what I mean."

No more knives, he could tell by looking at her. They were beyond knives. He was finally determined to talk; she wanted only to be silent. It was over, but it wouldn't be Tori who'd draw the curtain on their relationship. Whoever did that was to blame; whoever was chased away was the victim.

He took the knife in his hand again. Silver blade, black handle. It was a good knife. Then he realized the problem wasn't that Tori was a more or less normal young woman whose more or less normal needs had exceeded the boundaries of her more or less normal marriage. He was the problem: not because he had a disability, but because he hadn't let her go. He had accommodated her in everything so that she had had to resort to extremes: making him feel disabled.

"If you want to stay, stay, and we'll try once more. One last time. If you don't, then go. But go now."

It was a month until Christmas. Who wanted to move out before Christmas? The unsullied appointment book for the unsullied New Year was in his car. In *his* car.

She wasn't looking at him anymore; she was staring at the patterned surface of the bar, at the knife he'd put down again. Finally, she slid off the barstool and went into the bedroom. He could hear her packing, then calling her mother. Before going outside to wait for her mother she placed the key on the bar and said, "I'm going then."

...the postcard T. received from her uncle after he heard she wanted to marry me: "...and I'm confident that in good time you will abandon the wrong path you have chosen. Your Uncle Priest." By wrong path, the good uncle meant that his niece, who was of able body and thus, as such, "normal"—so, basically, of sound mind—intended to marry a disabled man. The man of God didn't take the trouble to get to know me. T.'s uncle was a priest in the Catholic Church and as a Brother Nicholas preacher in Flüeli-Ranft was an advocate of brotherly love. Of course, only among those who could walk, for there was much to pilgrimage in Flüeli-Ranft. T. married me all the same. She also divorced me; our wrong path had been another, however.

Now that Tori had not only left him, but Switzerland as well, Tori's mother could finally muster enthusiasm for K. She'd sometimes stand at his door with homemade bread, but he didn't want to talk about Tori. He praised the bread and Tori's mother divulged stories from her daughter's past, all of which amounted to the same thing (she'd "always known"), and all of which were channeled into K.'s notebook for his Tori project.

Even though he soon felt relieved, K. knew it would take him a while to get over his seven years with Tori. He found writing easy again. Walking wasn't going so well, but he was coping. He listened to Tori's mother talk about what a great guy he really was "at heart," with A-1 character, and this difficult fate, and that he never complained and always said he was doing well. K. resolved to start complaining more frequently. He fed the bread to the birds.

As time went by he was told that Tori was living in Siena with an Italian professor she'd met at the University of Constance. No one claimed to know his name or when exactly the two had met. Other sources indicated that Tori had bought a VW bus with Marinetti, their former media studies professor, and since then had been driving southward, destination South Pole. Either was fine with K.

"Typical Tori," Tori's mother said years later, when she called K. for the last time to rave about a homemade loaf of bread that she then didn't bring over. "Typical. She'll come to her senses, my Tori."

K. sometimes still saw Tori's mother coming out of the cathedral, her gaze directed heavenward. But he never saw Tori again.

Part ◪ Two
continuation

"Tori."

"Who?"

"Viktoria. My wife."

"What about her?"

"You asked me my wife's name. Her name is Viktoria. With a *K*."

"*K*?"

"Viktoria with a *K*, not a *C*. It's important to her."

"To who?"

"Vik-to-ri-a!"

"Don't yell."

"You're not listening to me."

"Of course, I'm listening."

Pause.

"I always listen!"

Pause.

"I am the world champion in listening!"

Pause.

"You see what it's gotten me..."

Pause.

"Another coffee?"

"No, thanks. I have to go."

"Me too. Always so much to do."

Pause.

"Besides, the coffee's not very good here."

Pause.

"Does she cook for you?"

"We cook for each other."

"Cook for each other. That's good. I cooked for you all sometimes. Sometimes we cooked together, you and I, on Sunday afternoons. Do you still remember?"

"Giant sandwich."

"Giant sandwich! Exactly! You take a giant cutting board, a giant knife, and two loaves of giant sandwich bread neatly cut by the giant father and then placed before the giant son to slice off the edges. The giant edges are then chopped up into teensy tiny pieces, which are put in a giant bowl for the giant bouillon. The soft parts of the bread are arranged on the giant cutting board so that they cover the entire wooden surface. Then a giant amount of quark-butter-chive spread is generously smeared on top. Layers of ham as foundation, then islands of salami, then pineapple rings, skewered giant radishes, onions, pickles, whatever one's giant heart desires. And then, the giant Spoerri was finished. But Spoerri wouldn't have enjoyed it because after the giant feast not the teensy tiniest crumblet was left for him to glue on to the plate and put under a glass cover. *Pause.* So, all in all, a giant treat. *Pause.* Of course, father and son left a giant mess in the kitchen and your mother got mad."

Pause.

"A gargantuan feast."

"What?"

"The giant sandwich."

"Gargan- what?"

"Gargantuan. An adjective meaning gigantic. From Gargantua, the giant in Rabelais' book."

"You went to college, not me."

"It was your book. I have the book from your library. Didn't you read it?"

"Don't know anymore. There were so many books."

"Three volumes in a slipcase. They were still wrapped."

"Then I probably didn't read them."

"Probably not."

"Gargantuan. I'll impress my artists with that. Gargantuan! Drop by the Hirschen sometime. I'm often there in the evenings with my artists."

"It's about time I get going."

"Are you living with your mother, you and your Viktoria-with-*K*?"

"Not with. We live in the same house…"

"On Alpsteinstrasse."

"In the basement apartment."

"Where I had to stay that time."

"That's where I have my office now."

Pause.

"Will the other two put in an appearance, too?"

"I don't know."

"Puck's still making mirrored cabinets?"

"Yes."

"And Mix? Still a councilman for that naysayer party. Read about him in the newspaper, too."

"Yes."

"That must really bug you!"

Pause.

"Saying no is good. You have to say no to everything. Always! See what happens when you don't."

Pause.

"Do they know you're here?"

"Yes."

"So you'll give them a report?"

"Yes."

"Whether the old man behaved himself or not."

"If you like."

"And then maybe they'll come, too."

"That's their decision."

"I won't beg. They can do what they want."

"And they will."

Pause.

"Is she waiting for you now?"

"Mother? No."

"I don't mean her. Your wife. Your Viktoria-with-*K*?"

"She's in Ferrara."

"In Ferrara. Really? What's she doing there, in Ferrara?"

"She's at school."

"At school. She can't do that here?"

"She's studying Romance languages."

"Romance languages?"

"Italian."

"I know. I'm not stupid."

"Ferrara is the city where Bassani's stories are set."

"Bassani?"

"An Italian writer. She's writing a paper about him."

"Shouldn't she be cooking for you? Who's cooking for you now?"

"My mother, sometimes."

"While your wife amuses herself in Italy?"

"Usually I cook myself."

"Can you cook?"

"Roast meat, salad dressings, fried eggs."

"I mean stand at the stove, that kind of thing."

"I cook things that don't take a lot of time."

"I do the same thing. Sometimes I have to sit down again after ten minutes. Enough time for a fried egg. No more giant sandwiches."

Pause.

"We have a bar near the kitchen so I only have to put the plate on the bar."

"Where the buffet was before. And the old farmhouse table? Where is that now? Sold?"

"Viktoria's using it as a desk."

"Where she's working on this..."

"Bassani."

"Bassani. I could've remembered. Your father is not old. He can still remember everything. Forgets nothing." *Pause.* "What did you do with the fireplace?"

"Made it smaller."

"Like everything, eh? Collection, business, family. Everything made smaller!"

"The old covering violated the fire prevention regulations."

"So it had to go."

226   Christoph Keller

"So it had to go."

Pause.

"Okay. I'll get the coffee."

"If you like. You all owe me a pile of money anyway. Millions! The house, the collection."

Pause.

Pause.

"A little hard for you to stand up. Not getting better either. What's it called again? Muscle wasting, right?"

"Spinal Muscular Atrophy."

"Doctors, all a bunch of—"

"So, take care."

"Come on, I'll walk you to your car. You came by car, didn't you?"

"That isn't necessary."

Pause.

"How come you're letting your wife spend an entire semester in Italy? I don't get it."

"Why shouldn't I? It is part of her degree."

"Is she pretty? I for one wouldn't let her out of my sight. Certainly not to the Italians. If she's pretty. Do you have a picture?"

Pause.

"You okay? The step here?"

Pause.

"There you have it. Even your father sometimes needs a cane for one confounded step."

Pause.

"Maybe you got this atrophy thing from me. Who knows? The way I'm walking."

Pause.

"These steps! These architects, they think they're something special if they can build steps everywhere."

Pause.

"What if she meets someone else?"

"She won't meet anyone else."

"I'd be more careful there. Especially you with your muscles. I bet you were lucky to get a woman to begin with."

Pause.

"How do you do it anyway?"

Pause.

"And then you let her go to Italy."

Pause.

"Don't walk so fast."

Pause.

"She'll screw you over, too. Just wait and see."

Pause.

"Is that your car? I could never afford that."

Pause.

"You okay? Oops, plopped himself down already. Well, not so bad, after all."

"So, take care."

"So you'll drop by the Hirschen? Or come to an opening?"

"Call me."

"You call me! Or just come. You're the one who wants something, after all. It wasn't me who was trying to kiss ass with a book now, was it?"

"We'll see."

"Do what you want. I, in any case, wouldn't let my wife go to Italy. Ferrara! Italia! *Occhi blu!* She's definitely doing it with this Bassani, your intellectual Viktoria-with-*K*!"

I s electrical engineering the free decision of the non-disabled for a disability? Who knows, maybe I'm unconsciously envied. Actually, I know I am. There's a lot I can't do, but there's a lot I don't have to do either. There are many small advantages. At some museums I don't have to pay the full admission price. More and more frequently I find parking spaces reserved for me. Considering what people are willing to do for a parking space that may even constitute a big advantage. I don't have to stand in line at the post office and I ride the bus for free. Though only in New York. In Switzerland, people with disabilities have to stand in line like everyone else—they do want their equal rights, after all. The question whether public transportation should be free or not for people like me isn't asked in Switzerland, because for the most part public transportation isn't wheelchair-accessible to people with disabilities anyway. And I don't have to go to war, an advantage that is potentially life-saving.

The main reason I am envied, however, I think, is that I really and truly profit from modern prostheses, while these same modern prostheses make non-disabled people into even more frenzied beings, effectively disabling them. Today's prostheses nudge me, the disabled person, closer to the non-disabled person, decreasing the difference between us. On the Internet, I am able to enter any store, can correspond with the entire world, and have access to all the information often denied me by the non-virtual world; in this way I have become to a large extent like everyone else again. In the professional world, however, an e-mail amounts to nothing more than increased pressure and higher

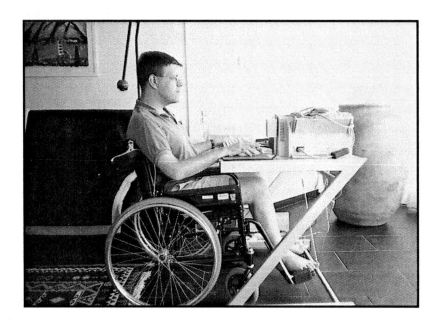

expectations, and a cell phone is merely a way for companies to keep their exhausted employees, now reachable day and night, on an even tighter rein. The non-disabled person and I are aligned in that we've agreed on the same prostheses, but for me the prostheses are more an advantage than a disadvantage—while they impose further restrictions on the non-disabled person, they give me more freedom of movement.

Next, we will become smaller. There's no longer any point in having such a large body when we don't really use it anymore. After all, our body is already a nuisance to us: cancer eats its way through our cells, bones break, pimples sprout on our faces. There's no point to our body; it makes us all into cripples at some time. Or is that the point?

And without bodies, movement is no longer necessary. All we need is a center of thinking and feeling. Our soul merely requires a hard disk. And this will become smaller and smaller. The ideal of our future form of existence is the smallest electronic unit of information: the bit.

1/0.

On/Off.

True/False.

This is, by the way, the solution to all the problems caused by humanity.

You can turn off your computer now.

230   Christoph Keller

T*ock.*

"Take it easy," the gallery owner mutters. He is sitting in his office in the atelier house. Although he knows he has to get up out of his chair, he stares ahead as if he could see his sluggish words floating through the room—and, in fact, in the semi-darkness between the narrow flight of stairs with its mooring rope banister and the all too clear demand ART IS SUPERFLUOUS. GO HOME, something does seem to rise up, gain in speed, and then disappear through the door in the corner opposite him and into the corridor. He looks at the clock.

He hears the front door again. Is Ms. Meili not at her perch, behind her little table in the corridor? He slips his bookkeeper's cap from his head and tosses it down next to the loupe he'd been using to study the contents of a new auction catalog. Once again a clock formerly in his possession had been subjected to the usual botched restoration job and is being offered below value. A spider's web covers Switzerland: it would be interesting to reconstruct the paths his dismembered collection had traveled from that summer in 1978 up to now, fall 1994. And he nearly loses himself in his musings again. *Knock-knock. Tick.* Of course, Ms. Meili forgot to unbolt the door again, and is sitting behind her table, staring at the door, wondering.

"The door!" he bellows.

"Take it easy," Ms. Meili shouts. Sometimes it's soothing to hear his own words coming from her mouth.

Sounds indicate that Ms. Meili is standing up. Wood on wood. *Tack-tack*. He heaves himself out of his chair. As if she had a wooden base. Did she? He grins. Is this why she always wears ankle-length skirts? She's been in his service for three years and yet he isn't even sure if she uses a cane or not. He reaches for his own, resolves at long last to buy a higher office chair, and sets off.

Another knock at the door (nothing can drive away a true art lover) and Ms. Meili is shouting her "come in!" This won't open the door either. When will she finally resign herself to the fact that a few weeks back he'd installed an additional bolt?

Who is it? *Tock*. A client? The bailiff? The Grim Reaper? Probably the landlord again, wanting to make sure his money, which he'd so very safely invested in art, is yielding a profit. The gallery owner is behind on the rent. Always has been. Catching his breath, he continues his journey to the door. He was able to string the landlord along awhile with paintings that actually belonged to his artists but then the landlord wanted more. "Now you belong to me, Föns," the landlord beamed when Föns handed him his certificate for ten percent of his art empire, antique shop, and gallery. Since then the landlord has been pestering

The atelier house.

him about the fluctuations in the art business even more frequently than he used to nag him with his overdue notices. He earned enough with his real estate and now wants to be a patron. A selfless sponsor of the arts. And this is a role he'll let him play. Making sure his share remains what it's worth, namely nothing, will be easy. At last, the gallery owner hears the metallic click of the new bolt.

In the corridor it occurs to the gallery owner that he has an opening today. His last one, as always. Who's showing? Claire. Claire Hofer, the artist, whose real name—as the wife of a banker, which is what she is in her less exciting life—is Wanda Mutz. She helps him look after the gallery; every so often her husband buys art for the teller area of his bank. He's thus far avoided setting foot in Claire's husband's bank, but how can he, caught in the net of greedy landlords, insatiable bankers, and the sticky threads his collection is pulling across the country, not show Claire? Besides her art is good, very good. What time is it? Not even six yet. *Tick.* The guests are early, as they always were.

"Mr. Metzler, welcome!" Ms. Meili cannot bring herself to greet the gallery's artists by their first names, even though she, like the gallery owner, refers to them as the gallery owner's children. "And you are Mr..."

"Keller," I say.

"Mr. Keller, Jr.!"

Ms. Meili is delighted and holds her hand out to me.

I give her a nod—there is no banister and I am holding on to the wall, behind which I partly disappear, outside her field of vision. Mr. Metzler—Larry to me—whom I met at the Hirschen the second time I went to see my father, offers to help me up the entrance steps, but this is a threshold I want to cross on my own.

"I am so pleased to finally meet you!" Ms. Meili cries, withdrawing her hand. "I devoured your books. I was especially amused by the one in which you let your father run off to the Val Müstair with that fashion floozy, who then turns around and walks out on him... Mr. Keller simply refuses to tell me whether it's a true story or not. He's just so happy you could come, even if, of course, he can't admit it. Not a peep. You know him. It's like pulling teeth. Oh, good, here he is finally! Mr. Keller, your son," as if she needed to acquaint father with son, and, likewise, "Mr. Keller, your father!"

While she talks I partly disappear behind the wall again and emerge on the second step.

"Welcome, son," my father says, standing behind Ms. Meili.

The first visitor, a woman, appears on the garden path. "You're— may I call you by your first name? I knew you were coming, Christoph!" I stand firmly on the second step and hold on to the wall to at least shake this hand. This woman, with her short boyish haircut and searching look, does not reveal who she is to me. She knows who I am, however; clearly everyone here does. "Can I help you?"

"Nice to meet you," I mumble and refuse her help. Too brusquely, though unintentionally so. Inexperienced helpers usually reach for the arm I'm supporting myself with, pulling me to the ground if I don't stop them in time. She lets go, is momentarily puzzled by my bad manners, but then smiles. I close my eyes so I no longer have to see myself sprawled on the ground in the entryway to the atelier house, surrounded by strange people—more visitors have since arrived—by Larry and my father, my legs outside the building, my upper body inside.

"You're sure you don't need any help?" Larry asks, still holding the door. I read fatigue and indifference in my father's face (had he been drinking?), and in Ms. Meili's, maternal regret that she cannot assist me. Behind her, next to the brochures and the gallery's printed materials, are stacks of my books and a postcard-sized piece of paper with the prices in my father's wide, green handwriting.

"You were doing better when I saw you at the Hirschen, weren't you?" he says.

I lift myself onto the last step, grab hold of the doorpost, and launch myself into the atelier house. I can finally shake Ms. Meili's hand and then my father's. Behind him, hanging on the wall, is the iron sculpture he stole from our garden.

"Nice," I say.

He gives me a conspiratorial wink. We enter the windowless gallery space, the room he'd walled up for a few months back in 1978, when he'd hidden his valuable items inside, concealing them first from the bankruptcy estate and then from us, his family.

"Isn't it?" my father says.

I nod. Nice here. Too nice.

There is a single piece of furniture in the gallery space: a long table on which there are snacks and refreshments for those attending the opening. Four large-scale abstract paintings hang in the room. This is the exhibition.

"This, by the way," Larry puts his hand on my arm, "is Claire, a colleague." Because things aren't moving quite fast enough for Claire, she adds: "It's my show!" and, laughing, takes me by the arm and leads me over to her paintings.

"Do you see what they're made of?"

I step closer. "Paper?"

Claire laughs. "Yes, it is paper, but what kind of paper? I'll give you a hint: my husband is a banker."

"Is it real?"

"And here he is, my husband, the banker who's made this all possible..."

Claire's husband, a bald, stocky man, who is shorter than his wife, shakes my hand and says: "Oh, they're just the bills we weren't using at the bank anymore, the discolored ones, the dog-eared ones, the out-of-circulation ones..."

"The paintings should be sold at face value," my father says, appearing behind them with two white wine glasses. In the meantime the first wave of visitors has fully arrived and the small room has become crowded. I lean on the edge of the table. "Only the ten-bill series will probably someday be worth less than the six thousand Claire wants for her gargantuan creations."

"Face value. That's good, Föns!" Claire says.

"These here are the twenties, here the fifties, the hundreds. No thousands, though—that was expecting too much, even from my generous husband."

Pretzels fall to the floor, wine glasses clink.

"Incidentally," Claire laughs, "just to be clear: the bills *aren't* real."

I am a writer, after all, making up lives for others, and always making up a bit of another life for myself, but the situation I had placed myself in on this particular evening is not one I'd been able to imagine. I gave so much thought to the physical obstacles that I wasn't able to envision obstacles of any other sort. I look at the people who fill the little room, and the gallery owner standing in their midst;

proudly, triumphantly. He had stolen from me, and from my brothers, he had cursed and repudiated us. And even though I know none of the gallery's visitors are thinking what I am thinking at this moment, they do seem to me, all the same, to be his audience. It's as if I am being paraded in front of them, that I am parading myself before them. My father appears to enjoy the betrayal, which wasn't his, but mine, my betrayal through having reestablished contact, through my having come. The trap into which I have fallen is perfect, for I set it myself. The sculpture he stole from us hangs as a trophy on the wall. And I, the son repudiated by his own father, cursed, despised for his illness, and (because of this?) taken to court, I stand beneath it, another trophy. Here, in his kingdom, where I can't and no longer want to be heir to the throne, his cruelty turns into self-congratulation. Here, his threats can be well-intentioned advice; in this setting, his legal proceedings are holy crusades against the infidels—just and fair battles on behalf of his collection, battles he won, even if his cases were always dismissed in court, even if he'd always destroyed everything around him in the process.

"Let's go upstairs," I say to Larry, "there are too many people here."

"Go on up," my father says, "look around, but don't steal anything."

"Don't you disappear, we still have something to discuss," Claire shouts.

"What?" the gallery owner wants to know, and Claire winks, "your successor, Föns." *Tick.*

But Kasperli *had* to go into the room.

I reach for Larry's arm so he can lead me past the people. In front of the staircase he crouches down, I wrap my arms around his neck, he straightens up, and there I am, lying on his back. As always, someone's standing by, surprised by the double-backed stair-climbing beast, and can't help staring. The steps disappear beneath my dangling feet, and, as I float higher—gradually, step by step—it becomes clearer to me that in these few small rooms, I will encounter the attic kingdom again. As if not a single decade, not a single year, not even an hour had elapsed, I will encounter everything that was, everything that could have been. Thonet chairs, iron clocks, mortar, rusted stethoscopes, Tiffany vases, *oignon* pocket watches, old Victrolas and album after album of His Master's Voice shellac records (Satchmo, his favorite), Rosenthal china, birdcages, antique Christmas tree decorations, wind-up Japanese dancing dolls, masks from Urnäsch and the Congo, garden gnomes from Thuringia, a medieval tooth extraction set in a quilted wooden case, porcelain music boxes, and everything imaginable made of pewter.

In the attic's workroom, c. 1968

Luckily the room was on the second floor. This way he could clime down easily. He had his rope ladder for a long time. He tied it to the windowsill and went down. He threw the rope ladder on the sill. This way he could bring down the ladder at any time with the pickaxe.

"Everything okay?" Larry asks.

Now Kasperli ran on the street, where the circus was. He ran around the circus grounds. Where he saw a poster.

"Let's go downstairs," I say.

Big excitement! the poster says. Attention! Bengil tiger on the loose! Great danger! A reward of 100 Francs for anyone who brings the tiger back alive and the chans of a life time: You can be:
Circus performer
Clown
Tightrope walker
Jugglr

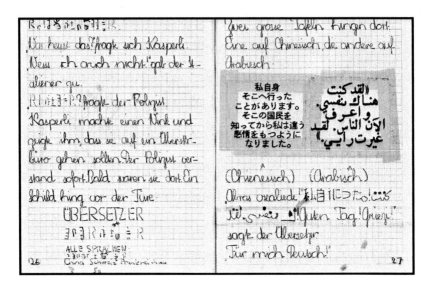

Tock.

To New York! To New York! Just don't forget the arm! Using the metal gripper, which lengthens my arm, I can snatch up objects from the ground while standing, or wangle things off the shelf from a sitting position. Not always successfully. Picking up papers from the floor takes a certain amount of agility, especially as I have to watch to my equilibrium at the same time, and the books I fish from the bookshelf could fall on my head—

Claire's thinking—*tick*—regarding who could succeed the gallery owner would be constructive were the gallery owner interested in something like a succession plan. But as soon as those present start putting suggestions forward—Claire? An association of artists who have shown in the gallery? Perhaps, even the son, who was skulking around the place again? The gallery owner waves them all off. There is only one person who can put a successor forward and there is only one person who is worth considering as successor. My father intends to succeed himself; he doesn't need anyone else. The king is also his own heir and reigns over this universe, which is as small and as large as Hadleyville—this is his whole kingdom. Should he go down, his kingdom will go with him.

We are already standing on the garden path, Larry, Claire and her husband, the banker, while the king fusses with bolting the door.

"And do you know why?" he yells, insulted, indignant, hurt, fiddling with his key ring as if it, too, has conspired against him. "Because I won't be leaving at all! I'll be hundred and twenty, and then immortal! I'm invincible, all right!" Finding the right key, he joggles it into the lock, turns it twice, and jiggles the door to assure himself it is securely shut. The opening is over; as usual no one bought anything, but art doesn't have to be a money-maker, as Jolanda Gut would misquote him in the newspaper the next day. What nonsense!

"Do you need help, Föns?" Claire says, stepping over to him.

Claire's husband and I stand at the fence, which separates the atelier house's yard from the parking lot, diagonally across which is the Hirschen. The banker touches my arm and says: "He was really treated a bit harshly, your father." I give him a questioning look. It turns out that back then Claire's husband worked for the bank that administered my father's bankruptcy. Now he's the manager of another bank. "He was made an example of because his was the first major bankruptcy after the sixties. It was a betrayal. He shattered the dream of the never-ending flow of cash and showed that failure was possible again. But it wasn't just about money," the banker philosophized, "more than a debtor, the public urgently needed a guilty party. Soon after, when one company after another started going under, people were used to failure, and those going bankrupt were treated more gently."

In the meantime, the gallery owner has set to work descending the entry steps. Holding firmly on to the doorpost he takes the first step backwards. Backwards, because this is the position he's in anyway. Then, seized by a playful confidence, he makes an elegant pirouette, and takes the next two steps neatly.

"See, invincible!" he shouts, marching off, across the moss-covered cobblestones, across the parking lot, to the Hirschen where he's reserved a table. I can distinctly hear him humming something to himself. It sounds like the famous melody from *High Noon*.

"Can he walk to his seat or does he need the boarding chair?" my aide asks the flight attendant over my head. I'm flying back to New York where Jan, my wife, will meet me at the airport. "If you're referring

to me," I say, having to look up at the man, "then please ask me. Just because I am in a wheelchair doesn't mean I can't provide information about myself." The aide is embarrassed and apologizes to me. Then he asks the flight attendant: "Is he being met in New York?"

A ground hostess at New York's Kennedy Airport pushes me, my bags on my lap, through customs—nothing to declare—and behind the barrier, Jan emerges from of the crowd. She greets me with a red rose, takes my hands, and dances around me. I bob up and down in my wheelchair beneath the weight of the bags as best I can. The wheelchair rattles along, the rose dances above our heads. Jan holds my hands in hers, I move my upper body, people are watching us, even here, a dancer in a wheelchair is an unusual sight.

In my appointment book, which covers the year of meetings with my father, from March 1994 to March 1995 (and likewise my separation and divorce from Viktoria, which also occurred during this period), there are ten entries, tentatively made, with abbreviations in pencil, as if I wanted to retain the option of erasing this information instead of returning to it some day.

Café Z. stands for Café Zimmermann, of course, where I met my father again for the first time. The entries *Hirschen* and *atelier house* appear more frequently. There is one place where the following is written: *70th b-day at the* Waaghaus. The *Waaghaus* is an old market building that was converted into an exhibition hall and meeting place for the St. Gallen city council. This was where the city held, in honor of the collector, gallery owner, and patron, the first and thus far only exhibition of my father's own artworks. Every so often I put an *F!* after these locational references, yet never once did I write *Father*.

I'd also jotted *air-raid shelter: F!* and the exact address. Behind a thirty-centimeter thick concrete door, in sixty square meters of space, he stored his holy relics: his own work. It had been his idea to meet there—after Claire had approached him at the Hirschen (following her opening and in my presence) about his successor.

"Hun-proof!" he shouted proudly when he pushed open the heavy door to the shelter. "You're the first person to set foot inside this place. Look around! Here lies Keller, the artist. The complete works, bomb-proofed. Collages, objects, charcoal drawings, paintings, sculptures, everything, and as always tons of it, you know me! Well? What do you think? Not bad, right? Pick something out. But not a sculpture, you have to earn a sculpture. And you know what? Why don't you drop by my apartment some time? Yes, come! Have a look at the whole business. You boys *are* my sons, after all. Should inherit it all, shouldn't you? I don't even know what will happen after I die. I need an heir to the throne, and that was always you. Of course, all this junk here is worth nothing, but I still have some real treasures back in the apartment. Come on, come inherit! Succeed me! When do you want to come? Tomorrow? Next week? Let's get it over and done with!"

And so in my appointment book under March 23, 1995, I find the address of his apartment marked with an *F!* This was the address he now lived at exclusively. He used the other apartment—the one where years earlier Puck had asked him to withdraw his legal action against us—only for storage. As his apartment was on the second floor of an elevator-less building, and in order not to be alone, I asked Larry to accompany me on this day as well.

We rang and the building door sprang open immediately. I got on Larry's back. As the second floor balustrade came into view, I was able to make out my father leaning on the railing in the dim stairwell light. The door to his apartment had been pulled shut behind him. He was watching us, curiously, astonished—offended? I looked up from Larry's back, nodded my head as if it were a second one Larry had sprouted, and mumbled a greeting into Larry's neck. My father continued his silence, but he seemed agitated. Then, I felt Larry shaking beneath me, sensed his hand clenching around the banister, and my father burst out laughing and shouted, "What a perverted sight!"

Larry managed the last step to the landing and lowered himself just a bit, allowing me to slowly slide off his back and onto my feet. Father moved away from the balustrade and positioned himself between us and the closed door of his apartment.

"Like two queers who can't wait till they're home going at it on the steps—that's what the two of you look like!"

Poor Larry was too exhausted to respond.

"Sorry, Larry, let's go," I said.

That would be best for him too, my father bellowed. He'd just gotten off the phone with his sister, he roared, and she also didn't see why he should see any of his sons after they'd left him in the lurch all those years. Now that he wasn't doing so well anymore, here they were, crawling back to inherit everything.

"Come on," I said to Larry and turned toward the stairs. Larry stood between my father and me. I wondered if my father was thinking how easy it would be for him to push me down the steps. And I wondered if this was why I had turned my back to (on) him: to finally achieve clarity?

"My sister is right! You're coming now because you and your brothers think I'm going to croak. But I won't do you this favor! Drop dead yourselves!"

What was he waiting for? What was Larry waiting for? I clutched the banister, stuck my foot out, as if testing the depth of a river. Readied to take a step. Retracted my foot.

"Larry—"

I stuck my foot out again, and this time I took the step. *Thud.* The step crashed into my foot, up my shin, dashed into my knee. I clasped the banister more firmly, and now, with my right leg securely planted on the step, I was able to drag the left one down after. *Thud.* My knee already throbbed, and after an entire flight of stairs it would ache badly for two or three days, but it was a pain I looked forward to.

"Föns," Larry said, "you invited Christoph here—"

"Because he tricked me, like always! Everything belongs to me! Before you and your brothers even get a single picture frame I'll burn everything! Myself, too!"

When Larry took me on his back again on the first landing my father, having suddenly turned whiny, shouted after us, saying I should stay after all and have a look in his apartment. He now cursed his sister. He pleaded. I saw him step over to the balustrade, but then I didn't look back anymore. Larry had to be careful that my feet, which grazed the steps, didn't throw off his balance, while I concentrated on the stairs disappearing beneath me.

My father didn't follow us, but his voice did: sounding like bottle Number Four from so long ago. Just another half bottle or even a mere sip and he'd fall asleep. We'd now reached the bottom of the stairs and

I heard him pleading, just as he did in my memory. I should stay, he implored, in spite of everything, I was one of his sons.

But once Larry had put me down, my father started swearing again. The doors clicked shut and I don't remember anymore which one was the first to close, the building door we'd now put behind us, or the door to the apartment, where my father had shut himself in once more.

The taxi stops in front of our building in New York's West Village. I pay the driver, while Jan gets out to take the wheelchair out of the trunk. The taxi driver pushes a button and the trunk springs open. A young African-American man standing on the corner, as if he'd been waiting for us, begins to walk in our direction. What does he want? While the (white) driver remains seated, waiting for his money, the stranger hauls the wheelchair out of the trunk. I watch how he pulls the chair open, pushes the seat straight, how he holds the wheelchair with something approaching tenderness.

The stranger sees that Jan is having trouble helping me out of the car and indicates to her to step aside. He takes me under my arms and pulls me up. Barely arrived in Manhattan and I'm embracing a stranger. How good it feels. He used a wheelchair himself, when he hurt his knee, the stranger says. Only once he sees I'm safely seated does he disappear into the crowd.

"Since I've known you, I pay attention to steps, elevators, accessibility, as if I've developed a new eye."
"I know," I say. "That's my eye."

New York, Spring 2000

"What is the matter now?" I said, querulously, very much startled by this change. "A simple halt," replied my uncle. "Is the eruption about to fail?" I asked. "I hope not."

—JULES VERNE, *Journey to the Center of the Earth.* Axel and Professor Lidenbrock, who are spewed out of the center of the earth by a volcano.

A*hhhh-iiieeeeh!*

The space is small, but I find everything I need in it. Light. Air. I have a view. Whenever I look up from my desk—which, in our studio apartment, also serves as the dining room table as well as the living room table—a silvery-gray squirrel is scurrying over one of the walls in the rear courtyard. There is always a cat lurking at a strategic junction of the labyrinth of walls that separates the tiny gardens from one another. If I want sky, I have only to roll to the window in my office chair. The cherry tree is in bloom, even though the nighttime hailstorm has knocked most of the petals off. When the wind is strong, the quickly growing bamboo reeds tap against our window, reminding me to ask the landlord to cut them back. I don't do it. I have time.

Broken glass has been embedded into the top of one of the garden walls. I observe how deftly our neighbor's young cat circumvents these dangerous traps. She darts after a squirrel. It doesn't seem to make any difference to her that she won't catch it.

I have—*Aaaah-iiieeh!*—peace and quiet. Sirens and the occasional car alarm or the beeping of a truck backing up can be heard here, though the sounds are muffled. Nothing compared to Seventh Avenue, which is just a block away. Here, birds chirp; there, engines drone. Admittedly, it has gotten louder here, too. The neighborhood is changing. Of the old bohemians—from Marcel Duchamp, who climbed the triumphal arch in Washington Square to proclaim the Independent Republic of Bohemia, to Allen Ginsberg, the poet laureate of the Village, who just a short while ago could still be seen ambling down the streets—there aren't too many left. Anyone who can afford the rent and who hasn't been living here for eons— well, he can't be a bohemian. *Aaah-iiieeeh-aaah-iiieh!*

Our building was a servants' quarters in the nineteenth century. It has only one-room apartments. Anything that is advertised as a two-room apartment is nothing more than one of these rooms through which our shameless landlord has put a wall. This way the illusion of a larger apartment is created, and he can demand even more rent. In the "bedroom" of these mini-apartments there is normally a bed that can be converted to a couch during the day and, next thing you know you're in the "living room." Clear the "dining table" and you're sitting in the "office." The entry area becomes larger by calling it "foyer," or a framed poster and a friend's painting on the wall turn it into a "gallery." In our case, it's also an extension of our "garage." The body of the wheelchair manages to fit inside the one closet we have, but the wheels have to be hung from two nails on the wall by our front door, adding a sculptural element to our "gallery."

Whoever moves out is—following a complete renovation of the room—replaced by the youngest possible renter. The landlord likes students best, as students never stay very long. Students also possess that quality held in high esteem by landlords: they are loud. This in turn reminds the older, concerned-about-peace-and-quiet tenants, that perhaps it's about time they start looking around for lodging more suited to their age. But the veterans of our building pay so little rent that they aren't about to let a little noise drive them out.

In our building, the record for attempting to live like an adult in twenty-three square meters of space is held by Daniel. He recently told us that he has lived here for thirty years, a fact that seemed to surprise him most of all. Daniel is short and stocky with a thick, black beard. He works nights and is, Jan thinks, a left-wing cartoonist. He is beginning to look a bit like a mole. Jules lives below us; he is a French chef who cooks for one of the jazz clubs in the neighborhood. In the mornings he listens to Jacques Brel or his wife yells at him. *Madame promène son cul sur les ramparts de Varsovie* permeates through our floor or: "Don't you know that I'm the smart one here, and you're the asshole!" Fran from New Jersey lives above us. She's working on spec, that is, at her own risk, on a television pilot series and considers herself an author in the tradition of Edith Wharton. She is endowed, she tells us, with a "primetime sensibility," and writing for primetime, she assures us whenever we run into her in the stairway, is "so much more prestigious" than writing for the afternoon shows. And then there's Karim Candyman, who no longer knows how long he's been living in our building. He is a caterer, but, even more, he's a "clutterer," a collector, or, so as not to do my father an injustice, a hoarder of everything. Karim doesn't let any of the other tenants into his apartment because he doesn't want word to get back to the landlord. It is forbidden in New York, the freest of all free cities, to hoard junk. As Karim has become a safety risk because of this law, he could be thrown out of his apartment at any time. *Aaaah-iii-eeeh!*

I don't even know how warm it is outside. The sun is shining. It could be eighty-five or thirty-five degrees. It is April. In here it's pleasant. I have water. I have juice. Music, if I want. As if our apartment weren't small enough already, I make it even a little smaller by wearing headphones while I work: that puts me in the "music room." Lunch, a sandwich, is ready. If I want, I can be hungry. I have names in my address book. Telephone, TV, fax, e-mail, the Internet. I don't have to use them. I'm sitting barefoot, because I like sitting barefoot, and because it is the only way I can get up from the office chair that I have here. I have everything. I am writing. I am here.

> There's something ticklish on my cheek, as if a warm finger were gliding over my face. It feels like a wasp, nature's model for the "helicopeter," which I was recently able to add to my toy soldier army. But THE RULE says it's still too early for scratching. It's even still too early for eyes to be opened—*Aaaah-iii-eeeh!—tick.*

Is it time? Jan is arriving around two o'clock to help me out of the building. If I want to refill my coffee, I have only to roll my office chair the two meters to the kitchen, where the coffee maker sits on top of our mini-refrigerator. But no more coffee; I'm going to roam through the city again this afternoon. And that requires, above all, two things: the battery of my electric wheelchair must be fully charged and my bladder must be completely empty—so that both are good for my eight-kilometer radius. Even if I can't be a flâneur—my dream job—I have, at least in New York, with my wheelchair, become a rolling flâneur—a *rôleur.*

> Morning wafts into my room carrying with it the aroma of freshly cut grass and damp earth. This is because I am digging a hole in the shadow of the fir tree, in the back near our garage. I found an ancient Icelandic parchment in the ground, an invitation— so dirty it was barely legible—to travel to the center of the earth. I'm headed in the right direction and my hole is already three quarters of a meter deep! And in the afternoon—

Jan is—*Aaaah-iiieeeh!*—home. I make a note of where she throws her key ring because she'll look for it before she can help me out of the apartment. It'll probably end up buried on the bed, under the mail she's brought. At first it bothered me that part of our apartment-leaving procedure is always Jan's search for her keys, until it dawned on me that instead of getting worked up about whether the constant misplacing of the keys was absolutely necessary, I could simply help her find them.

I push myself out of the office chair while Jan pulls the wheelchair and the Scalamobil out of the closet. A Scalamobil is a battery-operated device weighing about twenty-five kilograms that looks something like a lawnmower. Once it's attached, a person in a wheelchair, with the assistance of a second person, is able to negotiate certain flights of stairs. It takes Jan a couple minutes to "wiggle" the two devices together, and then I plop down into my wheelchair seat. We're ready. Jan pushes me into the corridor, where we frequently encounter fellow tenants who wish to let us go first. We always decline this friendly offer, as it takes about ten minutes before we're outside.

Jan opens the corridor door and hooks it onto the wall to keep it from closing. With a bit of a running start and a hefty jerk, we make it over the low threshold that our landlord fitted with a small rubber ramp. We are now on the landing. At this point, I ask Jan if she has turned on the Scalamobil's motor. I ask not because she might have forgotten, but because a procedure such as this one requires courage—for the person being transported, helplessly, in the wheelchair, but even more for the person who has to provide the assistance—and courage is best mustered when a slightly risky procedure like this one is ritualized.

Jan takes a deep breath—*Aaaah-iiieeeh!*—this, too, is part of the ritual—and holding the handles she tilts me backwards and wheels me carefully to the stairway's edge. This is the moment demanding the most courage (it is also when I find steps a personal affront). If the Scalamobil's braking wheels failed to sense the edge of the stairway and bring the device to a stop, I would slip away from Jan and fall down the steps. But we can depend on the braking wheels; they have yet to let us down.

The descent begins. The Scalamobil has four wheels that, rotating slowly, climb down the steps (and later, climb up again). During the descent, it is important that Jan keep me at the right angle: if she tips me too far forward, then I slide out of the chair; too far back, then I become too heavy for her and we'd both fall backwards. I don't want to think of what the full weight of me, my wheelchair, and the Scalamobil crashing down on her would do to *her* legs. To make this balancing act easier, I clutch at the banister, even if I'm deluding myself that this measure could help me break a fall. On the other hand, illusion is an important part of the ritual—of every ritual—for nothing can give us more of a sense of security than the illusion of security, whether we are crossing a street or sitting in an airplane. But there's one thing that becomes less and less illusionary each time we undertake the arduous procedure to negotiate these steps, and that is our love. For what we are doing here is an act of love; for me, in that I am entrusting myself to Jan, and for Jan, especially for Jan, in that she embarks on this daily stairway ritual along with me. Sometimes I think what a privilege it really is to be able to feel this certainty every day on every step.

So I go...?...roll...?...flow?...step by step, *clonk, ffft, clonk-ffft*, down the stairs, always one at a time, a bit like Foot, the stair-descending metal spring I played with in my attic. Having safely reached the bottom of the steps, Jan tips me forward and flat again and I wait while she goes to get the wheels of my wheelchair, which, with their motors, weigh about ten kilograms each. She fastens them to the wheelchair, unhooks the Scalamobil, and "walks" it—after all, it can take the steps, one by one—back up to the apartment. She returns with the battery (twelve kilograms), the metal supports that have to be attached to the back of the wheelchair to prevent it from tipping backward, and my bag. Before she can finish assembling the wheelchair, she has to get me over the high front door threshold and out onto the street. There I turn my motor on. We arrange my return time, give each other a kiss, and I roll off. *New York City—Aaaah-iiieeeh!—here I come!*

"Hey, Bill Gates, gimme something!" A panhandler comes toward me. Why I, in a wheelchair, of all people am supposed to be the richest American, I have no idea. Does the bum think Bill Gates has gotten himself a wheelchair as camouflage? The guy gets nothing, or otherwise I'll never be as rich as Bill.

More often than not it happens near Harlem and more often than not it's African-Americans who approach me, call out "You're strong, brother!" or clap me on the shoulder; but this time, it's a white man who heads my way in one of the Village post office branches.
"You'll be better every day," he says in a voice that allows no room for doubt. Not another one, I think ungratefully. Why on earth does my wheelchair attract them? "Well, that's good," I answer, wanting to get by him. The old man smiles and continues, "You're wonderful." He is wiser than I. I listen, eager as to what more he has to say about me. "You look good." Does he really mean me? Maybe he's not crazy at all. I examine him, look into this old, beautiful face. And, here it is again, this feeling of being a little privileged. Who else receives compliments on the street!
"You are a thirteen-million geniuses," the man proclaims. "You've made my day." "And you've made mine," I say, leaving the post office without having mailed my letters.

In an elevator, a woman lets her dog sniff me. The dog is in a training course, she says, and she needs to find out how her dog reacts to wheelchairs. I tell her that's all right, but I don't know how my new wheelchair will react to dogs.

I wait behind a parked car. Jan hails a cab and it pulls up next to her. DISABLED AND DOGS WELCOME it says on the door. When the driver sees me in a wheelchair, he turns on the off-duty sign. Jan shouts

Top: a ramp on W. 10th Street. Bottom left: a freestanding model spiral staircase in eastern Switzerland. The photograph on the bottom right shows the main entrance of the new building for the St. Gallen cantonal police, completed in 1999. The roughly twenty-five meter long wooden ramp had to be added after the fact, as the architects forgot to make the building, which cost millions, accessible to people with disabilities.

at him that he's only doing that because he doesn't want to take the wheelchair. Not true, replies the driver stepping on the gas. Before he's even rounded the next corner he switches on the for-hire sign again.

Ah, here he comes again, my friend, the wise old man, who just a few hours ago recognized the thirteen million geniuses in me! He stops and tells me he has come straight from Grace Church. And wasn't it crazy that so many innocent people were in prison. Before I can acknowledge this, he leans over me and wants to know if I, too, read about sex and sexuality. He does so all the time, he says. The man is hard to understand, while my thirteen-million-geniuses prophet spoke clearly. And didn't the latter have more teeth than the former? But it can't be that my seer is completely insane. He can only be just crazy enough to see every single genius in me.

Then he says "Dosvidania" in Russian, and as I wish him "Dosvidania" in return, he turns away. Only now do I see his nurse. She shrugs her shoulders, and her charge is already leaning over a baby in a baby carriage and asking it if it, too, reads about sex and sexuality all the time. Aaaah-iiieeeh!

When I'm out and about in this city, I am amazed simply because everywhere you look there is something to be amazed at. But what amazes me most of all is that I live here for a part of every year. I came here once when I was seventeen, twice when I was eighteen, and each time on my own two feet. And now, as if the eight-year-old boy—the one I was a quarter of a century ago when I was already dreaming of this city from an attic six thousand kilometers away—has actually sent me here in his stories and drawings, I live here. Twenty years later, I roll—*that* was not something I imagined, even if my first doctor predicted it clearly enough—through the streets of New York. Now, without a hyphen.

Can a person be beamed after all? Can the human body, as Puck once explained to me, break itself down in space in order to travel in time? Who says it can't? The human mind does it all the time. Would I otherwise be here? *Aaah-iiieeeh-aaah-iiieh!* Does it make a difference (for those who have let reality stifle their imaginations) that it was the other way around—that I brought that young boy with me on my journey? I am still just as curious about what awaits me around the next corner; I still think of the world as being a bit like that armoire missing its back panel that I considered my attic; and I still want, once I'm back in our tiny apartment, to write everything down—that may be my "collection of everything"—or at least keep it firmly in my memory. Even if Nana or Head-Foot or Foot may not be waiting for me around the next street corner—though I'm not even so sure of this—the creatures I do encounter may well be that fantastic, albeit always real—or are they?

"Why are you in a wheelchair?" A homeless woman. "Is everything going to be okay? It definitely will, I know it. You'll be walking again soon. Do you have a wife? Does she take good care of you? Really? She must take good care of you. Soon you'll be walking again. Definitely."

Jan and I see the crazy guy on Broadway almost every day—a vision that instills fear: tall, wiry beard, aggressive. Often he can be seen waving around a wood plank. Sometimes he chases cars down the street. He's always yelling something. By all means, avoid eye contact!

But today I'm at his mercy. As Jan disappears into a store, I see him coming toward me. He's still a block away, but she won't be back before he gets here and I can't roll away in the manual wheelchair, which we're

With Jan, 2000

using today. And he's heading right for me. I avoid his eyes. Why does Jan have to buy an ice cream now of all times? It was probably my idea: it has suddenly gotten so warm...

He's standing in front of me, the black guy, there's no escape. But he doesn't want to club me over the head with his wood plank. He doesn't even want money. He takes my white hand in his black one, rubs it over his beard—which isn't wiry at all, but soft—and bringing it to his lips says: "I prayed for you. Are you feeling better yet?"

Summer Morning, 2000

I did see my father one more time. Larry had invited me to an exhibition in eastern Switzerland in August 2000. I left a message on his answering machine asking whether the gallery—a converted warehouse—was wheelchair-accessible. When Jan and I returned home, his reply was waiting for us on our machine. Yes, the space was accessible, but he also wanted to let me know that he'd invited my father as well. After that time we visited him together, he continued, he would understand if I changed my mind, and yet he hoped I would still come.

I played the message a second time, as if this could banish the possibility of my father showing up, or as if the space were now no longer accessible after all, barricaded not by steps but by the undesirable presence of my father. Did Larry know he'd be coming and was he offering me a way out? Did I want a way out? I stood in my office in front of the answering machine and thought about how during the last years that father was still living with us, I used to wait in the living room for the moment he entered through the room's front door so I could steal out through the back one. I saw myself accelerating in my car when I spotted him coming toward me in his; I saw myself disappearing behind a shelf in the do-it-yourself section of the supermarket and picking up a bike lock when I spied him approaching. I erased the message.

I hadn't seen my father or had any other form of contact with him since our last encounter in the hallway in front of his apartment in March 1995. There was no longer any reason for contact. He didn't want it. He couldn't do it. Sometimes, usually at the flea market or at an opening, I'd run into an artist who knew him well and who'd also shown with him. I'd ask how my father was doing and usually he or she replied by assuring me that my father no longer drank. I sometimes also asked whether he'd inquired after his sons, which the artist always answered a bit too quickly in the affirmative. Then we'd talk about the clay water jug from Mali that I'd bought, or the old threshing flail that, because of its unusual shape, I could picture sculpture-like on the wall in our living room. "Just like your father," the artist would say to me, and I finally no longer minded hearing this.

In 1998, I learned from the newspaper that his gallery was closing twenty years after it had opened. In addition to the usual—Jolanda Gut authored the article—it said that my father, despite searching long and hard, hadn't found a successor. He had to leave the atelier house, which he'd been renting since 1960 and in which he'd founded the Atelier Gallery in 1978, his fateful year. Where on earth would everything go? But there was a silver lining to all this, the article continued, for now he could concentrate on restoring his antiques, which had always been his favorite thing to do. And finally he could also focus on his own artistic career, he said. It hadn't been given the attention it deserved because he'd always sacrificed himself for other artists. I cut the article out and put it with others I'd kept, inside the catalog that had been published on the occasion of his seventieth birthday exhibition.

The speaker had already opened the show when my father pushed his way into the wide circle that had formed around her. Like Kasimir Stanislavovitch in Bunin's story, who had snuck into the church where his daughter was getting married, my father had arrived late. But unlike Kasimir Stanislavovitch he made no effort to hide his presence. He stood with his legs apart, leaning on his cane, as always holding his ground, though now somewhat less firmly.

I sat facing him, about fifteen meters away. He looked in my direction. He must have seen me—how could he miss me in my wheelchair?—but he didn't let on. We both knew we'd seen each other. I looked toward him defiantly. I wanted to withstand his gaze. I wanted his attention, still, but my father just stood there. What was going through his head? Was he listening to the speaker? Had Larry warned him too, telling him that one of his sons might be coming?

When the speaker was finished—my father, still clasping the knob of his cane, was the only one who didn't applaud—a duo sang a song of what seemed like nothing but lengthened syllables to the accompaniment of a child's rattle and someone banging on a watering can. Larry's installation of colorful, semi-transparent plastic sheets, which hung on wire cables like articles of clothing, filled the far end of the gallery; at the front was a buffet, toward which the visitors now turned.

I waited. What would my father do? Someone tapped him on the shoulder and he turned away, his back now toward me. Jan suggested we go look at the installation. While I imagined how the slightest breeze would cause the brightly-colored plastic sheets to dance, Jan started setting them in motion with a few gentle pokes. We congratulated Larry on his show. Should we get going?

I looked over toward my father and thought of my brothers who like me could have used this—a—father; with our weakened muscles, we could have really used a strong father. I thought of my brothers and all they'd achieved despite everything. I thought of our mother, who reminded us over and over again that despite everything—always this "despite everything"—our father had also been able to be a good father. I thought of Jan, who told me should my muscles one day be too weak she would breathe for me; I thought that it was maybe even a little bit because of my weak muscles that I'd had the luck to find this love, a love that is worth more than all the muscles in the world. And I saw my father who'd deprived himself of all this perhaps only because he wasn't able to take the first step, not once, not with anyone.

"Let me speak to him," I said to Jan. She nodded and pushed me in my wheelchair toward my father.

I'm not even sure whether he was surprised as I rolled up to him. He stood with Larry in a small group of people. To my "hello" he said only his, "Well, who thought we'd meet again." His handshake was weak and he pulled his arm back immediately. He showed no sign of making the conversation easier for me: I'd taken the first step, after all—again.

"This is Jan, my wife," I said, "and this is my father."

They shook hands. Larry lingered on, reluctantly, while the others excused themselves.

"Heard something about you remarrying. Wasn't invited again, of course." Receiving no reaction from me, he continued, "You live in New York now?"

"And here."

"So, tell me, since you're the Russian expert: what's the real deal with this Putin?"

"Putin is the president of Russia."

"Yes, I know that. Is he any good?"

"Perfect German, speaks mobster Russian, KGB career."

"Does that mean he's an idiot?"

"It means he's acting in a certain Russian tradition."

"So he's an idiot."

Pause.

Larry suggested perhaps meeting for a coffee later and left.

"Garbage, isn't it?" my father said.

"What?"

"You know, Larry's garbage."

Pause.

"Well? How are you?"

"How am I supposed to be? Gallery's gone to the dogs; that was in the newspaper, of course. The art patron's now devoting himself more and more to his own art. That was also in the paper. What a load of nonsense! The art patron's now devoting himself more and more to his arthritis and a thousand other afflictions that these hotshot doctors can't seem to cure. They just sit around making piles from their fees and the drug industry, and they're all in cahoots."

"True."

"Exactly. But otherwise? Lousy. Gallery gone. No sooner had the gallery closed, all my artists walked out on me. Everything hurts all the time. A successor, of course, was not to be found."

"We have to go."

"Of course, you have to go. Okay then."

"Okay then."

He hesitated. "You know what's really funny?"

"What?"

"Who brought me here. Do you know who it was? The director of the canton of St. Gallen Invalid Insurance Administration!"

"That's really funny."

"The director of the Invalid Insurance is also bringing me home. I'm an invalid now, too. Isn't that funny?"

"We really have to go, father."

"Your chair there, the wheelchair, the Invalid Insurance's paying for it, right?"

"Yes."

"Well, then your old father's been doing something for you all along, after all, hasn't he? You see? Put in a good word with his friend, director of the Invalid Insurance."

Pause.

"Understands nothing about art, of course."

Pause.

"Constantly having trouble with his wife, too."

"Take care."

I gave him my hand. He withdrew his quickly again.

"Damn arthritis! Everything hurts. I can hardly manage the steps to my apartment anymore. You've no idea."

I nodded. Ultimately, he was right. Ultimately, I didn't have any idea what that would be like for someone else. Jan also shook my father's hand before turning me in my wheelchair away from him.

"Damn old age!" I heard him shout. "Just don't get old, I'm telling you!"

I raised my hand to wave at him but I didn't look back. Left him. Let my father go.

Today, once again, wild with joy.

Hard crash with the right front wheel of the wheelchair this afternoon: wheel broke off. Was lucky because it happened next to a restaurant. Had a beer while waiting for Jan, who went to get the car.

Finally filed the petition to provide Hadleyville with a wheelchair rail network. This would give wheelchair users—who, even in the year 2000, still can't use public transportation in my hometown—their independent rail network. Put your wheelchair on the tracks and zoom off! Was adopted with great enthusiasm, as expected. Woke up satisfied. Bang-bang!

My body is a storehouse for the same disease my brothers have; for this reason I know at any given point in my life with sobering accuracy what awaits me in five, in seven, years, just as for my brothers I probably function as a reminder of more mobile times.

Mix, who, like me, was once able to ski, uses a four-legged walker, which he pushes in front of him, for the route from his living room chair to the bathroom. Puck can now only get around in a wheelchair and routinely urinates into a Uribag, meaning he hasn't peed from a standing position in years. He owns cars he's no longer able to drive himself. Mix uses a scooter to get from his apartment to his car in the underground parking garage; it's his rowboat that brings him to his four-masted ship. Neither one of my brothers can hold a glass, and certainly not a full one, with an outstretched arm anymore, because glasses have become too heavy. (This is how those with SMA learn to view such things: it's not the arms that are too weak; rather the objects that can no longer be lifted are too heavy.)

Puck can't put his socks on himself; water has accumulated in Mix's ankles, a result of his physical inactivity and excessive weight. In order for Puck to stand for a few minutes every day and regulate his blood circulation, he purchased a wheelchair with what I call a "Hannibal-Lecter Device." As soon as his legs and torso are strapped in, a motor raises him into a standing position. All he needs to complete the Hannibal role is the mask. I tell him this and he laughs, tied in as he is.

In my case, a cane is no longer enough for me. I can't cross a room anymore; now I walk along the walls where my splayed fingers seek additional support. It took me a while to realize that the marks suddenly appearing on the walls at shoulder height are from my fingers. To get out of the shower I have developed my "shower pirouette," a three-quarters rotation to the left on my own axis; all of a sudden, it has become difficult for me to get out of the shower with a simple step to the right. I notice that sometimes I also employ the left pirouette to make it past an open door.

I've also noticed that sometimes I think of myself in the third person in order to ease the pain of a further loss. I think of Axel hesitating to begin the journey to the center of the earth. I intend to reread de Maistre's Voyage Around My Room *because I am curious how I will find it a dozen years later. Very rarely am I able to still surmount the steps leading from our living room to the yard and only try when Jan* or my mother is around. I tell myself the Swiss summers are too cool and rainy to sit outside anyway.

Thus far, none of the SMA Brothers have breathing problems. We all have a little scoliosis. Osteoporosis—no. 1, serious; no. 2, negligible; no. 3, mild—ensures that our bones break easily, which so far has meant three breaks for Puck (ankle, knee twice), a partial break for Mix (knee), and one break (ankle) for me. Puck has the "bone density of an eighty-four-year-old," Mix a Robert Morley paunch. I have an "athlete's heart." Puck's heart is also too big, the result of too much strain. But I don't actually believe a heart can be too big.

Sven Wingquist, *Self-Aligning Ball Bearing*, 1929, chrome-plated steel, The Museum of Modern Art. In 1907 Wingquist, a Swedish inventor, invented the ball bearing, which, among other things, is what allows chairs to swivel.

The Island Cathedral

T uesday, September 11. *Dearest, I don't know whether you'll receive this, as all telephone lines are currently down, but I'm trying. There's been a major terrorist attack, a hijacking of planes at Newark, which were then crashed into both towers of the World Trade Center. One tower has already collapsed. Another plane has hit the Pentagon, and another, if I have heard correctly, may have hit the Mall in DC. It's very hard to get accurate information. NY is closed off now to all traffic, so I just have to wait and see if I can get back to you. But I'm safely here at Sarah Lawrence. If you do get this e-mail, e-mail me back at the address above, it's another professor's computer that I'm using, and I'll try to check it later. Call C. or J. or K. or D. or whomever you can reach (if the phones are working) if you need help. I love you so much. Your Jan.*

On the Wednesday before September 11, 2001, I went to one of the first scheduled public readings given by Salman Rushdie. He read from his new novel and I thought of the bomb that for many years has been aimed at him. The bomb wasn't a knife or a gunshot from the audience directed toward the writer on the podium in the Barnes & Noble on Union Square in Manhattan, New York City. The bomb came six days later; it was first one plane filled with people, then two planes filled with people, and finally three, then four planes, and it was aimed at all of us.

And now I'm living in a cordoned-off war zone. I'm part of the crime scene—recognizable, like so many things, from American films. Certainly, I can't be the only one who had never been able to imagine standing, let alone living, inside of the yellow DO-NOT-CROSS-CRIME-SCENE plastic tape. Jan's and my apartment is on Waverly Place, between the first cordon on 14th Street and the second on Houston, which wasn't—yet?—evacuated. Purgatory. The third zone lies below Canal. Beyond Canal there is nothing. No electricity, no telephone, no people. The people who are down there now are either aid workers or dead. There, it is hell.

There is no World Trade Center anymore.

The world, at least the western financial world, is all of a sudden missing its two front teeth.

The Twin Towers, hit by two living bombs—with over a hundred people on board, several of whom were determined to do anything, even this—collapsed one right after the other. Much of the towers dissolved literally into air, smoke rising into the sky over the financial district, first toward Staten Island, then Brooklyn, and finally Manhattan itself. What we're breathing when we're out on the street is steel turned air, mixed with asbestos. And what we're also breathing is flesh and blood. During these days in New York we are breathing in people.

Like the images, which etched themselves in our collective memory in a matter of seconds, the stories are also everywhere. K. saw the bursting tower and the flood of people spilling toward him. S. felt the vibration, grabbed a pair of binoculars, ran to her East Village rooftop, and saw people jumping from the observation terrace on the 110th floor, some hand in hand, and wishes now she wouldn't have these images in her head for the rest of her life. A priest who was helping was laid out on an altar—where to go with a dead priest?—in a nearby church. L. was having an EKG at the time of the attack and afterward found it almost a little obscene that her old heart still beat with such vigor. The nearby cemeteries are ankle-deep in insurance policies, balance sheets, business transactions, which only a few hours before had been of unspeakable value. Now they are replaced by the omnipresent color copies: *Missing! Have you seen my husband-my wife-my mommy-my daughter-my best friend's girlfriend?* Stories everywhere. C. in tears on the phone. She can't locate her nephew, who works in a building opposite the WTC complex. After many uncertain hours, he turns up with a broken arm, the result of his having helped, we learn. A., Jan's brother, who worked with companies in the WTC that now no longer exist, offers to spend the night, sleeping in the chair beside my bed in case I need help. I think of the two men I read about in the paper, Mike and John, who risked their lives to carry a stranger, a woman in a wheelchair, down from the 68th floor.

My story is this one; the situation in which it takes place seems like the stage for a play—About what? Claustrophobia? Fear? Helplessness? Being paralyzed? War? Whatever it was about, it was a monologue: I was alone for all of September 11th, confined to my apartment. It was about me, on the phone with friends, D., J., C., K., A., soon Jan, how proud I am to know all of them, and others; me writing e-mails, informing the first worried friends and family in Europe, reassuring them because it reassured me; me watching television: attack, war— *ratatata!*—we'll strike back, we'll smoke 'em out of their holes, make no mistake; me in my chair, out of which I can raise myself with a bit of effort—Jan was going to be back at five o'clock, but was she really safe?—me packing a little emergency bag in case I'm evacuated after all; me later in bed—a bed which I cannot get out of without assistance—holding the telephone, which stopped working the moment I sat marooned and right after I had just told everyone: no, no need to come by, I'm okay so far, I have the phone. Disabled person behavior: whatever you do, don't be a burden on anyone, I probably thought unconsciously. That's my contribution: don't ask for the help that others needed more urgently. But I also think: if only someone were with me on this horrible September 11th. At least someone whom I could have held, or who could have held me: D., J., C., K., A., *Jan.*

They all offered. K. tried, D. tried. They couldn't get past the door code, which they didn't know by heart. The phone rang incessantly but inaudibly and my inbox filled. I was only able to empty it the next morning, when J. was there, and A. wanted to come again, and a little later Jan was home too; she'd been able to return to Manhattan. Manhattan, this temporarily cordoned-off island. Me in bed in the middle of the war zone, which, from here, I could only see on the screen of our television.

I had tried to reach the phone-charging station from bed and succeeded by unscrewing the plastic side table and using one of the three metal legs as a fishing rod. Holding the charger triumphantly in my hand, sitting on the edge of the bed in my pajamas, I noticed the little red light wasn't on: I'd managed to pull the cord out. Helplessly I stayed in bed, Kafka's beetle Samsa for the night, though at least with the TV remote. This attack disabled and paralyzed us all. The fact that I couldn't run was maybe even an advantage. At least, I'll never be able to run headlong into disaster. Now I was safe and had to remain so, whether I wanted to or not.

Is it war? Isn't it always war, only all of a sudden visible to us all?

✳✳✳

Wednesday, September 12. *It's the second day. I wake up in a war zone. J.'s helping, D.'s helping, C.'s helping, my mother-in-law calls to inform me I'm doing well and calls again a few hours later to tell Jan, once she managed to get back to me, that if Christoph isn't doing well he should make an effort next time to sound more panicked…*

No sooner am I outside—I leave our building for the first time—and I think why didn't I have the impulse *to leave the apartment. Is impulse also a muscle?*

I want to see what doesn't exist anymore, but then I see it again and again, a hundred times over, on the countless postcards that are everywhere. The felled Twin Towers are eerily omnipresent and now it begins to become real for me. I roll over to West Street, propelled by unbelievably blue sky, then dazzled by the shimmering blue of the river. Hundreds are standing here, holding signs with Peace, Compassion, You're Heroes, New York City, We Love You. *I realize nothing will be as it once was. The Village, New York, the world—all upside down. People are cheering the cops they still quite recently denounced as pigs (Diallo!). They are applauding the firefighters—so unbearably many of who have already died—the workers, and the trucks driving by us transporting rubble and (I cannot suppress the thought) overlooked body parts.*

Jan, who was waiting for me, comes up to me on the street. Bomb threat at St. Vincent's Hospital. A joke, a neighbor says, waving us aside. A joke!

But what if these monsters had thought ahead, had hoped their deed would succeed, and installed bombs in hospitals in advance, setting them off when they knew they'd be filled with wounded and dying?

What if the airplane bombs had poison gas on board or atomic bombs? What is it we are actually breathing in? Asbestos, we know that. You can't smell or taste asbestos, it collects in the lung and crystallizes, over time transforming the lung into a deadly "white lung."

Is that the poison bomb?

The people who are now working in the crater of the world just blocks away are breathing in this air, many of them will die of white lung in twenty years, but right now, we can't, we mustn't, speak of "in twenty years."

On television this evening they report that there have been bomb threats all over Manhattan but the one at the Empire State Building—one of the other major symbols of New York, America, the western world, so a target—has to be taken seriously, they say. A bomb-sniffing dog detected this threat. That was the end of that particular news item and the beginning of another worry. Sweet dreams.

✳✳✳

Thursday, September 13. We can't get away. We're stuck on the island, in our neighborhood, inside the crime scene, in our apartment, I in my chair. This is how being disabled feels as permanent state: you can't get away.

The face masks lie on the emergency bag. On them, it says: Warning! This respirator helps protect against certain dusts and mists. **Misuse may result in sickness or death.**

Poison gas. Radioactivity. Would they tell us? When? Gorbachev kept quiet for days after Chernobyl. What on earth are we breathing? What was really found in the Empire State Building?

There's no end to the bomb threats. I'd already packed the first version of my "go-bag" on Tuesday. Thought, if the time comes, I want to be able to snatch it up and go. First in, a handful of disks, mostly containing the *book I'm working on,* The Best Dancer, *my address book, Jan's poetry manuscript, pills, my sunglasses. Now I am packing number two, with passport, which I'd forgotten, some food, and cash. I don't think we'll use the go-bag. This war is being waged on our minds and we have to do something to calm our minds. I throw in the wasp sting medication although I don't even know if I am allergic. My mother is. Her dogs are. What if World War III has really broken out, as the Times is trumpeting, and a wasp ends up killing me?*

25th Street is the mortuary. Go there if you are missing someone.

C. is in the New York Times building. Go home, you're in a target. Avoid skyscrapers in Manhattan. Avoid skyscrapers *in Manhattan! Don't ride the subway! Avoid major streets and squares. Stay put. Stay home. Drink lots of water. Don't drink the water: It could be poisoned. And Jan's mammography at five? On Union Square, where they just closed the Barnes & Noble. Where (for me) everything started. Where Rushdie read. Have we now all become Rushdies?*

Over and over again, people running in panic on television, and I get confused about whether this is an endless replay of Tuesday morning or if these people are running right now!

The boot was raised and it came down on the anthill.

I am calm. Writing calms me. It's what I can do. I hear steps above me: the neighbor who didn't drop by once during that long Tuesday although he knew I was alone. The TV is reporting that the Brooklyn Bridge now can't be crossed on foot either. Bin Laden is named prime suspect. I can't get the images of Palestinians rejoicing over this massacre out of my head. What on earth have we turned our world into? How calm am I really?

Waverly Pl. *I am sitting on my still wheel-less wheelchair at the bottom of the half stairway that leads to our apartment. Jan is walking the Scalamobil back up. As I wait for my wheels, I stare at the street. This second-day-after is also absurdly beautiful. The blue of the sky, seemingly different. An odorless morning. Someone passes by, I give him a nod, and he turns his head away quickly. The next person, a woman, nods back.*

Everything's okay. New York is the friendliest city in the world, and now this atrocity has made it even friendlier. I stare at the sidewalk, the tree in front of me, the street, the buildings on the other side of the street, their windows, doors, stairs. The building directly across has been for sale for months now and I wonder whether it has become more or less expensive.

Walking (rolling) is like writing, it takes away fear.

"You realize you can forget your go-bag if there's an emergency," Jan says coming down the stairs with the wheelchair wheels.

Eerie—our blocked off zone. Barely any cars. Around the corner at St. Vincent's Hospital there are barriers. Aid workers, camera teams. I look around, try to see into the windows of the surrounding buildings. Inside televisions are on, showing, close-up, what's happening outside, but no one is standing at their windows.

I saw the first flag in the form of a tie around the neck of an African-American man. Flags are now hanging everywhere, in the transvestite karaoke club Lips, *from apartment windows, in supermarkets, flags perched on heads as baseball caps, as masks over people's mouths, wrapped as dresses around bodies. On the corner of 14th Street and 7th Avenue, one guy has clad himself from head to toe in American flags and, as if that still weren't enough, he's waving one too.*

Jan gets money from an ATM, a few twenty-dollar bills; this world is functioning as it always has. We leave the sector. Can you imagine? I write "We leave the sector," as if I am Graham Greene and in the Vienna of World War II, and the sentence came quite naturally. It is perverse, but the fact that I'm not bursting with fear is because all this somehow seems familiar to me. Not deja-vu, or is it? I'm rolling around in film and TV images.

The city police, the state police, the National Guard, are all standing by, are all friendly. They raise the yellow police tape and we go through

into the other city, into normal or more normal New York, which we
know, but can't really believe, is going about its daily life, or is at least
trying to.

My eyes burn, I notice this only now that I am wearing the mouth
mask. I smell the rubber part that's supposed to protect my nose against
scratches, and think this will poison me. Nevertheless I still manage to
smell the thick cloud of oil billowing from a McDonald's.

14th St and University Pl. *Out of the crowd, a familiar face emerges*
coming down from Broadway. It's Bill Clinton, on his way to the
financial district with his daughter and a few bodyguards, a modest
triumphal procession on foot. Shouts of We-need-you!, Thank-God-
you're-here!, *and* You're-our-President!, *and I roll up to him, too, hold*
out my hand and he takes it. I think: shaking the hands of cripples
always looks good in public, but just forget that for now, this hand feels
good simply because it feels like a hand. Bush wants to come tomorrow,
but all I can think is: no way would these attacks have happened under
Clinton. (And I can prove it! These attacks didn't happen under Clinton!)

The Beth Israel Medical Center. *Bag inspection. I ask whether the*
elevators are working. Yes, all of them, no problem, your bag, please.

The—friendly—official scarcely peeks into my bag; if I were a terrorist I'd use a wheelchair as camouflage. A secretary says I'm alive *into the phone, and this is already beginning to sound almost a little routine, she says:* Every frigging building is falling out of the sky right now—*it was* 7 World Trade Center, *the Millenium Hotel seemed unstable, we are in* 3F, *and are sent to* 4G. *Again an elevator, this time I see the sign that always sends a cold shiver down my spine: IN CASE OF FIRE USE STAIRS. Jan says they press your breasts as flat as a sheet of paper, and it feels awful. Ordinarily a doctor would look at the image right away; today the technician glanced at it, saying it looked okay, but a doctor will probably call nevertheless, don't worry, a doctor almost always calls after the first image. Jan asks me if I'm I glad to be in New York. I take a deep breath and say,* "Yes, I want to be here, this is now my city, too." *And she says,* "How I love this city, how I love New York City!"

14th St. and 4th Ave. *We return to the sector. It's enough for Jan to show her ID and say where we live. While she makes a few calls—*Was C. back home? Her nephew, our hero? Yes, everything's fine. D.? Going to a meeting this evening. S.? Is with friends. J.? Was evacuated for two hours, together with his friends, who had to leave their apartment downtown and now are camping at his place—*I ask the officers if they want a coffee, a sandwich, we'd be happy to get them something. They decline with thanks. Everyone's so friendly now, they say. The bomb threats? So far nothing's happened. And the bomb in the Empire State Building? Hadn't heard anything. I'm in the middle of carless Broadway and I look up. What are you doing, Jan asks, and I say I'm seeing if the Empire is still there.*

Washington Square Park. *So many people in the park, yet how quiet it is. Only one guy crouching in front of a boom box, listening forlornly to his song. Here, too, there are signs everywhere.* God forgive them, they don't know what they've done, *or* Destroy them all. *In front of the Washington Arch is the first wall of mourning I've seen: candles, photographs, pictures, photocopies of the missing. A dense, quiet crowd. Silenced, tear-stained faces. Photos are snapped, something is scribbled on a piece of paper, pinned to a photocopied face, a greeting, a hope, a farewell.*

✳✳✳

Friday, September 14. *All of a sudden, it's in all the newspapers—this word we could only imagine in bygone days or faraway places: WAR!*

✳✳✳

Saturday, September 15. *Fall has arrived, for us the second time this year. While I listen to Sinatra's* New York, New York *on the radio—the announcer: "I couldn't help it"—followed by the reading out of more of those killed on Tuesday in and around the World Trade Center, I* *think how I only just arrived in old New York from Switzerland the Tuesday before last. By a plane that at any time could have been turned into a bomb by a handful of lunatics. I try to picture myself back on that Tuesday when during the ride from the airport I saw the skyline of New York with its double towered cathedral of finance for the last time. I am not successful: the towers are gone.*

Jan and I want to take part in the silent vigil on Union Square—the candles are in the go-bag—but when we get there, Jan says it doesn't feel right. On the roof of a van, a cameraman points his camera like a gun at the crowd.

More reports of the missing now, more silent vigils. We keep stopping, we read the names, Gennie *and* Mark *and* Joseph, *look into the faces, and they seem more and more familiar to me, until I too feel the loss.*

D., with whom we are heading toward the "wound," hangs her face mask like a foulard around her neck, an accessory. "Soon you'll be able to get this mask with a Nike logo," I say. "Life must go on, of course." "The flags," she says. "There are so many of them, they're scaring me."

Only a few people on Greenwich Street. En route, stories: how people heard about the catastrophe, who saw it—from the street, from a window, on TV, live or the live video in endless replay, and which video. Who was where, that's now important. D. was the first to call us. Jan was already on her way to Sarah Lawrence. I immediately turned on the television, called C., J., or the other way around, it's only just five days ago and memory is already blurring the facts.

People carrying heavy bags or pulling suitcases on wheels come toward us; these are refugees. Really. A small stream of refugees files past us, leaving their broken apartments behind them, moving in with friends further uptown.

*Canal St. The barricade is visible from a distance. A few dozen people are standing here, can't get any further either. As expected, not much to see. Through the opera glasses—*opera glasses!—*just an inkling of*

what's already taken root in our memories. Memory sediment: debris, death, what we once were.

And yet we touched the wound. Mike, a UPS worker we meet a block away from the barricade, was—just months before—part of a police commando unit that no longer exists. A dozen or more of his former colleagues are dead. Mike's eyes fill with tears, but he wants to talk. I always wondered what sort of people hug strangers in the middle of the street and what prompts them to do so, and now one of these people is my wife Jan, another D., and still another is me.

Jan hesitates. M. is back in New York, a mutual friend will be there, and D., too, all meeting around the corner for dinner; did Jan want to join them, they asked. Of course she can leave me alone for a while and, yes, of course I'd like to come along too, but down and up the stairs again, her exhaustion, and mine. When she returns, she wants to know, tears in her eyes, if I am ready. For what? For death. I say I don't know, yes, maybe. Maybe this was why I was relatively calm, I continue, or, more likely, fatalistic—is that the pessimistic word for calm? Is this what my disability endows me with in such a situation? Then, firmly: "No, I am not ready for death." She wants to be, Jan says, but she doesn't want to die, because of me, because she has to help me. She thinks of these scenes, she continues, film scenes but now others have experienced these scenes in reality a mere few hundred meters away, falling out of a building holding each others' hands; she says she'll hold my hand no matter what.

I want to be ready, Jan says. And I say, I do, too.

Sunday, September 16. What sort of city do we live in now? Before, after. New York, New York. The skyline showcases itself as an all too simple puzzle picture, the difference between the first image and the second suggested by a cloud of smoke. On the street, hawkers are selling the last postcards with the skyline "before" for a high price. We now live in an injured world, rather, in a world that can no longer conceal its injury. We live in a city with a wound—onto which, admittedly, new stopgap bandages are slapped each day—and already we're hearing cries for new Twin Towers: they're to be higher, stronger—in any case, more expensive. The police, hated not so long ago, are now all heroes; and because the firefighters were already heroes before, they're now superheroes. All of a sudden, we want Giuliani to be mayor-for-life, or president, while the president, who just recently was still being denounced as a joke, papa's boy, and above all, illegally in power, is stylized by the media as the "great comforter," the savior, who needs only to lay his hand upon the wound; and yet, all he wanted was to be the country club president he already was in Texas, and now he's a warlord—woe is us, all of us.

The companies have already billeted themselves in New Jersey, doing business, and if still not quite as usual, the stock exchange, where the gangrene can be smelled, is already up and running again; stocks fell—and though no one may have wanted to venture the comparison, I'm sure it went through everyone's head—as far as some people had to jump from the towers, and, no, it isn't the comparison that's in bad taste, but that such a horrific thing should have come to pass, and yes, we now smell the link between the gleaming silver Twin Towers, the global logo of money, and the fact that the stock market is already back in operation, even if we don't want to, can't, or mustn't, think about it. G. now has more sun and is not cynical in the slightest when he says so. He lives near the former WTC, whose towers cast their heavy shadows on his street, Chambers; he notices this only now that the buildings no longer exist, he says. Maybe it will become somewhat warmer in the financial world, in New York, who knows, all over the world; New York was already a friendly city before, now, afterwards, it's even friendlier. We've moved closer together.

The city is in mourning. The faces of the dead are written on its body in the form of flyers with color-photocopied faces and the names belonging to them. Mark, Ray, Gennie, names of those I don't know, repeat themselves; the faces become familiar. We share the mourning. I am now at home here. It is pilgrimages that Jan and I or I alone undertake through our neighborhood. Huge walls of the missing near St. Vincent's, spontaneous chapels with constantly changing congregations on phone booths, in display windows, on trees. Union Square transformed into an open-air religious service. On the gate around the Washington Arch, which is being renovated, hundreds of copied faces look at me, burning their way into my heart, burning the candles, and brimming with tears, even the flowers seem to be in tears. A few sentences wail *war!*, most, however, whisper, *love, peace, forgiveness*, written on large bed sheets, even though I am forced to witness later, on the evening news, how awful a single belligerent sentence can be when the camera zooms in on it, takes it out of context, turns it into a sound bite, isolates it from all the conciliatory, anxious messages, and declares it to be "the mood down here." The Village's bohemian image has long since become cherished nostalgia: *Make-Love-Not-War*. And it is Gandhi's *an eye-for-an-eye-makes-the-whole-world-blind* that is now omnipresent and overshadowing the calls for war. In order that this not be forgotten again right away, we now have the wound for months, years, as a cruel reminder.

Our heroes now open the market place, I hear on TV again. During the night sirens startled us out of a restless sleep into a wide-awake certainty. Everyone is asking, is being asked, whether she or he is okay, as okay as can be expected under the circumstances, and whether one is missing loved ones. *Missing*—that is now the word for dead. How long is one allowed to hope, how long must one hope, when does one have to stop hoping? The city is bleeding. I hear that at Ground Zero—as the wound is now called, as if a title for the film version were already being sought—there are boxes with labels "arm, female," "wedding ring," or simply, "bodies." V. spoke to some of the workers digging through the World Trade wound. They say it now smells like burnt flesh across the entire financial district. There is a fire burning in the debris, and in the subterranean corridors. They tell her: Everything is roasting, people too—*the entire thing is one goddamn grill!*

Yes, God, even "God" has his role in this war that has now become visible, even here. In the name of one God (a different one, or is it all the same because, of course, there's supposed to only be one?), the planes crashed into the Pentagon and into the Twin Towers, and almost into the White House, and in the name of another God, there will be retaliation: God bless America; the American government has its finger on the button and its hand on the Bible. In his sermon in the National Cathedral, the president has already pledged to deliver us from evil: *It is our duty to rid the world of evil.* Reagan's Empire of Evil, which is now no longer embodied by the evil Soviet empire, but by Osama bin Laden, whom the Americans helped (back before he was an evildoer) build his future terrorist training camp to defeat the then (and soon to be again?) evil Russians. People are now praying all over the world, and that's part of what gives us this collective mourning and hope in New York now. But there's nothing scarier than religions wrapped in flags—there, where in the extreme they justify a bloodbath, but also here, where the word God sounds like a logo, like a branded product, his naming like product placement. God: through whom the war is now being justified—no, sold.

New York has also been made into this, a City of God: the mourning, the dead, the candles, the tears. The spirituality of those who are true believers as opposed to those who mobilize the beliefs of others for holy war. Doubt that Gandhi's eye-for-an-eye-makes-the-whole-world-blind is capable of achieving anything against the eye-for-an-eye of the governments. God and flags, religion and nationalism, this was always the deadliest combination and now it's everywhere you look in New York. The flags that are hung from windows, the flag at the grocery store, in the electrical store, hanging next to an (Arab) kiosk worker, even the bronze Buddha in the Asian food shop is waving one, the singing homeless man wrapped in flags, the street hawker who's peddling madonnas, skyline postcards, and little plastic flags, the flag bras, the flags painted on the face masks, the flag-waving army. *In God We Trust* is on every dollar bill and now God must pay off his debt and defend the dollar.

The first book I read—am able to read, "after"—is E.L. Doctorow's *City of God*, not Rushdie's ominously pertinent *Fury*. Behind me the financial skyline of lower Manhattan sunlit into an island cathedral, a religioplex. The island cathedral now missing its two main towers. The City of God, Augustine, Doctorow, us here, us everywhere. *What if there's no heaven, just a door?* There's a picture of Doctorow on the back of his book; behind his receding hairline, the Twin Towers of the World Trade Center rise into the gray sky of New York City.

The Meeting With Christoph Keller

a short story

Ooligan Press

*I write fiction and they tell me it's autobiography;
I write autobiography and they tell me it's fiction.*

—PHILIP ROTH, *Deception*

For my wife

-1-

I usually do dead people. I did the first Hrabal, to full critical acclaim. I did Eich, now considered "the standard Eich." Bulgakov is next on my list; maybe a Malamud; Sterne's in the pipeline. Every serious biographer has a Sterne in the pipeline. Then Dürrenmatt died, and I wanted to do him. His widow said over her dead body. That can be arranged, I thought, but it is the biographer's first and foremost duty to avoid personal involvement of any kind in the life or afterlife of her or his subject. We all remember Robert Frost's biographer, who lost a good deal of credibility when the news broke about his affair, and child, with the second Mrs. Frost.

For a grim winter (when even the heating gave in) I went back to Sterne while also secretly working on a Nabokov, until Nabokov somehow got wind of it. "You're not up to my standards!" I hear him hiss whenever I click on that file. I dream of a Giacometti, or rather a biography of his famous sculpture—*Man Walking, Tripping, Falling.* Like life, in three parts. But I'll never do it: the ideal biography is the one never written, existing only in the mind, and thus flawless. But for the time being, and to recover from my more serious work (I feel the need to justify myself) I'm doing a living writer. Minor as he is, he's unlikely to disturb my sleep.

Keller and I agreed not to meet until I'd completed his life. I've never even heard his voice, as we communicate online. "I'll also give you access to my thoughts and dreams," he wrote. I'm aware that e-mail correspondence already indicates a certain personal involvement; I'm dealing with that in my book. Keller signed a declaration waiving his rights to edit, change, or alter my text, or even suggest alterations in any form of communication whatsoever, including dreams and nightmares.

The book will be published under Keller's name, not mine. You'll find it in the non-fiction or memoir section at your local bookseller. Keller, the author of several critically praised but modestly selling fictions, is scarcely the kind of legendary figure who ordinarily attracts my attention. His new book, though, is a departure. These memories are premature as he admits himself. He mentions Klaus Mann's first of three memoirs written at the age of twenty-six. I let him know that, apart from his own attempts at writing in English and a gargantuan father problem, he's no Klaus Mann. While a father figure haunts his book, its focus is his life with a progressive disease that makes his muscles waste away. At some point, he won't be able to move anymore. Like the rest of us, he started off in life a "normal" boy, but now, at thirty-seven, he can only walk, or rather waddle, a few yards and doesn't have enough strength to lift a good-sized encyclopedia or even the manuscript of his own book, no matter who wrote it.

As far as I'm concerned, his prose is a mere spin-off of his medical condition; "Each sentence a muscle he doesn't have anymore," if I may quote myself. I wonder whether he'll try to talk me out of that statement. Or anything else. But then he can't. And he won't, as *The Best Dancer* will be his best book.

-2-

His voice sounded familiar. Of course, I wasn't surprised that he finally called.

"I'm proofreading," I snapped. "That's when I *really* don't want to hear from you. Wait till you get your copy. Meanwhile re-read our contract."

"Send me the galleys. What about meeting when you're finished? How does next Saturday sound?"

I saw him at his desk, sitting in his Sitag Synchro-sit 45S, calling me from his Brother faxphone 490DT, looking out his six-paned window...

"The children," he said.

"You never told me you have children."

"I'm watching the neighbor's children playing in the garden. Zoë and—"

"Chloë, I know."

"Send the galleys special delivery. I want to read them before we meet."

I said no. No to special delivery. No to meeting Christoph Keller.

He pressed the point. "Let's meet at The Golden Lion. I can't wait to sit there and read how you describe me sitting there taking notes—"

"For the scene that takes place in your last novel, *Time to Cart Away the Mountains*," I said, completing his sentence. "Try the cheese pies, they're delicious."

"Watch out for the threshold. I almost fell once. It could have unpredictable consequences."

- 3 -

I was late on purpose. I know—of course, I know—that Keller likes to arrive first. He wants to be seated; he doesn't want to be observed in the process of sitting down. Just outside The Golden Lion I saw his van on the curb. The wheelchair, what he calls his "lifeboat," or, if he's in a sunnier mood, his "convertible," was in the back. The van looked in need of a wash, but that's beyond the biographer's duties.

I peeked through the dirty window, and there he sat on a bench, at a corner table, cane leaning against a chair. The waitress put a beer in front of him. They chatted. She was tall and wore a short black skirt and black stockings. Her hair was long and black, too. As she walked away, Keller watched her. I knew he was thinking about her legs, not her muscles. That's when he turned around to look at me.

Next thing I knew, I was stumbling along the path—no more than a narrow slit between two slanting house fronts (the sky was barely visible)—that leads from the restaurant farther into town, pressing my hands against the walls of the houses to keep my balance. I was breathing hard when I reached Multergasse, the main drag. The sight of people soothed me. Although I was born in St. Gallen, I hadn't been back for almost twenty years, except for an occasional "slapdash weekend of unpacking and packing," as my mother once put it. "This is an insult, son. Better not come at all if you don't have time. I'll send you whatever you need." Seeing the old town again made me painfully aware of how much had changed since I left. The old bookstore Ribaux had been replaced by an office supply store called McPaper; the *wurst* stands now sold Starbucks coffee. I had changed, too.

I was seventeen, Francine nineteen, when we met. I was an exchange student living in St. Malo, France, for the summer. Francine's widowed father, Georges, insisted on an abortion, Francine insisted on having the child. When the summer was over, I went home to inform my parents that I would be staying on in St. Malo with my wife and son. My mother told me I was nuts. My father wasn't home.

I stopped by to tell my old French teacher that I had taken my homework seriously. For our summer reading he had assigned us Alain-

Fournier's novel *Le Grand Meaulnes*. Like Meaulnes, I had found my princess but, unlike him, I wasn't going to lose her. When I left Francine's semi-detached suburban palace to arrange my affairs in St. Gallen, I wrote her address with a shaky hand on a dozen scraps of paper and put them in the pockets of all my pants and vests. While I was gone, she tried to talk her father into looking forward to his French-Swiss grandson.

After all, Francine and I *were* jerks; fools not even in love. We had no clue, I much less than she. To provide for my wife and my boy, Georges gave us the two upstairs rooms in his house, and appointed me assistant cashier and first-and-only delivery boy of his grocery store, overlooking a marketplace older than mankind. St. Malo is too pretty to live in when you're seventeen. We named our son after his grandfather. We longed for freedom. We named our dream Paris. We both wanted to study literature.

Francine was a fragile creature, but when it came to something *she* wanted, you wound up the doll that broke. In any case, she had the *baccalauréat*, whereas I had abandoned my Swiss *Matura*, the door to university education. I became the family provider and mother, while Paris turned out to be Orléans, where I cooked and cleaned and changed little Georges's diapers while Francine completed her graduate degree and dissertation on Châteaubriand. Slowly I discovered that I had never really loved my wife, only what I had wanted her to be. I was twenty-one, married, had a three-year-old son, no money, no education, but still a few illusions. Again I ran away.

For a while, I lived in Geneva, working my ass off. It took me four years to get accepted by a university, and another five years to finish one, in this case the University of Zurich, where I studied German and French literature. I couldn't throw away everything I believed in. Of course, I was terrible at French. Each night I dreamt of my son, but he never had a face. What I saw was a light brown spot floating in an ocean of seaweed. I tried to imagine how my Georges lived, how he grew up and who he was, beyond the useless fact of being my son. I tried to describe him to myself and again I failed. I wrote, made desperate phone calls, sent thick letters with thin toys.

The closest I could get to Georges was his mother's new boyfriend, who turned out to be in command of the minutest details of her version of our story. "Get your own fucking life!" he yelled and chased me out of their front yard. I thought of shooting him. I thought of kidnapping my own son. Instead I started my first biography, my unfinished Sterne. Tristana says I should fight for Georges but I don't think she really means it. Tristana's a shrink's secretary dreaming of a shrink's office of her own. She owes a lot to my wife and knows it. We're still married, Francine and I, and I guess we always will be. Thus each intercourse with Tristana is adultery, which keeps our sex life juicy.

These days I live with Tristana in one of Zurich's commuter towns. I work mostly at home; she's the commuter. When she was a child, her mother used to lock her in the living room from noon till two. Her father didn't like to be disturbed listening to the news. When she was eighteen she threatened to become a whore to show daddy what he had done to her. Tristana sees herself as a victim. She wants to be a Jew. She sees a rabbi regularly to discuss the Jewish experience. If I satisfy her in bed, she calls me a *mensch*. If I don't, she wants me to get circumcised. I decided not to do the Malamud.

Tristana says I'm too absorbed in other people's lives. I tell her shrinks are, too.

"You dig in *dead* people's lives!" she screams.

She calls my biographer's art grave-robbing. Literary necrophilia, at best. I vaguely answer that this is my protection from getting too deep into mine.

"Grave?" she asks.

"Life."

Tristana never reads anything I write.

"You're morbid," she says.

- 4 -

When I returned the van was still there, parked illegally, but with no ticket on the windshield. There are certain privileges the international wheelchair logo will get you. I was thirsty. When I sat down in The Golden Lion the seat was warm. The manuscript lay on the table. Where was he? His cane leaned against the chair.

The waitress appeared beside me.

"Another beer?"

"Is Christoph Keller a regular?" As though I didn't know.

"Yes, I think so." She looked confused. Tall and skinny. Beautiful. Probably Slavic. "I mean yes, of course he's a regular. I just didn't know that was his name."

She came back with my beer. I felt dizzy. I admired her muscles, not her legs.

"Look, if this is your idea of flirting, then cut the crap. You've already had three beers today. Here's number four." She smiled and then scribbled a phone number on the manuscript. "I'm Ljuba."

After my second beer (or was it my fifth?) I decided to surprise my mother with a visit. I could already see myself approaching her in the garden where she would no doubt be hard at work, picking at the red currants or chasing snails, with the neighbor's kids, both of them, playing around her. I paid for five beers, and got up. I waved goodbye to Ljuba, but she was busy cleaning a table. I stumbled at the threshold and went down hard.

When I regained consciousness—if I really had been out—my muscles ached. Again—or still—I felt dizzy.

"Are you okay, Christoph?"

I tried to get up, but couldn't.

What's happening to me? I thought. It was no dream.

I watched how Ljuba's shapely calf muscles contracted as she helped me to my feet. For a short moment she was hugging me. I felt fine. Then when I was standing, she let go of me.

"I don't know," she said and handed me my cane. "You once told me the name of what it is you have but I can't remember now."

She walked me to the van. Ljuba wasn't just tall, she would easily qualify in basketball.

"Are you really okay?"

"Sure. I was just thinking that I had to give up basketball a while ago."

Ljuba held my arm firmer. Was she stroking me? It could have been the wind.

"Take care," she said, and headed back to the restaurant.

I had just turned the key in the ignition when Ljuba came running out again. I leaned over and threw open the passenger door.

"You forgot your book," she said.

- 5 -

I didn't drive off right away. I looked at my legs and thought I could see my muscles twitch through my thick cotton pants. I was late, as usual. I remembered that I was supposed to bring home sandwiches, but it was Saturday after five and the shops were closed. I decided to call for a delivery. By the time my wife got home the table would be set, the wine poured, the pizzas sliced and ready in the oven. I was already hungry.

Back home, I first went through the mail that sat on the kitchen bar. There was the invitation to an opening in New York. As if I'd fly there for an opening. A rejection slip. *We are interested in your work, but not enough to ask you to send us more. The editors.* A note from the editor of an anthology asking me to write something about writing. Junk mail. The doorknob rattled. Of course, I wasn't going to mention my fall.

The minute my wife enters, her things are everywhere: her pocketbook on the laundry basket by the door; her coat over a chair; her keys on a bookshelf (trying to draw her attention to Bulgakov's *The Master and Margarita*, which she still hasn't read); the groceries missed the kitchen and wound up on the sofa. Enthralled, I watched her shoes cuddling on the hallway floor.

"You didn't check the messages." She kissed me, and leaving the kitchen, and her pocketbook on the bar, asked: "So how was the meeting? I can't wait to hear."

Among the junk mail was a travel agency's leaflet offering a five-day trip to St. Malo where I'd spent my first romantic summer. I was seventeen. The girl got pregnant. We were jerks. Fools not even in love. She had an abortion and never heard from me again. That may be a story for that anthology, I thought. What it had to do with writing I'd find out in the process.

There was a vaguely familiar voice in the other room.

"Who's that? Did you see my pocketbook?"

Maybe the girl *did* have the baby. I took my cane and waddled into my office where my wife was listening to the messages. In the garden, the neighbor's kids were playing. Zoë-Moë-Shloë-something. Maybe I had a French son.

"Someone Lida or Lisa. You know her?"

I might have a grown-up daughter.

"Maybe a journalist."

It would be two-and-a-half decades too late to name her Ljuba.

"So how was meeting Keller? What's he like?"

"I'll tell you in a second. Let me make a phone call," I shouted as she left the room. "The manuscript is on the bar. Take a look. I haven't had a chance yet. And let's do take-out! I'm in a pizza mood."

"Hey, there's my pocketbook! You almost fell over it."

I had called him only once and yet I knew his number by heart.

"Hello." The voice sounded familiar, too. Of course, it did.

"Who is this?"

"You called. Shouldn't you say your name first?" There was an awkward silence.

"I'm trying to reach Christoph Keller," I said after a while. It was a strange connection. I could hear the echo of my own voice.

"He isn't home," the woman said. "He should be, though. Actually, I'm a little worried. When did he leave St. Gallen?"

"I don't know. He..."

"He what?"

"I waited in The Golden Lion for more than an hour."

"He stood you up?"

Again, the echo.

"I'm sorry. That's unlike him."

"I know," I said.

"What am I going to do?" she asked, helplessly.

"Be patient," I said and hung up.

My wife sat at the bar.

"It was great," I said.

"What was great?" she said, leafing absent-mindedly through the manuscript.

"Meeting Christoph Keller."

UPDATE

-6-

They did not accept Keller's book for publication nor did they reject it. They just let it sit the way they had done with previous projects of his and, to be fair, those of other writers as well.

There were his anthologies of Russian-born New York writers, then Nuyorican and finally Newarkian fiction (he claimed to be an expert in each field.) There was his moderately exciting pitch for an anthology of six dozen international authors, chosen by an incomprehensible function (or multiplication?) of age, language, faith, sex, criminal record, and zip code, who would simultaneously write the same story. There was his idea of publishing each New York-based writer's networking list (last name, first name, e-mail address, character references) in multimedia form, a project no publisher had to reject because the invited writers did. There was the (finished) novel he wanted to publish as a fragment, the way Kafka had done (this, they turned down politely—pointing out that Kafka did not want his work to be printed even posthumously—while choosing not to mention that they and, to be fair, other publishers had gone ahead and published it anyway). There were many more projects of his, among them, obviously, his collection of famous letters of rejection, both his and those of others.

Finish your book, they told him whenever he surprised them with a new literary endeavor. But each time he finished it, they said it's not quite there yet or now's not really the time for something like this.

"What you're referring to," he would furiously answer, "is my book about my *life* with a progressive disease. Do you know what a progressive disease does? It progresses, that's what it does! So while my disease keeps slowly progressing in my life, my disease in my book stops progressing. Thus what was once a true account becomes fictional, even false. *I* won't be able to recognize my old self!"

That was the nature of memoir writing, they said.

What could he do? He was under contract with them, and his muscle-wasting disease was incurable, thus wasting muscles whether they published his book or not. He kept exercising his muscles; he kept rewriting his book. He had started his true account in 1997. In 1999, he corrected his age in the manuscript for the first time. In 2000, he began the revisions of his life, rewriting it, but unable to relive it. In 2002, writing his fifth rewrite (thus the fifth revision of his life), he capitalized the words Time and Disease for the first time.

The year 2003 presented a particular challenge for them not to publish him: it was The International Year of His Disease. There'd be fund-raisers, conferences, even stamps featuring his disease. There'd be books, myriads of books with his disease in it. Just not his own book. They agreed that this must be particularly painful for him. But they postponed-rejected it on the basis of its lack of literariness, not on the basis of the author's personal state of health, progressive or not. And why did he want to get special treatment anyway? In his very unpublished book not so aptly titled *The Best Dancer* he writes that everybody's Life is progressing, and that Life was Itself an incurable Disease—a sentence, if not an idea, that needed serious editing, while Keller's obsession with capitalization needed to be addressed, too.

Did he take it well? Of course not. He probably grew bitter, blamed his publisher for his inability to invent the coherent, publishable, and marketable narrative of his own life, and eventually, he probably stopped writing altogether. I can only guess. The last I heard from him was a phone call after a decade of encouraging silence.

"'It's too close,' they keep telling me without specifying *what* exactly was too close," he yelled at me. He didn't bother introducing himself. "'Too close,' my ass! Does it hit *home*, is that what you're saying?" He made it sound as though I had rejected his book. "It's supposed to hit home! They're enough books out there that don't hit anything! What do you mean by *too close*? *Too close* to the reader? Do I have to spare them? Is it too painful for the reader? It was surely too painful for me to write! Is it *too close* to *you*? I'm going to show you *too close*!"

I hung up. A few days later, my newsclip service sent me a short note about him published in a local newspaper.

This is what Keller did (I had to make a few phone calls to flesh out the short article): he drove to his publishing house (which also happens to be mine); asked the gatekeeper, a friendly individual on the verge of a well-deserved early retirement, to help him into his wheelchair; brushed off the latter's attempts to push him toward the entrance; realized that he couldn't wheel himself up the modest incline; yelled something like, "Can't you see I need help?" at the gatekeeper; forced the gatekeeper to push him to the publishing house's iron gate; and hand-cuffed his wheelchair to the iron gate.

It was an overcast day and the first drops of rain were already falling. Keller's editor was recovering at home from a mysterious partial face paralysis and a selective loss of hearing. No one in the publishing house was aware that one of its authors was chained to the gate. The only journalist on the scene—Keller had summoned many—arrived without a camera.

It turned out that the day Keller had chosen to push his luck was one of two or three days a year the publisher himself paid an unannounced visit. Naturally, the publisher wondered what kind of person would handcuff himself to his publishing house.

"Call the cops," the publisher told his driver.

At the same time, a private Pilatus Porter four-seater plane approached the city. The pilot was a man in his early fifties, the copilot a man in his late fifties. They were friends, never suspicious or even envious of each other. Thus the pilot was truly amazed when his friend produced a handgun and pointed it first at his head, then at the tall blue-ish glass-metal construction gleaming in the morning sun, which he, the pilot, owned.

"There must be another way to settle this. For the sake of our friendship, *please!*"

But the copilot stubbornly directed him with his gun toward the iridescent tower. The pilot, the richest—and thus most influential—man in the city, had never thought that one day he'd find himself weighing a bullet shot through his head against becoming a bullet shooting through his own publishing house (which, of course, was only an insignificant division of his corporation). On what floor would his life end? Which window was it going to be? Would it be his (usually empty) own office?

"Friendship, my ass," the former friend said.

That's when the city's air control realized that they had a problem. Within minutes (there's always a U.S. airbase nearby) the sky filled with lean jets.

At the same time, the cops arrived on the premises to end Keller's act of authorial disobedience. They unchained him from the gate, but refused to arrest him. Keller apologized to the gatekeeper, but not to the publisher. He was already in his car, jammed in the traffic between Kafkastrasse and Familie-Mann-Brücke, when the radio reported that a hijacked plane was threatening the city's safety.

It took the police five hours to talk the hijacker into abandoning his bloody scheme. At gunpoint, and only a few hundred yards above the ground, the pilot agreed in writing to not publish his former friend's take-the-money-and-run memoir, ghostwritten by an intern, who under these circumstances had to be fired immediately.

No one got hurt. Yes, the intern lost her job, but wasn't that a small sacrifice in light of what could have happened? The Pilatus Porter safely landed on the U.S. airbase without making even a blip of a headline. The official explanation was that a technical flaw had made the plane circle above the city until a technician could tell the pilot what button to push. The city, learning that it hadn't really been attacked, calmed down. The publishing house's reputation remained intact. Now everything was water under the bridge. The pilot resumed his friendship with his former friend. The face of Keller's editor recovered fully, and he regained most of his hearing. The owner's friend received a polite letter of rejection.

Keller's book never saw the light of day.

But *he* did. He made his peace with not publishing his account of a life with a progressive disease and considered it something of a medical victory over a literary disease. He even found joy in rewriting his book every year, parallel to the year-by-year progression of his disease, and thus he was able to both update his work-in-progress and his life.

He was offered, and accepted, a permanent position as a writer of rejection letters for his publishing house. It was an occupation he could perform at home. The mailman was happy to carry the daily cartons from his mailbox to his desk. This occupation gave Keller satisfaction. He could finally live a fulfilled life as a full member of society. He could finally be of use as a human being.

-7-

What can I say, I'm old now. I'm not even interested in what year it is anymore. I haven't "lost it," as Georges, my son, recently suggested. If anything, I've "had it," but that's a different story.

So Keller lived happily ever after, I assume, and I changed my name. This turned my life upside down. I was the author of several critically praised but modestly selling books of fiction. I became the author of several modestly praised but bestselling biographies of movie stars.

Usually, I do dead people. I wrote a Cary Grant to some critical acclaim. I did a tremendously successful Bette Davis. A Bergman (Ingrid, not Ingmar) is on my list. I have a Charles Laughton in the pipeline. Every serious biographer has a Laughton in the pipeline. Of course, I did the biography of the movie star I'm now married to under a nom-de-plume.

Once in a while I think of writing the book Keller really wanted to write. It could be a fictionalized autobiography. It could be my memoir of him, the way I experienced him. It could be a postmodern exercise in who's writing whose life. It could simply be a novel. Or it could, and maybe should, be, plainly and simply, a good book.

Written in English by Christoph Keller.

Author and publisher would like to express their gratitude to the Hecht-Levi Foundation and Mr. Wolfgang Schürer. Their generous help made this book possible.

- QUOTATIONS -

1. Emily Dickenson, 1896.

2. Xavier de Maistre, *Voyage Around My Room*, translated from the French, with a Notice of the Author's Life. Published by H. A. Riverside Press, 1871.

3. François Rabelais, *Five Books of the Lives, Heroic Deeds and Sayings of Gargantua and his Son Pantagruel*, translated into English by Sir Thomas Urquhart of Cromarty and Peter Antony Motteux. Published by A.H. Bullen, 1904.

4. Franz Kafka, *The Metamorphosis: Great Books Edition (Penguin Great Books of the 20th Century)*, translated by Malcolm Pasley. Published by Penguin Books, 2000.

5. *Works of Jules Verne*, Charles F. Horne, Ed. Published by Vincent Parke and Company, 1911

6. Philip Roth, *Deception*. Published by Simon & Schuster, 1990.

Do royal fairytales have to end as royal dramas?

- *ILLUSTRATIONS* -

1. Private.
2. Marcel Duchamp, *Bicycle Wheel*. The illustration shows the third version from 1951; the original from 1913 is lost. Metal wheel mounted on painted stool, The Museum of Modern Art, New York.
3. Private.
4. *Sometimes we gazed through a succession of arches, its course very like the aisles of a Gothic cathedral.* Illustration to Jules Verne's *Journey to the Center of the Earth.*
"Well," said the Professor quickly, "what is the matter?"
"The fact is, I am dreadfully tired," was my earnest reply.
"What," cried my uncle, "tired after a three hours' walk, and by so easy a road?"
"Easy enough, I dare say, but very fatiguing."
"But how can that be, when all we have to do is to go downwards."
"I beg your pardon, sir. For some time I have noticed that we are going upwards."
"Upwards," cried my uncle, shrugging his shoulders, "how can that be?" (*Works of Jules Verne*, Charles F. Horne, Ed. Published by Vincent Parke and Company, 1911)
5. Private.
6. Private.
7. Carl Liner, portrait of my mother, 1955.
8. Private.
9. Private.
10. Private.
11. Private.
12. Private.
13. Gustave Doré in: François Rabelais, *Gargantua and Pantagruel*, translated into English by Sir Thomas Urquhart of Cromarty and Peter Antony Motteux, Chapter 1.XIII.
14. Private.

15. Private.
16. Private.
17. Private.
18. Private.
19. Gustave Doré in: François Rabelais, *Gargantua and Pantagruel*, translated into English by Sir Thomas Urquhart of Cromarty and Peter Antony Motteux, Chapter I.XVII.
20. Private.
21. Private.
22. Private.
23. Private.
24. Artist's rendition of drawings "beetle" and "the Samsa flat" by Vladimir Nabokov in: Vladimir Nabokov, Lectures on Literature, edited by Fredson Bowers. New York: Harcourt Brace Jovanovich, 1980. Copyright by the Estate of Vladimir Nabokov.
25. Private.
26. Artist's rendition of an illustration from the St. Galler Tagblatt.
27. Artist's rendition of Solomon R. Guggenheim Museum in New York City, by Frank Lloyd Wright, 1959.
28. Private.
29. Kurt Adler, *Chromosomes III*, private collection.
30. Private.
31. Private.
32. Private.
33. Swiss military and civil defense record book. Montage. Copyright by the Swiss Confederation.
34. Peter Greenaway, *Stairs*, 1994. Photo: Christoph Gevrey, www.cri.ch/stairs/img0067.jpg. Does art have to be wheelchair accessible? If you can't even expect it from art, who can you expect it from?
35. Vice President Dick Cheney, Inauguration Day, 2009.
36. Alberto Giacometti, *The Chariot*, 1950, The Museum of Modern Art, New York (illus. from: Christian Klemm, in collaboration with Carolyn Lachner, Tobia Bezzola, Anne Umland: *Alberto Giacometti*. Berlin: Nicolaische Verlagsbuchhandlung, 2001, p. 167. "He resumes walking, limping. He tells me he was very happy when he found out that his operation—after an accident—would leave him lame. That is why I will chance this: his statues still give me the impression that they are

taking refuge, finally, in the secret infirmity that grants them solitude."
(Jean Genet on Giacometti in "The studio of Alberto Giacometti" in
Jean Genet, *Fragments of the Artwork*, translated by Charlotte Mandell.
Stanford, Calif.: Stanford University Press, 2003).

37. Artist's rendition of film poster for *El jardín de las delicias*, Spanish
version by Carlos Saura, 1972.

38. Private.

39. Private.

40. Private

41. Private.

42. Private.

43. Private.

44. Text page in Christoph Keller, *Kasperli*, notebook 8, "The Circus,"
pp. 26–27, G. Fischer printing, 1974.

45. Private.

46. Private.

47. Photo by Jonathan Santlofer, 2000. From one of Jan's poems about,
among other things, loss (before she met me): "And what are they singing
about?:/the liner notes say a woman who threatens their friendship, which
they vow to uphold./But I say they're singing life,/how we're always
losing something,/how beautiful that is." – " Und was besingen sie?/
Das Beiheft sagt, eine Frau, die beider Freundschaftsschwur bedroht./
Aber ich sage, sie singen das Leben,/wie wir immer was verlieren,/wie
schön das ist." (Jan Heller Levi in: *Switzerland or Somewhere / Schweiz
oder Sonstwo*, poems, in German and English, translated by Christine
Frick-Gerke. St. Gallen: Sabon Verlag, 2000).

48. Private.

49. Sven Wingquist, *Self-Aligning Ball Bearing*, 1929, chrome-plated
steel, The Museum of Modern Art, New York.

50. Private.

51. Private.

52. Private.

53. Private.

54. Private.

55. Kurt Adler, *Hommage à Duchamp*, 2001, wheelchair front wheels
mounted on a wood base (drilled), rubber, metal. Private collection.

- *CREDITS* -

Ooligan is a general trade press that publishes books honoring the cultural and natural diversity of the Pacific Northwest. Founded in 2001 as a teaching press, Ooligan is staffed by students pursuing master's degrees in the Department of English at Portland State University. This apprenticeship program is led by a core faculty of publishing professionals dedicated to the art and craft of publishing.

The following students contributed to the publication of *The Best Dancer*:

Katrina Hill (Acquiring Editors)
Vinnie Kinsella
    Kylin Larsson (Acquisitions)
    Megan Wellman (Acquisitions)
Rachel S. Tobie (Design Managers)
Marie Miller
Matthew Warren
    Kari Smit (Cover Design)
    Matthew Warren (Interior Design)
    Jennifer Lawrence (Copyright Research & Permissions)
Haili Graff (Managing Editors)
Lauren Shapiro
Leah Sims
Mel Wells
Ian VanWyhe
    Ryan Hume (Senior Editor)
    Matt Schrunk (Senior Editor)
    Malini Kochhar (Contributing Editor)
    Pamela Ivey (Contributing Editor)
    Sandra Argüello (Contributing Editor)
    Melissa Tessitor (Contributing Editor)
    Kathryn Foster (Contributing Editor)

- A NOTE ON THE TRANSLATION -

The English translation of this book was done in close collaboration with the author and deviates significantly in some places from the original German edition due to changes made during the translation process. "The Island Cathedral" chapter was added for the English edition. "The Meeting with Christoph Keller" chapter was written by the author in English.

Kurt Adler, *Hommage à Duchamp*, 2001, private collection.